ST IVES

S^T IVES

THE ADVENTURES OF A FRENCH PRISONER IN ENGLAND

ROBERT LOUIS STEVENSON

CHAPTERS XXXI TO XXXV
BY JENNI CALDER

WITH RESEARCH AND A
FOREWORD BY R. J. STOREY

RICHARD DREW
PUBLISHING
GLASGOW

First published in 1897 by William Heinemann

This edition first published 1990 by
Richard Drew Publishing Ltd
6 Clairmont Gardens
Glasgow G3 7LW   Scotland

The publisher acknowledges the financial assistance of the
Scottish Arts Council in the publication of this work.

British Library Cataloguing in Publication Data
Stevenson, Robert Louis, *1850-1894*
St Ives: being the adventures of a French prisoner in
England. — this ed., *completed by Jenni Calder.*
I. Title II. Calder, Jenni
823′.8 [F]

ISBN 0-86267-272-4

Printed and bound in Great Britain by
Cox & Wyman Ltd, Reading

FOREWORD

BY R. J. STOREY

A CASUAL reading some years ago of Stevenson's letters from Samoa brought me sharply to attention when a familiar name presented itself from among tentative chapter-headings for *St. Ives*. This was 'The True Blooded Yankee', which I knew as arguably the most colourful of the privateers operating in British waters in the war with the United States of 1812-14. The heading pleased but surprised me. I had pursued an amateur interest in the ship over many years, and was aware that little concerning her would have been available to Stevenson from most standard sources.

The Beinecke Library at Yale afforded closer scrutiny of the sequence of chapter headings, supporting the conclusion that Stevenson had intended to use *The True Blooded Yankee* in the escape of St. Ives from Scotland. She had much to commend her for this purpose, including a spectacular raid on a Scottish harbour at the time assigned by RLS to the escape. Yet she plays no part in the ending written by Arthur Quiller-Couch, who opted instead for a convoluted episode which he acutely regretted. 'Q', as he was known, was handicapped by his refusal to believe, until too late, that American ships had operated on the British coast. His scepticism is not surprising, as the extent of this activity has been recognised by few. Stevenson, I should have known, had reason to be better informed than most; but to appreciate this and the significance of *The True Blooded Yankee*, some background is necessary.

Though Britain effectively won the War of 1812 through a naval blockade of the United States, her own shipping was badly mauled by the Americans. The small US Navy played an impressive part, but most of the damage was done by privateers. These were fast, well-armed vessels owned by civilians, often groups of merchants, and licensed by government to take prizes. Their prime objective was profit. Most privateer captains were under orders not to risk loss or capture, but with Britain already extended in operations against the French, they had a good deal of scope. About one thousand British ships became prizes, and although many of these were eventually recaptured, the shock to national pride was profound. Even a convoy system instituted by the Admiralty failed to halt the toll.

Probably not more than a score of privateers ventured as far as the British coast, but their depredations were spectacular. Several took prizes valued at more than half a million dollars in a single cruise. They caused near panic among the merchants and insurers of the main ports, and the Prince Regent was petitioned for improved protection. The American captains, some of whom were of British origin, relished the situation. One sent an elaborate scroll to Lloyd's Coffee House, declaring that he was personally placing '. . . all the ports, harbours, bays, creeks, rivers, inlets, outlets, islands and sea coast of the United Kingdom of Great Britain and Ireland in a state of strict and rigorous blockade.' Another, the master of the aptly named *Shark*, conveyed his compliments to 'the Gentlemen at the Commercial Rooms, Bristol', acknowledging their concern.

Remoter parts of the Scottish and Irish coasts were favoured hunting-grounds of the Americans. A letter of June, 1813, from the master of the *Daphne*, which had been laden with slates from Easdale bound for Leith, conveys the manner of their operations:

'Being 3 leagues W by S from Cape Wrath, saw a strange vessel coming out of the sea, which proved to be an American privateer, mounting 10 guns, having 70 men on board, 30 days from Broad Island. She had captured two brigs before us; on the 27th at four in the afternoon we were captured. At eight that night he took two sloops, one brig and a schooner, abreast of the Cape. He lightened the *Daphne* and sent her to America, and put me and my crew aboard the *Six Sisters* of Inverkeithing, and sent us about our business after taking both my quadrants and all my charts. They behaved very well to us while on board the privateer. They took the *Hope* of Kirkwall the same morning as the *Daphne*, but not thinking her worthwhile, put the crew on board and sent her away. The Captain's father was a Greenock man, and I have every reason to believe there are too many Scots and English on board her.'

The last sentence of this account was well enough founded. American crews commonly included former British seamen. Although many could claim United States citizenship, they remained vulnerable to impressment by the Royal Navy, or to execution if suspected of desertion. The practice of stopping American ships on the high seas and impressing their seamen was one of the immediate causes of the War of 1812. Bitterness on this score might understandably have been reflected in harsh treatment of British prisoners, yet the reverse seems to have been more usual, as in the case of the *Daphne*. Another account of a capture on the West Highland coast states that 'The master, William Wilson, being confined in a high state of mental derangement, the captain of the privateer allowed them to depart after detaining them four hours. The Americans very humanely sent their surgeon on board to bleed the master . . .'

Clearly, where prizes were taken, no amount of courtesy could compensate for the loss. Newspapers of the time contain numerous accounts of captures which must have spelled ruin where small shipowners were involved. Thus on 30 July, 1813, the *Glasgow Herald* reported:

'We are sorry to learn that American privateers continue to infest the coasts . . . A very fine vessel, belonging to Mr. MacDonald of Lochinver, with salt and other stores for the herring fishery, was captured a few days ago within half a mile of his dwelling house.'

Not surprisingly there was fear of attack by land, as a report from Broadford, Skye, of 3 July, 1813, makes clear:

'. . . It is remarked here, the hardship of the coast being unprotected, we have not a redcoat to turn out, although the Yankees should take into their head to annoy us on shore. The local militia (3rd Inverness) has been dismissed, and the volunteers also; and the Isle of Skye, though in importance not inconsiderable, is quite defenceless.'

The privateer that gave most ground for such apprehension was *The True Blooded Yankee*, the vessel identified by Stevenson. She was an altogether formidable craft, with 18 guns, a crew of 180, and a turn of speed which led one Royal Navy captain to say, 'She outsailed everything, and not one of our cruisers could touch her.' She made three cruises in British and Irish waters, and in the course of one of these, lasting thirty-seven days, captured twenty-seven vessels (one of them, with cargo, worth over 400,000 dollars), and took two hundred and seventy prisoners. She was also reported to have held an Irish island for six days and to have destroyed several vessels in a Scottish harbour. Evidence of the Irish episode is lacking, but there is proof of the Scottish raid. On 4 December, 1813, a young exciseman at Bowmore, on the island of Islay, wrote to his father in Glasgow:

'We had a serious alarm here on Wednesday night in consequence of an American brig of war anchoring in the bay in the dusk of the evening. There were above her in the bay eight vessels; of which four were fine brigs with valuable cargoes, two sloops, a Danish galliot that had been stranded in the late storm, and the packet, which was lying alongside of the quay. Two boats with pilots that went out to the American were detained and the men put in irons.

'There having been some communication between the Americans and the Danes, information was sent ashore by the latter that it was the intention of the enemy to destroy the vessels in the harbour, and to land at midnight and burn the town. The confusion caused by this intelligence was indescribable; a number of women and children with the most valuable of the effects being hurriedly removed into the country—while the men, in the absence of every description of the military, mustered what arms and ammunition were in the town and neighbourhood, and kept watch along the shore.

'The night was extremely dark; but about 2 o'clock the Americans, who had removed six of the vessels without firing a gun, and without even the sound of an oar being heard, set one of them on fire; she burned for about two hours, but the cargo not being of inflammable materials, the fire was not to be compared to that of the next devoted vessel, which being laden with wood and hemp, illumined the whole country around. At daybreak we had the satisfaction of seeing the enemy set sail, after destroying three vessels in addition to the two burnt. One brig was given up to the captain, and the crews of all the rest put on board of her. The packet was not touched. The American had 180 men on board, and was 12 days out from Brest. Expresses were immediately sent off to Greenock, and we trust we shall hear of her capture.'

The True Blooded Yankee returned to her base at Brest some weeks later, after a cat-and-mouse game with the Royal Navy. (Part of this time may well have been spent in concealment on the Irish coast, including occupation of the island referred to earlier.) Contemporary newspaper reports make clear the alarm she generated. An innocent merchantman lying off Portpatrick caused a turn-out of the Dumfriesshire militia, with 'sailors, boatmen, robberymen and townsmen, armed with marlin spikes, boat-hooks, spades, pitch-forks, fowling-pieces and every other weapon they could procure, determined to oppose the landing of the Americans.'

Some months later it was reported that *The True Blooded Yankee* had set out on another predatory cruise, with express instructions to operate as she had in Islay: 'to sink, burn and destroy, and not to capture with the intention of carrying into port.'

In 1964 I visited Islay in the slender hope that there might be oral tradition of the raid. I was delighted to find vivid material in both English and Gaelic. A belief had grown up that the villain of the piece was John Paul Jones, on whom the name of the privateer of 1813 had been conferred as *The Bloody Yankee*. There appears to be nothing in British or American sources to support the idea that Jones ever visited Islay. He had in fact been dead for over twenty years at the time of *The True Blooded Yankee's* raid, and in almost all respects tradition strikingly confirms the account of the Bowmore exciseman in 1813.

On Islay, the fullest material was given to me by Gilbert Clark, of Port Charlotte, an outstanding island historian who died in 1989 at the age of 84. He was remarkable for his measured assessment of local tradition, and I recorded several hours of conversation with him. Other islanders provided versions of the affair, and from these and Gilbert Clark's own account, with commentary, the following emerge as central features of the Islay tradition.

Neil Connell, the miller of Ardnish, and his nephew, a boy named MacAllister, put out to the American ship to pilot her up Lochindaal, on which the main settlement of Bowmore, with its distillery, is situated. On boarding her they saw men in irons sitting on the deck, and it was made clear that they were themselves prisoners. The miller was ordered to proceed with his piloting. On their way up Lochindaal he attempted to run the ship aground, but was checked by one of the crew, who said in Gaelic 'Tuilleadh uisge air do mhuileann, a mhuillear' ('More water on your mill, miller'). In Bowmore the Americans burned almost all the ships in the harbour. The fires lit the night sky, and people several miles away fled into the hills, fearing 'the whole island would be up in flames.' On leaving Bowmore the next day, the Americans bombarded the shore of the loch, and released the miller and his nephew before making for the open sea. They made good their escape after a close encounter with a British man-of-war, using their fine turn of speed ('she could cut the wind in two').

The Americans are said to have given the miller a new boat which contained silver taken, according to some versions, from Islay House, seat of the Campbells of Shawfield. This echoes the seizure of plate in a raid by John Paul Jones on the house of the Earl of Selkirk, near Kirkcudbright, In 1778. The Islay House story was dismissed by Gilbert Clark, and lacks corroboration.

Evidence is not lacking for the fact that *The True Blooded Yankee* used her guns as she left Islay. Two of her cannonballs were used in shot-putting competitions at island games until well into the present century. The location of one of them was known in 1964.

Yet for all the stir caused by *The True Blooded Yankee* in 1813-14, and the folk memory in Islay one hundred and fifty years later, she and the other privateers operating off the British Isles seem largely to have dropped from historical ken. Most authorities treat the topic in scant detail. How then did Stevenson, in Samoa, settle on this particular vessel? It is clear from his letters that he wanted more information ('Were all your privateers voiceless?' he asked the American painter, William Low), but he had already identified his ship. This much may have been possible from material sent out to him (the idea of *St. Ives* came from a reading of the *Annual Register* for 1814), and he may even have seen an account published in 1856 by Captain George Coggeshall, himself a Yankee privateersman, though this seems doubtful.

More significant perhaps is the fact that the topic must already have been broadly familiar to the Stevenson family. RLS's grandfather, Robert, would have been well aware of the proximity of US vessels during the War of 1812 while pursuing his work as a master builder of lighthouses. The Islay episode could hardly have escaped him—the family firm built several of the island's lights —and the whereabouts of *The True Blooded Yankee* would have been a subject of keen interest.

It is difficult to conceive that Stevenson would not have inherited knowledge of such colourful affairs. He refers to the American threat in his fragment, 'Records of a Family of Engineers'. His grandfather accompanied Walter Scott and the Commissioners of Northern Lights on their celebrated circumnavigation of Scotland in 1814, during which there was a mild scare, of which Scott wrote later:

'... that our little expedition might not want the dignity of danger, we were favoured with a distant glimpse of what was said to be an American cruiser, and had opportunity to consider what a pretty figure we should have made had the voyage ended in our being carried captive to the United States.'

Whether or not Stevenson knew much detail of the operations of *The True Blooded Yankee*, he had clearly recognised her potential for *St. Ives* when at the outset he gave her name to the chapter succeeding that which dealt with the hero's escape by balloon. Later he inserted a chapter title 'The East Wind Blows' following 'The Balloon Ascension', confirming that the ensuing action was to take place west of the Pentlands. Islay is due west.

These indications do not seem to have benefitted Quiller-Couch in his conclusion of the book after Stevenson's death. 'Q' provides a balloon flight, as RLS intended, and a rescue of her crew by a ship—but a British ship, and in the English Channel. St. Ives is conveyed to America and later to France in a process of unnecessary complication. This involves the Colenso episode, in which a captain of that name saves the balloonists while on his way to the United States to discharge a debt of honour by surrendering his ship to the Americans.

Quiller-Couch maintained a detailed correspondence with Stevenson's literary executor, Sidney Colvin, on the conclusion of *St. Ives*. His letters, now held at Princeton University Library, make clear that although he had been told by Belle Strong, RLS's step-daughter and amanuensis, that a privateer was to be involved he either knew nothing of *The True Blooded Yankee*, or if he did, could not accept it as plausible. He was thus sorely handicapped in making sense of Stevenson's intentions, and at several points expresses his frustration to Colvin:

4 June, 1897: '...It is abundantly clear that no balloon could travel more than 1000 miles (and 500 would be a goodish voyage) and that no American privateer would be near the British coast in 1813-14. Supposing the balloon to reach the English Channel, or the Atlantic off Ushant, we might possibly make the rescuer an American merchantman running home from a French port...'

29 June, 1897: '...I fancy Anne must be picked up by an *English packet* and *then* captured by the American. I have searched the books and don't see how to manage it otherwise, if he has to go to America. Shouldn't have thought that necessary; but so it's ordained, and so it must be worked.'

18 July, 1897: '...It has been a chapter of heart-breaking difficulty. I believe—if one may say it—that RLS himself would have been hard put to it to make the thing probable: and can hardly hope that you'll like it at all. It has seemed to me throughout that to make it plausible at all one must make it extravagant—if that's not too much of a paradox. But as soon as you take the adventure seriously it becomes absurd...'

22 July, 1897: '...I *hate* the balloon business; but have better hopes of the rest...'

1 August, 1897: '...To my horror and dismay I find, against all probabilities, American privateers did occasionally visit the coasts of Britain in 1813; but I hope 'Captain Colenso', as I have called him, will do as a substitute...'

13 August, 1897: '...Am sorry about Capt Colenso—would spare no pains to write entire new chapter if time could or can be given...'

15 August, 1897: '...I am still distressed about Capt Colenso.'

A scrupulous craftsman, Quiller-Couch deserves sympathy. His scepticism about American activity in British waters was understandable, and would be a common enough reaction today. Moreover, the guidance he received from the Stevenson household may not have been of much help. RLS's attention to *St. Ives* had been sporadic, and latterly he had deserted it in favour of *Weir of Hermiston*. Part of his dictation to Belle Strong had been through a kind of sign language, when forbidden to speak for fear of haemorrhage. A list of chapter headings in Belle's hand shows that 'The True Blooded Yankee' became simply 'The Privateer', and it is likely that her indications to 'Q' on the matter were less than precise. She wrote later of her work for Stevenson on *St. Ives*: 'I loved helping him and found it thrilling, for he never would tell me what came next.'

There seems to have been an expectation, reflected in the letter to Colvin of 29 June, 1897, that St. Ives would return to France after first being taken to America by the privateer. If Belle Strong was right about this (although 'Q' questions the necessity), it may have been with a transatlantic edition in mind. As likely is the supposition that an American privateer would have its base in the States, as indeed most did. Yet *The True Blooded Yankee* was owned by a Rhode Islander living in Paris, and sailed out of Brest. If Stevenson knew these facts—and had lived—he would almost certainly have employed them to advantage in simplifying St. Ives' return to France, as Jenni Calder has now done. That this was at least his original intention is strongly suggested by the heading 'In France Again' for the chapter immediately following 'The True Blooded Yankee'.

Quiller-Couch's concern to do justice to Stevenson is clearly evident in his letters. It seems entirely arguable that he would have welcomed a revision more closely reflecting Stevenson's intentions. Both writers, I believe, would have applauded Jenni Calder's skilful evocation of fact within the spirit of the novel.

ACKNOWLEDGEMENTS

In addition to the late Gilbert Clark and others on Islay, I must thank especially Dr. John White, of Cambridge, Mass.; Miss M. G. Wynne, Yale University Library; Prof. J. B. Hattendorf, US Naval War College; Dr. P. MacMahon, National Library of Ireland; Dr. J. De Courcy Ireland; Dr. R. Rines; Sheriff A. A. MacDonald; Mr. David Angus; Mr. J. G. Graham; and above all my wife, Lisa (not least for aid with Gaelic).

I am also grateful to the Morris L Parrish Collection of Victorian Novelists, Princeton University Library and the Beinecke Rare Book and Manuscript Library, Yale University for allowing me to reproduce material in their keeping, and to Michael Joseph Ltd. for permission to quote from *This Life I've Loved*, by Isobel Osbourne Strong Field.

PREFACE

ROBERT Louis Stevenson left Edinburgh in the summer of 1887. He would never return to Scotland, except in his imagination. He spent the next seven years first in the United States, then voyaging in the Pacific, and finally in Vailima, the home he established near Apia, in Samoa. In those years he wrote a great deal about the Pacific, but when he died, on 3 December 1894, almost all his work in progress concerned Scotland. Amongst this was *St. Ives*, only six chapters from completion.

St. Ives is an adventure story, 'a rattling, touch-and-go tale of adventure', as one early reviewer described it. It is in a very different vein from *Weir of Hermiston*, also unfinished at his death, and from the work that stemmed from his South Sea experiences. It is clear that he wrote it under pressure: he had a large house and an extended, and somewhat improvident, family to maintain, and needed to write something that would attract a wide readership. He described the book in a letter to his cousin Bob Stevenson as 'a tissue of adventures, the central character not very well done, no philosophic pith under the yarn; and, in short, if people will read it, that's all I ask; and if they won't, damn them! I like doing it though . . .'

Stevenson had always liked adventure, but his adventure stories had always been more than yarns. *St. Ives* is perhaps his only work that is simply a yarn, without the moral undercurrents which are apparent in most of his writing, and which often have the force of a whirlpool. But he knew what he was doing, and had also, in his essay 'A Gossip on Romance' (1882), discussed just that kind of tale. 'There is a vast deal in life and letters . . . where the interest turns not upon what a man shall choose to do, but on how he manages to do it; not on the passionate slips and hesitations of the conscience, but on the problems of the body and of the practical intelligence, in clean open-air adventure, the shock of arms, or the diplomacy of life.' The story of the French prisoner-of-war St. Ives, precipitated from incident to incident, responding to character and action in a spirit of serendipity, fits the pattern Stevenson describes here.

The adventure story creates its own dynamic, and part of it lies in the extraordinary freedom of the characters. St. Ives grows up an orphan, which means that he is free of filial responsibilities (a freedom Stevenson himself never had), and although he is proud of being 'a soldier of Napoleon' he has no strong external loyalties. He is very much his own man. We meet him first as a prisoner in Edinburgh Castle, but once he has escaped from that physical restraint he is liberated also from all the inhibitions that generally hinder free movement. That is the appeal; we read the story not for the attractiveness of the hero (for he isn't entirely attractive) nor for its message (for there is no message) but for the sheer charm of incident.

There is, however, more in *St. Ives* than incident. The novel begins and ends in Scotland, and in it Stevenson lovingly recreates the scenes of his youth. The Castle itself, the streets of Edinburgh he knew so well, Swanston and the Pentland Hills—these are at the heart of the novel. The distance in time and miles if anything sharpened his sense of place, which had always been one of the strongest elements of his writing. And place lends authority to the characters, to Miss Gilchrist, the formidable guardian of Flora, to Major Chevenix, St. Ives's dry but decent rival in love, to Mr. Robbie, the mild and eccentric lawyer. If Flora herself does not quite live up to her early promise, the congenial realities of Swanston Cottage, the associations with food and wine and comfort, help to breathe life into her.

Stevenson's pleasure in the writing of the tale is communicated at many points, particularly when his hero is north of the Border. Much of it derives not only from the influence of place but from what is in effect the recreation of aspects of his own youth. The 'University of Cramond' incident, for example, is resonant with Stevenson's own high-spirited activities as a student, and we know from his letters that the past was much in his mind. But there are times when he falters, and relies on sheer extravagance to rescue his hero—and himself. His letters indicate that he was finding the later chapters a struggle to write. In the autumn of 1894 he set the novel aside briefly, but went back to it in an effort to meet his commitment to serial publication. He hoped to finish it by the end of the year, but death intervened.

Stevenson had many problems with the writing of *St. Ives*. The story is set in the time of the Napoleonic Wars and Stevenson was concerned to get both the background and the details right. To this end he sent off for books and information, but he did not always get what he needed, and sometimes what he needed did not come in time, and he had to rewrite in consequence.

There was one problem of detail Stevenson never, so far as we know, resolved, which concerned his intentions as to the ending of the book. The problem was inherited by Arthur Quiller-Couch, who after Stevenson's death was approached by Sidney Colvin to provide the outstanding chapters. The difficulties are described in his foreword by R. J. Storey, whose researches have uncovered material, and vital links, that certainly eluded 'Q'. Colvin, friend, adviser and editor of Stevenson, had first asked Conan Doyle to finish *St. Ives*. Quiller-Couch was a second choice, but he had a reputation as an adventure story writer and a parodist, and was an appropriate one. He took up the task enthusiastically. He wrote at speed, again to meet the demands of serial publication, and was aware that he was not able to continue the story in quite the way he believed Stevenson had planned. He kept to the spirit of the novel, captured, though at times overdid, Stevenson's style, and brought the tale to a satisfactory, if perhaps over-embellished, conclusion. The completed novel was published in 1897, and since then has been the accepted version.

It would no doubt remain the accepted version were it not for the discoveries of R. J. Storey and his tracing of the connections between the activities of American privateers off the west coast of Scotland and Stevenson's *St. Ives*. It was his suggestion that I might rewrite the last chapters to bring them closer to Stevenson's intentions that initiated this new version. Quiller-Couch's six chapters have been replaced by five. I have used the material researched by Mr. Storey in Chapter 34. The rest is devised from the evidence left behind by Stevenson himself, the clues in the earlier part of the novel, and from my knowledge of Stevenson's interests and involvements. And of course it is not possible to write fiction, even someone else's fiction, without a fair measure of imagination.

Stevenson had written thirty chapters of *St. Ives* when he died. He left his hero in Edinburgh, a hunted man, determined to clear his name, protect his inheritance and win Flora Gilchrist. He is being pursued by his cousin, seeking vengeance, and by the law, which considers him a murderer. In the final chapters the entanglement with the law has to be sorted out, the cousin dealt with, and a reunion with Flora accomplished. In the Quiller-Couch version St. Ives returns, by balloon and boat, to France via America, has a final encounter with his cousin, and is last seen back in Edinburgh with his bride. In the course of tying up loose ends 'Q' introduced a number of new characters and entertaining episodes. In this version all the incident that was purely Quiller-Couch's invention has gone, and some that is my own invention has been introduced: but the invention is, I hope, true to the spirit and experience of RLS.

It is not possible to get under the skin of an author, dead or alive. I have not tried to impersonate Stevenson, himself impersonating his hero, but have worked from my understanding of the novel and the author. In my preparation for rewriting I visited the island of Islay, the most significant new feature in the story, and am most grateful to the people I spoke to there, especially Catriona Bell, Anne Clark, James Macaulay and Margaret MacTaggart. I am grateful, too, to my father, David Daiches, for his comments and suggestions, to Gordon Jarvie, for his invaluable and sympathetic editing, to E. J. Mehew for drawing attention to some errors in Stevenson's original text, and to Richard Drew, for his enthusiastic encouragement from the outset of the project. Most of all, I owe thanks to Bob Storey, who began it all with a suggestion over lunch in the Magnum, not a stone's throw from where St. Ives encountered Dalmahoy and the other members of the University of Cramond, on their way to an evening of delightful but almost disastrous inebriation within sight of the Firth of Forth.

Jenni Calder
South Queensferry
January 1990

CONTENTS

St. Ives

CHAPTER I

A TALE OF A LION RAMPANT

It was in the month of May 1813 that I was so unlucky as to fall at last into the hands of the enemy. My knowledge of the English language had marked me out for a certain employment. Though I cannot conceive a soldier refusing to incur the risk, yet to be hanged for a spy is a disgusting business; and I was relieved to be held a prisoner of war. Into the Castle of Edinburgh, standing in the midst of that city on the summit of an extraordinary rock, I was cast with several hundred fellow-sufferers, all privates like myself, and the more part of them, by an accident, very ignorant, plain fellows. My English, which had brought me into that scrape, now helped me very materially to bear it. I had a thousand advantages. I was often called to play the part of an interpreter, whether of orders or complaints, and thus brought in relations, sometimes of mirth, sometimes almost of friendship, with the officers in charge. A young lieutenant singled me out to be his adversary at chess, a game in which I was extremely proficient, and would reward me for my gambits with excellent cigars. The major of the battalion took lessons of French from me while at breakfast, and was sometimes so obliging as to have me join him at the meal. Chevenix was his name. He was stiff as a drum-major and selfish as an Englishman, but a fairly conscientious pupil and a fairly upright man. Little did I suppose that his ramrod body and frozen face would, in the end, step in between me and all my dearest wishes; that upon this precise, regular, icy soldier-man my fortunes should so nearly shipwreck! I never liked, but yet I trusted him; and though it may seem but a trifle, I found his snuff-box with the bean in it come very welcome.

For it is strange how grown men and seasoned soldiers can go back in life; so that after but a little while in prison, which

is after all the next thing to being in the nursery, they grow
absorbed in the most pitiful, childish interests, and a sugar
biscuit or a pinch of snuff become things to follow after and
scheme for!

We made but a poor show of prisoners. The officers had
been all offered their parole, and had taken it. They lived
mostly in suburbs of the city, lodging with modest families,
and enjoyed their freedom and supported the almost continual
evil tidings of the Emperor as best they might. It chanced I
was the only gentleman among the privates who remained. A
great part were ignorant Italians, of a regiment that had
suffered heavily in Catalonia. The rest were mere diggers of
the soil, treaders of grapes or hewers of wood, who had been
suddenly and violently preferred to the glorious state of soldiers.
We had but the one interest in common : each of us who had
any skill with his fingers passed the hours of his captivity in
the making of little toys and *articles of Paris* ; and the prison
was daily visited at certain hours by a concourse of people of
the country, come to exult over our distress, or—it is more
tolerant to suppose—their own vicarious triumph. Some moved
among us with a decency of shame or sympathy. Others were
the most offensive personages in the world, gaped at us as if we
had been baboons, sought to evangelise us to their rustic,
northern religion, as though we had been savages, or tortured
us with intelligence of disasters to the arms of France. Good,
bad, and indifferent, there was one alleviation to the annoyance
of these visitors; for it was the practice of almost all to purchase
some specimen of our rude handiwork. This led, amongst the
the prisoners, to a strong spirit of competition. Some were
neat of hand, and (the genius of the French being always distinguished) could place upon sale little miracles of dexterity
and taste. Some had a more engaging appearance ; fine
features were found to do as well as fine merchandise, and an
air of youth in particular (as it appealed to the sentiment of
pity in our visitors) to be a source of profit. Others again
enjoyed some acquaintance with the language, and were able
to recommend the more agreeably to purchasers such trifles as
they had to sell. To the first of these advantages I could lay
no claim, for my fingers were all thumbs. Some at least of the
others I possessed ; and finding much entertainment in our
commerce, I did not suffer my advantages to rust. I have
never despised the social arts, in which it is a national boast
that every Frenchman should excel. For the approach of
particular sorts of visitors, I had a particular manner of address,
and even of appearance, which I could readily assume and

change on the occasion rising. I never lost an opportunity to
flatter either the person of my visitor, if it should be a lady,
or, if it should be a man, the greatness of his country in war.
And in case my compliments should miss their aim, I was
always ready to cover my retreat with some agreeable pleasantry,
which would often earn me the name of an 'oddity' or a 'droll
fellow.' In this way, although I was so left-handed a toy-
maker, I made out to be rather a successful merchant; and
found means to procure many little delicacies and alleviations,
such as children or prisoners desire.

I am scarcely drawing the portrait of a very melancholy man.
It is not indeed my character; and I had, in a comparison with
my comrades, many reasons for content. In the first place, I
had no family: I was an orphan and a bachelor; neither wife
nor child awaited me in France. In the second, I had never
wholly forgot the emotions with which I first found myself a
prisoner; and although a military prison be not altogether a
garden of delights, it is still preferable to a gallows. In the
third, I am almost ashamed to say it, but I found a certain
pleasure in our place of residence: being an obsolete and
really mediæval fortress, high placed and commanding extraordinary prospects, not only over sea, mountain, and champaign
but actually over the thoroughfares of a capital city, which we
could see blackened by day with the moving crowd of the
inhabitants, and at night shining with lamps. And lastly,
although I was not insensible to the restraints of prison or the
scantiness of our rations, I remembered I had sometimes eaten
quite as ill in Spain, and had to mount guard and march
perhaps a dozen leagues into the bargain. The first of my
troubles, indeed, was the costume we were obliged to wear.
There is a horrible practice in England to trick out in ridiculous
uniforms, and as it were to brand in mass, not only convicts but
military prisoners, and even the children in charity schools. I
think some malignant genius had found his masterpiece of irony
in the dress which we were condemned to wear: jacket, waistcoat, and trousers of a sulphur or mustard yellow, and a shirt or
blue-and-white striped cotton. It was conspicuous, it was
cheap, it pointed us out to laughter—we, who were old soldiers,
used to arms, and some of us showing noble scars,—like a set or
lugubrious zanies at a fair. The old name of that rock on which
our prison stood was (I have heard since then) the *Painted Hill.*
Well, now it was all painted a bright yellow with our costumes;
and the dress of the soldiers who guarded us being of course
the essential British red rag, we made up together the elements
of a lively picture of hell. I have again and again looked round

upon my fellow-prisoners, and felt my anger rise, and choked upon tears, to behold them thus parodied. The more part, as I have said, were peasants, somewhat bettered perhaps by the drill-sergeant, but for all that ungainly, loutish fellows, with no more than a mere barrack-room smartness of address: indeed, you could have seen our army nowhere more discreditably represented than in this Castle of Edinburgh. And I used to see myself in fancy, and blush. It seemed that my more elegant carriage would but point the insult of the travesty. And I remembered the days when I wore the coarse but honourable coat of a soldier; and remembered further back how many of the noble, the fair, and the gracious had taken a delight to tend my childhood. . . . But I must not recall these tender and sorrowful memories twice; their place is further on, and I am now upon another business. The perfidy of the Britannic Government stood nowhere more openly confessed than in one particular of our discipline: that we were shaved twice in the week. To a man who has loved all his life to be fresh shaven, can a more irritating indignity be devised? Monday and Thursday were the days. Take the Thursday, and conceive the picture I must present by Sunday evening! And Saturday, which was almost as bad, was the great day for visitors.

Those who came to our market were of all qualities, men and women, the lean and the stout, the plain and the fairly pretty. Sure, if people at all understood the power of beauty, there would be no prayers addressed except to Venus; and the mere privilege of beholding a comely woman is worth paying for. Our visitors, upon the whole, were not much to boast of; and yet, sitting in a corner and very much ashamed of myself and my absurd appearance, I have again and again tasted the finest, the rarest, and the most ethereal pleasures in a glance of an eye that I should never see again—and never wanted to. The flower of the hedgerow and the star in heaven satisfy and delight us: how much more the look of that exquisite being who was created to bear and rear, to madden and rejoice, mankind!

There was one young lady in particular, about eighteen or nineteen, tall, of a gallant carriage, and with a profusion of hair in which the sun found threads of gold. As soon as she came in the courtyard (and she was a rather frequent visitor) it seemed I was aware of it. She had an air of angelic candour, yet of a high spirit; she stepped like a Diana, every movement was noble and free. One day there was a strong east wind; the banner was straining at the flagstaff; below us the smoke of the city chimneys blew hither and thither in a thousand crazy variations; and away out on the Forth we could see the ships lying down to it and scudding. I was thinking what a vile day it was, when she appeared. Her hair blew in the wind with changes of colour; her garments moulded her with the accuracy of sculpture; the ends of her shawl fluttered about her ear and were caught in again with an inimitable deftness. You have seen a pool on a gusty day, how it suddenly sparkles and flashes like a thing alive? So this lady's face had become animated and coloured; and as I saw her standing, somewhat inclined, her lips parted, a divine trouble in her eyes, I could have clapped my hands in applause, and was ready to acclaim her a genuine daughter of the winds. What put it in my head, I know not: perhaps because it was a Thursday and I was new from the razor; but I determined to engage her attention no later than that day. She was approaching that part of the court in which I sat with my merchandise, when I observed her handkerchief to escape from her hands and fall to the ground; the next moment the wind had taken it up and carried it within my reach. I was on foot at once: I had forgot my mustard-coloured clothes, I had forgot the private soldier and his salute. Bowing deeply, I offered her the slip of cambric.

'Madam,' said I, 'your handkerchief. The wind brought it me.'

I met her eyes fully.

'I thank you, sir,' said she.

'The wind brought it me,' I repeated. 'May I not take it for an omen? You have an English proverb, "It's an ill wind that blows nobody good."'

'Well,' she said, with a smile, '"One good turn deserves another." I will see what you have.'

She followed me to where my wares were spread out under lee of a piece of cannon.

'Alas, mademoiselle!' said I, 'I am no very perfect craftsman. This is supposed to be a house, and you see the chimneys are awry. You may call this a box if you are very indulgent; but see where my tool slipped! Yes, I am afraid you may go from one to another, and find a flaw in everything. *Failures for Sale* should be on my signboard. I do not keep a shop; I keep a Humorous Museum.' I cast a smiling glance about my display, and then at her, and instantly became grave. 'Strange, is it not,' I added, 'that a grown man and a soldier should be engaged upon such trash, and a sad heart produce anything so funny to look at?'

An unpleasant voice summoned her at this moment by the name of Flora, and she made a hasty purchase and rejoined her party.

A few days after she came again. But I must first tell you how she came to be so frequent. Her aunt was one of those terrible British old maids, of which the world has heard much ; and having nothing whatever to do, and a word or two of French, she had taken what she called an *interest in the French prisoners*. A big, bustling, bold old lady, she flounced about our market-place with insufferable airs of patronage and con- descension. She bought, indeed, with liberality, but her manner of studying us through a quizzing-glass, and playing cicerone to her followers, acquitted us of any gratitude. She had a tail behind her of heavy, obsequious old gentlemen, or dull, giggling misses, to whom she appeared to be an oracle. 'This one can really carve prettily : is he not a quiz with his big whiskers ?' she would say. 'And this one,' indicating myself with her gold eye-glass, 'is, I assure you, quite an oddity.' The oddity, you may be certain, ground his teeth. She had a way of standing in our midst, nodding around, and addressing us in what she imagined to be French : '*Bienne, hommes ! ça va bienne ?*' I took the freedom to reply in the same lingo : '*Bienne, femme ! ça va couci-couci tout d'même, la bourgeoise !*' And at that, when we had all laughed with a little more heartiness than was entirely civil, 'I told you he was quite an oddity !' says she in triumph. Needless to say, these passages were before I had remarked the niece.

The aunt came on the day in question with a following rather more than usually large, which she manœuvred to and fro about the market and lectured to at rather more than usual length, and with rather less than her accustomed tact. I kept my eyes down, but they were ever fixed in the same direction, quite in vain. The aunt came and went, and pulled us out, and showed us off, like caged monkeys ; but the niece kept herself on the outskirts of the crowd and on the opposite side of the courtyard, and departed at last as she had come, without a sign. Closely as I had watched her, I could not say her eyes had ever rested on me for an instant ; and my heart was over- whelmed with bitterness and blackness. I tore out her detested image ; I felt I was done with her for ever ; I laughed at myself savagely, because I had thought to please ; when I lay down at night sleep forsook me, and I lay, and rolled, and gloated on her charms, and cursed her insensibility, for half the night. How trivial I thought her ! and how trivial her sex ! A man might be an angel or an Apollo, and a mustard-coloured coat would wholly blind them to his merits. I was a prisoner, a slave, a contemned and despicable being, the butt of her sniggering countrymen. I would take the lesson: no proud daughter of my foes should have the chance to mock at me again; none in the future should have the chance to think I had looked at her with admiration. You cannot imagine any one of a more resolute and independent spirit, or whose bosom was more wholly mailed with patriotic arrogance, than I. Before I dropped asleep, I had remembered all the infamies of Britain, and debited them in an overwhelming column to Flora.

The next day, as I sat in my place, I became conscious there was some one standing near; and behold, it was herself! I kept my seat, at first in the confusion of my mind, later on from policy; and she stood, and leaned a little over me, as in pity. She was very still and timid; her voice was low. Did I suffer in my captivity? she asked me. Had I to complain of any hardship?

'Mademoiselle, I have not learned to complain,' said I. 'I am a soldier of Napoleon.'

She sighed. 'At least you must regret *La France*,' said she, and coloured a little as she pronounced the words, which she did with a pretty strangeness of accent.

'What am I to say?' I replied. 'If you were carried from this country, for which you seem so wholly suited, where the very rains and winds seem to become you like ornaments, would you regret, do you think? We must surely all regret! the son to his mother, the man to his country; these are native feelings.'

'You have a mother?' she asked.

'In heaven, mademoiselle,' I answered. 'She, and my father also, went by the same road to heaven as so many others of the fair and brave: they followed their queen upon the scaffold. So, you see, I am not so much to be pitied in my prison,' I continued: 'there are none to wait for me; I am alone in the world. 'Tis a different case, for instance, with yon poor fellow in the cloth cap. His bed is next to mine, and in the night I hear him sobbing to himself. He has a tender character, full of tender and pretty sentiments; and in the dark at night, and sometimes by day when he can get me apart with him, he laments a mother and a sweetheart. Do you know what made him take me for a confidant?'

She parted her lips with a look, but did not speak. The look burned all through me with a sudden vital heat.

'Because I had once seen, in marching by, the belfry of his village!' I continued. 'The circumstance is quaint enough. It seems to bind up into one the whole bundle of those human

instincts that make life beautiful, and people and places dear
—and from which it would seem I am cut off!'

I rested my chin on my knee and looked before me on the
ground. I had been talking until then to hold her; but I was
now not sorry she should go: an impression is a thing so delicate to produce and so easy to overthrow! Presently she
seemed to make an effort.

'I will take this toy,' she said, laid a five-and-sixpenny piece
in my hand, and was gone ere I could thank her.

I retired to a place apart near the ramparts and behind a
gun. The beauty, the expression of her eyes, the tear that
had trembled there, the compassion in her voice, and a kind
of wild elegance that consecrated the freedom of her movements, all combined to enslave my imagination and inflame my
heart. What had she said? Nothing to signify; but her eyes
had met mine, and the fire they had kindled burned inextin-
guishably in my veins. I loved her; and I did not fear to
hope. Twice I had spoken with her; and in both interviews
I had been well inspired, I had engaged her sympathies, I had
found words that she must remember, that would ring in her
ears at night upon her bed. What mattered if I were half
shaved and my clothes a caricature? I was still a man, and I
had drawn my image on her memory. I was still a man, and,
as I trembled to realise, she was still a woman. Many waters
cannot quench love; and love, which is the law of the world,
was on my side. I closed my eyes, and she sprang up on the
background of the darkness, more beautiful than in life. 'Ah!'
thought I, 'and you too, my dear, you too must carry away with
you a picture, that you are still to behold again and still to em-
bellish. In the darkness of night, in the streets by day, still
you are to have my voice and face, whispering, making love
for me, encroaching on your shy heart. Shy as your heart is,
it is lodged there—*I* am lodged there; let the hours do their
office—let time continue to draw me ever in more lively, ever
in more insidious colours.' And then I had a vision of myself,
and burst out laughing.

A likely thing, indeed, that a beggar-man, a private soldier,
a prisoner in a yellow travesty, was to awake the interest of
this fair girl! I would not despair; but I saw the game must
be played fine and close. It must be my policy to hold myself
before her, always in a pathetic or pleasing attitude; never to
alarm or startle her; to keep my own secret locked in my
bosom like a story of disgrace, and let hers (if she could be
induced to have one) grow at its own rate; to move just so
fast, and not by a hair's-breadth any faster, than the inclina-

tion of her heart. I was the man, and yet I was passive, tied by the foot in prison. I could not go to her; I must cast a spell upon her at each visit, so that she should return to me; and this was a matter of nice management. I had done it the last time—it seemed impossible she should not come again after our interview; and for the next I had speedily ripened a fresh plan. A prisoner, if he has one great disability for a lover, has yet one considerable advantage: there is nothing to distract him, and he can spend all his hours ripening his love and preparing its manifestations. I had been then some days upon a piece of carving,—no less than the emblem of Scotland, the Lion Rampant. This I proceeded to finish with what skill I was possessed of; and when at last I could do no more to it (and, you may be sure, was already regretting I had done so much), added on the base the following dedication.—

À LA BELLE FLORA

LE PRISONNIER RECONNAISSANT

A. D. ST. Y. D. K.

I put my heart into the carving of these letters. What was done with so much ardour, it seemed scarce possible that any should behold with indifference; and the initials would at least suggest to her my noble birth. I thought it better to suggest: I felt that mystery was my stock-in-trade; the contrast between my rank and manners, between my speech and my clothing, and the fact that she could only think of me by a combination of letters, must all tend to increase her interest and engage her heart.

This done, there was nothing left for me but to wait and to hope. And there is nothing further from my character: in love and in war, I am all for the forward movement; and these days of waiting made my purgatory. It is a fact that I loved her a great deal better at the end of them; for love comes, like bread, from a perpetual rehandling. And besides, I was fallen into a panic of fear. How, if she came no more, how was I to continue to endure my empty days? how was I to fall back and find my interest in the major's lessons, the lieutenant's chess, in a twopenny sale in the market, or a halfpenny addition to the prison fare?

Days went by, and weeks; I had not the courage to calculate, and to-day I have not the courage to remember; but at last she was there. At last I saw her approach me in the company of a boy about her own age, and whom I divined at once to be her brother.

I rose and bowed in silence.

'This is my brother, Mr. Ronald Gilchrist,' said she. 'I have told him of your sufferings. He is so sorry for you!'

'It is more than I have the right to ask,' I replied; 'but among gentlefolk these generous sentiments are natural. If your brother and I were to meet in the field, we should meet like tigers; but when he sees me here disarmed and helpless, he forgets his animosity.' (At which, as I had ventured to expect, this beardless champion coloured to the ears for pleasure.) 'Ah, my dear young lady,' I continued, 'there are many of your countrymen languishing in my country, even as I do here. I can but hope there is found some French lady to convey to each of them the priceless consolation of her sympathy. You have given me alms; and more than alms—hope; and while you were absent I was not forgetful. Suffer me to be able to tell myself that I have at least tried to make a return; and for the prisoner's sake deign to accept this trifle.'

So saying, I offered her my lion, which she took, looked at in some embarrassment, and then, catching sight of the dedication, broke out with a cry.

'Why, how did you know my name?' she exclaimed.

'When names are so appropriate, they should be easily guessed,' said I, bowing. 'But indeed, there was no magic in the matter. A lady called you by name on the day I found your handkerchief, and I was quick to remark and cherish it.'

'It is very, very beautiful,' said she, 'and I shall be always proud of the inscription.—Come, Ronald, we must be going.' She bowed to me as a lady bows to her equal, and passed on (I could have sworn) with a heightened colour.

I was overjoyed: my innocent ruse had succeeded; she had taken my gift without a hint of payment, and she would scarce sleep in peace till she had made it up to me. No greenhorn in matters of the heart, I was besides aware that I had now a resident ambassador at the court of my lady. The lion might be ill chiselled; it was mine. My hands had made and held it; my knife—or, to speak more by the mark, my rusty nail— had traced those letters; and simple as the words were, they would keep repeating to her that I was grateful and that I found her fair. The boy had looked like a gawky, and blushed at a compliment; I could see besides that he regarded me with considerable suspicion; yet he made so manly a figure of a lad, that I could not withhold from him my sympathy. And as for the impulse that had made her bring and introduce him, I could not sufficiently admire it. It seemed to me finer than wit, and more tender than a caress. It said (plain as language), 'I do not and I cannot know you. Here is my brother —you can know him; this is the way to me—follow it.'

CHAPTER II

A TALE OF A PAIR OF SCISSORS

I was still plunged in these thoughts when the bell was rung that discharged our visitors into the street. Our little market was no sooner closed than we were summoned to the distribution, and received our rations, which we were then allowed to eat according to fancy in any part of our quarters.

I have said the conduct of some of our visitors was unbearably offensive; it was possibly more so than they dreamed—as the sight-seers at a menagerie may offend in a thousand ways, and quite without meaning it, the noble and unfortunate animals behind the bars; and there is no doubt but some of my compatriots were susceptible beyond reason. Some of these old whiskerandos, originally peasants, trained since boyhood in victorious armies, and accustomed to move among subject and trembling populations, could ill brook their change of circumstance. There was one man of the name of Goguelat, a brute of the first water, who had enjoyed no touch of civilisation beyond the military discipline, and had risen by an extreme heroism of bravery to a grade for which he was otherwise unfitted—that of *maréchal des logis* in the 22nd of the line. In so far as a brute can be a good soldier, he was a good soldier; the Cross was on his breast, and gallantly earned; but in all things outside his line of duty the man was no other than a brawling, bruising ignorant pillar of low pothouses. As a gentleman by birth, and a scholar by taste and education, I was the type of all that he least understood and most detested; and the mere view of our visitors would leave him daily in a transport of annoyance, which he would make haste to wreak on the nearest victim, and too often on myself.

It was so now. Our rations were scarce served out, and I had just withdrawn into a corner of the yard, when I perceived him drawing near. He wore an air of hateful mirth; a set of young fools, among whom he passed for a wit, followed

11

him with looks of expectation; and I saw I was about to be the object of some of his insufferable pleasantries. He took a place beside me, spread out his rations, drank to me derisively from his measure of prison beer, and began. What he said it would be impossible to print; but his admirers, who believed their wit to have surpassed himself, actually rolled among the gravel. For my part, I thought at first I should have died. I had not dreamed the wretch was so observant; but hate sharpens the ears, and he had counted our interviews and actually knew Flora by her name. Gradually my coolness returned to me, accompanied by a volume of living anger that surprised myself.

'Are you nearly done?' I asked. 'Because if you are, I am about to say a word or two myself.'

'Oh, fair play!' said he. 'Turn about! The Marquis of Carabas to the tribune.'

'Very well,' said I. 'I have to inform you that I am a gentleman. You do not know what that means, hey? Well, I will tell you. It is a comical sort of animal; springs from another strange set of creatures they call ancestors; and, in common with toads and other vermin, has a thing that he calls feelings. The lion is a gentleman; he will not touch carrion. I am a gentleman, and I cannot bear to soil my fingers with such a lump of dirt. Sit still, Philippe Goguelat! sit still and do not say a word, or I shall know you are a coward; the eyes of our guards are upon us. Here is your health!' said I, and pledged him in the prison beer. 'You have chosen to speak in a certain way of a young child,' I continued, 'who might be your daughter, and who was giving alms to me and some others of us mendicants. If the Emperor'—saluting—'if my Emperor could hear you, he would pluck off the Cross from your gross body. I cannot do that; I cannot take away what His Majesty has given; but one thing I promise you—I promise you, Goguelat, you shall be dead to-night.'

I had borne so much from him in the past, I believe he thought there was no end to my forbearance, and he was at first amazed. But I have the pleasure to think that some of my expressions had pierced through his thick hide; and besides, the brute was truly a hero of valour, and loved fighting for itself. Whatever the cause, at least, he had soon pulled himself together, and took the thing (to do him justice) handsomely.

'And I promise you, by the devil's horns, that you shall have the chance!' said he, and pledged me again; and again I did him scrupulous honour.

The news of this defiance spread from prisoner to prisoner
with the speed of wings ; every face was seen to be illuminated
like those of the spectators at a horse-race ; and indeed you
must first have tasted the active life of a soldier, and then
mouldered for a while in the tedium of a jail, in order to understand, perhaps even to excuse, the delight of our companions.
Goguelat and I slept in the same squad, which greatly simpli-
fied the business ; and a committee of honour was accordingly
formed of our shed-mates. They chose for president a sergeant-
major in the 4th Dragoons, a greybeard of the army, an excellent military subject, and a good man. He took the most
serious view of his functions, visited us both, and reported our
replies to the committee. Mine was of a decent firmness. I
told him the young lady of whom Goguelat had spoken had on
several occasions given me alms. I reminded him that, if we
were now reduced to hold out our hands and sell pill-boxes for
charity, it was something very new for soldiers of the Empire.
We had all seen bandits standing at a corner of a wood truck-
ling for copper halfpence, and after their benefactors were gone
spitting out injuries and curses. ' But,' said I, ' I trust that
none of us will fall so low. As a Frenchman and a soldier, I
owe that young child gratitude, and am bound to protect her
character, and to support that of the army. You are my elder
and my superior : tell me if I am not right.'

' He was a quiet-mannered old fellow, and patted me with
three fingers on the back. ' *C'est bien, mon enfant,*' says he,
and returned to his committee.

Goguelat was no more accommodating than myself. ' I do not
like apologies nor those that make them,' was his only answer.
And there remained nothing but to arrange the details of the
meeting. So far as regards place and time we had no choice ;
we must settle the dispute at night, in the dark, after a round
had passed by, and in the open middle of the shed under which
we slept. The question of arms was more obscure. We had a
good many tools, indeed, which we employed in the manufacture of our toys ; but they were none of them suited for a single
combat between civilised men, and, being nondescript, it was
found extremely hard to equalise the chances of the combatants. At length a pair of scissors was unscrewed ; and a couple
of tough wands being found in a corner of the courtyard, one
blade of the scissors was lashed solidly to each with resined
twine—the twine coming I know not whence, but the resin
from the green pillars of the shed, which still sweated from the
axe. It was a strange thing to feel in one's hand this weapon,
which was no heavier than a riding-rod, and which it was diffi-

cult to suppose would prove more dangerous. A general oath was administered and taken, that no one should interfere in the duel nor (suppose it to result seriously) betray the name of the survivor. And with that, all being then ready, we composed ourselves to await the moment.

The evening fell cloudy; not a star was to be seen when the first round of the night passed through our shed and wound off along the ramparts; and as we took our places, we could still hear, over the murmurs of the surrounding city, the sentries challenging its further passage. Leclos, the sergeant-major, set us in our stations, engaged our wands, and left us. To avoid blood-stained clothing, my adversary and I had stripped to the shoes; and the chill of the night enveloped our bodies like a wet sheet. The man was better at fencing than myself; he was vastly taller than I, being of a stature almost gigantic, and proportionately strong. In the inky blackness of the shed, it was impossible to see his eyes; and from the suppleness of the wands, I did not like to trust to a parade. I made up my mind accordingly to profit, if I might, by my defect; and as soon as the signal should be given, to throw myself down and lunge at the same moment. It was to play my life upon one card: should I not mortally wound him, no defence would be left me; what was yet more appalling, I thus ran the risk of bringing my own face against his scissor with the double force of our assaults, and my face and eyes are not that part of me that I would the most readily expose.

'*Allez!*' said the sergeant-major.

Both lunged in the same moment with an equal fury, and but for my manœuvre both had certainly been spitted. As it was, he did no more than strike my shoulder, while my scissor plunged below the girdle into a mortal part; and that great bulk of a man, falling from his whole height, knocked me immediately senseless.

When I came to myself I was laid in my own sleeping-place, and could make out in the darkness the outline of perhaps a dozen heads crowded around me. I sat up. 'What is it?' I exclaimed.

'Hush!' said the sergeant-major. 'Blessed be God, all is well.' I felt him clasp my hand, and there were tears in his voice. ''Tis but a scratch, my child; here is papa, who is taking good care of you. Your shoulder is bound up; we have dressed you in your clothes again, and it will all be well.'

At this I began to remember. 'And Goguelat?' I gasped.

'He cannot bear to be moved; he has his bellyful; 'tis a bad business, said the sergeant-major.

The idea of having killed a man with such an instrument as half a pair of scissors seemed to turn my stomach. I am sure I might have killed a dozen with a firelock, a sabre, a bayonet, or any accepted weapon, and been visited by no such sickness of remorse. And to this feeling every unusual circumstance of our rencounter, the darkness in which we had fought, our nakedness, even the resin on the twine, appeared to contribute. I ran to my fallen adversary, kneeled by him, and could only sob his name.

He bade me compose myself. 'You have given me the key of the fields, comrade,' said he. '*Sans rancune!*'

At this my horror redoubled. Here had we two expatriated Frenchmen engaged in an ill-regulated combat like the battles of beasts. Here was he, who had been all his life so great a ruffian, dying in a foreign land of this ignoble injury, and meeting death with something of the spirit of a Bayard. I insisted that the guards should be summoned and a doctor brought. 'It may still be possible to save him,' I cried.

The sergeant-major reminded me of our engagement. 'If you had been wounded,' said he, 'you must have lain there till the patrol came by and found you. It happens to be Goguelat—and so must he! Come, child, time to go to by-by.' And as I still resisted, 'Champdivers!' he said, 'this is weakness. You pain me.'

'Ay, off to your beds with you!' said Goguelat, and named us in a company with one of his jovial gross epithets.

Accordingly the squad lay down in the dark and simulated, what they certainly were far from experiencing, sleep. It was not yet late. The city, from far below, and all around us, sent up a sound of wheels and feet and lively voices. Yet awhile, and the curtain of the cloud was rent across, and in the space of sky between the eaves of the shed and the irregular outline of the ramparts a multitude of stars appeared. Meantime, in the midst of us lay Goguelat, and could not always withhold himself from groaning.

We heard the round far off; heard it draw slowly nearer. Last of all, it turned the corner and moved into our field of vision: two file of men and a corporal with a lantern, which he swung to and fro, so as to cast its light in the recesses of the yards and sheds.

'Hullo!' cried the corporal, pausing as he came by Goguelat.

He stooped with his lantern. All our hearts were flying.

'What devil's work is this?' he cried, and with a startling voice summoned the guard.

We were all afoot upon the instant; more lanterns and soldiers crowded in front of the shed; an officer elbowed his way in. In the midst was the big naked body, soiled with blood. Some one had covered him with his blanket; but as he lay there in agony, he had partly thrown it off.

'This is murder!' cried the officer. 'You wild beasts, you will hear of this to-morrow.'

As Goguelat was raised and laid upon a stretcher, he cried to us a cheerful and blasphemous farewell.

CHAPTER III

THERE was never any talk of a recovery, and no time was lost in getting the man's deposition. He gave but the one account of it : that he had committed suicide because he was sick of seeing so many Englishmen. The doctor vowed it was impossible, the nature and direction of the wound forbidding it. Goguelat replied that he was more ingenious than the other thought for, and had propped up the weapon in the ground and fallen on the point—'just like Nebuchadnezzar,' he added, winking to the assistants. The doctor, who was a little, spruce, ruddy man of an impatient temper, pished and pshawed and swore over his patient. 'Nothing to be made of him !' he cried. 'A perfect heathen. If we could only find the weapon !' But the weapon had ceased to exist. A little resined twine was perhaps blowing about in the castle gutters ; some bits of broken stick may have trailed in corners ; and behold, in the pleasant air of the morning, a dandy prisoner trimming his nails with a pair of scissors !

Finding the wounded man so firm, you may be sure the authorities did not leave the rest of us in peace. No stone was left unturned. We were had in again and again to be examined, now singly, now in twos and threes. We were threatened with all sorts of impossible severities and tempted with all manner of improbable rewards. I suppose I was five times interrogated, and came off from each with flying colours. I am like old Souvaroff, I cannot understand a soldier being taken aback by any question ; he should answer, as he marches on the fire, with an instant briskness and gaiety. I may have been short of bread, gold or grace ; I was never yet found wanting in an answer. My comrades, if they were not all so ready, were none of them less staunch ; and I may say here at once that the inquiry came to nothing at the time, and the death of Goguelat remained a mystery of the prison. Such were the veterans of France ! And yet I should be disingenuous if I did not own this was a case apart ; in ordinary circumstances, some one might have stumbled or been intimidated into an admission; and what bound us together with a closeness beyond that of mere comrades was a secret to which we were all committed and a design in which all were equally engaged. No need to inquire as to its nature: there is only one desire, and only one kind of design, that blooms in prisons. And the fact that our tunnel was near done supported and inspired us.

I came off in public, as I have said, with flying colours; the sittings of the court of inquiry died away like a tune that no one listens to; and yet I was unmasked—I, whom my very adversary defended, as good as confessed, as good as told the nature of the quarrel, and by so doing prepared for myself in the future a most anxious, disagreeable adventure. It was the third morning after the duel, and Goguelat was still in life, when the time came round for me to give Major Chevenix a lesson. I was fond of this occupation; not that he paid me much—no more, indeed, than eighteenpence a month, the customary figure, being a miser in the grain; but because I liked his breakfasts and (to some extent) himself. At least, he was a man of education; and of the others with whom I had any opportunity of speech, those that would not have held a book upsidedown would have torn the pages out for pipe-lights. For I must repeat again that our body of prisoners was exceptional: there was in Edinburgh Castle none of that educational busyness that distinguished some of the other prisons, so that men entered them unable to read, and left them fit for high employments. Chevenix was handsome, and surprisingly young to be a major: six feet in his stockings, well set up, with regular features and very clear grey eyes. It was impossible to pick a fault in him, and yet the sum-total was displeasing. Perhaps he was too clean; he seemed to bear about with him the smell of soap. Cleanliness is good, but I cannot bear a man's nails to seem japanned. And certainly he was too self-possessed and cold. There was none of the fire of youth, none of the swiftness of the soldier, in this young officer. His kindness was cold, and cruel cold; his deliberation exasperating. And perhaps it was from this character, which is very much the opposite of my own, that even in these days, when he was of service to me, I approached him with suspicion and reserve.

I looked over his exercise in the usual form, and marked six faults.

'H'm. Six,' says he, looking at the paper. 'Very annoying! I can never get it right.'

'Oh, but you make excellent progress!' I said. I would

not discourage him, you understand, but he was congenitally unable to learn French. Some fire, I think, is needful, and he had quenched his fire in soapsuds.

He put the exercise down, leaned his chin upon his hand, and looked at me with clear, severe eyes.

'I think we must have a little talk,' said he.

'I am entirely at your disposition,' I replied; but I quaked, for I knew what subject to expect.

'You have been some time giving me these lessons,' he went on, 'and I am tempted to think rather well of you. I believe you are a gentleman.'

'I have that honour, sir,' said I.

'You have seen me for the same period. I do not know how I strike you; but perhaps you will be prepared to believe that I also am a man of honour,' said he.

'I require no assurances; the thing is manifest,' and I bowed.

'Very well, then,' said he. 'What about this Goguelat?'

'You heard me yesterday before the court,' I began. 'I was awakened only——'

'Oh yes; I "heard you yesterday before the court," no doubt,' he interrupted, 'and I remember perfectly that you were "awakened only." I could repeat the most of it by rote, indeed. But do you suppose that I believed you for a moment?'

'Neither would you believe me if I were to repeat it here,' said I.

'I may be wrong—we shall soon see,' says he; 'but my impression is that you will not "repeat it here." My impression is that you have come into this room, and that you will tell me something before you go out.'

I shrugged my shoulders.

'Let me explain,' he continued. 'Your evidence, of course, is nonsense. I put it by, and the court put it by.'

'My compliments and thanks!' said I.

'You *must* know—that's the short and the long,' he proceeded. 'All of you in shed B are bound to know. And I want to ask you where is the common-sense of keeping up this farce, and maintaining this cock-and-bull story between friends. Come, come, my good fellow, own yourself beaten, and laugh at it yourself.'

'Well, I hear you, go ahead,' said I. 'You put your heart in it.'

He crossed his legs slowly. 'I can very well understand,' he began, 'that precautions have had to be taken. I dare say

an oath was administered. I can comprehend that perfectly.'
(He was watching me all the time with his cold, bright eyes.)
'And I can comprehend that, about an affair of honour, you
would be very particular to keep it.'

'About an affair of. honour?' I repeated, like a man quite
puzzled.

'It was not an affair of honour, then?' he asked.

'What was not? I do not follow,' said I.

He gave no sign of impatience; simply sat awhile silent, and
began again in the same placid and good-natured voice: 'The
court and I were at one in setting aside your evidence. It
could not deceive a child. But there was a difference between
myself and the other officers, because *I knew my man* and they
did not. They saw in you a common soldier, and I knew you
for a gentleman. To them your evidence was a leash of lies,
which they yawned to hear you telling. Now, I was asking
myself, how far will a gentleman go? Not surely so far as to
help hush a murder up? So that—when I heard you tell how
you knew nothing of the matter, and were only awakened by
the corporal, and all the rest of it—I translated your statements
into something else. Now, Champdivers,' he cried, springing
up lively and coming towards me with animation, 'I am going
to tell you what that was, and you are going to help me to see
justice done: how, I don't know, for of course you are under
oath—but somehow. Mark what I'm going to say.'   .

At that moment he laid a heavy, hard grip upon my shoulder;
and whether he said anything more or came to a full stop at
once, I am sure I could not tell you to this day. For, as the
devil would have it, the shoulder he laid hold of was the one
Goguelat had pinked. The wound was but a scratch; it was
healing with the first intention; but in the clutch of Major
Chevenix it gave me agony. My head swam; the sweat poured
off my face; I must have grown deadly pale.

He removed his hand as suddenly as he had laid it there.

'What is wrong with you?' said he.

'It is nothing,' said I. 'A qualm. It has gone by.'

'Are you sure?' said he. 'You are as white as a sheet.'

'Oh no, I assure you! Nothing whatever. I am my own
man again,' I said, though I could scarce command my tongue.

'Well, shall I go on again?' says he. 'Can you follow me?'

'Oh, by all means!' said I, and mopped my streaming face
upon my sleeve, for you may be sure in those days I had no
handkerchief.

'If you are sure you can follow me. That was a very sudden
and sharp seizure,' he said doubtfully. 'But if you are sure,

all right, and here goes. An affair of honour among you fellows would, naturally, be a little difficult to carry out, perhaps it would be impossible to have it wholly regular. And yet a duel might be very irregular in form, and, under the peculiar circumstances of the case, loyal enough in effect. Do you take me? Now, as a gentleman and a soldier.'

His hand rose again at the words and hovered over me. I could bear no more, and winced away from him. 'No,' I cried, 'not that. Do not put your hand upon my shoulder. I cannot bear it. It is rheumatism,' I made haste to add. 'My shoulder is inflamed and very painful.'

He returned to his chair and deliberately lighted a cigar.

'I am sorry about your shoulder,' he said at last. 'Let me send for the doctor.'

'Not in the least,' said I. 'It is a trifle. I am quite used to it. It does not trouble me in the smallest. At any rate, I don't believe in doctors.'

'All right,' said he, and sat and smoked a good while in a silence which I would have given anything to break. 'Well,' he began presently, 'I believe there is nothing left for me to learn. I presume I may say that I know all.'

'About what?' said I boldly.

'About Goguelat,' said he.

'I beg your pardon. I cannot conceive,' said I.

'Oh,' says the major, 'the man fell in a duel, and by your hand! I am not an infant.'

'By no means,' said I. 'But you seem to me to be a good deal of a theorist.'

'Shall we test it?' he asked. 'The doctor is close by. If there is not an open wound on your shoulder, I am wrong. If there is——' He waved his hand. 'But I advise you to think twice. There is a deuce of a nasty drawback to the experiment—that what might have remained private between us two becomes public property.'

'Oh, well!' said I, with a laugh, 'anything rather than a doctor! I cannot bear the breed.'

His last words had a good deal relieved me, but I was still far from comfortable.

Major Chevenix smoked awhile, looking now at his cigar ash, now at me. 'I'm a soldier myself,' he says presently, 'and I've been out in my time and hit my man. I don't want to run any one into a corner for an affair that was at all necessary or correct. At the same time, I want to know that much, and I'll take your word of honour for it. Otherwise, I shall be very sorry, but the doctor must be called in.'

'I neither admit anything nor deny anything,' I returned. 'But if this form of words will suffice you, here is what I say: I give you my parole, as a gentleman and a soldier, there has nothing taken place amongst us prisoners that was not honourable as the day.'

'All right,' says he. 'That was all I wanted. You can go now, Champdivers.'

And as I was going out he added, with a laugh: 'By the bye, I ought to apologise: I had no idea I was applying the torture!'

The same afternoon the doctor came into the courtyard with a piece of paper in his hand. He seemed hot and angry, and had certainly no mind to be polite.

'Here!' he cried. 'Which of you fellows knows any English? 'Oh!'—spying me—'there you are, what's your name! *You*'ll do. Tell these fellows that the other fellow's dying. He's booked; no use talking; I expect he'll go by evening. And tell them I don't envy the feelings of the fellow who spiked him. Tell them that first.'

I did so.

'Then you can tell 'em,' he resumed, 'that the fellow, Goggle—what's his name?—wants to see some of them before he gets his marching orders. If I got it right, he wants to kiss or embrace you, or some sickening stuff. Got that? Then here's a list he's had written, and you'd better read it out to them—I can't make head or tail of your beastly names—and they can answer *present*, and fall in against that wall.'

It was with a singular movement of incongruous feelings that I read the first name on the list. I had no wish to look again on my own handiwork; my flesh recoiled from the idea; and how could I be sure what reception he designed to give me? The cure was in my own hand; I could pass that first name over—the doctor would not know—and I might stay away. But to the subsequent great gladness of my heart, I did not dwell for an instant on the thought, walked over to the designated wall, faced about, read out the name 'Champdivers,' and answered myself with the word 'Present.'

There were some half dozen on the list, all told; and as soon as we were mustered, the doctor led the way to the hospital, and we followed after, like a fatigue party, in single file. At the door he paused, told us 'the fellow' would see each of us alone, and, as soon as I had explained that, sent me by myself into the ward. It was a small room, whitewashed; a south window stood open on a vast depth of air and a spacious and distant prospect; and from deep below, in the Grassmarket, the voices of hawkers came up clear and far away. Hard by, on a little bed, lay Goguelat. The sunburn had not yet faded from his face, and the stamp of death was already there. There was something wild and unmannish in his smile, that took me by the throat; only death and love know or have ever seen it. And when he spoke, it seemed to shame his coarse talk.

He held out his arms as if to embrace me. I drew near with incredible shrinkings, and surrendered myself to his arms with overwhelming disgust. But he only drew my ear down to his lips.

'Trust me,' he whispered. '*Je suis bon bougre, moi.* I'll take it to hell with me, and tell the devil.'

Why should I go on to reproduce his grossness and trivialities? All that he thought, at that hour, was even noble, though he could not clothe it otherwise than in the language of a brutal farce. Presently he bade me call the doctor; and when that officer had come in, raised a little up in his bed, pointed first to himself and then to me, who stood weeping by his side, and several times repeated the expression, 'Frinds— frinds—dam frinds.'

To my great surprise, the doctor appeared very much affected. He nodded his little bob-wigged head at us, and said repeatedly, 'All right, Johnny—me comprong.'

Then Goguelat shook hands with me, embraced me again, and I went out of the room sobbing like an infant.

How often have I not seen it, that the most unpardonable fellows make the happiest exits! It is a fate we may well envy them. Goguelat was detested in life; in the last three days, by his admirable staunchness and consideration, he won every heart; and when word went about the prison the same evening that he was no more, the voice of conversation became hushed as in a house of mourning.

For myself I was like a man distracted; I cannot think what ailed me: when I awoke the following day, nothing remained of it; but that night I was filled with a gloomy fury of the nerves. I had killed him; he had done his utmost to protect me; I had seen him with that awful smile. And so illogical and useless is this sentiment of remorse, that I was ready, at a word or a look, to quarrel with somebody else. I presume the disposition of my mind was imprinted on my face; and when, a little after, I overtook, saluted and addressed the doctor, he looked on me with commiseration and surprise.

I had asked him if it was true.

'Yes,' he said, 'the fellow's gone.'

'Did he suffer much?' I asked.

'Devil a bit; passed away like a lamb,' said he. He looked on me a little, and I saw his hand go to his fob. 'Here, take that! no sense in fretting,' he said, and, putting a silver two-penny-bit in my hand, he left me.

I should have had that twopenny framed to hang upon the wall, for it was the man's one act of charity in all my knowledge of him. Instead of that, I stood looking at it in my hand and laughed out bitterly, as I realised his mistake; then went to the ramparts, and flung it far into the air like blood money. The night was falling; through an embrasure and across the gardened valley I saw the lamplighters hasting along Princes Street with ladder and lamp, and looked on moodily. As I was so standing a hand was laid upon my shoulder, and I turned about. It was Major Chevenix, dressed for the evening, and his neckcloth really admirably folded. I never denied the man could dress.

'Ah!' said he, 'I thought it was you, Champdivers. So he's gone?'

I nodded.

'Come, come,' said he, 'you must cheer up. Of course it's very distressing, very painful and all that. But do you know, it ain't such a bad thing either for you or me? What with his death and your visit to him I am entirely reassured.'

So I was to owe my life to Goguelat at every point.

'I had rather not discuss it,' said I.

'Well,' said he, 'one word more, and I'll agree to bury the subject. What did you fight about?'

'Oh, what do men ever fight about?' I cried.

'A lady?' said he.

I shrugged my shoulders.

'Deuce you did!' said he. 'I should scarce have thought it of him.'

And at this my ill-humour broke fairly out in words. 'He!' I cried. 'He never dared to address her—only to look at her and vomit his vile insults! She may have given him sixpence: if she did, it may take him to heaven yet!'

At this I became aware of his eyes set upon me with a considering look, and brought up sharply.

'Well, well,' said he. 'Good night to you, Champdivers. Come to me at breakfast-time to-morrow, and we'll talk of other subjects.'

I fully admit the man's conduct was not bad: in writing it down so long after the events I can even see that it was good.

CHAPTER IV

I was surprised one morning, shortly after, to find myself the object of marked consideration by a civilian and a stranger. This was a man of the middle age; he had a face of a mulberry colour, round black eyes, comical tufted eyebrows, and a protuberant forehead; and was dressed in clothes of a Quakerish cut. In spite of his plainness, he had that inscrutable air of a man well-to-do in his affairs. I conceived he had been some while observing me from a distance, for a sparrow sat betwixt us quite unalarmed on the breech of a piece of cannon. So soon as our eyes met, he drew near and addressed me in the French language, which he spoke with a good fluency but an abominable accent.

'I have the pleasure of addressing Monsieur le Vicomte Anne de Kéroual de Saint-Yves?' said he.

'Well,' said I, 'I do not call myself all that; but I have a right to, if I chose. In the meanwhile I call myself plain Champdivers, at your disposal. It was my mother's name, and good to go soldiering with.'

'I think not quite,' said he; 'for if I remember rightly, your mother also had the particle. Her name was Florimonde de Champdivers.'

'Right again!' said I, 'and I am extremely pleased to meet a gentleman so well informed in my quarterings. Is monsieur Born himself?' This I said with a great air of assumption, partly to conceal the degree of curiosity with which my visitor had inspired me, and in part because it struck me as highly incongruous and comical in my prison garb and on the lips of a private soldier.

He seemed to think so too, for he laughed.

'No, sir,' he returned, speaking this time in English; 'I am not "*born*," as you call it, and must content myself with *dying*, of which I am equally susceptible with the best of you. My name is Mr. Romaine—Daniel Romaine—a solicitor of London City, at your service; and, what will perhaps interest you more, I am here at the request of your great-uncle, the Count.'

'What!' I cried, 'does M. de Kéroual de St.-Yves remember the existence of such a person as myself, and will he deign to count kinship with a soldier of Napoleon?'

'You speak English well,' observed my visitor.

'It has been a second language to me from a child,' said I. 'I had an English nurse; my father spoke English with me; and I was finished by a countryman of yours and a dear friend of mine, a Mr. Vicary.'

A strong expression of interest came into the lawyer's face.

'What!' he cried, 'you knew poor Vicary?'

'For more than a year,' said I; 'and shared his hiding-place for many months.'

'And I was his clerk, and have succeeded him in business,' said he. 'Excellent man! It was on the affairs of M. de Kéroual that he went to that accursed country, from which he was never destined to return. Do you chance to know his end, sir?'

'I am sorry,' said I, 'I do. He perished miserably at the hands of a gang of banditti, such as we call *chauffeurs*. In a word, he was tortured, and died of it. See,' I added, kicking off one shoe, for I had no stockings; 'I was no more than a child, and see how they had begun to treat myself.'

He looked at the mark of my old burn with a certain shrinking. 'Beastly people!' I heard him mutter to himself.

'The English may say so with a good grace,' I observed politely.

Such speeches were the coin in which I paid my way among this credulous race. Ninety per cent. of our visitors would have accepted the remark as natural in itself and creditable to my powers of judgment, but it appeared my lawyer was more acute.

'You are not entirely a fool, I perceive,' said he.

'No,' said I; 'not wholly.'

'And yet it is well to beware of the ironical mood,' he continued. 'It is a dangerous instrument. Your great-uncle has, I believe, practised it very much, until it is now become a problem what he means.'

'And that brings me back to what you will admit is a most natural inquiry,' said I. 'To what do I owe the pleasure of this visit? how did you recognise me? and how did you know I was here?'

Carefully separating his coat skirts, the lawyer took a seat beside me on the edge of the flags.

'It is rather an odd story,' says he, 'and, with your leave,

I 'll answer the second question first. It was from a certain resemblance you bear to your cousin, M. le Vicomte.'

' I trust, sir, that I resemble him advantageously ?' said I.

' I hasten to reassure you,' was the reply : 'you do. To my eyes, M. Alain de St.-Yves has scarce a pleasing exterior. And yet, when I knew you were here, and was actually looking for you—why, the likeness helped. As for how I came to know your whereabouts, by an odd enough chance, it is again M. Alain we have to thank. I should tell you, he has for some time made it his business to keep M. de Kéroual informed of your career; with what purpose I leave you to judge. When he first brought the news of your—that you were serving Buonaparte, it seemed it might be the death of the old gentleman, so hot was his resentment. But from one thing to another, matters have a little changed. Or I should rather say, not a little. We learned you were under orders for the Peninsula, to fight the English ; then that you had been commissioned for a piece of bravery, and were again reduced to the ranks. And from one thing to another (as I say), M. de Kéroual became used to the idea that you were his kinsman and yet served with Buonaparte, and filled instead with wonder that he should have another kinsman who was so remarkably well informed of events in France. And it now became a very disagreeable question, whether the young gentleman was not a spy ? In short, sir, in seeking to disserve you, he had accumulated against himself a load of suspicions.'

My visitor now paused, took snuff, and looked at me with an air of benevolence.

' Good God, sir !' says I, 'this is a curious story.'

' You will say so before I have done,' said he. ' For there have two events followed. The first of these was an encounter of M. de Kéroual and M. de Mauséant.'

' I know the man to my cost,' said I : 'it was through him I lost my commission.'

' Do you tell me so?' he cried. ' Why, here is news !'

' Oh, I cannot complain !' said I. ' I was in the wrong. I did it with my eyes open. If a man gets a prisoner to guard and lets him go, the least he can expect is to be degraded.'

' You will be paid for it,' said he. ' You did well for yourself and better for your king.'

' If I had thought I was injuring my emperor,' said I, ' I would have let M. de Mauséant burn in hell ere I had helped him, and be sure of that ! I saw in him only a private person in a difficulty : I let him go in private charity ; not even to profit myself will I suffer it to be misunderstood.'

'Well, well,' said the lawyer, 'no matter now. This is a foolish warmth—a very misplaced enthusiasm, believe me! The point of the story is that M. de Mauséant spoke of you with gratitude, and drew your character in such a manner as greatly to affect your uncle's views. Hard upon the back of which, in came your humble servant, and laid before him the direct proof of what we had been so long suspecting. There was no dubiety permitted. M. Alain's expensive way of life, his clothes and mistresses, his dicing and racehorses, were all explained: he was in the pay of Buonaparte, a hired spy, and a man that held the strings of what I can only call a convolution of extremely fishy enterprises. To do M. de Kéroual justice, he took it in the best way imaginable, destroyed the evidences of the one great-nephew's disgrace—and transferred his interest wholly to the other.'

'What am I to understand by that?' said I.

'I will tell you,' says he. 'There is a remarkable inconsistency in human nature which gentlemen of my cloth have a great deal of occasion to observe. Selfish persons can live without chick or child, they can live without all mankind except perhaps the barber and the apothecary; but when it comes to dying, they seem physically unable to die without an heir. You can apply this principle for yourself. Viscount Alain, though he scarce guesses it, is no longer in the field. Remains, Viscount Anne.'

'I see,' said I, 'you give a very unfavourable impression of my uncle, the Count.'

'I had not meant it,' said he. 'He has led a loose life— sadly loose—but he is a man it is impossible to know and not to admire; his courtesy is exquisite.'

'And so you think there is actually a chance for me?' I asked.

'Understand,' said he: 'in saying as much as I have done, I travel quite beyond my brief. I have been clothed with no capacity to talk of wills, or heritages, or your cousin. I was sent here to make but the one communication: that M. de Kéroual desires to meet his great-nephew.'

'Well,' said I, looking about me on the battlements by which we sat surrounded, 'this is a case in which Mahomet must certainly come to the mountain.'

'Pardon me,' said Mr. Romaine; 'you know already your uncle is an aged man; but I have not yet told you that he is quite broken up, and his death shortly looked for. No, no, there is no doubt about it—it is the mountain that must come to Mahomet.'

'From an Englishman, the remark is certainly significant,' said I; 'but you are of course, and by trade, a keeper of men's secrets, and I see you keep that of Cousin Alain, which is not the mark of a truculent patriotism, to say the least.'

'I am first of all the lawyer of your family!' says he.

'That being so,' said I,' I can perhaps stretch a point myself. This rock is very high, and it is very steep; a man might come by a devil of a fall from almost any part of it, and yet I believe I have a pair of wings that might carry me just so far as to the bottom. Once at the bottom I am helpless.'

'And perhaps it is just then that I could step in,' returned the lawyer. 'Suppose by some contingency, at which I make no guess, and on which I offer no opinion——'

But here I interrupted him. 'One word ere you go further. I am under no parole,' said I.

'I understood so much,' he replied, 'although some of you French gentry find their word sit lightly on them.'

'Sir, I am not one of those,' said I.

'To do you plain justice, I do not think you one,' said he. 'Suppose yourself, then, set free and at the bottom of the rock,' he continued, 'although I may not be able to do much, I believe I can do something to help you on your road. In the first place I would carry this, whether in an inside pocket or my shoe. And he passed me a bundle of bank notes.

'No harm in that,' said I, at once concealing them.

'In the second place,' he resumed, 'it is a great way from here to where your uncle lives—Amersham Place, not far from Dunstable; you have a great part of Britain to get through; and for the first stages, I must leave you to your own luck and ingenuity. I have no acquaintance here in Scotland, or at least' (with a grimace) 'no dishonest ones. But further to the south, about Wakefield, I am told there is a gentleman called Burchell Fenn, who is not so particular as some others, and might be willing to give you a cast forward. In fact, sir, I believe it's the man's trade: a piece of knowledge that burns my mouth. But that is what you get by meddling with rogues; and perhaps the biggest rogue now extant, M. de Saint-Yves, is your cousin, M. Alain.'

'If this be a man of my cousin's,' I observed, 'I am perhaps better to keep clear of him?'

'It was through some paper of your cousin's that we came across his trail,' replied the lawyer. 'But I am inclined to think, so far as anything is safe in such a nasty business, you might apply to the man Fenn. You might even, I think, use the Viscount's name; and the little trick of family resemblance might come in. How, for instance, if you were to call yourself his brother?'

'It might be done,' said I. 'But look here a moment? You propose to me a very difficult game: I have apparently a devil of an opponent in my cousin; and, being a prisoner of war, I can scarcely be said to hold good cards. For what stakes, then, am I playing?'

'They are very large,' said he. 'Your great-uncle is immensely rich—immensely rich. He was wise in time; he smelt the revolution long before; sold all that he could, and had all that was movable transported to England through my firm. There are considerable estates in England; Amersham Place itself is very fine; and he has much money, wisely invested. He lives, indeed, like a prince. And of what use is it to him? He has lost all that was worth living for—his family, his country; he has seen his king and queen murdered; he has seen all these miseries and infamies,' pursued the lawyer, with a rising inflection and a heightening colour; and then broke suddenly off,—'In short, sir, he has seen all the advantages of that government for which his nephew carries arms, and he has the misfortune not to like them.'

'You speak with a bitterness that I suppose I must excuse,' said I; 'yet which of us has the more reason to be bitter? This man, my uncle, M. de Kéroual, fled. My parents, who were less wise perhaps, remained. In the beginning, they were even republicans; to the end they could not be persuaded to despair of the people. It was a glorious folly, for which, as a son, I reverence them. First one and then the other perished. If I have any mark of a gentleman, all who taught me died upon the scaffold, and my last school of manners was the prison of the Abbaye. Do you think you can teach bitterness to a man with a history like mine?'

'I have no wish to try,' said he. 'And yet there is one point I cannot understand: I cannot understand that one of your blood and experience should serve the Corsican. I cannot understand it: it seems as though everything generous in you must rise against that—domination.'

'And perhaps,' I retorted, 'had your childhood passed among wolves, you would have been overjoyed yourself to see the Corsican Shepherd.'

'Well, well,' replied Mr. Romaine, 'it may be. There are things that do not bear discussion.

And with a wave of his hand he disappeared abruptly down a flight of steps and under the shadow of a ponderous arch.

CHAPTER V

THE lawyer was scarce gone before I remembered many omissions; and chief among these, that I had neglected to get Mr. Burchell Fenn's address. Here was an essential point neglected; and I ran to the head of the stairs to find myself already too late. The lawyer was beyond my view; in the archway that led downward to the castle gate, only the red coat and the bright arms of a sentry glittered in the shadow; and I could but return to my place upon the ramparts.

I am not very sure that I was properly entitled to this corner. But I was a high favourite; not an officer, and scarce a private, in the castle would have turned me back, except upon a thing of moment; and whenever I desired to be solitary, I was suffered to sit here behind my piece of cannon unmolested. The cliff went down before me almost sheer, but mantled with a thicket of climbing trees; from farther down, an outwork raised its turret; and across the valley I had a view of that long terrace of Princes Street which serves as a promenade to the fashionable inhabitants of Edinburgh. A singularity in a military prison, that it should command a view on the chief thoroughfare!

It is not necessary that I should trouble you with the train of my reflections, which turned upon the interview I had just concluded and the hopes that were now opening before me. What is more essential, my eye (even while I thought) kept following the movement of the passengers on Princes Street, as they passed briskly to and fro—met, greeted, and bowed to each other—or entered and left the shops, which are in that quarter, and, for a town of the Britannic provinces, particularly fine. My mind being busy upon other things, the course of my eye was the more random; and it chanced that I followed, for some time, the advance of a young gentleman with a red head and a white great-coat, for whom I cared nothing at the moment, and of whom it is probable I shall be gathered to my fathers without learning more. He seemed to have a large acquaintance:

31

his hat was for ever in his hand; and I daresay I had already observed him exchanging compliments with half a dozen, when he drew up at last before a young man and a young lady whose tall persons and gallant carriage I thought I recognised.

It was impossible at such a distance that I could be sure, but the thought was sufficient, and I craned out of the embrasure to follow them as long as possible. To think that such emotions, that such a concussion of the blood, may have been inspired by a chance resemblance, and that I may have stood and thrilled there for a total stranger! This distant view, at least, whether of Flora or of some one else, changed in a moment the course of my reflections. It was all very well, and it was highly needful, I should see my uncle; but an uncle, a great-uncle at that, and one whom I had never seen, leaves the imagination cold; and if I were to leave the castle, I might never again have the opportunity of finding Flora. The little impression I had made, even supposing I had made any, how soon it would die out! how soon I should sink to be a phantom memory, with which (in after days) she might amuse a husband and children! No, the impression must be clenched, the wax impressed with the seal, ere I left Edinburgh. And at this the two interests that were now contending in my bosom came together and became one. I wished to see Flora again; and I wanted some one to further me in my flight and to get me new clothes. The conclusion was apparent. Except for persons in the garrison itself, with whom it was a point of honour and military duty to retain me captive, I knew, in the whole country of Scotland, these two alone. If it were to be done at all, they must be my helpers. To tell them of my designed escape while I was still in bonds, would be to lay before them a most difficult choice. What they might do in such a case, I could not in the least be sure of, for (the same case arising) I was far from sure what I should do myself. It was plain I must escape first. When the harm was done, when I was no more than a poor wayside fugitive, I might apply to them with less offence and more security. To this end it became necessary that I should find out where they lived and how to reach it; and feeling a strong confidence that they would soon return to visit me, I prepared a series of baits with which to angle for my information. It will be seen the first was good enough.

Perhaps two days after, Master Ronald put in an appearance by himself. I had no hold upon the boy, and pretermitted my design till I should have laid court to him and engaged his interest. He was prodigiously embarrassed, not having previously addressed me otherwise than by a bow and blushes;

and he advanced to me with an air of one stubbornly performing a duty, like a raw soldier under fire. I laid down my carving; greeted him with a good deal of formality, such as I thought he would enjoy; and finding him to remain silent, branched off into narratives of my campaigns such as Goguelat himself might have scrupled to endorse. He visibly thawed and brightened; drew more near to where I sat; forgot his timidity so far as to put many questions; and at last, with another blush, informed me he was himself expecting a commission.

'Well,' said I, 'they are fine troops, your British troops in the Peninsula. A young gentleman of spirit may well be proud to be engaged at the head of such soldiers.'

'I know that,' he said; 'I think of nothing else. I think shame to be dangling here at home and going through with this foolery of education, while others, no older than myself, are in the field.'

'I cannot blame you,' said I. 'I have felt the same myself.'

'There are—there are no troops, are there, quite so good as ours?' he asked.

'Well,' said I, 'there is a point about them: they have a defect,—they are not to be trusted in a retreat. I have seen them behave very ill in a retreat.'

'I believe that is our national character,' he said—God forgive him!—with an air of pride.

'I have seen your national character running away at least, and had the honour to run after it!' rose to my lips, but I was not so ill advised as to give it utterance. Every one should be flattered, but boys and women without stint; and I put in the rest of the afternoon narrating to him tales of British heroism, for which I should not like to engage that they were all true.

'I am quite surprised,' he said at last. 'People tell you the French are insincere. Now, I think your sincerity is beautiful. I think you have a noble character. I admire you very much. I am very grateful for your kindness to—to one so young,' and he offered me his hand.

'I shall see you again soon?' said I.

'Oh, now! Yes, very soon,' said he. 'I—I wish to tell you. I would not let Flora—Miss Gilchrist, I mean—come to-day. I wished to see more of you myself. I trust you are not offended: you know, one should be careful about strangers.'

I approved his caution, and he took himself away: leaving me in a mixture of contrarious feelings, part ashamed to have played on one so gullible, part raging that I should have burned so much incense before the vanity of England; yet, in the

bottom of my soul, delighted to think I had made a friend—
or, at least, begun to make a friend—of Flora's brother.

As I had half expected, both made their appearance the next
day. I struck so fine a shade betwixt the pride that is allowed
to soldiers and the sorrowful humility that befits a captive, that
I declare, as I went to meet them, I might have afforded a subject for a painter. So much was high comedy, I must confess;
but so soon as my eyes lighted full on her dark face and eloquent
eyes, the blood leaped into my cheeks—and that was nature!
I thanked them, but not the least with exultation; it was my
cue to be mournful, and to take the pair of them as one.

'I have been thinking,' I said, 'you have been so good to
me, both of you, stranger and prisoner as I am, that I have
been thinking how I could testify to my gratitude. It may
seem a strange subject for a confidence, but there is actually
no one here, even of my comrades, that knows me by my name
and title. By these I am called plain Champdivers, a name to
which I have a right, but not the name which I should bear,
and which (but a little while ago) I must hide like a crime.
Miss Flora, suffer me to present to you the Vicomte Anne de
Kéroual de Saint-Yves, a private soldier.'

'I knew it!' cried the boy; 'I knew he was a noble!'

And I thought the eyes of Miss Flora said the same, but
more persuasively. All through this interview she kept them
on the ground, or only gave them to me for a moment at a
time, and with a serious sweetness.

'You may conceive, my friends, that this is rather a painful
confession,' I continued. 'To stand here before you, vanquished, a prisoner in a fortress, and take my own name upon
my lips, is painful to the proud. And yet I wished that you
should know me. Long after this, we may yet hear of one
another—perhaps Mr. Gilchrist and myself in the field and
from opposing camps—and it would be a pity if we heard and
did not recognise.'

They were both moved; and began at once to press upon
me offers of service, such as to lend me books, get me
tobacco if I used it, and the like. This would have been all
mighty welcome, before the tunnel was ready. Now it signified
no more to me than to offer the transition I required.

'My dear friends,' I said—'for you must allow me to call you
that, who have no others within so many hundred leagues—
perhaps you will think me fanciful and sentimental; and
perhaps indeed I am; but there is one service that I would beg
of you before all others. You see me set here on the top of this
rock in the midst of your city. Even with what liberty I have,

I have the opportunity to see a myriad roofs, and I dare to say, thirty leagues of sea and land. All this hostile! Under all these roofs my enemies dwell; wherever I see the smoke of a house rising, I must tell myself that some one sits before the chimney and reads with joy of our reverses. Pardon me, dear friends, I know that you must do the same, and I do not grudge at it! With you, it is all different. Show me your house then, were it only the chimney, or, if that be not visible, the quarter of the town in which it lies! So, when I look all about me, I shall be able to say: *"There is one house in which I am not quite unkindly thought of."*'

Flora stood a moment.

'It is a pretty thought,' said she, 'and, as far as regards Ronald and myself, a true one. Come, I believe I can show you the very smoke out of our chimney.'

So saying, she carried me round the battlements towards the opposite or southern side of the fortress, and indeed to a bastion almost immediately overlooking the place of our projected flight. Thence we had a view of some foreshortened suburbs at our feet, and beyond of a green, open, and irregular country rising towards the Pentland Hills. The face of one of these summits (say two leagues from where we stood) is marked with a procession of white scars. And to this she directed my attention.

'You see these marks?' she said. 'We call them the Seven Sisters. Follow a little lower with your eye, and you will see a fold of the hill, the tops of some trees, and a tail of smoke out of the midst of them. That is Swanston Cottage, where my brother and I are living with my aunt. If it gives you pleasure to see it, I am glad. We, too, can see the castle from a corner in the garden, and we go there in the morning often —do we not, Ronald?—and we think of you, M. de Saint-Yves; but I am afraid it does not altogether make us glad.'

'Mademoiselle!' said I, and indeed my voice was scarce under command, 'if you knew how your generous words—how even the sight of you—relieved the horrors of this place, I believe, I hope, I know, you would be glad. I will come here daily and look at that dear chimney and these green hills, and bless you from the heart, and dedicate to you the prayers of this poor sinner. Ah! I do not say they can avail!'

'Who can say that, M. de Saint-Yves?' she said softly. 'But I think it is time we should be going.'

'High time,' said Ronald, whom (to say the truth) I had a little forgotten.

On the way back, as I was laying myself out to recover lost

ground with the youth, and to obliterate, if possible, the memory of my last and somewhat too fervent speech, who should come past us but the major? I had to stand aside and salute as he went by, but his eyes appeared entirely occupied with Flora.

'Who is that man?' she asked.

'He is a friend of mine,' said I. 'I give him lessons in French, and he has been very kind to me.'

'He stared,' she said,—'I do not say, rudely; but why should he stare?'

'If you do not wish to be stared at, mademoiselle, suffer me to recommend a veil,' said I.

She looked at me with what seemed anger. 'I tell you the man stared,' she said.

And Ronald added: 'Oh, I don't think he meant any harm. I suppose he was just surprised to see us walking about with a pr—with M. Saint-Yves.'

But the next morning, when I went to Chevenix's rooms, and after I had dutifully corrected his exercise—'I compliment you on your taste,' said he to me.

'I beg your pardon?' said I.

'Oh no, I beg yours,' said he. 'You understand me perfectly, just as I do you.'

I murmured something about enigmas.

'Well, shall I give you the key to the enigma?' said he, leaning back. 'That was the young lady whom Goguelat insulted and whom you avenged. I do not blame you. She is a heavenly creature.'

'With all my heart, to the last of it!' said I. 'And to the first also, if it amuses you! You are become so very acute of late that I suppose you must have your own way.'

'What is her name?' he asked.

'Now, really!' said I. 'Do you think it likely she has told me?'

'I think it certain,' said he.

I could not restrain my laughter. 'Well, then, do you think it likely I would tell you?' I cried.

'Not a bit,' said he. 'But come, to our lesson!'

CHAPTER VI

THE ESCAPE

THE time for our escape drew near, and the nearer it came the less we seemed to enjoy the prospect. There is but one side on which this castle can be left either with dignity or safety; but as there is the main gate and guard, and the chief street of the upper city, it is not to be thought of by escaping prisoners. In all other directions an abominable precipice surrounds it, down the face of which (if anywhere at all) we must regain our liberty. By our concurrent labours in many a dark night, working with the most anxious precautions against noise, we had made out to pierce below the curtain about the south-west corner, in a place they call the *Devil's Elbow*. I have never met that celebrity; nor (if the rest of him at all comes up to what they called his elbow) have I the least desire of his acquaintance. From the heel of the masonry, the rascally, breakneck precipice descended sheer among waste lands, scattered suburbs of the city, and houses in the building. I had never the heart to look for any length of time—the thought that I must make the descent in person some dark night robbing me of breath; and, indeed, on anybody not a seaman or a steeple-jack, the mere sight of the *Devil's Elbow* wrought like an emetic.

I don't know where the rope was got, and doubt if I much cared. It was not that which gravelled me, but whether, now that we had it, it would serve our turn. Its length, indeed, we made a shift to fathom out; but who was to tell us how that length compared with the way we had to go? Day after day, there would be always some of us stolen out to the *Devil's Elbow* and making estimates of the descent, whether by a bare guess or the dropping of stones. A private of pioneers remembered the formula for that—or else remembered part of it and obligingly invented the remainder. I had never any real confidence in that formula; and even had we got it from a book, there were difficulties in the way of the application that might have daunted Archimedes. We durst not drop any considerable pebble lest the sentinels should hear, and those

37

that we dropped we could not hear ourselves. We had never a watch—or none that had a second-hand; and though every one of us could guess a second to a nicety, all somehow guessed it differently. In short, if any two set forth upon this enterprise, they invariably returned with two opinions, and often with a black eye in the bargain. I looked on upon these proceedings, although not without laughter, yet with impatience and disgust. I am one that cannot bear to see things botched or gone upon with ignorance; and the thought that some poor devil was to hazard his bones upon such premises, revolted me. Had I guessed the name of that unhappy first adventurer, my sentiments might have been livelier still.

The designation of this personage was indeed all that remained for us to do; and even in that we had advanced so far that the lot had fallen on Shed B. It had been determined to mingle the bitter and the sweet; and whoever went down first, the whole of his shed-mates were to follow next in order. This caused a good deal of joy in Shed B, and would have caused more if it had not still remained to choose our pioneer. In view of the ambiguity in which we lay as to the length of the rope and the height of the precipice—and that this gentleman was to climb down from fifty to seventy fathoms on a pitchy night, on a rope entirely free, and with not so much as an infant child to steady it at the bottom, a little backwardness was perhaps excusable. But it was, in our case, more than a little. The truth is, we were all womanish fellows about a height; and I have myself been put, more than once, *hors de combat* by a less affair than the rock of Edinburgh Castle.

We discussed it in the dark and between the passage of the rounds; and it was impossible for any body of men to show a less adventurous spirit. I am sure some of us, and myself first among the number, regretted Goguelat. Some were persuaded it was safe, and could prove the same by argument; but if they had good reasons why some one else should make the trial, they had better still why it should not be themselves. Others, again, condemned the whole idea as insane; among these, as ill-luck would have it, a seaman of the fleet; who was the most dispiriting of all. The height, he reminded us, was greater than the tallest ship's mast, the rope entirely free; and he as good as defied the boldest and strongest to succeed. We were relieved from this dead-lock by our serjeant-major of dragoons.

'Comrades,' said he, 'I believe I rank you all; and for that reason, if you really wish it, I will be the first myself. At the same time, you are to consider what the chances are that I may prove to be the last, as well. I am no longer young—I was sixty near a month ago. Since I have been a prisoner, I have made for myself a little *bedaine*. My arms are all gone to fat. And you must promise not to blame me, if I fall and play the devil with the whole thing.'

'We cannot hear of such a thing!' said I. 'M. Laclas is the oldest man here; and, as such, he should be the very last to offer. It is plain, we must draw lots.'

'No,' said M. Laclas; 'you put something else in my head! There is one here who owes a pretty candle to the others, for they have kept his secret. Besides, the rest of us are only rabble; and he is another affair altogether. Let Champdivers —let the noble go the first.'

I confess there was a notable pause before the noble in question got his voice. But there was no room for choice. I had been so ill-advised, when I first joined the regiment, as to take ground on my nobility. I had been often rallied on the matter in the ranks, and had passed under the by-names of *Monseigneur* and *the Marquis*. It was now needful I should justify myself and take a fair revenge.

Any little hesitation I may have felt passed entirely unnoticed, from the lucky incident of a round happening at that moment to go by. And during the interval of silence there occurred something that sent my blood to the boil. There was a private in our shed called Clausel, a man of a very ugly disposition. He had made one of the followers of Goguelat; but, whereas Goguelat had always a kind of monstrous gaiety about him, Clausel was no less morose than he was evil-minded. He was sometimes called *the General*, and sometimes by a name too ill-mannered for repetition. As we all sat listening, this man's hand was laid on my shoulder, and his voice whispered in my ear: 'If you don't go, I 'll have you hanged, Marquis!'

As soon as the round was past—'Certainly, gentlemen!' said I. 'I will give you a lead, with all the pleasure in the world. But, first of all, there is a hound here to be punished. M. Clausel has just insulted me, and dishonoured the French army; and I demand that he run the gauntlet of this shed.'

There was but one voice asking what he had done, and, as soon as I had told them, but one voice agreeing to the punishment. The General was, in consequence, extremely roughly handled, and the next day was congratulated by all who saw him on his *new decorations*. It was lucky for us that he was one of the prime movers and believers in our project of escape, or he had certainly revenged himself by a denunciation. As for his feelings towards myself, they appeared, by his looks, to surpass humanity; and I made up my mind to give him a wide berth in the future.

Had I been to go down that instant, I believe I could have carried it well. But it was already too late—the day was at hand. The rest had still to be summoned. Nor was this the extent of my misfortune; for the next night, and the night after, were adorned with a perfect galaxy of stars, and showed every cat that stirred in a quarter of a mile. During this interval, I have to direct your sympathies on the Vicomte de Saint-Yves! All addressed me softly, like folk round a sickbed. Our Italian corporal, who had got a dozen of oysters from a fishwife, laid them at my feet, as though I were a Pagan idol; and I have never since been wholly at my ease in the society of shellfish. He who was the best of our carvers brought me a snuff-box, which he had just completed, and which, while it was yet in hand, he had often declared he would not part with under fifteen dollars. I believe the piece was worth the money too! And yet the voice stuck in my throat with which I must thank him. I found myself, in a word, to be fed up like a prisoner in a camp of anthropophagi, and honoured like the sacrificial bull. And what with these annoyances, and the risky venture immediately ahead, I found my part a trying one to play.

It was a good deal of a relief when the third evening closed about the castle with volumes of sea-fog. The lights of Princes Street sometimes disappeared, sometimes blinked across at us no brighter than the eyes of cats; and five steps from one of the lanterns on the ramparts it was already groping dark. We made haste to lie down. Had our jailers been upon the watch, they must have observed our conversation to die out unusually soon. Yet I doubt if any of us slept. Each lay in his place, tortured at once with the hope of liberty and the fear of a hateful death. The guard call sounded; the hum of the town declined by little and little. On all sides of us, in their different quarters, we could hear the watchman cry the hours along the street. Often enough, during my stay in England, have I listened to these gruff or broken voices; or perhaps gone to my window when I lay sleepless, and watched the old gentleman hobble by upon the causeway with his cape and his cap, his hanger and his rattle. It was ever a thought with me how differently that cry would re-echo in the chamber of lovers, beside the bed of death, or in the condemned cell. I might be said to hear it that night myself in the condemned cell! At length a fellow with a voice like a bull's began to roar out in the opposite thoroughfare:

' Past yin o'cloak, and a dark, haary moarnin'.'

At which we were all silently afoot.

As I stole about the battlements towards the—gallows, I was about to write—the sergeant-major, perhaps doubtful of my resolution, kept close by me, and occasionally proffered the most indigestible reassurances in my ear. At last I could bear them no longer.

' Be so obliging as to let me be!' said I. 'I am neither a coward nor a fool. What do *you* know of whether the rope be long enough? But I shall know it in ten minutes!'

The good old fellow laughed in his moustache, and patted me.

It was all very well to show the disposition of my temper before a friend alone; before my assembled comrades the thing had to go handsomely. It was then my time to come on the stage; and I hope I took it handsomely.

' Now, gentlemen,' said I, 'if the rope is ready, here is the criminal!'

The tunnel was cleared, the stake driven, the rope extended. As I moved forward to the place, many of my comrades caught me by the hand and wrung it, an attention I could well have done without.

' Keep an eye on Clausel!' I whispered to Laclas; and with that, got down on my elbows and knees, took the rope in both hands, and worked myself, feet foremost, through the tunnel. When the earth failed under my feet, I thought my heart would have stopped; and a moment after I was demeaning myself in mid-air like a drunken jumping-jack. I have never been a model of piety, but at this juncture prayers and a cold sweat burst from me simultaneously.

The line was knotted at intervals of eighteen inches; and to the inexpert it may seem as if it should have been even easy to descend. The trouble was, this devil of a piece of rope appeared to be inspired, not with life alone, but with a personal malignity against myself. It turned to the one side, paused for a moment, and then spun me like a toasting-jack to the other; slipped like an eel from the clasp of my feet; kept me all the time in the most outrageous fury of exertion; and dashed me at intervals against the face of the rock. I had no eyes to see with; and I doubt if there was anything to see but darkness. I must occasionally have caught a gasp of breath, but it was quite unconscious. And the whole forces of my mind were so consumed with losing hold and getting it again, that I could scarce have told whether I was going up or coming down.

Of a sudden I knocked against the cliff with such a thump as almost bereft me of my sense ; and, as reason twinkled back, I was amazed to find that I was in a state of rest, that the face of the precipice here inclined outwards at an angle which relieved me almost wholly of the burthen of my own weight, and that one of my feet was safely planted on a ledge. I drew one of the sweetest breaths in my experience, hugged myself against the rope, and closed my eyes in a kind of ecstasy of relief. It occurred to me next to see how far I was advanced on my unlucky journey, a point on which I had not a shadow of a guess. I looked up : there was nothing above me but the blackness of the night and the fog. I craned timidly forward and looked down. There, upon a floor of darkness, I beheld a certain pattern of hazy lights, some of them aligned as in thoroughfares, others standing apart as in solitary houses ; and before I could well realise it, or had in the least estimated my distance, a wave of nausea and vertigo warned me to lie back and close my eyes. In this situation I had really but the one wish, and that was : something else to think of ! Strange to say, I got it : a veil was torn from my mind, and I saw what a fool I was—what fools we had all been—and that I had no business to be thus dangling between earth and heaven by my arms. The only thing to have done was to have attached me to a rope and lowered me, and I had never the wit to see it till that moment !

I filled my lungs, got a good hold on my rope, and once more launched myself on the descent. As it chanced, the worst of the danger was at an end, and I was so fortunate as to be never again exposed to any violent concussion. Soon after I must have passed within a little distance of a bush of wallflower, for the scent of it came over me with that impression of reality which characterises scents in darkness. This made me a second land-mark, the ledge being my first. I began accordingly to com-pute intervals of time : so much to the ledge, so much again to the wallflower, so much more below. If I were not at the bottom of the rock, I calculated I must be near indeed to the end of the rope, and there was no doubt that I was not far from the end of my own resources. I began to be light-headed and to be tempted to let go,—now arguing that I was certainly arrived within a few feet of the level and could safely risk a fall, anon persuaded I was still close at the top and it was idle to continue longer on the rock. In the midst of which I came to a bearing on plain ground, and had nearly wept aloud. My hands were as good as flayed, my courage entirely exhausted, and, what with the long strain and the sudden relief, my limbs shook under me with more than the violence of ague, and I was glad to cling to the rope.

But this was no time to give way. I had (by God's single mercy) got myself alive out of that fortress; and now I had to try to get the others, my comrades. There was about a fathom of rope to spare; I got it by the end, and searched the whole ground thoroughly for anything to make it fast to. In vain: the ground was broken and stony, but there grew not there so much as a bush of furze.

'Now then,' thought I to myself, 'here begins a new lesson, and I believe it will prove richer than the first. I am not strong enough to keep this rope extended. If I do not keep it extended the next man will be dashed against the precipice. There is no reason why he should have my extravagant good luck. I see no reason why he should not fall—nor any place for him to fall on but my head.'

From where I was now standing there was occasionally visible, as the fog lightened, a lamp in one of the barrack windows, which gave me a measure of the height he had to fall and the horrid force that he must strike me with. What was yet worse, we had agreed to do without signals: every so many minutes by Laclas' watch another man was to be started from the battlements. Now, I had seemed to myself to be about half an hour in my descent, and it seemed near as long again that I waited, straining on the rope for my next comrade to begin. I began to be afraid that our conspiracy was out, that my friends were all secured, and that I should pass the remainder of the night, and be discovered in the morning, vainly clinging to the rope's end like a hooked fish upon an angle. I could not refrain, at this ridiculous image, from a chuckle of laughter. And the next moment I knew, by the jerking of the rope, that my friend had crawled out of the tunnel and was fairly launched on his descent. It appears it was the sailor who had insisted on succeeding me: as soon as my continued silence had assured him the rope was long enough, Gautier, for that was his name, had forgot his former arguments, and shown himself so extremely forward, that Laclas had given way. It was like the fellow, who had no harm in him beyond an instinctive selfishness. But he was like to have paid pretty dearly for the privilege. Do as I would, I could not keep the rope as I could have wished it; and he ended at last by falling on me from a height of several yards, so that we both rolled together on the ground. As soon as he could breathe he cursed me beyond belief, wept over his finger, which he had broken, and cursed me again. I bade him be still and think shame of himself to

be so great a cry-baby. Did he not hear the round going by
above? I asked; and who could tell but what the noise of his
fall was already remarked, and the sentinels at the very
moment leaning upon the battlements to listen?

The round, however, went by, and nothing was discovered;
the third man came to the ground quite easily; the fourth was,
of course, child's play; and before there were ten of us collected, it seemed to me that, without the least injustice to
my comrades, I might proceed to take care of myself.

I knew their plan: they had a map and an almanack, and
designed for Grangemouth, where they were to steal a ship.
Suppose them to do so, I had no idea they were qualified to
manage it after it was stolen. Their whole escape, indeed, was
the most haphazard thing imaginable; only the impatience of
captives and the ignorance of private soldiers would have entertained so misbegotten a device; and though I played the good
comrade and worked with them upon the tunnel, but for the
lawyer's message I should have let them go without me. Well,
now they were beyond my help, as they had always been
beyond my counselling; and, without word said or leave taken,
I stole out of the little crowd. It is true I would rather have
waited to shake hands with Laclas, but in the last man who
had descended I thought I recognised Clausel, and since the
scene in the shed my distrust of Clausel was perfect. I believed
the man to be capable of any infamy, and events have since
shown that I was right.

CHAPTER VII

SWANSTON COTTAGE

I HAD two views. The first was, naturally, to get clear of Edinburgh Castle and the town, to say nothing of my fellow-prisoners; the second to work to the southward so long as it was night, and be near Swanston Cottage by morning. What I should do there and then, I had no guess, and did not greatly care, being a devotee of a couple of divinities called Chance and Circumstance. Prepare, if possible; where it is impossible, work straight forward, and keep your eyes open and your tongue oiled. Wit and a good exterior—there is all life in a nutshell.

I had at first a rather chequered journey: got involved in gardens, butted into houses, and had even once the misfortune to awake a sleeping family, the father of which, as I suppose, menaced me from the window with a blunderbuss. Altogether, though I had been some time gone from my companions, I was still at no great distance, when a miserable accident put a period to the escape. Of a sudden the night was divided by a scream. This was followed by the sound of something falling, and that again by the report of a musket from the Castle battlements. It was strange to hear the alarm spread through the city. In the fortress drums were beat and a bell rung backward. On all hands the watchmen sprang their rattles. Even in that limbo or no-man's-land where I was wandering, lights were made in the houses; sashes were flung up; I could hear neighbouring families converse from window to window, and at length I was challenged myself.

'Wha's that?' cried a big voice.

I could see it proceeded from a big man in a big nightcap, leaning from a one-pair window; and as I was not yet abreast of his house, I judged it was more wise to answer. This was not the first time I had had to stake my fortunes on the goodness of my accent in a foreign tongue; and I have always found the moment inspiriting, as a gambler should. Pulling around

45

me a sort of great-coat I had made of my blanket, to cover my sulphur-coloured livery,—'A friend!' said I.

'What like's all this collieshangie?' said he.

I had never heard of a collieshangie in my days, but with the racket all about us in the city, I could have no doubt as to the man's meaning.

'I do not know, sir, really,' said I; 'but I suppose some of the prisoners will have escaped.'

'Bedamned!' says he.

'Oh, sir, they will be soon taken,' I replied: 'it has been found in time. Good morning, sir!'

'Ye walk late, sir?' he added.

'Oh, surely not,' said I, with a laugh. 'Earlyish, if you like!' which brought me finally beyond him, highly pleased with my success.

I was now come forth on a good thoroughfare, which led (as well as I could judge) in my direction. It brought me almost immediately through a piece of street, whence I could hear close by the springing of a watchman's rattle, and where I suppose a sixth part of the windows would be open, and the people, in all sorts of night gear, talking with a kind of tragic gusto from one to another. Here, again, I must run the gauntlet of a half-dozen questions, the rattle all the while sounding nearer; but as I was not walking inordinately quick, as I spoke like a gentleman, and the lamps were too dim to show my dress, I carried it off once more. One person, indeed, inquired where I was off to at that hour.

I replied vaguely and cheerfully, and as I escaped at one end of this dangerous pass I could see the watchman's lantern entering by the other. I was now safe on a dark country highway, out of sight of lights and out of the fear of watchmen. And yet I had not gone above a hundred yards before a fellow made an ugly rush at me from the roadside. I avoided him with a leap, and stood on guard, cursing my empty hands, wondering whether I had to do with an officer or a mere footpad, and scarce knowing which to wish. My assailant stood a little; in the thick darkness I could see him bob and sidle as though he were feinting at me for an advantageous onfall. Then he spoke.

'My goo' frien',' says he, and at the first word I pricked my ears, 'my goo' frien', will you oblishe me with lil neshary infamation? Whish roa' t' Cramond?'

I laughed out clear and loud, stepped up to the convivialist, took him by the shoulders and faced him about. 'My good friend,' said I, 'I believe I know what is best for you much better than yourself, and may God forgive you the fright you have given me! There, get you gone to Edinburgh!' And I gave a shove, which he obeyed with the passive agility of a ball, and disappeared incontinently in the darkness down the road by which I had myself come.

Once clear of this foolish fellow, I went on again up a gradual hill, descended on the other side through the houses of a country village, and came at last to the bottom of the main ascent leading to the Pentlands and my destination. I was some way up when the fog began to lighten; a little farther, and I stepped by degrees into a clear starry night, and saw in front of me, and quite distinct, the summits of the Pentlands, and behind, the valley of the Forth and the city of my late captivity buried under a lake of vapour. I had but one encounter—that of a farm-cart, which I heard, from a great way ahead of me, creaking nearer in the night, and which passed me about the point of dawn like a thing seen in a dream, with two silent figures in the inside nodding to the horse's steps. I presume they were asleep; by the shawl about her head and shoulders, one of them should be a woman. Soon, by concurrent steps, the day began to break and the fog to subside and roll away. The east grew luminous and was barred with chilly colours, and the Castle on its rock, and the spires and chimneys of the upper town, took gradual shape, and arose, like islands, out of the receding cloud. All about me was still and sylvan; the road mounting and winding, with nowhere a sign of any passenger, the birds chirping, I suppose for warmth, the boughs of the trees knocking together, and the red leaves falling in the wind.

It was broad day, but still bitter cold and the sun not up, when I came in view of my destination. A single gable and chimney of the cottage peeped over the shoulder of the hill; not far off, and a trifle higher on the mountain, a tall old white-washed farmhouse stood among the trees, beside a falling brook; beyond were rough hills of pasture. I bethought me that shepherd folk were early risers, and if I were once seen skulking in that neighbourhood it might prove the ruin of my prospects; took advantage of a line of hedge, and worked myself up in its shadow till I was come under the garden wall of my friends' house. The cottage was a little quaint place of many rough-cast gables and grey roofs. It had something the air of a rambling infinitesimal cathedral, the body of it rising in the midst two storeys high, with a steep-pitched roof, and sending out upon all hands (as it were chapter-houses, chapels, and transepts) one-storeyed and dwarfish projections. To add to this appearance, it was grotesquely decorated with crockets and **gargoyles**, ravished from some mediæval church. The place seemed hidden away, being not only concealed in the trees of the garden, but, on the side on which I approached it, buried as high as the eaves by the rising of the ground. About the walls of the garden there went a line of well-grown elms and beeches, the first entirely bare, the last still pretty well covered with red leaves, and the centre was occupied with a thicket of laurel and holly, in which I could see arches cut and paths winding.

I was now within hail of my friends, and not much the better. The house appeared asleep; yet if I attempted to wake any one, I had no guarantee it might not prove either the aunt with the gold eyeglasses (whom I could only remember with trembling), or some ass of a servant-maid who should burst out screaming at sight of me. Higher up I could hear and see a shepherd shouting to his dogs and striding on the rough sides of the mountain, and it was clear I must get to cover without loss of time. No doubt the holly thickets would have proved a very suitable retreat, but there was mounted on the wall a sort of signboard not uncommon in the country of Great Britain, and very damping to the adventurous: SPRING GUNS AND MAN-TRAPS was the legend that it bore. I have learned since that these advertisements, three times out of four, were in the nature of Quaker guns on a disarmed battery, but I had not learned it then, and even so, the odds would not have been good enough. For a choice, I would a hundred times sooner be returned to Edinburgh Castle and my corner in the bastion, than to leave my foot in a steel trap or have to digest the contents of an automatic blunderbuss. There was but one chance left—that Ronald or Flora might be the first to come abroad; and in order to profit by this chance if it occurred, I got me on the cope of the wall in a place where it was screened by the thick branches of a beech, and sat there waiting.

As the day wore on, the sun came very pleasantly out. I had been awake all night, I had undergone the most violent agitations of mind and body, and it is not so much to be wondered at, as it was exceedingly unwise and foolhardy, that I should have dropped into a doze. From this I awakened to the characteristic sound of digging, looked down, and saw immediately below me the back view of a gardener in a stable waistcoat. Now he would appear steadily immersed in his business; anon, to my more immediate terror, he would straighten his back, stretch his arms, gaze about the otherwise deserted garden, and relish a deep pinch of snuff. It was my first thought to drop from the wall upon the other side. A glance sufficed to show me that even the way by which I had come was now cut off, and the field behind me already occupied by a couple of shepherds' assistants and a score or two of sheep. I have named the talismans on which I habitually depend, but here was a conjuncture in which both were wholly useless. The copestone of a wall arrayed with broken bottles is no favourable rostrum; and I might be as eloquent as Pitt, and as fascinating as Richelieu, and neither the gardener nor the shepherd lads would care a halfpenny. In short, there was no escape possible from my absurd position: there I must continue to sit until one or other of my neighbours should raise his eyes and give the signal for my capture.

The part of the wall on which (for my sins) I was posted could be scarce less than twelve feet high on the inside; the leaves of the beech which made a fashion of sheltering me were already partly fallen; and I was thus not only perilously exposed myself, but enabled to command some part of the garden walks and (under an evergreen arch) the front lawn and windows of the cottage. For long nothing stirred except my friend with the spade; then I heard the opening of a sash; and presently after saw Miss Flora appear in a morning wrapper and come strolling hitherward between the borders, pausing and visiting her flowers—herself as fair. *There* was a friend; *here*, immediately beneath me, an unknown quantity — the gardener: how to communicate with the one and not attract the notice of the other? To make a noise was out of the question; I dared scarce to breathe. I held myself ready to make a gesture as soon as she should look, and she looked in every possible direction but the one. She was interested in the vilest tuft of chickweed, she gazed at the summit of the mountain, she came even immediately below me and conversed on the most fastidious topics with the gardener; but to the top of that wall she would not dedicate a glance! At last she began to retrace her steps in the direction of the cottage; whereupon, becoming quite desperate, I broke off a piece of plaster, took a happy aim, and hit her with it in the nape of the neck. She clapped her hand to the place, turned about, looked on all sides for an explanation, and spying me (as indeed I was parting the branches to make it the more easy), half uttered and half swallowed down again a cry of surprise.

The infernal gardener was erect upon the instant. 'What's your wull, miss?' said he.

Her readiness amazed me. She had already turned and was gazing in the opposite direction. 'There's a child among the artichokes,' she said.

'The Plagues of Egypt'! *I'll* see to them!' cried the gardener truculently, and with a hurried waddle disappeared among the evergreens.

That moment she turned, she came running towards me, her arms stretched out, her face incarnadined for the one moment with heavenly blushes, the next pale as death. 'Monsieur de Saint-Yves!' she said.

'My dear young lady,' I said, 'this is the damnedest liberty —I know it! But what else was I to do?'

'You have escaped?' said she.

'If you call this escape,' I replied.

'But you cannot possibly stop there!' she cried.

'I know it,' said I. 'And where am I to go?'

She struck her hands together. 'I have it!' she exclaimed. 'Come down by the beech trunk—you must leave no footprint in the border—quickly, before Robie can get back! I am the hen-wife here: I keep the key; you must go into the hen-house —for the moment.'

I was by her side at once. Both cast a hasty glance at the blank windows of the cottage and so much as was visible of the garden alleys; it seemed there was none to observe us. She caught me by the sleeve and ran. It was no time for compliments; hurry breathed upon our necks; and I ran along with her to the next corner of the garden, where a wired court and a board hovel standing in a grove of trees advertised my place of refuge. She thrust me in without a word; the bulk of the fowls were at the same time emitted; and I found myself the next moment locked in alone with half a dozen sitting hens. In the twilight of the place all fixed their eyes on me severely, and seemed to upbraid me with some crying impropriety. Doubtless the hen has always a puritanic appearance, although (in its own behaviour) I could never observe it to be more particular than its neighbours. But conceive a British hen!

CHAPTER VIII

THE HEN-HOUSE

I was half an hour at least in the society of these distressing bipeds, and alone with my own reflections and necessities. I was in great pain of my flayed hands, and had nothing to treat them with; I was hungry and thirsty, and had nothing to eat or to drink; I was thoroughly tired, and there was no place for me to sit. To be sure there was the floor, but nothing could be imagined less inviting.

At the sound of approaching footsteps, my good-humour was restored. The key rattled in the lock, and Master Ronald entered, closed the door behind him, and leaned his back to it.

'I say, you know!' he said, and shook a sullen young head.

'I know it's a liberty,' said I.

'It's infernally awkward: my position is infernally embarrassing,' said he.

'Well,' said I, 'and what do you think of mine?'

This seemed to pose him entirely, and he remained gazing upon me with a convincing air of youth and innocence. I could have laughed, but I was not so inhumane.

'I am in your hands,' said I, with a little gesture. 'You must do with me what you think right.'

'Ah, yes!' he cried: 'if I knew!'

'You see,' said I, 'it would be different if you had received your commission. Properly speaking, you are not yet a combatant; I have ceased to be one; and I think it arguable that we are just in the position of one ordinary gentleman to another, where friendship usually comes before the law. Observe, I only say *arguable*. For God's sake, don't think I wish to dictate an opinion. These are the sort of nasty little businesses, inseparable from war, which every gentleman must decide for himself. If I were in your place——'

'Ay, what would you do, then?' says he.

'Upon my word, I do not know,' said I. 'Hesitate, as you are doing, I believe.'

'I will tell you,' he said. 'I have a kinsman, and it is what *he* would think, that I am thinking. It is General Graham of Lynedoch—Sir Thomas Graham. I scarcely know him, but I believe I admire him more than I do God.'

'I admire him a good deal myself,' said I, 'and have good reason to. I have fought with him, been beaten, and run away. *Veni, victus sum, evasi.*'

'What!' he cried. 'You were at Barossa?'

'There and back, which many could not say,' said I. 'It was a pretty affair and a hot one, and the Spaniards behaved abominably, as they usually did in a pitched field; the Marshal Duke of Belluno made a fool of himself, and not for the first time; and your friend Sir Thomas had the best of it, so far as there was any best. He is a brave and ready officer.'

'Now, then, you will understand!' said the boy. 'I wish to please Sir Thomas: what would he do?'

'Well, I can tell you a story,' said I, 'a true one too, and about this very combat of Chiclana, or Barossa as you call it. I was in the Eighth of the Line; we lost the eagle of the First Battalion, more betoken, but it cost you dear. Well, we had repulsed more charges than I care to count, when your 87th Regiment came on at a foot's pace, very slow but very steady; in front of them a mounted officer, his hat in his hand, white-haired, and talking very quietly to the battalions. Our Major, Vigo-Roussillon, set spurs to his horse and galloped out to sabre him, but seeing him an old man, very handsome, and as composed as if he were in a coffee-house, lost heart and galloped back again. Only, you see, they had been very close together for the moment, and looked each other in the eyes. Soon after the Major was wounded, taken prisoner, and carried into Cadiz. One fine day they announced to him the visit of the General, Sir Thomas Graham. "Well, sir," said the General, taking him by the hand, "I think we were face to face upon the field." It was the white-haired officer!'

'Ah!' cried the boy,—his eyes were burning.

'Well, and here is the point,' I continued. 'Sir Thomas fed the Major from his own table from that day, and served him with six covers.'

'Yes, it is a beautiful—a beautiful story,' said Ronald. 'And yet somehow it is not the same—is it?'

'I admit it freely,' said I.

The boy stood awhile brooding. 'Well, I take my risk of it,' he cried. 'I believe it's treason to my sovereign—I believe there is an infamous punishment for such a crime—and yet I'm hanged if I can give you up'

I was as much moved as he. 'I could almost beg you to do otherwise,' I said. 'I was a brute to come to you, a brute and a coward. You are a noble enemy; you will make a noble soldier.' And with rather a happy idea of a compliment for this warlike youth, I stood up straight and gave him the salute.

He was for a moment confused; his face flushed. 'Well, well, I must be getting you something to eat, but it will not be for six,' he added, with a smile: 'only what we can get smuggled out. There is my aunt in the road, you see,' and he locked me in again with the indignant hens.

I always smile when I recall that young fellow; and yet, if the reader were to smile also, I should feel ashamed. If my son shall be only like him when he comes to that age, it will be a brave day for me and not a bad one for his country.

At the same time I cannot pretend that I was sorry when his sister succeeded in his place. She brought me a few crusts of bread and a jug of milk, which she had handsomely laced with whisky after the Scottish manner.

'I am so sorry,' she said: 'I dared not bring you anything more. We are so small a family, and my aunt keeps such an eye upon the servants. I have put some whisky in the milk— it is more wholesome so—and with eggs you will be able to make something of a meal. How many eggs will you be wanting to that milk? for I must be taking the others to my aunt—that is my excuse for being here. I should think three or four. Do you know how to beat them in? or shall I do it?'

Willing to detain her a while longer in the hen-house, I displayed my bleeding palms; at which she cried out aloud.

'My dear Miss Flora, you cannot make an omelette without breaking eggs,' said I; 'and it is no bagatelle to escape from Edinburgh Castle. One of us, I think, was even killed.'

'And you are as white as a rag, too,' she exclaimed, 'and can hardly stand! Here is my shawl, sit down upon it here in the corner, and I will beat your eggs. See, I have brought a fork too; I should have been a good person to take care of Jacobites or Covenanters in old days! You shall have more to eat this evening; Ronald is to bring it you from town. We have money enough, although no food that we can call our own. Ah, if Ronald and I kept house, you should not be lying in this shed! He admires you so much.'

'My dear friend,' said I, 'for God's sake do not embarrass me with more alms. I loved to receive them from that hand, so long as they were needed; but they are so no more, and whatever else I may lack—and I lack everything—it is not money.' I pulled out my sheaf of notes and detached the top one: it was written for ten pounds, and signed by that very famous individual, Abraham Newlands. 'Oblige me, as you would like me to oblige your brother if the parts were reversed, and take this note for the expenses. I shall need not only food, but clothes.'

'Lay it on the ground,' said she. 'I must not stop my beating.'

'You are not offended?' I exclaimed.

She answered me by a look that was a reward in itself, and seemed to imply the most heavenly offers for the future. There was in it a shadow of reproach, and such warmth of communicative cordiality as left me speechless. I watched her instead till her hens' milk was ready.

'Now,' said she, 'taste that.'

I did so, and swore it was nectar. She collected her eggs and crouched in front of me to watch me eat. There was about this tall young lady at the moment an air of motherliness delicious to behold. I am like the English general, and to this day I still wonder at my moderation.

'What sort of clothes will you be wanting?' said she.

'The clothes of a gentleman,' said I. 'Right or wrong, I think it is the part I am best qualified to play. Mr. St. Ives (for that's to be my name upon the journey) I conceive as rather a theatrical figure, and his make-up should be to match.'

'And yet there is a difficulty,' said she. 'If you got coarse clothes the fit would hardly matter. But the clothes of a fine gentleman—O, it is absolutely necessary that these should fit! And above all, with your'—she paused a moment—'to our ideas somewhat noticeable manners.'

'Alas for my poor manners!' said I. 'But my dear friend Flora, these little noticeabilities are just what mankind has to suffer under. Yourself, you see, you're very noticeable even when you come in a crowd to visit poor prisoners in the Castle.'

I was afraid I should frighten my good angel visitant away, and without the smallest breath of pause went on to add a few directions as to stuffs and colours.

She opened big eyes upon me. 'O, Mr. St. Ives!' she cried—'if that is to be your name—I do not say they would not be becoming; but for a journey, do you think they would be wise? I am afraid'—she gave a pretty break of laughter—'I am afraid they would be daft-like!'

'Well, and am I not daft?' I asked her.

'I do begin to think you are,' said she.

'There it is, then!' said I. 'I have been long enough a figure of fun. Can you not feel with me that perhaps the bitterest thing in this captivity has been the clothes? Make me a captive—bind me with chains if you like—but let me be still myself. You do not know what it is to be a walking travesty—among foes,' I added bitterly.

'O, but you are too unjust!' she cried. 'You speak as though any one ever dreamed of laughing at you. But no one did. We were all pained to the heart. Even my aunt—though sometimes I do think she was not quite in good taste—you should have seen her and heard her at home! She took so much interest. Every patch in your clothes made us sorry; it should have been a sister's work.'

'That is what I never had—a sister,' said I. 'But since you say that I did not make you laugh——'

'O, Mr. St. Ives! never!' she exclaimed. 'Not for one moment. It was all too sad. To see a gentleman——'

'In the clothes of a harlequin, and begging?' I suggested.

'To see a gentleman in distress, and nobly supporting it,' she said.

'And do you not understand, my fair foe,' said I, 'that even if all were as you say—even if you had thought my travesty were becoming—I should be only the more anxious, for my sake, for my country's sake, and for the sake of your kindness, that you should see him whom you have helped as God meant him to be seen? that you should have something to remember him by at least more characteristic than a misfitting sulphur-yellow suit, and half a week's beard?'

'You think a great deal too much of clothes,' she said. 'I am not that kind of girl.'

'And I am afraid I am that kind of a man,' said I. 'But do not think of me too harshly for that. I talked just now of something to remember by. I have many of them myself, of these beautiful reminders, of these keepsakes, that I cannot be parted from until I lose memory and life. Many of them are great things, many of them are high virtues—charity, mercy, faith. But some of them are trivial enough. Miss Flora, do you remember the day that I first saw you, the day of the strong east wind? Miss Flora, shall I tell you what you wore?'

We had both risen to our feet, and she had her hand already on the door to go. Perhaps this attitude emboldened me to profit by the last seconds of our interview; and it certainly rendered her escape the more easy.

'O, you are too romantic!' she said, laughing; and with that my sun was blown out, my enchantress had fled away, and I was again left alone in the twilight with the lady hens.

CHAPTER IX

THREE IS COMPANY, AND FOUR NONE

The rest of the day I slept in the corner of the hen-house upon Flora's shawl. Nor did I awake until a light shone suddenly in my eyes, and starting up with a gasp (for, indeed, at the moment I dreamed I was still swinging from the Castle battlements) I found Ronald bending over me with a lantern. It appeared it was past midnight, that I had slept about sixteen hours, and that Flora had returned her poultry to the shed and I had heard her not. I could not but wonder if she had stooped to look at me as I slept. The puritan hens now slept irremediably; and being cheered with the promise of supper I wished them an ironical good-night, and was lighted across the garden and noiselessly admitted to a bedroom on the ground floor of the cottage. There I found soap, water, razors—offered me diffidently by my beardless host—and an outfit of new clothes. To be shaved again without depending on the barber of the gaol was a source of a delicious, if a childish joy. My hair was sadly too long, but I was none so unwise as to make an attempt on it myself. And, indeed, I thought it did not wholly misbecome me as it was, being by nature curly. The clothes were about as good as I expected. The waistcoat was of toilenet, a pretty piece, the trousers of fine kerseymere, and the coat sat extraordinarily well. Altogether, when I beheld this changeling in the glass, I kissed my hand to him.

'My dear fellow,' said I, 'have you no scent?'

'Good God, no!' cried Ronald. 'What do you want with scent?'

'Capital thing on a campaign,' said I. 'But I can do without.'

I was now led, with the same precautions against noise, into the little bow-windowed dining-room of the cottage. The shutters were up, the lamp guiltily turned low; the beautiful Flora greeted me in a whisper; and when I was set down to table, the pair proceeded to help me with precautions that might have seemed excessive in the Ear of Dionysius.

'She sleeps up there,' observed the boy, pointing to the ceiling; and the knowledge that I was so imminently near to the resting-place of that gold eyeglass touched even myself with some uneasiness.

Our excellent youth had imported from the city a meat pie, and I was glad to find it flanked with a decanter of really admirable wine of Oporto. While I ate, Ronald entertained me with the news of the city, which had naturally rung all day with our escape: troops and mounted messengers had followed each other forth at all hours and in all directions; but according to the last intelligence no recapture had been made. Opinion in town was very favourable to us: our courage was applauded, and many professed regret that our ultimate chance of escape should be so small. The man who had fallen was one Sombref, a peasant; he was one who slept in a different part of the Castle; and I was thus assured that the whole of my former companions had attained their liberty, and Shed A was untenanted.

From this we wandered insensibly into other topics. It is impossible to exaggerate the pleasure I took to be thus sitting at the same table with Flora, in the clothes of a gentleman, at liberty and in the full possession of my spirits and resources; of all of which I had need, because it was necessary that I should support at the same time two opposite characters, and at once play the cavalier and lively soldier for the eyes of Ronald, and to the ears of Flora maintain the same profound and sentimental note that I had already sounded. Certainly there are days when all goes well with a man; when his wit, his digestion, his mistress are in a conspiracy to spoil him, and even the weather smiles upon his wishes. I will only say of myself upon that evening that I surpassed my expectations, and was privileged to delight my hosts. Little by little they forgot their terrors and I my caution; until at last we were brought back to earth by a catastrophe that might very easily have been foreseen, but was not the less astonishing to us when it occurred.

I had filled all the glasses. 'I have a toast to propose,' I whispered, 'or rather three, but all so inextricably interwoven that they will not bear dividing. I wish first to drink to the health of a brave and therefore a generous enemy. He found me disarmed, a fugitive and helpless. Like the lion, he disdained so poor a triumph; and when he might have vindicated an easy valour, he preferred to make a friend. I wish that we should next drink to a fairer and a more tender foe. She found me in prison; she cheered me with a priceless sympathy; what she has done since, I know she has done in mercy, and I only pray—I dare scarce hope—her mercy may prove to have been merciful. And I wish to conjoin with these, for the first, and perhaps the last time, the health—and I fear I may already say the memory—of one who has fought, not always without success, against the soldiers of your nation; but who came here, vanquished already, only to be vanquished again by the loyal hand of the one, by the unforgettable eyes of the other.'

It is to be feared I may have lent at times a certain resonancy to my voice; it is to be feared that Ronald, who was none the better for his own hospitality, may have set down his glass with something of a clang. Whatever may have been the cause, at least, I had scarce finished my compliment before we were aware of a thump upon the ceiling overhead. It was to be thought some very solid body had descended to the floor from the level (possibly) of a bed. I have never seen consternation painted in more lively colours than on the faces of my hosts. It was proposed to smuggle me forth into the garden, or to conceal my form under a horsehair sofa which stood against the wall. For the first expedient, as was now plain by the approaching footsteps, there was no longer time; from the second I recoiled with indignation.

'My dear creatures,' said I, 'let us die, but do not let us be ridiculous.'

The words were still upon my lips when the door opened and my friend of the gold eyeglass appeared, a memorable figure, on the threshold. In one hand she bore a bedroom candlestick; in the other, with the steadiness of a dragoon, a horse-pistol. She was wound about in shawls which did not wholly conceal the candid fabric of her nightdress, and surmounted by a nightcap of portentous architecture. Thus accoutred, she made her entrance; laid down the candle and pistol, as no longer called for; looked about the room with a silence more eloquent than oaths; and then, in a thrilling voice—'To whom have I the pleasure?' she said, addressing me with a ghost of a bow.

'Madam, I am charmed, I am sure,' said I. 'The story is a little long; and our meeting, however welcome, was for the moment entirely unexpected by myself. I am sure——' but here I found I was quite sure of nothing, and tried again. 'I have the honour,' I began, and found I had the honour to be only exceedingly confused. With that, I threw myself outright upon her mercy. 'Madam, I must be more frank with you,' I resumed. 'You have already proved your charity and compassion for the French prisoners, I am one of these; and if my

appearance be not too much changed, you may even yet recognise in me that *Oddity* who had the good fortune more than
once to make you smile.'

Still gazing upon me through her glass, she uttered an uncompromising grunt; and then, turning to her niece—'Flora,'
said she, 'how comes he here?'

The culprits poured out for a while an antiphony of explanations, which died out at last in a miserable silence.

'I think at least you might have told your aunt,' she
snorted.

'Madam,' I interposed, 'they were about to do so. It is my
fault if it be not done already. But I made it my prayer that
your slumbers might be respected, and this necessary formula of
my presentation should be delayed until to-morrow in the
morning.'

The old lady regarded me with undissembled incredulity, to
which I was able to find no better repartee than a profound and
I trust graceful reverence.

'French prisoners are very well in their place,' she said,
'but I cannot see that their place is in my private dining-
room.'

'Madam,' said I, 'I hope it may be said without offence, but
(except the Castle of Edinburgh) I cannot think upon the spot
from which I would so readily be absent.'

At this, to my relief, I thought I could perceive a vestige of
a smile to steal upon that iron countenance and to be bitten
immediately in.

'And if it is a fair question, what do they call ye?' she asked.

'At your service, the Vicomte Anne de St.-Yves,' said I.

'Mosha the Viscount,' said she, 'I am afraid you do us plain
people a great deal too much honour.'

'My dear lady,' said I, 'let us be serious for a moment. What
was I to do? Where was I to go? And how can you be angry
with these benevolent children who took pity on one so unfortunate as myself? Your humble servant is no such terrific
adventurer that you should come out against him with horse-
pistol and '—smiling—'bedroom candlesticks. It is but a young
gentleman in extreme distress, hunted upon every side, and
asking no more than to escape from his pursuers. I know your
character, I read it in your face'—the heart trembled in my
body as I said these daring words. 'There are unhappy
English prisoners in France at this day, perhaps at this hour.
Perhaps at this hour they kneel as I do; they take the hand of
her who might conceal and assist them; they press it to their
lips as I do——'

'Here, here!' cried the old lady, breaking from my solicitations. 'Behave yourself before folk! Saw ever anyone the match of that? And on earth, my dears, what are we to do with him?'

'Pack him off, my dear lady,' said I: 'pack off the impudent fellow double-quick! And if it may be, and if your good heart allows it, help him a little on the way he has to go.'

'What's this pie?' she cried stridently. 'Where is this pie from, Flora?'

No answer was vouchsafed by my unfortunate and (I may say) extinct accomplices.

'Is that my port?' she pursued. 'Hough! Will somebody give me a glass of my port wine?'

I made haste to serve her.

She looked at me over the rim with an extraordinary expression. 'I hope ye liked it?' said she.

'It is even a magnificent wine,' said I.

'Aweel, it was my father laid it down,' said she. 'There were few knew more about port wine than my father, God rest him!' She settled herself in a chair with an alarming air of resolution. 'And so there is some particular direction that you wish to go in?' said she.

'O,' said I, following her example, 'I am by no means such a vagrant as you suppose. I have good friends, if I could get to them, for which all I want is to be once clear of Scotland; and I have money for the road.' And I produced my bundle.

'English bank-notes?' she said. 'That's not very handy for Scotland. It's been some fool of an Englishman that's given you these, I'm thinking. How much is it?'

'I declare to heaven I never thought to count!' I exclaimed. 'But that is soon remedied.'

And I counted out ten notes of ten pound each, all in the name of Abraham Newlands, and five bills of country bankers for as many guineas.

'One hundred and twenty six pound five,' cried the old lady. 'And you carry such a sum about you, and have not so much as counted it! If you are not a thief, you must allow you are very thief-like.'

'And yet, madam, the money is legitimately mine,' said I.

She took one of the bills and held it up. 'Is there any probability, now, that this could be traced?' she asked.

'None, I should suppose; and if it were, it would be no matter,' said I. 'With your usual penetration, you guessed right. An Englishman brought it me. It reached me, through the hands of his English solicitor, from my great-uncle, the Comte de Kéroual de Saint-Yves, I believe the richest *émigré* in London.'

'I can do no more than take your word for it,' said she.

'And I trust, madam, not less,' said I.

'Well,' said she, 'at this rate the matter may be feasible. I will cash one of these five-guinea bills, less the exchange, and give you silver and Scots notes to bear you as far as the border. Beyond that, Mosha the Viscount, you will have to depend upon yourself.'

I could not but express a civil hesitation as to whether the amount would suffice, in my case, for so long a journey.

'Ay,' said she, 'but you havenae heard me out. For if you are not too fine a gentleman to travel with a pair of drovers, I believe I have found the very thing, and the Lord forgive me for a treasonable old wife! There are a couple stopping up by with the shepherd-man at the farm; to-morrow they will take the road for England, probably by skriegh of day—and in my opinion you had best be travelling with the stots,' said she.

'For Heaven's sake do not suppose me to be so effeminate a character!' I cried. 'An old soldier of Napoleon is certainly beyond suspicion. But, dear lady, to what end? and how is the society of these excellent gentlemen supposed to help me?'

'My dear sir,' said she, 'you do not at all understand your own predicament, and must just leave your matters in the hands of those who do. I dare say you have never even heard tell of the drove-roads or the drovers; and I am certainly not going to sit up all night to explain it to you. Suffice it, that it is me who is arranging this affair—the more shame to me!—and that is the way ye have to go. Ronald,' she continued, 'away up-by to the shepherds; rowst them out of their beds, and make it perfectly distinct that Sim is not to leave till he has seen *me*.'

Ronald was nothing loath to escape from his aunt's neighbourhood, and left the room and the cottage with a silent expedition that was more like flight than mere obedience. Meanwhile the old lady turned to her niece.

'And I would like to know what we are to do with him the night!' she cried.

'Ronald and I meant to put him in the hen-house,' said the encrimsoned Flora.

'And I can tell you he is to go to no such a place,' replied the aunt. 'Hen-house, indeed! If a guest he is to be, he shall sleep in no mortal hen-house. Your room is the most fit, I think, if he will consent to occupy it on so great a suddenty. And as for you, Flora, you shall sleep with me.'

I could not help admiring the prudence and tact of this old dowager, and of course it was not for me to make objections. Ere I well knew how, I was alone with a flat candlestick, which is not the most sympathetic of companions, and stood studying the snuff in a frame of mind between triumph and chagrin. All had gone well with my flight: the masterful lady who had arrogated to herself the arrangement of the details gave me every confidence; and I saw myself already arriving at my uncle's door. But, alas! it was another story with my love affair. I had seen and spoken with her alone; I had ventured boldly; I had been not ill received; I had seen her change colour, had enjoyed the undissembled kindness of her eyes; and now, in a moment, down comes upon the scene that apocalyptic figure with the nightcap and the horse-pistol, and with the very wind of her coming behold me separated from my love! Gratitude and admiration contended in my breast with the extreme of natural rancour. My appearance in her house at past midnight had an air (I could not disguise it from myself) that was insolent and underhand, and could not but minister to the worst suspicions. And the old lady had taken it well. Her generosity was no more to be called in question than her courage, and I was afraid that her intelligence would be found to match. Certainly, Miss Flora had to support some shrewd looks, and certainly she had been troubled. I could see but the one way before me: to profit by an excellent bed, to try to sleep soon, to be stirring early, and to hope for some renewed occasion in the morning. To have said so much and yet to say no more, to go out into the world upon so half-hearted a parting, was more than I could accept.

It is my belief that the benevolent fiend sat up all night to baulk me. She was at my bedside with a candle long ere day, roused me, laid out for me a damnable misfit of clothes, and bade me pack my own (which were wholly unsuited to the journey) in a bundle. Sore grudging, I arrayed myself in a suit of some country fabric, as delicate as sackcloth and about as becoming as a shroud; and, on coming forth, found the dragon had prepared for me a hearty breakfast. She took the head of the table, poured out the tea, and entertained me as I ate with a great deal of good sense and a conspicuous lack of charm. How often did I not regret the change!—how often compare her, and condemn her in the comparison, with her charming niece! But if my entertainer was not beautiful, she had certainly been busy in my interest. Already she was in communication with my destined fellow-travellers; and the device on which she had struck appeared entirely suitable. I was a young Englishman who had outrun the constable; warrants were out against me in Scotland, and it had become needful I should pass the border without loss of time, and privately.

'I have given a very good account of you,' said she, 'which I hope you may justify. I told them there was nothing against you beyond the fact that you were put to the horn (if that is the right word) for debt.'

'I pray God you have the expression incorrectly, ma'am,' said I. 'I do not give myself out for a person easily alarmed; but you must admit there is something barbarous and mediæval in the sound well qualified to startle a poor foreigner.'

'It is the name of a process in Scots Law, and need alarm no honest man,' said she. 'But you are a very idle-minded young gentleman; you must still have your joke, I see: I only hope you will have no cause to regret it.'

'I pray you not to suppose, because I speak lightly, that I do not feel deeply,' said I. 'Your kindness has quite conquered me; I lay myself at your disposition, I beg you to believe, with real tenderness; I pray you to consider me from henceforth as the most devoted of your friends.'

'Well, well,' she said, 'here comes your devoted friend the drover. I'm thinking he will be eager for the road; and I will not be easy myself till I see you well off the premises, and the dishes washed, before my servant-woman wakes. Praise God, we have gotten one that is a treasure at the sleeping!'

The morning was already beginning to be blue in the trees of the garden, and to put to shame the candle by which I had breakfasted. The lady rose from table, and I had no choice but to follow her example. All the time I was beating my brains for any means by which I should be able to get a word apart with Flora, or find the time to write her a billet. The windows had been open while I breakfasted, I suppose to ventilate the room from any traces of my passage there; and, Master Ronald appearing on the front lawn, my ogre leaned forth to address him.

'Ronald,' she said, 'wasn't that Sim that went by the wall?'

I snatched my advantage. Right at her back there was pen, ink, and paper laid out. I wrote: 'I love you'; and before I had time to write more, or so much as to blot what I had written, I was again under the guns of the gold eyeglasses.

'It's time,' she began; and then, as she observed my occupation, 'Umph!' she broke off. 'Ye have something to write?' she demanded.

'Some notes, madam,' said I, bowing with alacrity.

'Notes,' she said ; 'or a note?'

'There is doubtless some *finesse* of the English language that I do not comprehend,' said I.

'I'll contrive, however, to make my meaning very plain to ye, Mosha le Viscount,' she continued. 'I suppose you desire to be considered a gentleman?'

'Can you doubt it, madam?' said I.

'I doubt very much, at least, whether you go to the right way about it,' she said. 'You have come here to me, I cannot very well say how; I think you will admit you owe me some thanks, if it was only for the breakfast I made ye. But what are you to me? A waif young man, not so far to seek for looks and manners, with some English notes in your pocket and a price upon your head. I am a lady; I have been your hostess, with however little will; and I desire that this random acquaintance of yours with my family will cease and determine.'

I believe I must have coloured. 'Madam,' said I, 'the notes are of no importance; and your least pleasure ought certainly to be my law. You have felt, and you have been pleased to express, a doubt of me. I tear them up.' Which you may be sure I did thoroughly.

'There's a good lad!' said the dragon, and immediately led the way to the front lawn.

The brother and sister were both waiting us here, and, as well as I could make out in the imperfect light, bore every appearance of having passed through a rather cruel experience. Ronald seemed ashamed to so much as catch my eye in the presence of his aunt, and was the picture of embarrassment. As for Flora, she had scarce the time to cast me one look before the dragon took her by the arm, and began to march across the garden in the extreme first glimmer of the dawn without exchanging speech. Ronald and I followed in equal silence.

There was a door in that same high wall on the top of which I had sat perched no longer gone than yesterday morning. This the old lady set open with a key; and on the other side we were aware of a rough-looking, thick-set man, leaning with his arms (through which was passed a formidable staff) on a dry-stone dyke. Him the old lady immediately addressed.

'Sim,' said she, 'this is the young gentleman.'

Sim replied with an inarticulate grumble of sound, and a movement of one arm and his head, which did duty for a salutation.

'Now, Mr. St. Ives,' said the old lady, 'it's high time for you to be taking the road. But first of all let me give the change of your five-guinea bill. Here are four pounds of it in British Linen notes, and the balance in small silver, less sixpence. Some charge a shilling, I believe, but I have given you the benefit of the doubt. See and guide it with all the sense that you possess.'

'And here, Mr. St. Ives,' said Flora, speaking for the first time, 'is a plaid which you will find quite necessary on so rough a journey. I hope you will take it from the hands of a Scotch friend,' she added, and her voice trembled.

'Genuine holly: I cut it myself,' said Ronald, and gave me as good a cudgel as a man could wish for in a row.

The formality of these gifts, and the waiting figure of the driver, told me loudly that I must be gone. I dropped on one knee and bade farewell to the aunt, kissing her hand. I did the like—but with how different a passion!—to her niece; as for the boy, I took him to my arms and embraced him with a cordiality that seemed to strike him speechless. 'Farewell!' and 'Farewell!' I said. 'I shall never forget my friends. Keep me sometimes in memory. Farewell!' With that I turned my back and began to walk away; and had scarce done so, when I heard the door in the high wall close behind me. Of course this was the aunt's doing; and of course, if I know anything of human character, she would not let me go without some tart expressions. I declare, even if I had heard them, I should not have minded in the least, for I was quite persuaded that, whatever admirers I might be leaving behind me in Swanston Cottage, the aunt was not the least sincere.

CHAPTER X

THE DROVERS

It took me a little effort to come abreast of my new companion; for though he walked with an ugly roll and no great appearance of speed, he could cover the ground at a good rate when he wanted to. Each looked at the other: I with natural curiosity, he with a great appearance of distaste. I have heard since that his heart was entirely set against me; he had seen me kneel to the ladies, and diagnosed me for a 'gesterin' eediot.'

'So, ye 're for England, are ye?' said he.

I told him yes.

'Weel, there 's waur places, I believe,' was his reply; and he relapsed into a silence which was not broken during a quarter of an hour of steady walking.

This interval brought us to the foot of a bare green valley, which wound upwards and backwards among the hills. A little stream came down the midst and made a succession of clear pools; near by the lowest of which I was aware of a drove of shaggy cattle, and a man who seemed the very counterpart of Mr. Sim making a breakfast upon bread and cheese. This second drover (whose name proved to be Candlish) rose on our approach.

'Here 's a mannie that 's to gang through with us,' said Sim. 'It was the auld wife, Gilchrist, wanted it.'

'Aweel, aweel,' said the other; and presently, remembering his manners, and looking on me with a solemn grin, 'A fine day!' says he.

I agreed with him, and asked him how he did.

'Brawly,' was the reply; and without further civilities, the pair proceeded to get the cattle under way. This, as well as almost all the herding, was the work of a pair of comely and intelligent dogs, directed by Sim or Candlish in little more than monosyllables. Presently we were ascending the side of the mountain by a rude green track, whose presence I had not hitherto observed. A continual sound of munching and the crying of a great quantity of moor birds accompanied our progress, which the deliberate pace and perennial appetite of the cattle rendered wearisomely slow. In the midst my two conductors marched in a contented silence that I could not but admire. The more I looked at them, the more I was impressed by their absurd resemblance to each other. They were dressed in the same coarse homespun, carried similar sticks, were equally begrimed about the nose with snuff, and each wound in an identical plaid of what is called the shepherd's tartan. In a back view they might be described as indistinguishable; and even from the front they were much alike. An incredible coincidence of humours augmented the impression. Thrice and four times I attempted to pave the way for some exchange of thought, sentiment, or—at the least of it—human words. An *Ay* or an *Nhm* was the sole return, and the topic died on the hill-side without echo. I can never deny that I was chagrined; and when, after a little more walking, Sim turned towards me and offered me a ram's horn of snuff, with the question 'Do ye use it?' I answered, with some animation, 'Faith, sir, I would use pepper to introduce a little cordiality.' But even this sally failed to reach, or at least failed to soften, my companions.

At this rate we came to the summit of a ridge, and saw the track descend in front of us abruptly into a desert vale, about a league in length, and closed at the farther end by no less barren hilltops. Upon this point of vantage Sim came to a halt, took off his hat, and mopped his brow.

'Weel,' he said, 'here we're at the top o' Howden.'

'The top o' Howden, sure eneuch,' said Candlish.

'Mr. St. Ivey, are ye dry?' said the first.

'Now, really,' said I, 'is not this Satan reproving sin?'

'What ails ye, man?' said he. 'I'm offerin' ye a dram.'

'Oh, if it be anything to drink,' said I, 'I am as dry as my neighbours.'

Whereupon Sim produced from the corner of his plaid a black bottle, and we all drank and pledged each other. I found these gentlemen followed upon such occasions an invariable etiquette, which you may be certain I made haste to imitate. Each wiped his mouth with the back of his left hand, held up the bottle in his right, remarked with emphasis, 'Here's to ye!' and swallowed as much of the spirit as his fancy prompted. This little ceremony, which was the nearest thing to manners I could perceive in either of my companions, was repeated at becoming intervals, generally after an ascent. Occasionally we shared a mouthful of ewe-milk cheese and an inglorious form of bread, which I understood (but am far from engaging my honour on the point) to be called 'shearer's bannock.' And that may be said to have concluded our whole active intercourse for the first day.

I had the more occasion to remark the extraordinarily desolate nature of that country, through which the drove road continued, hour after hour and even day after day, to wind. A continual succession of insignificant shaggy hills, divided by the course of ten thousand brooks, through which we had to wade, or by the side of which we encamped at night; infinite perspectives of heather, infinite quantities of moorfowl; here and there, by a stream side, small and pretty clumps of willows or the silver birch; here and there, the ruins of ancient and inconsiderable fortresses—made the unchanging characters of the scene. Occasionally, but only in the distance, we could perceive the smoke of a small town or of an isolated farmhouse or cottage on the moors; more often, a flock of sheep and its attendant shepherd, or a rude field of agriculture perhaps not yet harvested. With these alleviations, we might almost be said to pass through an unbroken desert—sure, one of the most impoverished in Europe; and when I recalled to mind that we were yet but a few leagues from the chief city (where the law courts sat every day with a press of business, soldiers garrisoned the castle, and men of admitted parts were carrying on the practice of letters and the investigations of science), it gave me a singular view of that poor, barren, and yet illustrious country through which I travelled. Still more, perhaps, did it commend the wisdom of Miss Gilchrist in sending me with these uncouth companions and by this unfrequented path.

My itinerary is by no means clear to me; the names and distances I never clearly knew, and have now wholly forgotten; and this is the more to be regretted as there is no doubt that, in the course of those days, I must have passed and camped among sites which have been rendered illustrious by the pen of Walter Scott. Nay, more, I am of opinion that I was still more favoured by fortune, and have actually met and spoken with that inimitable author. Our encounter was of a tall, stoutish, elderly gentleman, a little grizzled, and of a rugged but cheerful and engaging countenance. He sat on a hill pony, wrapped in a plaid over his green coat, and was accompanied by a horse-woman, his daughter, a young lady of the most charming appearance. They overtook us on a stretch of heath, reined up as they came alongside, and accompanied us for perhaps a quarter of an hour before they galloped off again across the hillsides to our left. Great was my amazement to find the

unconquerable Mr. Sim thaw immediately on the accost of this
strange gentleman, who hailed him with a ready familiarity,
proceeded at once to discuss with him the trade of droving and
the prices of cattle, and did not disdain to take a pinch from
the inevitable ram's horn. Presently I was aware that the
stranger's eye was directed on myself; and there ensued a
conversation, some of which I could not help overhearing at the
time, and the rest have pieced together more or less plausibly
from the report of Sim.

'Surely that must be an *amateur drover* ye have gotten there?'
the gentleman seems to have asked.

Sim replied, I was a young gentleman that had a reason of
his own to travel privately.

'Well, well, ye must tell me nothing of that. I am in the
law, you know, and *tace* is the Latin for a candle,' answered the
gentleman. 'But I hope it's nothing bad.'

Sim told him it was no more than debt.

'Oh, Lord, if that be all!' cried the gentleman; and turning
to myself, 'Well, sir,' he added, 'I understand you are taking
a tramp through our forest here for the pleasure of the thing?'

'Why, yes, sir,' said I; 'and I must say I am very well
entertained.'

'I envy you,' said he. 'I have jogged many miles of it
myself when I was younger. My youth lies buried about here
under every heather-bush, like the soul of the licentiate Lucius.
But you should have a guide. The pleasure of this country is
much in the legends, which grow as plentiful as blackberries.'
And directing my attention to a little fragment of a broken
wall no greater than a tombstone, he told me for an example a
story of its earlier inhabitants. Years after it chanced that I
was one day diverting myself with a Waverley Novel, when
what should I come upon but the identical narrative of my
green-coated gentleman upon the moors! In a moment the
scene, the tones of his voice, his northern accent, and the very
aspect of the earth and sky and temperature of the weather,
flashed back into my mind with the reality of dreams. The
unknown in the green-coat had been the Great Unknown! I
had met Scott; I had heard a story from his lips; I should have
been able to write, to claim acquaintance, to tell him that his
legend still tingled in my ears. But the discovery came too
late, and the great man had already succumbed under the load
of his honours and misfortunes.

Presently, after giving us a cigar apiece, Scott bade us farewell and disappeared with his daughter over the hills. And
when I applied to Sim for information, his answer of 'The

Shirra, man! A'body kens the Shirra!' told me, unfortunately, nothing.

A more considerable adventure falls to be related. We were now near the border. We had travelled for long upon the track beaten and browsed by a million herds, our predecessors, and had seen no vestige of that traffic which had created it. It was early in the morning when we at last perceived, drawing near to the drove road, but still at a distance of about half a league, a second caravan, similar to but larger than our own. The liveliest excitement was at once exhibited by both my comrades. They climbed hillocks, they studied the approaching drove from under their hand, they consulted each other with an appearance of alarm that seemed to me extraordinary. I had learned by this time that their stand-off manners implied, at least, no active enmity; and I made bold to ask them what was wrong.

'Bad yins,' was Sim's emphatic answer.

All day the dogs were kept unsparingly on the alert, and the drove pushed forward at a very unusual and seemingly unwelcome speed. All day Sim and Candlish, with a more than ordinary expenditure both of snuff and of words, continued to debate the position. It seems that they had recognised two of our neighbours on the road—one Faa, and another by the name of Gillies. Whether there was an old feud between them still unsettled I could never learn; but Sim and Candlish were prepared for every degree of fraud or violence at their hands. Candlish repeatedly congratulated himself on having left 'the watch at home with the mistress'; and Sim perpetually brandished his cudgel, and cursed his ill-fortune that it should be sprung.

'I willna care a damn to gie the daashed scoon'rel a fair clout wi' it,' he said. 'The daashed thing micht come sindry in ma hand.'

'Well, gentlemen,' said I, 'suppose they do come on, I think we can give a very good account of them.' And I made my piece of holly, Ronald's gift, the value of which I now appreciated, sing about my head.

'Ay, man? Are ye stench?' inquired Sim, with a gleam of approval in his wooden countenance.

The same evening, somewhat wearied with our day-long expedition, we encamped on a little verdant mound, from the midst of which there welled a spring of clear water scarce great enough to wash the hands in. We had made our meal and lain down, but were not yet asleep, when a growl from one of the collies set us on the alert. All three sat up, and on a second impulse all lay down again, but now with our cudgels ready. A man must be an alien and an outlaw, an old soldier and a young man in the bargain, to take adventure easily. With no idea as to the rights of the quarrel or the probable consequences of the encounter, I was as ready to take part with my two drovers, as ever to fall in line on the morning of a battle. Presently there leaped three men out of the heather; we had scarce time to get to our feet before we were assailed; and in a moment each one of us was engaged with an adversary whom the deepening twilight scarce permitted him to see. How the battle sped in other quarters I am in no position to describe. The rogue that fell to my share was exceedingly agile and expert with his weapon; had and held me at a disadvantage from the first assault; forced me to give ground continually, and at last, in mere self-defence, to let him have the point. It struck him in the throat, and he went down like a ninepin and moved no more.

It seemed this was the signal for the engagement to be discontinued. The other combatants separated at once; our foes were suffered, without molestation, to lift up and bear away their fallen comrade; so that I perceived this sort of war to be not wholly without laws of chivalry, and perhaps rather to partake of the character of a tournament than of a battle *à outrance*. There was no doubt, at least, that I was supposed to have pushed the affair too seriously. Our friends the enemy removed their wounded companion with undisguised consternation; and they were no sooner over the top of the brae, than Sim and Candlish roused up their wearied drove and set forth on a night march.

'I'm thinking Faa's unco bad,' said the one.

'Ay,' said the other, 'he lookit dooms gash.'

'He did that,' said the first.

And their weary silence fell upon them again.

Presently Sim turned to me. 'Ye're unco ready with the stick,' said he.

'Too ready, I'm afraid,' said I. 'I am afraid Mr. Faa (if that be his name) has got his gruel.'

'Weel, I wouldnae wonder,' replied Sim.

'And what is likely to happen?' I inquired.

'Aweel,' said Sim, snuffing profoundly, 'if I were to offer an opeenion, it would not be conscientious. For the plain fac' is, Mr. St. Ivy, that I div not ken. We have had crackit heids— and rowth of them—ere now; and we have had a broken leg or maybe twa; and the like of that we drover bodies make a kind of a practice like to keep among oursel's. But a corp we have none of us ever had to deal with, and I could set nae leemit to what Gillies micht consider proper in the affair.   Forbye that, he would be in raither a hobble himsel', if he was to gang hame wantin' Faa.   Folk are awfu' throng with their questions, and parteecularly when they 're no wantit.'

'That 's a fac',' said Candlish.

I considered this prospect ruefully; and then making the best of it, ' Upon all which accounts,' said I, ' the best will be to get across the border and there separate.   If you are troubled, you can very truly put the blame upon your late companion; and if I am pursued, I must just try to keep out of the way.'

'Mr. St. Ivy,' said Sim, with something resembling enthusiasm, 'no' a word mair!   I have met in wi' mony kinds o' gentry ere now; I hae seen o' them that was the tae thing, and I hae seen o' them that was the tither; but the wale of a gentleman like you I have no sae very frequently seen the bate of.'

Our night march was accordingly pursued with unremitting diligence.   The stars paled, the east whitened, and we were still, both dogs and men, toiling after the wearied cattle.   Again and again Sim and Candlish lamented the necessity: it was ' fair ruin on the bestial,' they declared; but the thought of a judge and a scaffold hunted them ever forward.   I myself was not so much to be pitied.   All that night, and during the whole of the little that remained before us of our conjunct journey, I enjoyed a new pleasure, the reward of my prowess, in the now loosened tongue of Mr. Sim.   Candlish was still obdurately tæciturn: it was the man's nature; but Sim, having finally appraised and approved me, displayed without reticence a rather garrulous habit of mind and a pretty talent for narration.   The pair were old and close companions, co-existing in these endless moors in a brotherhood of silence such as I have heard attributed to the trappers of the west.   It seems absurd to mention love in connection with so ugly and snuffy a couple; at least, their trust was absolute; and they entertained a surprising admiration for each other's qualities; Candlish exclaiming that Sim was 'grand company!' and Sim frequently assuring me in an aside that for ' a rale, auld, stench bitch, there was nae the bate of Candlish in braid Scotland.'   The two dogs appeared to be entirely included in this family compact, and I remarked that their exploits and traits of character were constantly and minutely observed by the two masters.   Dog stories particularly abounded with them; and not only the dogs of the present but those of the past contributed their quota.   'But that was naething,' Sim would begin: 'there was a herd in Manor, they ca'd him Tweedie—ye'll mind Tweedie, Can'lish?' 'Fine, that!' said Candlish. 'Aweel, Tweedie had a dog——' The story I have forgotten; I dare say it was dull, and I suspect it was not true; but indeed, my travels with the drovers had rendered me indulgent, and perhaps even credulous, in the matter of dog stories. Beautiful, indefatigable beings! as I saw them at the end of a long day's journey frisking, barking, bounding, striking attitudes, slanting a bushy tail, manifestly playing to the spectator's eye, manifestly rejoicing in their grace and beauty—and turned to observe Sim and Candlish unornamentally plodding in the rear with the plaids about their bowed shoulders and the drop at their snuffy nose—I thought I would rather claim kinship with the dogs than with the men! My sympathy was unreturned; in their eyes I was a creature light as air; and they would scarce spare me the time for a perfunctory caress or perhaps a hasty lap of the wet tongue, ere they were back again in sedulous attendance on those dingy deities, their masters—and their masters, as like as not, damning their stupidity.

Altogether the last hours of our tramp were infinitely the most agreeable to me, and I believe to all of us; and by the time we came to separate, there had grown up a certain familiarity and mutual esteem that made the parting harder. It took place about four of the afternoon on a bare hillside from which I could see the ribbon of the great north road, henceforth to be my conductor. I asked what was to pay.

'Naething,' replied Sim.

'What in the name of folly is this?' I exclaimed. 'You have led me, you have fed me, you have filled me full of whisky, and now you will take nothing!'

'Ye see we indentit for that,' replied Sim.

'Indented?' I repeated; 'what does the man mean?'

'Mr. St. Ivy,' said Sim, 'this is a maitter entirely between Candlish and me and the auld wife, Gilchrist. You had naething to say to it; weel, ye can have naething to do with it, then.'

'My good man,' said I, 'I can allow myself to be placed in no such ridiculous position. Mrs. Gilchrist is nothing to me, and I refuse to be her debtor.'

'I dinna exac'ly see what way ye're gaun to help it,' observed my drover.

'By paying you here and now,' said I.

'There's aye twa to a bargain, Mr. St. Ives,' said he.

'You mean that you will not take it?' said I.

'There or thereabout,' said he. 'Forbye, that it would set

ye a heap better to keep your siller for them you awe it to. Ye're young, Mr. St. Ivy, and thoughtless; but it's my belief that, wi' care and circumspection, ye may yet do credit to yoursel'. But just you bear this in mind: that him that *awes* siller should never *gie* siller.'

Well, what was there to say? I accepted his rebuke, and bidding the pair farewell, set off alone upon my southward way.

'Mr. St. Ivy,' was the last word of Sim, 'I was never muckle ta'en up in Englishry; but I think that I really ought to say that ye seem to me to have the makings of quite a decent lad.'

CHAPTER XI

THE GREAT NORTH ROAD

It chanced that as I went down the hill these last words of my friend the drover echoed not unfruitfully in my head. I had never told these men the least particulars as to my race or fortune, as it was a part, and the best part, of their civility to ask no questions: yet they had dubbed me without hesitation English. Some strangeness in the accent they had doubtless thus explained. And it occurred to me, that if I could pass in Scotland for an Englishman, I might be able to reverse the process and pass in England for a Scot. I thought, if I was pushed to it, I could make a struggle to imitate the brogue; after my experience with Candlish and Sim, I had a rich provision of outlandish words at my command; and I felt I could tell the tale of Tweedie's dog so as to deceive a native. At the same time, I was afraid my name of St. Ives was scarcely suitable; till I remembered there was a town so called in the province of Cornwall, thought I might yet be glad to claim it for my place of origin, and decided for a Cornish family and a Scots education. For a trade, as I was equally ignorant of all, and as the most innocent might at any moment be the means of my exposure, it was best to pretend to none. And I dubbed myself a young gentleman of a sufficient fortune and an idle, curious habit of mind, rambling the country at my own charges, in quest of health, information, and merry adventures.

At Newcastle, which was the first town I reached, I completed my preparations for the part, before going to the inn, by the purchase of a knapsack and a pair of leathern gaiters. My plaid I continued to wear from sentiment. It was warm, useful to sleep in if I were again benighted, and I had discovered it to be not unbecoming for a man of gallant carriage. Thus equipped, I supported my character of the light-hearted pedestrian not amiss. Surprise was indeed expressed that I should have selected such a season of the year; but I pleaded some delays of business, and smilingly claimed to be an eccentric. The devil was in it, I would say, if any season of the year was not good enough for me; I was not made of sugar, I was no mollycoddle to be afraid of an ill-aired bed or a sprinkle of snow; and I would knock upon the table with my fist and call for t'other bottle, like the noisy and free-hearted young gentleman I was. It was my policy (if I may so express myself) to talk much and say little. At the inn tables, the country, the state of the roads, the business interest of those who sat down with me, and the course of public events, afforded me a considerable field in which I might discourse at large and still communicate no information about myself. There was no one with less air of reticence; I plunged into my company up to the neck; and I had a long cock-and-bull story of an aunt of mine which must have convinced the most suspicious of my innocence. 'What!' they would have said, 'that young ass to be concealing anything! Why, he has deafened me with an aunt of his until my head aches. He only wants you should give him a line, and he would tell you his whole descent from Adam downward, and his whole private fortune to the last shilling.' A responsible solid fellow was even so much moved by pity for my inexperience as to give me a word or two of good advice : that I was but a young man after all—I had at this time a deceptive air of youth that made me easily pass for one-and-twenty, and was, in the circumstances, worth a fortune—that the company at inns was very mingled, that I should do well to be more careful, and the like; to all which I made answer that I meant no harm myself and expected none from others, or the devil was in it. 'You are one of those d——d prudent fellows that I could never abide with,' said I. 'You are the kind of man that has a long head. That's all the world, my dear sir : the long-heads and the short-horns! Now, I am a short-horn.' 'I doubt,' says he, 'that you will not go very far without getting sheared.' I offered to bet with him on that, and he made off, shaking his head.

But my particular delight was to enlarge on politics and the war. None damned the French like me; none was more bitter against the Americans. And when the north-bound mail arrived, crowned with holly, and the coachman and guard hoarse with shouting victory, I went even so far as to entertain the company to a bowl of punch, which I compounded myself with no illiberal hand, and doled out to such sentiments as the following :—

'Our glorious victory on the Nivelle!' 'Lord Wellington, God bless him! and may victory ever attend upon his arms!' and, 'Soult, poor devil! and may he catch it again to the same tune!'

Never was oratory more applauded to the echo—never any one was more of the popular man than I. I promise you, we made a night of it. Some of the company supported each other, with the assistance of boots, to their respective bed-chambers, while the rest slept on the field of glory where we had left them; and at the breakfast table the next morning there was an extraordinary assemblage of red eyes and shaking fists. I observed patriotism to burn much lower by daylight. Let no one blame me for insensibility to the reverses of France! God knows how my heart raged. How I longed to fall on that herd of swine and knock their heads together in the moment of their revelry! But you are to consider my own situation and its necessities; also a certain lightheartedness, eminently Gallic, which forms a leading trait in my character, and leads me to throw myself into new circumstances with the spirit of a schoolboy. It is possible that I sometimes allowed this impish humour to carry me further than good taste approves: and I was certainly punished for it once.

This was in the episcopal city of Durham. We sat down, a considerable company, to dinner, most of us fine old vatted English tories of that class which is often so enthusiastic as to be inarticulate. I took and held the lead from the beginning; and, the talk having turned on the French in the Peninsula, I gave them authentic details (on the authority of a cousin of mine, an ensign) of certain cannibal orgies in Galicia, in which no less a person than General Caffarelli had taken a part. I always disliked that commander, who once ordered me under arrest for insubordination; and it is possible that a spice of vengeance added to the rigour of my picture. I have forgotten the details; no doubt they were high-coloured. No doubt I rejoiced to fool these jolter-heads; and no doubt the sense of security that I drank from their dull, gasping faces encouraged me to proceed extremely far. And for my sins, there was one silent little man at table who took my story at the true value. It was from no sense of humour, to which he was quite dead. It was from no particular intelligence, for he had not any. The bond of sympathy, of all things in the world, had rendered him clairvoyant.

Dinner was no sooner done than I strolled forth into the streets with some design of viewing the cathedral; and the little man was silently at my heels. A few doors from the inn, in a dark place of the street, I was aware of a touch on my arm, turned suddenly, and found him looking up at me with eyes pathetically bright.

'I beg your pardon, sir; but that story of yours was parti-

cularly rich. He—he! Particularly racy,' said he. 'I tell
you, sir, I took you wholly! I *smoked* you! I believe you and
I, sir, if we had a chance to talk, would find we had a good
many opinions in common. Here is the "Blue Bell," a very
comfortable place. They draw good ale, sir. Would you be
so condescending as to share a pot with me?'

There was something so ambiguous and secret in the little
man's perpetual signalling, that I confess my curiosity was much
aroused. Blaming myself, even as I did so, for the indiscretion,
I embraced his proposal, and we were soon face to face over a
tankard of mulled ale. He lowered his voice to the least at-
tenuation of a whisper.

'Here, sir,' said he, 'is to the Great Man. I think you take
me? No?' He leaned forward till our noses touched. 'Here
is to the Emperor!' said he.

I was extremely embarrassed, and, in spite of the creature's
innocent appearance, more than half alarmed. I thought him
too ingenious, and, indeed, too daring for a spy. Yet if he
were honest he must be a man of extraordinary indiscretion,
and therefore very unfit to be encouraged by an escaped
prisoner. I took a half course, accordingly—accepted his toast
in silence, and drank it without enthusiasm.

He proceeded to abound in the praises of Napoleon, such as
I had never heard in France, or at least only on the lips of
officials paid to offer them.

'And this Caffarelli, now,' he pursued: 'he is a splendid
fellow, too, is he not? I have not heard vastly much of him
myself. No details, sir—no details! We labour under huge
difficulties here as to unbiassed information.'

'I believe I have heard the same complaint in other countries,' I could not help remarking. 'But as to Caffarelli, he is
neither lame nor blind, he has two legs and a nose in the middle
of his face. And I care as much about him as you care for the
dead body of Mr. Perceval!'

He studied me with glowing eyes.

'You cannot deceive me!' he cried. 'You have served under
him. You are a Frenchman! I hold by the hand, at last, one
of that noble race, the pioneers of the glorious principles of
liberty and brotherhood. Hush! No, it is all right. I thought
there had been somebody at the door. In this wretched, en-
slaved country we dare not even call our souls our own. The
spy and the hangman, sir—the spy and the hangman! And
yet there is a candle burning, too. The good leaven is working,
sir—working underneath. Even in this town there are a few
brave spirits, who meet every Wednesday. You must stay over

a day or so, and join us. We do not use this house. Another, and a quieter. They draw fine ale, however—fair, mild ale. You will find yourself among friends, among brothers. You will hear some very daring sentiments expressed !' he cried, expanding his small chest. ' Monarchy, Christianity—all the trappings of a bloated past—the Free Confraternity of Durham and Tyneside deride.'

Here was a devil of a prospect for a gentleman whose whole design was to avoid observation ! The Free Confraternity had no charms for me ; daring sentiments were no part of my baggage ; and I tried, instead, a little cold water.

' You seem to forget, sir, that my Emperor has re-established Christianity,' I observed.

' Ah, sir, but that was policy !' he exclaimed. ' You do not understand Napoleon. I have followed his whole career. I can explain his policy from first to last. Now for instance in the Peninsula, on which you were so very amusing, if you will come to a friend's house who has a map of Spain, I can make the whole course of the war quite clear to you, I venture to say, in half an hour.

This was intolerable. Of the two extremes, I found I preferred the British tory ; and, making an appointment for the morrow, I pleaded sudden headache, escaped to the inn, packed my knapsack, and fled, about nine at night, from this accursed neighbourhood. It was cold, starry, and clear, and the road dry, with a touch of frost. For all that, I had not the smallest intention to make a long stage of it ; and about ten o'clock, spying on the right-hand side of the way the lighted windows of an alehouse, I determined to bait there for the night.

It was against my principle, which was to frequent only the dearest inns ; and the misadventure that befell me was sufficient to make me more particular in the future. A large company was assembled in the parlour, which was heavy with clouds of tobacco smoke, and brightly lighted up by a roaring fire of coal. Hard by the chimney stood a vacant chair in what I thought an enviable situation, whether for warmth or the pleasure of society ; and I was about to take it, when the nearest of the company stopped me with his hand.

' Beg thy pardon, sir,' said he ; ' but that there chair belongs to a British soldier.'

A chorus of voices enforced and explained. It was one of Lord Wellington's heroes. He had been wounded under Rowland Hill. He was Colbourne's right-hand man. In short, this favoured individual appeared to have served with every separate corps, and under every individual general in the Peninsula. Of course I apologised. I had not known. The devil was in it if a soldier had not a right to the best in England. And with that sentiment, which was loudly applauded, I found a corner of a bench, and awaited, with some hopes of entertainment, the return of the hero. He proved, of course, to be a private soldier. I say of course, because no officer could possibly enjoy such heights of popularity. He had been wounded before San Sebastian, and still wore his arm in a sling. What was a great deal worse for him, every member of the company had been plying him with drink. His honest yokel's countenance blazed as if with fever, his eyes were glazed and looked the two ways, and his feet stumbled as, amidst a murmur of applause, he returned to the midst of his admirers.

Two minutes afterwards I was again posting in the dark along the highway; to explain which sudden movement of retreat I must trouble the reader with a reminiscence of my services.

I lay one night with the out-pickets in Castile. We were in close touch with the enemy; the usual orders had been issued against smoking, fires, and talk, and both armies lay as quiet as mice, when I saw the English sentinel opposite making a signal by holding up his musket. I repeated it, and we both crept together in the dry bed of a stream, which made the demarcation of the armies. It was wine he wanted, of which we had a good provision, and the English had quite run out. He gave me the money, and I, as was the custom, left him my firelock in pledge, and set off for the canteen. When I returned with a skin of wine, behold, it had pleased some uneasy devil of an English officer to withdraw the outposts! Here was a situation with a vengeance, and I looked for nothing but ridicule in the present and punishment in the future. Doubtless our officers winked pretty hard at this interchange of courtesies, but doubtless it would be impossible to wink at so gross a fault, or rather so pitiable a misadventure as mine; and you are to conceive me wandering in the plains of Castile, benighted, charged with a wine-skin for which I had no use, and with no knowledge whatever of the whereabouts of my musket, beyond that it was somewhere in my Lord Wellington's army. But my Englishman was either a very honest fellow, or else extremely thirsty, and at last contrived to advertise me of his new position. Now, the English sentry in Castile, and the wounded hero in the Durham public-house, were one and the same person; and if he had been a little less drunk, or myself less lively in getting away, the travels of M. St. Ives might have come to an untimely end.

I suppose this woke me up; it stirred in me besides a spirit of opposition, and in spite of cold, darkness, the highwaymen and the footpads, I determined to walk right on till breakfast-time : a happy resolution, which enabled me to observe one of those traits of manners which at once depict a country and condemn it. It was near midnight when I saw, a great way ahead of me, the light of many torches; presently after, the sound of wheels reached me, and the slow tread of feet, and soon I had joined myself to the rear of a sordid, silent, and lugubrious procession, such as we see in dreams. Close on a hundred persons marched by torchlight in unbroken silence; in their midst a cart, and in the cart, on an inclined platform, the dead body of a man—the centre-piece of this solemnity, the hero whose obsequies we were come forth at this unusual hour to celebrate. It was but a plain, dingy old fellow of fifty or sixty, his throat cut, his shirt turned over as though to show the wound. Blue trousers and brown socks completed his attire, if we can talk so of the dead. He had a horrid look of a waxwork. In the tossing of the lights he seemed to make faces and mouths at us, to frown, and to be at times upon the point of speech. The cart, with this shabby and tragic freight, and surrounded by its silent escort and bright torches, continued for some distance to creak along the high-road, and I to follow it in amazement, which was soon exchanged for horror. At the corner of a lane the procession stopped, and, as the torches ranged themselves along the hedgerow-side, I became aware of a grave dug in the midst of the thoroughfare, and a provision of quicklime piled in the ditch. The cart was backed to the margin, the body slung off the platform and dumped into the grave with an irreverent roughness. A sharpened stake had hitherto served it for a pillow. It was now withdrawn, held in its place by several volunteers, and a fellow with a heavy mallet (the sound of which still haunts me at night) drove it home through the bosom of the corpse. The hole was filled with quicklime, and the bystanders, as if relieved of some oppression, broke at once into a sound of whispered speech.

My shirt stuck to me, my heart had almost ceased beating, and I found my tongue with difficulty.

'I beg your pardon,' I gasped to a neighbour, 'what is this? what has he done? is it allowed?'

'Why, where do you come from?' replied the man.

'I am a traveller, sir,' said I, 'and a total stranger in this

part of the country. I had lost my way when I saw your
torches, and came by chance on this—this incredible scene.
Who was the man?'

'A suicide,' said he. 'Ay, he was a bad one, was Johnnie
Green.'

It appeared this was a wretch who had committed many
barbarous murders, and being at last upon the point of discovery fell of his own hand. And the nightmare at the cross-
roads was the regular punishment, according to the laws of
England, for an act which the Romans honoured as a virtue!
Whenever an Englishman begins to prate of civilisation (as,
indeed, it's a defect they are rather prone to), I hear the
measured blows of a mallet, see the bystanders crowd with
torches about the grave, smile a little to myself in conscious
superiority—and take a thimbleful of brandy for the stomach's
sake.

I believe it must have been at my next stage, for I remember
going to bed extremely early, that I came to the model of a good
old-fashioned English inn, and was attended on by the picture of
a pretty chambermaid. We had a good many pleasant passages
as she waited table or warmed my bed for me with a devil of a
brass warming pan, fully larger than herself; and as she was no
less pert than she was pretty, she may be said to have given rather
better than she took. I cannot tell why (unless it were for the
sake of her saucy eyes), but I made her my confidante, told her
I was attached to a young lady in Scotland, and received the
encouragement of her sympathy, mingled and connected with a
fair amount of rustic wit. While I slept the down-mail stopped
for supper; it chanced that one of the passengers left behind
a copy of the *Edinburgh Courant*, and the next morning my
pretty chambermaid set the paper before me at breakfast, with
the remark that there was some news from my lady-love. I
took it eagerly, hoping to find some further word of our escape, in
which I was disappointed; and I was about to lay it down, when
my eye fell on a paragraph immediately concerning me. Faa
was in hospital, grievously sick, and warrants were out for the
arrest of Sim and Candlish. These two men had shown themselves very loyal to me. This trouble emerging, the least I
could do was to be guided by a similar loyalty to them. Suppose
my visit to my uncle crowned with some success, and my finances
re-established, I determined I should immediately return to
Edinburgh, put their case in the hands of a good lawyer, and
await events. So my mind was very lightly made up to what
proved a mighty serious matter. Candlish and Sim were all very
well in their way, and I do sincerely trust I should have been

at some pains to help them, had there been nothing else. But in truth my heart and my eyes were set on quite another matter, and I received the news of their tribulation almost with joy. That is never a bad wind that blows where we want to go, and you may be sure there was nothing unwelcome in a circumstance that carried me back to Edinburgh and Flora. From that hour I began to indulge myself with the making of imaginary scenes and interviews, in which I confounded the aunt, flattered Ronald, and now in the witty, now in the sentimental manner, declared my love and received the assurance of its return. By means of this exercise my resolution daily grew stronger, until at last I had piled together such a mass of obstinacy as it would have taken a cataclysm of nature to subvert.

'Yes,' said I to the chambermaid, 'here is news of my lady-love indeed, and very good news too.'

All that day, in the teeth of a keen winter wind, I hugged myself in my plaid, and it was as though her arms were flung around me.

CHAPTER XII

At last I began to draw near, by reasonable stages, to the neighbourhood of Wakefield; and the name of Mr. Burchell Fenn came to the top in my memory. This was the gentleman (the reader may remember) who made a trade of forwarding the escape of French prisoners. How he did so: whether he had a signboard, *Escapes forwarded, apply within*; what he charged for his services, or whether they were gratuitous and charitable, were all matters of which I was at once ignorant and extremely curious. Thanks to my proficiency in English, and Mr. Romaine's bank-notes, I was getting on swimmingly without him; but the trouble was that I could not be easy till I had come to the bottom of these mysteries, and it was my difficulty that I knew nothing of him beyond the name. I knew not his trade beyond that of Forwarder of Escapes—whether he lived in town or country, whether he were rich or poor, nor by what kind of address I was to gain his confidence. It would have a very bad appearance to go along the highwayside asking after a man of whom I could give so scanty an account; and I should look like a fool, indeed, if I were to present myself at his door and find the police in occupation! The interest of the conundrum, however, tempted me, and I turned aside from my direct road to pass by Wakefield; kept my ears pricked, as I went, for any mention of his name, and relied for the rest on my good fortune. If Luck (who must certainly be feminine) favoured me as far as to throw me in the man's way, I should owe the lady a candle; if not, I could very readily console myself. In this experimental humour, and with so little to help me, it was a miracle that I should have brought my enterprise to a good end; and there are several saints in the calendar who might be happy to exchange with St. Ives!

I had slept that night in a good inn at Wakefield, made my breakfast by candle-light with the passengers of an up-coach, and set off in a very ill temper with myself and my surround-

84

ings. It was still early; the air raw and cold; the sun low, and soon to disappear under a vast canopy of rain-clouds that had begun to assemble in the north-west, and from that quarter invaded the whole width of the heaven. Already the rain fell in crystal rods; already the whole face of the country sounded with the discharge of drains and ditches; and I looked forward to a day of downpour and the hell of wet clothes, in which particular I am as dainty as a cat. At a corner of the road, and by the last glint of the drowning sun, I spied a covered cart, of a kind that I thought I had never seen before, preceding me at the foot's pace of jaded horses. Anything is interesting to a pedestrian that can help him to forget the miseries of a day of rain; and I bettered my pace and gradually overtook the vehicle.

The nearer I came, the more it puzzled me. It was much such a cart as I am told the calico printers use, mounted on two wheels, and furnished with a seat in front for the driver. The interior closed with a door, and was of a bigness to contain a good load of calico, or (at a pinch and if it were necessary) four or five persons. But, indeed, if human beings were meant to travel there, they had my pity! They must travel in the dark, for there was no sign of a window; and they would be shaken all the way like a phial of doctor's stuff, for the cart was not only ungainly to look at—it was besides very imperfectly balanced on the one pair of wheels, and pitched unconscionably. Altogether, if I had any glancing idea that the cart was really a carriage, I had soon dismissed it; but I was still inquisitive as to what it should contain, and where it had come from. Wheels and horses were splashed with many different colours of mud, as though they had come far and across a considerable diversity of country. The driver continually and vainly plied his whip. It seemed to follow they had made a long, perhaps an all-night, stage; and that the driver, at that early hour of a little after eight in the morning, already felt himself belated. I looked for the name of the proprietor on the shaft, and started outright. Fortune had favoured the careless: it was Burchell Fenn!

'A wet morning, my man,' said I.

The driver, a loutish fellow, shock-headed and turnip-faced, returned not a word to my salutation, but savagely flogged his horses. The tired animals, who could scarce put the one foot before the other, paid no attention to his cruelty; and I continued without effort to maintain my position alongside, smiling to myself at the futility of his attempts, and at the same time pricked with curiosity as to why he made them. I made no such formidable a figure as that a man should flee when I accosted him; and my conscience not being entirely clear, I was more accustomed to be uneasy myself than to see others timid. Presently he desisted, and put back his whip in the holster with the air of a man vanquished.

'So you would run away from me?' said I. 'Come, come, that's not English.'

'Beg pardon, master: no offence meant,' he said, touching his hat.

'And none taken!' cried I. 'All I desire is a little gaiety by the way.'

I understood him to say he didn't 'take with gaiety.'

'Then I will try you with something else,' said I. 'Oh, I can be all things to all men, like the apostle! I dare to say I have travelled with heavier fellows than you in my time, and done famously well with them. Are you going home?'

'Yes, I'm a goin' home, I am,' he said.

'A very fortunate circumstance for me!' said I. 'At this rate we shall see a good deal of each other, going the same way; and, now I come to think of it, why should you not give me a cast? There is room beside you on the bench.'

With a sudden snatch, he carried the cart two yards into the roadway. The horses plunged and came to a stop. 'No, you don't!' he said, menacing me with the whip. 'None o' that with me.'

'None of what?' said I. 'I asked you for a lift, but I have no idea of taking one by force.'

'Well, I've got to take care of the cart and 'orses, I have,' says he. 'I don't take up with no runagate vagabones, you see, else.'

'I ought to thank you for your touching confidence,' said I, approaching carelessly nearer as I spoke. 'But I admit the road is solitary hereabouts, and no doubt an accident soon happens. Little fear of anything of the kind with you! I like you for it, like your prudence, like that pastoral shyness of disposition. But why not put it out of my power to hurt? Why not open the door and bestow me here in the box, or whatever you please to call it?' And I laid my hand demonstratively on the body of the cart.

He had been timorous before; but at this, he seemed to lose the power of speech a moment, and stared at me in a perfect enthusiasm of fear.

'Why not?' I continued. 'The idea is good. I should be safe in there if I were the monster Williams himself. The great thing is to have me under lock and key. For it does lock; it is locked now,' said I, trying the door. '*A propos*, what have you for a cargo? It must be precious.'

He found not a word to answer.

Rat-tat-tat, I went upon the door like a well-drilled footman. 'Any one at home?' I said, and stooped to listen.

There came out of the interior a stifled sneeze, the first of an uncontrollable paroxysm; another followed immediately on the heels of it; and then the driver turned with an oath, laid the lash upon the horses with so much energy that they found their heels again, and the whole equipage fled down the road at a gallop.

At the first sound of the sneeze, I had started back like a man shot. The next moment, a great light broke on my mind, and I understood. Here was the secret of Fenn's trade: this was how he forwarded the escape of prisoners, hawking them by night about the country in his covered cart. There had been Frenchmen close to me; he who had just sneezed was my countryman, my comrade, perhaps already my friend! I took to my heels in pursuit. 'Hold hard!' I shouted. 'Stop! It's all right! Stop!' But the driver only turned a white face on me for a moment, and redoubled his efforts, bending forward, plying his whip and crying to his horses; these lay themselves down to the gallop and beat the highway with flying hoofs; and the cart bounded after them among the ruts and fled in a halo of rain and spattering mud. But a minute since, and it had been trundling along like a lame cow; and now it was off as though drawn by Apollo's coursers. There is no telling what a man can do, until you frighten him!

It was as much as I could do myself, though I ran valiantly, to maintain my distance; and that (since I knew my countrymen so near) was become a chief point with me. A hundred yards farther on the cart whipped out of the high-road into a lane embowered with leafless trees, and became lost to view. When I saw it next, the driver had increased his advantage considerably, but all danger was at an end, and the horses had again declined into a hobbling walk. Persuaded that they could not escape me, I took my time, and recovered my breath as I followed them.

Presently the lane twisted at right angles, and showed me a gate and the beginning of a gravel sweep; and a little after, as I continued to advance, a red brick house about seventy years old, in a fine style of architecture, and presenting a front of many windows to a lawn and garden. Behind, I could see outhouses and the peaked roofs of stacks; and I judged that a manor-house had in some way declined to be the residence of a tenant-farmer, careless alike of appearances and substantial comfort. The marks of neglect were visible on every side, in flower-bushes straggling beyond the borders, in the ill-kept turf, and in the broken windows that were incongruously patched with paper or stuffed with rags. A thicket of trees, mostly evergreen, fenced the place round and secluded it from the eyes of prying neighbours. As I came in view of it, on that melancholy winter's morning, in the deluge of the falling rain, and with the wind that now rose in occasional gusts and hooted over the old chimneys, the cart had already drawn up at the front-door steps, and the driver was already in earnest discourse with Mr. Burchell Fenn. He was standing with his hands behind his back—a man of a gross, misbegotten face and body, dewlapped like a bull and red as a harvest moon ; and in his jockey cap, blue coat and top boots, he had much the air of a good, solid tenant-farmer.

The pair continued to speak as I came up the approach, but received me at last in a sort of goggling silence. I had my hat in my hand.

'I have the pleasure of addressing Mr. Burchell Fenn ?' said I.

'The same, sir,' replied Mr. Fenn, taking off his jockey cap in answer to my civility, but with the distant look and the tardy movements of one who continues to think of something else. 'And who may you be ?' he asked.

'I shall tell you afterwards,' said I. 'Suffice it, in the meantime, that I come on business.'

He seemed to digest my answer laboriously, his mouth gaping, his little eyes never straying from my face.

'Suffer me to point out to you, sir,' I resumed, 'that this is a devil of a wet morning ; and that the chimney corner, and possibly a glass of something hot, are clearly indicated.'

Indeed, the rain was now grown to be a deluge ; the gutters of the house roared ; the air was filled with the continuous, strident crash. The stolidity of his face, on which the rain streamed, was far from reassuring me. On the contrary, I was aware of a distinct qualm of apprehension, which was not at all lessened by a view of the driver, craning from his perch to observe us with the expression of a fascinated bird. So we stood silent, when the prisoner again began to sneeze from the body of the cart ; and at the sound, prompt as a transformation, the driver had whipped up his horses and was shambling off round the corner of the house, and Mr. Fenn, recovering his wits with a gulp, had turned to the door behind him.

'Come in, come in, sir,' he said. 'I beg your pardon, sir ; the lock goes a trifle hard.'

Indeed, it took him a surprising time to open the door, which

was not only locked on the outside, but the lock seemed re-
bellious from disuse; and when at last he stood back and
motioned me to enter before him, I was greeted on the threshold by that peculiar and convincing sound of the rain echoing
over empty chambers. The entrance-hall, in which I now
found myself, was of a good size and good proportions; potted
plants occupied the corners; the paved floor was soiled with
muddy footprints and encumbered with straw; on a mahogany
hall-table, which was the only furniture, a candle had been
stuck and suffered to burn down—plainly a long while ago, for
the gutterings were green with mould. My mind, under these
new impressions, worked with unusual vivacity. I was here
shut off with Fenn and his hireling in a deserted house, a
neglected garden, and a wood of evergreens: the most eligible
theatre for a deed of darkness. There came to me a vision of
two flagstones raised in the hall-floor, and the driver putting
in the rainy afternoon over my grave, and the prospect displeased
me extremely. I felt I had carried my pleasantry as far as was
safe; I must lose no time in declaring my true character, and I
was even choosing the words in which I was to begin, when the
hall-door was slammed-to behind me with a bang, and I turned,
dropping my stick as I did so, in time—and not any more than
time—to save my life.

The surprise of the onslaught and the huge weight of my
assailant gave him the advantage. He had a pistol in his right
hand of a portentous size, which it took me all my strength to
keep deflected. With his left arm he strained me to his bosom,
so that I thought I must be crushed or stifled. His mouth was
open, his face crimson, and he panted aloud with hard animal
sounds. The affair was as brief as it was hot and sudden. The
potations which had swelled and bloated his carcase had
already weakened the springs of energy. One more huge
effort, that came near to overpower me, and in which the pistol
happily exploded, and I felt his grasp slacken and weakness
come on his joints; his legs succumbed under his weight, and
he grovelled on his knees on the stone floor. 'Spare me!'
he gasped.

I had not only been abominably frightened; I was shocked
besides: my delicacy was in arms, like a lady to whom violence
should have been offered by a similar monster. I plucked
myself from his horrid contact, I snatched the pistol—even
discharged, it was a formidable weapon—and menaced him
with the butt. 'Spare you!' I cried, 'you beast!'

His voice died in his fat inwards, but his lips still vehemently
framed the same words of supplication. My anger began to

pass off, but not all my repugnance; the picture he made revolted me, and I was impatient to be spared the further view of it.

'Here,' said I, 'stop this performance : it sickens me. I am not going to kill you, do you hear ? I have need of you.'

A look of relief, that I could almost have called beautiful, dawned on his countenance. 'Anything—anything you wish,' said he.

Anything is a big word, and his use of it brought me for a moment to a stand. 'Why, what do you mean ?' I asked. 'Do you mean that you will blow the gaff on the whole business ?'

He answered me Yes with eager asseverations.

'I know Monsieur de Saint-Yves is in it ; it was through his papers we traced you,' I said. 'Do you consent to make a clean breast of the others ?'

'I do—I will !' he cried. 'The 'ole crew of 'em ; there's good names among 'em. I'll be king's evidence.'

'So that all shall hang except yourself? You damned villain !' I broke out. 'Understand at once that I am no spy or thief-taker. I am a kinsman of Monsieur de St. Yves—here in his interest. Upon my word, you have put your foot in it prettily, Mr. Burchell Fenn ! Come, stand up ; don't grovel there. Stand up, you lump of iniquity !'

He scrambled to his feet. He was utterly unmanned, or it might have gone hard with me yet ; and I considered him hesitating, as, indeed, there was cause. The man was a double-dyed traitor : he had tried to murder me, and I had first baffled his endeavours and then exposed and insulted him. Was it wise to place myself any longer at his mercy ? With his help I should doubtless travel more quickly ; doubtless also far less agreeably ; and there was everything to show that it would be at a greater risk. In short, I should have washed my hands of him on the spot, but for the temptation of the French officers, whom I knew to be so near, and for whose society I felt so great and natural an impatience. If I was to see anything of my countrymen, it was clear I had first of all to make my peace with Mr. Fenn ; and that was no easy matter. To make friends with any one implies concessions on both sides ; and what could I concede ? What could I say of him, but that he had proved himself a villain and a fool, and the worse man ?

'Well,' said I, 'here has been rather a poor piece of business, which I dare say you can have no pleasure in calling to mind ; and, to say truth, I would as readily forget it myself. Suppose we try. Take back your pistol, which smells very ill ; put it in your pocket or wherever you had it concealed. There ! Now let us meet for the first time.—Give you good morning, Mr. Fenn! I hope you do very well. I come on the recommendation of my kinsman, the Vicomte de St. Yves.'

'Do you mean it?' he cried. 'Do you mean you will pass over our little scrimmage?'

'Why, certainly!' said I. 'It shows you are a bold fellow, who may be trusted to forget the business when it comes to the point. There is nothing against you in the little scrimmage, unless that your courage is greater than your strength. You are not so young as you once were, that is all.'

'And I beg of you, sir, don't betray me to the Vis-count,' he pleaded. 'I'll not deny but what my 'eart failed me a trifle; but it was only a word, sir, what anybody might have said in the 'eat of the moment, and over with it.'

'Certainly,' said I. 'That is quite my own opinion.'

'The way I came to be anxious about the Vis-count,' he continued, 'is that I believe he might be induced to form an 'asty judgment. And the business, in a pecuniary point of view, is all that I could ask; only trying, sir—very trying. It's making an old man of me before my time. You might have observed yourself, sir, that I 'aven't got the knees I once 'ad. The knees and the breathing, there's where it takes me. But I'm very sure, sir, I address a gentleman as would be the last to make trouble between friends.'

'I am sure you do me no more than justice,' said I; 'and I shall think it quite unnecessary to dwell on any of these passing circumstances in my report to the Vicomte.'

'Which you do favour him (if you'll excuse me being so bold as to mention it) exac'ly!' said he. 'I should have known you anywheres. May I offer you a pot of 'ome-brewed ale, sir? By your leave! This way, if you please. I am 'eartily grateful—'eartily pleased to be of any service to a gentleman like you, sir, which is related to the Vis-count, and really a fambly of which you might well be proud! Take care of the step, sir. You have good news of 'is 'ealth, I trust? as well as that of Monseer the Count?'

God forgive me! the horrible fellow was still puffing and panting with the fury of his assault, and already he had fallen into an obsequious, wheedling familiarity like that of an old servant,—already he was flattering me on my family connections!

I followed him through the house into the stable-yard, where I observed the driver washing the cart in a shed. He must have heard the explosion of the pistol. He could not choose but hear it: the thing was shaped like a little blunderbuss, charged to the mouth, and made a report like a piece of field artillery. He had heard, he had paid no attention; and now, as we came forth by the back-door, he raised for a moment a pale and tell-tale face that was as direct as a confession. The rascal had expected to see Fenn come forth alone; he was waiting to be called on for that part of sexton, which I had already allotted to him in fancy.

I need not detain the reader very long with any description of my visit to the back-kitchen; of how we mulled our ale there, and mulled it very well; nor of how we sat talking, Fenn like an old, faithful, affectionate dependant, and I—well! I myself fallen into a mere admiration of so much impudence, that transcended words, and had very soon conquered animosity. I took a fancy to the man, he was so vast a humbug. I began to see a kind of beauty in him, his *aplomb* was so majestic. I never knew a rogue to cut so fat; his villainy was ample, like his belly, and I could scarce find it in my heart to hold him responsible for either. He was good enough to drop into the autobiographical; telling me how the farm, in spite of the war and the high prices, had proved a disappointment; how there was 'a sight of cold, wet land as you come along the 'igh-road'; how the winds and rains and the seasons had been misdirected, it seemed 'o' purpose'; how Mrs. Fenn had died—'I lost her coming two year agone; a remarkable fine woman, my old girl, sir! if you'll excuse me,' he added, with a burst of humility. In short, he gave me an opportunity of studying John Bull, as I may say, stuffed naked—his greed, his usuriousness, his hypocrisy, his perfidy of the back-stairs, all swelled to the superlative—such as was well worth the little disarray and fluster of our passage in the hall.

CHAPTER XIII

As soon as I judged it safe, and that was not before Burchell
Fenn had talked himself back into his breath and a complete
good humour, I proposed he should introduce me to the French
officers, henceforth to become my fellow-passengers. There
were two of them, it appeared, and my heart beat as I approached the door. The specimen of Perfidious Albion whom
I had just been studying gave me the stronger zest for my
fellow-countrymen. I could have embraced them; I could
have wept on their necks. And all the time I was going to a
disappointment.

It was in a spacious and low room, with an outlook on the
court, that I found them bestowed. In the good days of that
house the apartment had probably served as a library, for there
were traces of shelves along the wainscot. Four or five
mattresses lay on the floor in a corner, with a frowsy heap of
bedding; near by was a basin and a cube of soap; a rude
kitchen-table and some deal chairs stood together at the far
end; and the room was illuminated by no less than four
windows, and warmed by a little, crazy, sidelong grate, propped
up with bricks in the vent of a hospitable chimney, in which a
pile of coals smoked prodigiously and gave out a few starveling
flames. An old, frail, white-haired officer sat in one of the
chairs, which he had drawn close to this apology for a fire. He
was wrapped in a camlet cloak, of which the collar was turned
up, his knees touched the bars, his hands were spread in the
very smoke, and yet he shivered for cold. The second—a big,
florid, fine animal of a man, whose every gesture labelled him
the cock of the walk and the admiration of the ladies—had
apparently despaired of the fire, and now strode up and down,
sneezing hard, bitterly blowing his nose, and proffering a continual stream of bluster, complaint, and barrack-room oaths.

Fenn showed me in with the brief form of introduction:
'Gentlemen all, this here's another fare!' and was gone again

at once. The old man gave me but the one glance out of lack-lustre eyes; and even as he looked a shiver took him as sharp as a hiccough. But the other, who represented to admiration the picture of a Beau in a Catarrh, stared at me arrogantly.

'And who are you, sir?' he asked.

I made the military salute to my superiors.

'Champdivers, private, Eighth of the Line,' said I.

'Pretty business!' said he. 'And you are going on with us? Three in a cart, and a great trolloping private at that! And who is to pay for you, my fine fellow?' he inquired.

'If monsieur comes to that,' I answered civilly, 'who paid for him?'

'Oh, if you choose to play the wit!' said he,—and began to rail at large upon his destiny, the weather, the cold, the danger and the expense of the escape, and, above all, the cooking of the accursed English. It seemed to annoy him particularly that I should have joined their party. 'If you knew what you were doing, thirty thousand millions of pigs! you would keep yourself to yourself! The horses can't drag the cart; the roads are all ruts and swamps. No longer ago than last night the Colonel and I had to march half the way—thunder of God!—half the way to the knees in mud—and I with this infernal cold—and the danger of detection! Happily we met no one: a desert—a real desert—like the whole abominable country! Nothing to eat—no, sir, there is nothing to eat but raw cow and greens boiled in water—nor to drink but Worcestershire sauce! Now I, with my catarrh, I have no appetite; is it not so? Well, if I were in France, I should have a good soup with a crust in it, an omelette, a fowl in rice, a partridge in cabbages—things to tempt me, thunder of God! But here—day of God!—what a country! And cold, too! They talk about Russia—this is all the cold I want! And the people—look at them! What a race! Never any handsome men; never any fine officers!'—and he looked down compla-cently for a moment at his waist—'And the women—what faggots! No, that is one point clear, I cannot stomach the English!'

There was something in this man so antipathetic to me, as sent the mustard into my nose. I can never bear your bucks and dandies, even when they are decent-looking and well dressed; and the Major—for that was his rank—was the image of a flunkey in good luck. Even to be in agreement with him, or to seem to be so, was more than I could make out to endure.

'You could scarce be expected to stomach them,' said I civilly, 'after having just digested your parole.'

He whipped round on his heel and turned on me a countenance which I dare say he imagined to be awful; but another fit
of sneezing cut him off ere he could come the length of speech.

'I have not tried the dish myself,' I took the opportunity to
add. 'It is said to be unpalatable. Did monsieur find it so?'

With surprising vivacity the Colonel woke from his lethargy.
He was between us ere another word could pass.

'Shame, gentlemen!' he said. 'Is this a time for Frenchmen
and fellow-soldiers to fall out? We are in the midst of our
enemies; a quarrel, a loud word, may suffice to plunge us back
into irretrievable distress. *Monsieur le Commandant,* you have
been gravely offended. I make it my request, I make it my
prayer—if need be, I give you my orders—that the matter shall
stand by until we come safe to France. Then, if you please, I
will serve you in any capacity. And for you, young man, you
have shown all the cruelty and carelessness of youth. This
gentleman is your superior; he is no longer young'—at which
word you are to conceive the Major's face. 'It is admitted he
has broken his parole. I know not his reason, and no more do
you. It might be patriotism in this hour of our country's
adversity, it might be humanity, necessity; you know not what
in the least, and you permit yourself to reflect on his honour.
To break parole may be a subject for pity and not derision. I
have broken mine—I, a colonel of the Empire. And why? I
have been years negotiating my exchange, and it cannot be
managed; those who have influence at the Ministry of War
continually rush in before me, and I have to wait, and my
daughter at home is in a decline. I am going to see my
daughter at last, and it is my only concern lest I should have
delayed too long. She is ill, and very ill,—at death's door.
Nothing is left me but my daughter, my Emperor, and my
honour; and I give my honour, blame me for it who dare!'

At this my heart smote me.

'For God's sake,' I cried, 'think no more of what I have
said! A parole? what is a parole against life and death and
love? I ask your pardon; this gentleman's also. As long as I
shall be with you, you shall not have cause to complain of me
again. I pray God you will find your daughter alive and
restored.'

'That is past praying for,' said the Colonel; and immediately
the brief fire died out of him, and, returning to the hearth, he
relapsed into his former abstraction.

But I was not so easy to compose. The knowledge of the
poor gentleman's trouble, and the sight of his face, had filled
me with the bitterness of remorse; and I insisted upon shaking

hands with the Major (which he did with a very ill grace), and abounded in palinodes and apologies.

'After all,' said I, 'who am I to talk? I am in the luck to be a private soldier; I have no parole to give or to keep; once I am over the rampart, I am as free as air. I beg you to believe that I regret from my soul the use of these ungenerous expressions. Allow me . . . Is there no way in this damned house to attract attention? Where is this fellow, Fenn?'

I ran to one of the windows and threw it open. Fenn, who was at the moment passing below in the court, cast up his arms like one in despair, called to me to keep back, plunged into the house, and appeared next moment in the doorway of the chamber.

'Oh, sir!' says he, 'keep away from those there windows. A body might see you from the back lane.'

'It is registered,' said I. 'Henceforward I will be a mouse for precaution and a ghost for invisibility. But in the meantime, for God's sake, fetch us a bottle of brandy! Your room is as damp as the bottom of a well, and these gentlemen are perishing of cold.'

So soon as I had paid him (for everything, I found, must be paid in advance), I turned my attention to the fire, and whether because I threw greater energy into the business, or because the coals were now warmed and the time ripe, I soon started a blaze that made the chimney roar again. The shine of it, in that dark, rainy day, seemed to reanimate the Colonel like a blink of sun. With the outburst of the flames, besides, a draught was established, which immediately delivered us from the plague of smoke; and by the time Fenn returned, carrying a bottle under his arm and a single tumbler in his hand, there was already an air of gaiety in the room that did the heart good.

I poured out some of the brandy.

'Colonel,' said I, 'I am a young man and a private soldier. I have not been long in this room, and already I have shown the petulance that belongs to the one character and the ill manners that you may look for in the other. Have the humanity to pass these slips over, and honour me so far as to accept this glass.'

'My lad,' says he, waking up and blinking at me with an air of suspicion, 'are you sure you can afford it?'

I assured him I could.

'I thank you, then: I am very cold.' He took the glass out, and a little colour came in his face. 'I thank you again,' said he. 'It goes to the heart.'

The Major, when I motioned him to help himself, did so with a good deal of liberality; continued to do so for the rest of the morning, now with some sort of apology, now with none at all; and the bottle began to look foolish before dinner was served. It was such a meal as he had himself predicted: beef, greens, potatoes, mustard in a teacup, and beer in a brown jug that was all over hounds, horses, and hunters, with a fox at the far end and a gigantic John Bull—for all the world like Fenn—sitting in the midst in a bob-wig and smoking tobacco. The beer was a good brew, but not good enough for the Major; he laced it with brandy—for his cold, he said; and in this curative design the remainder of the bottle ebbed away. He called my attention repeatedly to the circumstance; helped me pointedly to the dregs, threw the bottle in the air and played tricks with it; and at last, having exhausted his ingenuity, and seeing me remain quite blind to every hint, he ordered and paid for another himself.

As for the Colonel, he ate nothing, sat sunk in a muse, and only awoke occasionally to a sense of where he was, and what he was supposed to be doing. On each of these occasions he showed a gratitude and kind courtesy that endeared him to me beyond expression. 'Champdivers, my lad, your health!' he would say. 'The Major and I had a very arduous march last night, and I positively thought I should have eaten nothing, but your fortunate idea of the brandy has made quite a new man of me—quite a new man.' And he would fall to with a great air of heartiness, cut himself a mouthful, and, before he had swallowed it, would have forgotten his dinner, his company, the place where he then was, and the escape he was engaged on, and become absorbed in the vision of a sick-room and a dying girl in France. The pathos of this continual pre-occupation, in a man so old, sick, and over-weary, and whom I looked upon as a mere bundle of dying bones and death-pains, put me wholly from my victuals: it seemed there was an element of sin, a kind of rude bravado of youth, in the mere relishing of food at the same table with this tragic father; and though I was well enough used to the coarse, plain diet of the English, I ate scarce more than himself. Dinner was hardly over before he succumbed to a lethargic sleep; lying on one of the mattresses with his limbs relaxed, and his breath seemingly suspended—the very image of dissolution.

This left the Major and myself alone at the table. You must not suppose our *tête-à-tête* was long, but it was a lively period while it lasted. He drank like a fish or an Englishman; shouted, beat the table, roared out songs, quarrelled, made it up again, and at last tried to throw the dinner-plates through the window, a feat of which he was at that time quite incapable. For a party of fugitives, condemned to the most rigorous discretion, there was never seen so noisy a carnival; and through it all the Colonel continued to sleep like a child. Seeing the Major so well advanced, and no retreat possible, I made a fair wind of a foul one, keeping his glass full, pushing him with toasts; and sooner than I could have dared to hope, he became drowsy and incoherent. With the wrong-headedness of all such sots, he would not be persuaded to lie down upon one of the mattresses until I had stretched myself upon another. But the comedy was soon over; soon he slept the sleep of the just, and snored like a military music; and I might get up again and face (as best I could) the excessive tedium of the afternoon.

I had passed the night before in a good bed; I was denied the resource of slumber; and there was nothing open for me but to pace the apartment, maintain the fire, and brood on my position. I compared yesterday and to-day—the safety, comfort, jollity, open-air exercise and pleasant roadside inns of the one, with the tedium, anxiety, and discomfort of the other. I remembered that I was in the hands of Fenn, who could not be more false—though he might be more vindictive—than I fancied him. I looked forward to nights of pitching in the covered cart, and days of monotony in I knew not what hiding-places; and my heart failed me, and I was in two minds whether to slink off ere it was too late, and return to my former solitary way of travel. But the Colonel stood in the path. I had not seen much of him; but already I judged him a man of a childlike nature—with that sort of innocence and courtesy that, I think, is only to be found in old soldiers or old priests—and broken with years and sorrow. I could not turn my back on his distress; could not leave him alone with the selfish trooper who snored on the next mattress. 'Champdivers, my lad, your health!' said a voice in my ear, and stopped me —and there are few things I am more glad of in the retrospect than that it did.

It must have been about four in the afternoon—at least the rain had taken off, and the sun was setting with some wintry pomp—when the current of my reflections was effectually changed by the arrival of two visitors in a gig. They were farmers of the neighbourhood, I suppose—big, burly fellows in great-coats and top-boots, mightily flushed with liquor when they arrived, and, before they left, inimitably drunk. They stayed long in the kitchen with Burchell, drinking, shouting, singing, and keeping it up; and the sound of their merry minstrelsy kept me a kind of company. The night fell, and the shine of the fire brightened and blinked on the panelled wall. Our illuminated windows must have been visible not only from the back lane of which Fenn had spoken, but from the court where the farmers' gig awaited them. In the far end of the firelit room lay my companions, the one silent, the other clamorously noisy, the images of death and drunkenness. Little wonder if I were tempted to join in the choruses below, and sometimes could hardly refrain from laughter, and sometimes, I believe, from tears—so unmitigated was the tedium, so cruel the suspense, of this period.

At last, about six at night, I should fancy, the noisy minstrels appeared in the court, headed by Fenn with a lantern, and knocking together as they came. The visitors clambered noisily into the gig, one of them shook the reins, and they were snatched out of sight and hearing with a suddenness that partook of the nature of prodigy. I am well aware there is a Providence for drunken men, that holds the reins for them and presides over their troubles; doubtless he had his work cut out for him with this particular gigful! Fenn rescued his toes with an ejaculation from under the departing wheels, and turned at once with uncertain steps and devious lantern to the far end of the court. There, through the open doors of a coach-house, the shock-headed lad was already to be seen drawing forth the covered cart. If I wished any private talk with our host, it must be now or never.

Accordingly I groped my way downstairs, and came to him as he looked on at and lighted the harnessing of the horses.

'The hour approaches when we have to part,' said I; 'and I shall be obliged if you will tell your servant to drop me at the nearest point for Dunstable. I am determined to go so far with our friends, Colonel X and Major Y, but my business is peremptory, and it takes me to the neighbourhood of Dunstable.'

Orders were given to my satisfaction, with an obsequiousness that seemed only inflamed by his potations.

CHAPTER XIV

TRAVELS OF THE COVERED CART

My companions were aroused with difficulty : the Colonel, poor old gentleman, to a sort of permanent dream, in which you could say of him only that he was very deaf and anxiously polite ; the Major still maudlin drunk. We had a dish of tea by the fireside, and then issued like criminals into the scathing cold of the night. For the weather had in the meantime changed. Upon the cessation of the rain, a strict frost had succeeded. The moon, being young, was already near the zenith when we started, glittered everywhere on sheets of ice, and sparkled in ten thousand icicles. A more unpromising night for a journey it was hard to conceive. But in the course of the afternoon the horses had been well roughed ; and King (for such was the name of the shock-headed lad) was very positive that he could drive us without misadventure. He was as good as his word ; indeed, despite a gawky air, he was simply invaluable in his present employment, showing marked sagacity in all that concerned the care of horses, and guiding us by one short cut after another for days, and without a fault.

The interior of that engine of torture, the covered cart, was fitted with a bench, on which we took our places ; the door was shut ; in a moment, the night closed upon us solid and stifling ; and we felt that we were being driven carefully out of the courtyard. Careful was the word all night, and it was an alleviation of our miseries that we did not often enjoy. In general, as we were driven the better part of the night and day, often at a pretty quick pace and always through a labyrinth of the most infamous country lanes and by-roads, we were so bruised upon the bench, so dashed against the top and sides of the cart, that we reached the end of a stage in truly pitiable case, sometimes flung ourselves down without the formality of eating, made but one sleep of it until the hour of departure returned, and were only properly awakened by the first jolt of the renewed journey. There were interruptions, at times, that we hailed as alleviations. At times the cart was bogged, once

100

it was upset, and we must alight and lend the driver the assistance of our arms ; at times, too (as on the occasion when I had first encountered it), the horses gave out, and we had to trail alongside in mud or frost until the first peep of daylight, or the approach to a hamlet or a high road, bade us disappear like ghosts into our prison.

The main roads of England are incomparable for excellence, of a beautiful smoothness, very ingeniously laid down, and so well kept that in most weathers you could take your dinner off any part of them without distaste. On them, to the note of the bugle, the mail did its sixty miles a day ; innumerable chaises whisked after the bobbing postboys ; or some young blood would flit by in a curricle and tandem, to the vast delight and danger of the lieges. On them, the slow-pacing waggons made a music of bells, and all day long the travellers on horse-back and the travellers on foot (like happy Mr. St. Ives so little a while before !) kept coming and going, and baiting and gaping at each other, as though a fair were due, and they were gathering to it from all England. No, nowhere in the world is travel so great a pleasure as in that country. But unhappily our one need was to be secret ; and all this rapid and animated picture of the road swept quite apart from us, as we lumbered up hill and down dale, under hedge and over stone, among circuitous byways. Only twice did I receive, as it were, a whiff of the highway. The first reached my ears alone. I might have been anywhere. I only knew I was walking in the dark night and among ruts, when I heard very far off, over the silent country that surrounded us, the guard's horn wailing its signal to the next post-house for a change of horses. It was like the voice of the day heard in darkness, a voice of the world heard in prison, the note of a cock crowing in the mid-seas—in short, I cannot tell you what it was like, you will have to fancy for yourself—but I could have wept to hear it. Once we were belated : the cattle could hardly crawl, the day was at hand, it was a nipping, rigorous morning, King was lashing his horses, I was giving an arm to the old Colonel, and the Major was coughing in our rear. I must suppose that King was a thought careless, being nearly in desperation about his team, and, in spite of the cold morning, breathing hot with his exertions. We came, at last, a little before sunrise to the summit of a hill, and saw the high-road passing at right angles through an open country of meadows and hedgerow pollards ; and not only the York mail, speeding smoothly at the gallop of the four horses, but a post-chaise besides, with the post-boy titupping briskly, and the traveller himself putting his head

out of the window, but whether to breathe the dawn, or the
better to observe the passage of the mail, I do not know. So
that we enjoyed for an instant a picture of free life on the road,
in its most luxurious forms of despatch and comfort. And
thereafter, with a poignant feeling of contrast in our hearts, we
must mount again into our wheeled dungeon.

We came to our stages at all sorts of odd hours, and they
were in all kinds of odd places. I may say at once that my
first experience was my best. Nowhere again were we so well
entertained as at Burchell Fenn's. And this, I suppose, was
natural, and indeed inevitable, in so long and secret a journey.
The first stop, we lay six hours in a barn standing by itself in a
poor, marshy orchard, and packed with hay ; to make it more
attractive, we were told it had been the scene of an abominable
murder, and was now haunted. But the day was beginning
to break, and our fatigue was too extreme for visionary terrors.
The second or third, we alighted on a barren heath about
midnight, built a fire to warm us under the shelter of some
thorns, supped like beggars on bread and a piece of cold bacon,
and slept like gipsies with our feet to the fire. In the meanwhile, King was gone with the cart, I know not where, to get
a change of horses, and it was late in the dark morning when
he returned and we were able to resume our journey. In the
middle of another night, we came to a stop by an ancient,
whitewashed cottage of two stories ; a privet hedge surrounded
it ; the frosty moon shone blankly on the upper windows ; but
through those of the kitchen the firelight was seen glinting on
the roof and reflected from the dishes on the wall. Here,
after much hammering on the door, King managed to arouse an
old crone from the chimney-corner chair, where she had been
dozing in the watch ; and we were had in, and entertained
with a dish of hot tea. This old lady was an aunt of Burchell
Fenn's — and an unwilling partner in his dangerous trade.
Though the house stood solitary, and the hour was an unlikely
one for any passenger upon the road, King and she conversed
in whispers only. There was something dismal, something
of the sick-room, in this perpetual, guarded sibilation. The
apprehensions of our hostess insensibly communicated themselves to every one present. We ate like mice in a cat's ear ;
if one of us jingled a teaspoon, all would start ; and when the
hour came to take the road again, we drew a long breath of
relief, and climbed to our places in the covered cart with a
positive sense of escape. The most of our meals, however,
were taken boldly at hedgerow alehouses, usually at untimely
hours of the day, when the clients were in the field or the

farmyard at labour. I shall have to tell presently of our last
experience of the sort, and how unfortunately it miscarried ;
but as that was the signal for my separation from my fellow-
travellers, I must first finish with them.

I had never any occasion to waver in my first judgment of
the Colonel. The old gentleman seemed to me, and still seems
in the retrospect, the salt of the earth. I had occasion to see
him in the extremes of hardship, hunger and cold ; he was
dying, and he looked it ; and yet I cannot remember any hasty,
harsh, or impatient word to have fallen from his lips. On the
contrary, he ever showed himself careful to please ; and even
if he rambled in his talk, rambled always gently—like a humane,
half-witted old hero, true to his colours to the last. I would
not dare to say how often he awoke suddenly from a lethargy,
and told us again, as though we had never heard it, the story
of how he had earned the cross, how it had been given him by
the hand of the Emperor, and of the innocent—and, indeed,
foolish—sayings of his daughter when he returned with it on his
bosom. He had another anecdote which he was very apt to
give, by way of a rebuke, when the Major wearied us beyond
endurance with dispraises of the English. This was an account
of the *braves gens* with whom he had been boarding. True
enough, he was a man so simple and grateful by nature, that
the most common civilities were able to touch him to the heart,
and would remain written in his memory ; but from a thousand
inconsiderable but conclusive indications, I gathered that this
family had really loved him, and loaded him with kindness.
They made a fire in his bedroom, which the sons and daughters
tended with their own hands ; letters from France were looked
for with scarce more eagerness by himself than by these alien
sympathisers ; when they came, he would read them aloud in
the parlour to the assembled family, translating as he went.
The Colonel's English was elementary ; his daughter not in the
least likely to be an amusing correspondent ; and, as I conceived
these scenes in the parlour, I felt sure the interest centred in
the Colonel himself, and I thought I could feel in my own
heart that mixture of the ridiculous and the pathetic, the con-
test of tears and laughter, which must have shaken the bosoms
of the family. Their kindness had continued till the end. It
appears they were privy to his flight, the camlet cloak had been
lined expressly for him, and he was the bearer of a letter from
the daughter of the house to his own daughter in Paris. The
last evening, when the time came to say good-night, it was tacitly
known to all that they were to look upon his face no more.
He rose, pleading fatigue, and turned to the daughter, who had

been his chief ally: 'You will permit me, my dear—to an old and very unhappy soldier—and may God bless you for your goodness!' The girl threw her arms about his neck and sobbed upon his bosom; the lady of the house burst into tears; '*et je vous le jure, le père se mouchait!*' quoth the Colonel, twisting his moustaches with a cavalry air, and at the same time blinking the water from his eyes at the mere recollection.

It was a good thought to me that he had found these friends in captivity; that he had started on this fatal journey from so cordial a farewell. He had broken his parole for his daughter: that he should ever live to reach her sick-bed, that he could continue to endure to an end the hardships, the crushing fatigue, the savage cold, of our pilgrimage, I had early ceased to hope. I did for him what I was able,—nursed him, kept him covered, watched over his slumbers, sometimes held him in my arms at the rough places of the road. 'Champdivers,' he once said, 'you are like a son to me—like a son.' It is good to remember, though at the time it put me on the rack. All was to no purpose. Fast as we were travelling towards France, he was travelling faster still to another destination. Daily he grew weaker and more indifferent. An old rustic accent of Lower Normandy reappeared in his speech, from which it had long been banished, and grew stronger; old words of the *patois*, too: *Ouistreham, matrassé*, and others, the sense of which we were sometimes unable to guess. On the very last day he began again his eternal story of the cross and the Emperor. The Major, who was particularly ill, or at least particularly cross, uttered some angry words of protest. '*Pardonnez-moi, monsieur le commandant, mais c'est pour monsieur,*' said the Colonel: 'Monsieur has not yet heard the circumstance, and is good enough to feel an interest.' Presently after, however, he began to lose the thread of his narrative; and at last: '*Qué que j'ai? Je m'embrouille!*' says he, '*Suffit: s'm'a la donné, et Berthe en était bien contente.*' It struck me as the falling of the curtain or the closing of the sepulchre doors.

Sure enough, in but a little while after, he fell into a sleep as gentle as an infant's, which insensibly changed into the sleep of death. I had my arm about his body at the time and remarked nothing, unless it were that he once stretched himself a little, so kindly the end came to that disastrous life. It was only at our evening halt that the Major and I discovered we were travelling alone with the poor clay. That night we stole a spade from a field—I think near Market Bosworth—and a little farther on, in a wood of young oak trees and by the light of King's lantern, we buried the old soldier of the Empire with both prayers and tears.

We had needs invent Heaven if it had not been revealed to us ; there are some things that fall so bitterly ill on this side Time ! As for the Major, I have long since forgiven him. He broke the news to the poor Colonel's daughter; I am told he did it kindly; and sure, nobody could have done it without tears ! His share of purgatory will be brief; and in this world, as I could not very well praise him, I have suppressed his name. The Colonel's also, for the sake of his parole. *Requiescat.*

CHAPTER XV

THE ADVENTURE OF THE ATTORNEY'S CLERK

I HAVE mentioned our usual course, which was to eat in inconsiderable wayside hostelries, known to King. It was a dangerous business; we went daily under fire to satisfy our appetite, and put our head in the lion's mouth for a piece of bread. Sometimes, to minimise the risk, we would all dismount before we came in view of the house, straggle in severally, and give what orders we pleased, like disconnected strangers. In like manner we departed, to find the cart at an appointed place, some half a mile beyond. The Colonel and the Major had each a word or two of English—God help their pronunciation! But they did well enough to order a rasher and a pot or call a reckoning; and, to say truth, these country folks did not give themselves the pains, and had scarce the knowledge, to be critical.

About nine or ten at night the pains of hunger and cold drove us to an alehouse in the flats of Bedfordshire, not far from Bedford itself. In the inn kitchen was a long, lean, characteristic-looking fellow of perhaps forty, dressed in black. He sat on a settle by the fireside, smoking a long pipe, such as they call a yard of clay. His hat and wig were hanged upon the knob behind him, his head as bald as a bladder of lard, and his expression very shrewd, cantankerous, and inquisitive. He seemed to value himself above his company, to give himself the airs of a man of the world among that rustic herd; which was often no more than his due; being, as I afterwards discovered, an attorney's clerk. I took upon myself the more ungrateful part of arriving last; and by the time I entered on the scene the Major was already served at a side table. Some general conversation must have passed, and I smelled danger in the air. The Major looked flustered, the attorney's clerk triumphant, and three or four peasants in smock-frocks (who sat about the fire to play chorus) had let their pipes go out.

'Give you good evening, sir!' said the attorney's clerk to me.

106

'The same to you, sir,' said I.

'I think this one will do,' quoth the clerk to the yokels with a wink; and then, as soon as I had given my order, 'Pray, sir, whither are you bound?' he added.

'Sir,' said I, 'I am not one of those who speak either of their business or their destination in houses of public entertainment.'

'A good answer,' said he, 'and an excellent principle. Sir, do you speak French?'

'Why, no, sir,' said I. 'A little Spanish at your service.'

'But you know the French accent, perhaps?' said the clerk.

'Well do I do that!' said I. 'The French accent? Why, I believe I can tell a Frenchman in ten words.'

'Here is a puzzle for you, then!' he said. 'I have no material doubt myself, but some of these gentlemen are more backward. The lack of education, you know. I make bold to say that a man cannot walk, cannot hear, and cannot see, without the blessings of education.'

He turned to the Major, whose food plainly stuck in his throat.

'Now, sir,' pursued the clerk, 'let me have the pleasure to hear your voice again. Where are you going, did you say?'

'Sare, I am go—ing to Lon—don,' said the Major.

I could have flung my plate at him to be such an ass, and to have so little a gift of languages where that was the essential.

'What think ye of that?' said the clerk. 'Is that French enough?'

'Good God!' cried I, leaping up like one who should suddenly perceive an acquaintance, 'is this you, Mr. Dubois? Why, who would have dreamed of encountering you so far from home?' As I spoke, I shook hands with the Major heartily; and turning to our tormentor, 'Oh, sir, you may be perfectly reassured! This is a very honest fellow, a late neighbour of mine in the city of Carlisle.'

I thought the attorney looked put out; I little knew the man!

'But he is French,' said he, 'for all that?'

'Ay, to be sure!' said I. 'A Frenchman of the emigration! None of your Buonaparté lot. I will warrant his views of politics to be as sound as your own.'

'What is a little strange,' said the clerk quietly, 'is that Mr. Dubois should deny it.'

I got it fair in the face, and took it smiling; but the shock was rude, and in the course of the next words I contrived to do what I have rarely done, and make a slip in my English. I kept my liberty and life by my proficiency all these months, and for once that I failed, it is not to be supposed that I would make a public exhibition of the details. Enough, that it was a very little error, and one that might have passed ninety-nine times in a hundred. But my limb of the law was as swift to pick it up as though he had been by trade a master of languages.

'Aha!' cries he; 'and you are French, too! Your tongue bewrays you. Two Frenchmen coming into an alehouse, severally and accidentally, not knowing each other, at ten of the clock at night, in the middle of Bedfordshire? No, sir, that shall not pass! You are all prisoners escaping, if you are nothing worse. Consider yourselves under arrest. I have to trouble you for your papers.'

'Where is your warrant, if you come to that?' said I. 'My papers! A likely thing that I would show my papers on the *ipse dixit* of an unknown fellow in a hedge alehouse!'

'Would you resist the law?' says he.

'Not the law, sir!' said I. 'I hope I am too good a subject for that. But for a nameless fellow with a bald head and a pair of gingham small-clothes, why certainly! 'Tis my birthright as an Englishman. Where's *Magna Charta*, else?'

'We will see about that,' says he; and then, addressing the assistants, 'where does the constable live?'

'Lord love you, sir!' cried the landlord, 'what are you thinking of? The constable at past ten at night! Why, he's abed and asleep, and good and drunk two hours agone!'

'Ah that a' be!' came in chorus from the yokels.

The attorney's clerk was put to a stand. He could not think of force; there was little sign of martial ardour about the landlord, and the peasants were indifferent—they only listened, and gaped, and now scratched a head, and now would get a light to their pipes from the embers on the hearth. On the other hand, the Major and I put a bold front on the business and defied him, not without some ground of law. In this state of matters he proposed I should go along with him to one Squire Merton, a great man of the neighbourhood, who was in the commission of the peace, the end of his avenue but three lanes away. I told him I would not stir a foot for him if it were to save his soul. Next he proposed I should stay all night where I was, and the constable could see to my affair in the morning, when he was sober. I replied I should go when and where I pleased; that we were lawful travellers in the fear of God and the king, and I for one would suffer myself to be stayed by nobody. At the same time, I was thinking the matter had lasted altogether too long, and I determined to bring it to an end at once.

'See here,' said I, getting up, for till now I had remained

carelessly seated, 'there's only one way to decide a thing like this—only one way that's right *English*—and that's man to man. Take off your coat, sir, and these gentlemen shall see fair play.'

At this there came a look in his eye that I could not mistake. His education had been neglected in one essential and eminently British particular : he could not box. No more could I, you may say ; but then I had the more impudence—and I had made the proposal.

'He says I'm no Englishman, but the proof of the pudding is the eating of it,' I continued. And here I stripped my coat and fell into the proper attitude, which was just about all I knew of this barbarian art. 'Why, sir, you seem to me to hang back a little,' said I. 'Come, I'll meet you ; I'll give you an appetiser—though hang me if I can understand the man that wants any enticement to hold up his hands.' I drew a bank-note out of my fob and tossed it to the landlord. 'There are the stakes,' said I. 'I'll fight you for first blood, since you seem to make so much work about it. If you tap my claret first, there are five guineas for you, and I'll go with you to any squire you choose to mention. If I tap yours, you'll perhaps let on that I'm the better man, and allow me to go about my lawful business at my own time and convenience, by God ; is that fair, my lads ?' says I, appealing to the company.

'Ay, ay,' said the chorus of chawbacons ; 'he can't say no fairer nor that, he can't. Take off thy coat, master !'

The limb of the law was now on the wrong side of public opinion, and, what heartened me to go on, the position was rapidly changing in our favour. Already the Major was paying his shot to the very indifferent landlord, and I could see the white face of King at the back-door, making signals of haste.

'Oho !' quoth my enemy, 'you are as full of doubles as a fox, are you not ? But I see through you ; I see through and through you. You would change the venue, would you ?'

'I may be transparent, sir,' says I, 'but if you'll do me the favour to stand up, you'll find I can hit dam hard.'

'Which is a point, if you will observe, that I had never called in question,' said he. 'Why, you ignorant clowns,' he proceeded, addressing the company, 'can't you see the fellow's gulling you before your eyes ? Can't you see that he has changed the point upon me ? I say he's a French prisoner, and he answers that he can box ! What has that to do with it ? I would not wonder but what he can dance, too—they're all dancing masters over there. I say, and I stick to it, that he's a Frenchy. He says he isn't. Well then, let him out with his papers, if he has them ! If he had, would he not show them ? If he had, would he not jump at the idea of going to Squire Merton, a man you all know? Now, you are all plain, straightforward Bedfordshire men, and I wouldn't ask a better lot to appeal to. You're not the kind to be talked over with any French gammon, and he's plenty of that. But let me tell him, he can take his pigs to another market; they'll never do here; they'll never go down in Bedfordshire. Why! look at the man! Look at his feet! Has anybody got a foot in the room like that? See how he stands! do any of you fellows stand like that? Does the landlord, there? Why, he has Frenchman wrote all over him, as big as a sign-post!'

This was all very well; and in a different scene I might even have been gratified by his remarks; but I saw clearly, if I were to allow him to talk, he might turn the tables on me altogether. He might not be much of a hand at boxing; but I was much mistaken, or he had studied forensic eloquence in a good school. In this predicament I could think of nothing more ingenious than to burst out of the house, under the pretext of an ungovernable rage. It was certainly not very ingenious—it was elementary, but I had no choice.

'You white-livered dog!' I broke out. 'Do you dare to tell me you're an Englishman, and won't fight? But I'll stand no more of this! I leave this place, where I've been insulted! Here! what's to pay? Pay yourself!' I went on, offering the landlord a handful of silver, 'and give me back my bank-note!'

The landlord, following his usual policy of obliging everybody, offered no opposition to my design. The position of my adversary was now thoroughly bad. He had lost my two companions. He was on the point of losing me also. There was plainly no hope of arousing the company to help; and watching him with a corner of my eye, I saw him hesitate for a moment. The next, he had taken down his hat and his wig, which was of black horsehair; and I saw him draw from behind the settle a vast hooded great-coat and a small valise. 'The devil!' thought I: 'is the rascal going to follow me?'

I was scarce clear of the inn before the limb of the law was at my heels. I saw his face plain in the moonlight; and the most resolute purpose showed in it, along with an unmoved composure. A chill went over me. 'This is no common adventure,' thinks I to myself. 'You have got hold of a man of character, St. Ives! A bite-hard, a bull-dog, a weasel is on your trail; and how are you to throw him off?' Who was he? By some of his expressions I judged he was a hanger-on of courts. But in what character had he followed the assizes? As a simple spectator, as a lawyer's clerk, as a criminal himself, or —last and worst supposition—as a Bow-street 'runner'?

The cart would wait for me, perhaps, half a mile down our onward road, which I was already following. And I told myself that in a few minutes' walking, Bow-street runner or not, I should have him at my mercy. And then reflection came to me in time. Of all things, one was out of the question. Upon no account must this obtrusive fellow see the cart. Until I had killed or shook him off, I was quite divorced from my companions—alone, in the midst of England, on a frosty by-way leading whither I knew not, with a sleuth-hound at my heels, and never a friend but the holly-stick!

We came at the same time to a crossing of lanes. The branch to the left was overhung with trees, deeply sunken and dark. Not a ray of moonlight penetrated its recesses; and I took it at a venture. The wretch followed my example in silence; and for some time we crunched together over frozen pools without a word. Then he found his voice, with a chuckle.

'This is not the way to Mr. Merton's,' said he.

'No?' said I. 'It is mine, however.'

'And therefore mine,' said he.

Again we fell silent; and we may thus have covered half a mile before the lane, taking a sudden turn, brought us forth again into the moonshine. With his hooded great-coat on his back, his valise in his hand, his black wig adjusted, and footing it on the ice with a sort of sober doggedness of manner, my enemy was changed almost beyond recognition: changed in everything but a certain dry, polemical, pedantic air, that spoke of a sedentary occupation and high stools. I observed, too, that his valise was heavy; and, putting this and that together, hit upon a plan.

'A seasonable night, sir,' said I. 'What do you say to a bit of running? The frost has me by the toes.'

'With all the pleasure in life,' says he.

His voice seemed well assured, which pleased me little. However, there was nothing else to try, except violence, for which it would always be too soon. I took to my heels accordingly, he after me; and for some time the slapping of our feet on the hard road might have been heard a mile away. He had started a pace behind me, and he finished in the same position. For all his extra years and the weight of his valise, he had not lost a hair's breadth. The devil might race him for me—I had enough of it!

And, besides, to run so fast was contrary to my interests. We could not run long without arriving somewhere. At any moment we might turn a corner and find ourselves at the lodge-gate of some Squire Merton, in the midst of a village whose constable was sober, or in the hands of a patrol. There was no help for it—I must finish with him on the spot, as long as it was possible. I looked about me, and the place seemed suitable; never a light, never a house—nothing but stubble-fields, fallows, and a few stunted trees. I stopped and eyed him in in the moonlight with an angry stare.

'Enough of this foolery!' said I.

He had turned, and now faced me full, very pale, but with no sign of shrinking.

'I am quite of your opinion,' said he. 'You have tried me at the running; you can try me next at the high jump. It will be all the same. It must end the one way.'

I made my holly whistle about my head.

'I believe you know what way!' said I. 'We are alone, it is night, and I am wholly resolved. Are you not frightened?'

'No,' he said, 'not in the smallest. I do not box, sir; but I am not a coward, as you may have supposed. Perhaps it will simplify our relations if I tell you at the outset that I walk armed.'

Quick as lightning I made a feint at his head; as quickly he gave ground, and at the same time I saw a pistol glitter in his hand.

'No more of that, Mr. French-Prisoner!' he said. 'It will do me no good to have your death at my door.'

'Faith, nor me either!' said I; and I lowered my stick and considered the man, not without a twinkle of admiration. 'You see,' I said, 'there is one consideration that you appear to overlook: there are a great many chances that your pistol may miss fire.'

'I have a pair,' he returned. 'Never travel without a brace of barkers.'

'I make you my compliment,' said I. 'You are able to take care of yourself, and that is a good trait. But, my good man! let us look at this matter dispassionately. You are not a coward, and no more am I; we are both men of excellent sense; I have good reason, whatever it may be, to keep my concerns to myself and to walk alone. Now I put it to you pointedly, am I likely to stand it? Am I likely to put up with your continued and—excuse me—highly impudent *ingérence* into my private affairs?'

'Another French word,' says he composedly.

'Oh! damn your French words!' cried I. 'You seem to be a Frenchman yourself!'

'I have had many opportunities by which I have profited,' he explained. 'Few men are better acquainted with the similarities and differences, whether of idiom or accent, of the two languages.'

'You are a pompous fellow, too!' said I.

'Oh, I can make distinctions, sir,' says he. 'I can talk with Bedfordshire peasants; and I can express myself becomingly, I hope, in the company of a gentleman of education like yourself.'

'If you set up to be a gentleman——' I began.

'Pardon me,' he interrupted: 'I make no such claim. I only see the nobility and gentry in the way of business. I am quite a plain person.'

'For the Lord's sake,' I exclaimed, 'set my mind at rest upon one point. In the name of mystery, who and what are you?'

'I have no cause to be ashamed of my name, sir,' said he, 'nor yet my trade. I am Thomas Dudgeon, at your service, clerk to Mr. Daniel Romaine, solicitor of London; High Holborn is our address, sir.'

It was only by the ecstasy of the relief that I knew how horribly I had been frightened. I flung my stick on the road.

'Romaine?' I cried. 'Daniel Romaine? An old hunks with a red face and a big head, and got up like a Quaker? My dear friend, to my arms!'

'Keep back, I say!' said Dudgeon weakly.

I would not listen to him. With the end of my own alarm, I felt as if I must infallibly be at the end of all dangers likewise; as if the pistol that he held in one hand were no more to be feared than the valise that he carried with the other, and now put up like a barrier against my advance.

'Keep back, or I declare I will fire,' he was crying. 'Have a care, for God's sake! My pistol——'

He might scream as he pleased. Willy nilly, I folded him to my breast, I pressed him there, I kissed his ugly mug as it had never been kissed before and would never be kissed again; and in the doing so knocked his wig awry and his hat off. He bleated in my embrace; so bleats the sheep in the arms of the butcher. The whole thing, on looking back, appears incomparably reckless and absurd; I no better than a madman for offering to advance on Dudgeon, and he no better than a fool for not shooting me while I was about it. But all's well that ends well; or, as the people in these days kept singing and whistling on the streets :—

> 'There's a sweet little cherub that sits up aloft
> And looks out for the life of poor Jack.'

'There!' said I, releasing him a little, but still keeping my hands on his shoulders, '*je vous ai bel et bien embrassé*—and, as you would say, there is another French word.' With his wig over one eye, he looked incredibly rueful and put out. 'Cheer up, Dudgeon; the ordeal is over, you shall be embraced no more. But do, first of all, for God's sake, put away your pistol; you handle it as if you were a cockatrice; some time or other, depend upon it, it will certainly go off. Here is your hat. No, let me put it on square, and the wig before it. Never suffer any stress of circumstances to come between you and the duty you owe to yourself. If you have nobody else to dress for, dress for God!

> 'Put your wig straight
> On your bald pate,
> Keep your chin scraped,
> And your figure draped.

Can you match me that? The whole duty of man in a quatrain! And remark, I do not set up to be a professional bard; these are the outpourings of a *dilettante*.'

'But, my dear sir!' he exclaimed.

'But, my dear sir!' I echoed, 'I will allow no man to interrupt the flow of my ideas. Give me your opinion on my quatrain, or I vow we shall have a quarrel of it.'

'Certainly you are quite an original,' he said.

'Quite,' said I; 'and I believe I have my counterpart before me.'

'Well, for a choice,' says he, smiling, 'and whether for sense or poetry, give me

> '"Worth makes the man, and want of it the fellow:
> The rest is all but leather and prunello."'

'Oh, but that's not fair—that's Pope! It's not original, Dudgeon. Understand me,' said I, wringing his breast-button, 'the first duty of all poetry is to be mine, sir—mine. Inspiration now swells in my bosom, because—to tell you the plain truth, and descend a little in style—I am devilish relieved at the turn things have taken. So, I dare say, are you yourself, Dudgeon, if you would only allow it. And *à propos*, let me ask you a home question. Between friends, have you ever fired that pistol?'

'Why, yes, sir,' he replied. 'Twice—at hedgesparrows.'

'And you would have fired at me, you bloody-minded man?' I cried.

'If you go to that, you seemed mighty reckless with your stick,' said Dudgeon.

'Did I indeed? Well, well, 'tis all past history; ancient as King Pharamond—which is another French word, if you cared to accumulate more evidence,' says I. 'But happily we are now the best of friends, and have all our interests in common.'

'You go a little too fast, if you'll excuse me, Mr. —— : I do not know your name, that I am aware,' said Dudgeon.

'No, to be sure!' said I. 'Never heard of it!'

'A word of explanation——' he began.

'No, Dudgeon!' I interrupted. 'Be practical; I know what you want, and the name of it is supper. *Rien ne creuse comme l'émotion.* I am hungry myself, and yet I am more accustomed to warlike palpitations than you, who are but a hunter of hedgesparrows. Let me look at your face critically: your bill of fare is three slices of cold rare roast beef, a Welsh rabbit, a pot of stout, and a glass or two of sound tawny port, old in bottle—the right milk of Englishmen.' Methought there seemed a brightening in his eye and a melting about his mouth at this enumeration.

'The night is young,' I continued; 'not much past eleven, for a wager. Where can we find a good inn? And remark that I say *good*, for the port must be up to the occasion—not a headache in a pipe of it.'

'Really, sir,' he said, smiling a little, 'you have a way of carrying things——'

'Will nothing make you stick to the subject?' I cried; 'you have the most irrelevant mind! How do you expect to rise in your profession? The inn?'

'Well, I will say you are a facetious gentleman!' said he. 'You must have your way, I see. We are not three miles from Bedford by this very road.'

'Done!' cried I. 'Bedford be it!'

I tucked his arm under mine, possessed myself of the valise, and walked him off unresisting. Presently we came to an open piece of country lying a thought downhill. The road was smooth and free of ice, the moonshine thin and bright over the meadows and the leafless trees. I was now honestly done with the purgatory of the covered cart; I was close to my great-uncle's; I had no more fear of Mr. Dudgeon; which were all grounds enough for jollity. And I was aware, besides, of us two as of a pair of tiny and solitary dolls under the vast frosty cupola of the midnight; the rooms decked, the moon burnished, the least of the stars lighted, the floor swept and waxed, and

nothing wanting but for the band to strike up and the dancing
to begin.   In the exhilaration of my heart I took the music on
myself—

> ' Merrily danced the Quaker's wife,
> And merrily danced the Quaker.'

I broke into that animated and appropriate air, clapped my
arm about Dudgeon's waist, and away down the hill at a
dancing step!   He hung back a little at the start, but the
impulse of the tune, the night, and my example, were not to
be resisted.   A man made of putty must have danced, and
even Dudgeon showed himself to be a human being.   Higher
and higher were the capers that we cut; the moon repeated in
shadow our antic footsteps and gestures; and it came over my
mind of a sudden—really like balm—what appearance of man
I was dancing with, what a long bilious countenance he had
shown under his shaven pate, and what a world of trouble the
rascal had given me in the immediate past.

Presently we began to see the lights of Bedford.   My Puritanic companion stopped and disengaged himself.

'This is a trifle *infra dig.*, sir, is it not?' said he.   'A party
might suppose we had been drinking.'

'And so you shall be, Dudgeon,' said I.   'You shall not
only be drinking, you old hypocrite, but you shall be drunk—
dead drunk, sir—and the boots shall put you to bed!   We'll
warn him when we go in.   Never neglect a precaution; never
put off till to-morrow what you can do to-day!'

But he had no more frivolity to complain of.   We finished
our stage and came to the inn-door with decorum, to find the
house still alight and in a bustle with many late arrivals;
to give our orders with a prompt severity which ensured
obedience, and to be served soon after at a side-table, close to
the fire and in a blaze of candle-light, with such a meal as
I had been dreaming of for days past.   For days, you are to
remember, I had been skulking in the covered cart, a prey
to cold, hunger, and an accumulation of discomforts that might
have daunted the most brave; and the white table napery, the
bright crystal, the reverberation of the fire, the red curtains,
the Turkey carpet, the portraits on the coffee-room wall, the
placid faces of the two or three late guests who were silently
prolonging the pleasures of digestion, and (last, but not by any
means least) a glass of an excellent light dry port, put me in a
humour only to be described as heavenly.   The thought of the
Colonel, of how he would have enjoyed this snug room and
roaring fire, and of his cold grave in the wood by Market
Bosworth, lingered on my palate, *amari aliquid*, like an after-

taste, but was not able—I say it with shame—entirely to dispel my self-complacency. After all, in this world every dog hangs by its own tail. I was a free adventurer, who had just brought to a successful end—or, at least, within view of it—an adventure very difficult and alarming; and I looked across at Mr. Dudgeon, as the port rose to his cheeks, and a smile, that was semi-confidential and a trifle foolish, began to play upon his leathery features, not only with composure, but with a suspicion of kindness. The rascal had been brave, a quality for which I would value the devil; and if he had been pertinacious in the beginning, he had more than made up for it before the end.

'And now, Dudgeon, to explain,' I began. 'I know your master, he knows me, and he knows and approves of my errand. So much I may tell you, that I am on my way to Amersham Place.'

'Oho!' quoth Dudgeon, 'I begin to see.'

'I am heartily glad of it,' said I, passing the bottle, 'because that is about all I can tell you. You must take my word for the remainder. Either believe me or don't. If you don't, let's take a chaise; you can carry me to-morrow to High Holborn, and confront me with Mr. Romaine; the result of which will be to set your mind at rest—and to make the holiest disorder in your master's plans. If I judge you aright (for I find you a shrewd fellow), this will not be at all to your mind. You know what a subordinate gets by officiousness; if I can trust my memory, old Romaine has not at all the face that I should care to see in anger; and I venture to predict surprising results upon your weekly salary—if you are paid by the week, that is. In short, let me go free, and 'tis an end of the matter; take me to London, and 'tis only a beginning—and, by my opinion, a beginning of troubles. You can take your choice.'

'And that is soon taken,' said he. 'Go to Amersham to-morrow, or go to the devil if you prefer—I wash my hands of you and the whole transaction. No, you don't find me putting my head in between Romaine and a client! A good man of business, sir, but hard as millstone grit. I might get the sack, and I shouldn't wonder! But, it's a pity, too,' he added, and sighed, shook his head, and took his glass off sadly.

'That reminds me,' said I. 'I have a great curiosity, and you can satisfy it. Why were you so forward to meddle with poor Mr. Dubois? Why did you transfer your attentions to me? And generally, what induced you to make yourself such a nuisance?'

He blushed deeply.

'Why, sir,' says he, 'there *is* such a thing as patriotism, I hope.'

CHAPTER XVI

By eight the next morning Dudgeon and I had made our parting. By that time we had grown to be extremely familiar; and I would very willingly have kept him by me, and even carried him to Amersham Place. But it appeared he was due at the public-house where we had met, on some affairs of my great-uncle the Count, who had an outlying estate in that part of the shire. If Dudgeon had had his way the night before, I should have been arrested on my uncle's land and by my uncle's agent, a culmination of ill-luck.

A little after noon I started, in a hired chaise, by way of Dunstable. The mere mention of the name Amersham Place made every one supple and smiling. It was plainly a great house, and my uncle lived there in style. The fame of it rose as we approached, like a chain of mountains; at Bedford they touched their caps, but in Dunstable they crawled upon their bellies. I thought the landlady would have kissed me; such a flutter of cordiality, such smiles, such affectionate attentions were called forth, and the good lady bustled on my service in such a pother of ringlets and with such a jingling of keys. 'You're probably expected, sir, at the Place? I do trust you may 'ave better accounts of his lordship's 'elth, sir. We understood that his lordship, Mosha de Carwell, was main bad. Ha, sir, we shall all feel his loss, poor, dear, noble gentleman; and I'm sure nobody more polite! They do say, sir, his wealth is enormous, and before the Revolution, quite a prince in his own country! But I beg your pardon, sir; 'ow I do run on, to be sure; and doubtless all beknown to you already! For you do resemble the family, sir. I should have known you anywheres by the likeness to the dear viscount. Ha, poor gentleman, he must 'ave a 'eavy 'eart these days.'

In the same place I saw out of the inn-windows a man-servant passing in the livery of my house, which you are to think I had never before seen worn, or not that I could remember. I had often enough, indeed, pictured myself advanced to be a Marshal, a Duke of the Empire, a Grand Cross of the Legion of Honour, and some other kickshaws of the kind, with a perfect rout of flunkeys correctly dressed in my own colours. But it is one thing to imagine, and another to see ; it would be one thing to have these liveries in a house of my own in Paris—it was quite another to find them flaunting in the heart of hostile England ; and I fear I should have made a fool of myself, if the man had not been on the other side of the street, and I at a one-pane window. There was something illusory in this transplantation of the wealth and honours of a family, a thing by its nature so deeply rooted in the soil ; something ghostly in this sense of home-coming so far from home.

From Dunstable I rolled away into a crescendo of similar impressions. There are certainly few things to be compared with these castles, or rather country seats, of the English nobility and gentry ; nor anything at all to equal the servility of the population that dwells in their neighbourhood. Though I was but driving in a hired chaise, word of my destination seemed to have gone abroad, and the women curtseyed and the men louted to me by the wayside. As I came near, I began to appreciate the roots of this widespread respect. The look of my uncle's park wall, even from the outside, had something of a princely character ; and when I came in view of the house itself, a sort of madness of vicarious vain-glory struck me dumb and kept me staring. It was about the size of the Tuileries. It faced due north ; and the last rays of the sun, that was setting like a red-hot shot amidst a tumultuous gathering of snow clouds, were reflected on the endless rows of windows. A portico of Doric columns adorned the front, and would have done honour to a temple. The servant who received me at the door was civil to a fault—I had almost said, to offence ; and the hall to which he admitted me through a pair of glass doors was warmed and already partly lighted by a liberal chimney heaped with the roots of beeches.

'Vicomte Anne de St. Yves,' said I, in answer to the man's question ; whereupon he bowed before me lower still, and stepping upon one side introduced me to the truly awful presence of the major-domo. I have seen many dignitaries in my time, but none who quite equalled this eminent being ; who was good enough to answer to the unassuming name of Dawson. From him I learned that my uncle was extremely low, a doctor in close attendance, Mr. Romaine expected at any moment, and that my cousin, the Vicomte de St. Yves, had been sent for the same morning.

'It was a sudden seizure, then?' I asked.

Well, he would scarcely go as far as that. It was a decline, a fading away, sir; but he was certainly took bad the day before, had sent for Mr. Romaine, and the major-domo had taken it on himself a little later to send word to the Viscount. 'It seemed to me, my lord,' said he, 'as if this was a time when all the fambly should be called together.'

I approved him with my lips, but not in my heart. Dawson was plainly in the interests of my cousin.

'And when can I expect to see my great-uncle, the Count?' said I.

In the evening, I was told; in the meantime he would show me to my room, which had been long prepared for me, and I should be expected to dine in about an hour with the doctor, if my lordship had no objections.

My lordship had not the faintest.

'At the same time,' I said, 'I have had an accident: I have unhappily lost my baggage, and am here in what I stand in. I don't know if the doctor be a formalist, but it is quite impossible I should appear at table as I ought.'

He begged me to be under no anxiety. 'We have been long expecting you,' said he. 'All is ready.'

Such I found to be the truth. A great room had been prepared for me; through the mullioned windows the last flicker of the winter sunset interchanged with the reverberation of a royal fire; the bed was open, a suit of evening clothes was airing before the blaze, and from the far corner a boy came forward with deprecatory smiles. The dream in which I had been moving seemed to have reached its pitch. I might have quitted this house and room only the night before; it was my own place that I had come to; and for the first time in my life I understood the force of the words home and welcome.

'This will be all as you would want, sir?' said Mr. Dawson. 'This 'ere boy, Rowley, we place entirely at your disposition. 'E's not exactly a trained vallet, but Mossho Powl, the Viscount's gentleman, 'ave give him the benefick of a few lessons, and it is 'oped that he may give sitisfection. Hanythink that you may require, if you will be so good as to mention the same to Rowley, I will make it my business myself, sir, to see you sitisfied.'

So saying, the eminent and already detested Mr. Dawson took his departure, and I was left alone with Rowley. A man who may be said to have wakened to consciousness in the prison of the Abbaye, among those ever graceful and ever tragic figures of the brave and fair, awaiting the hour of the guillotine and denuded of every comfort, I had never known the luxuries or the amenities of my rank in life. To be attended on by servants I had only been accustomed to in inns. My toilet had long been military, to a moment, at the note of a bugle, too often at a ditch-side. And it need not be wondered at if I looked on my new valet with a certain diffidence. But I remembered that if he was my first experience of a valet, I was his first trial as a master. Cheered by which consideration, I demanded my bath in a style of good assurance. There was a bathroom contiguous; in an incredibly short space of time the hot water was ready; and soon after, arrayed in a shawl dressing-gown, and in a luxury of contentment and comfort, I was reclined in an easy-chair before the mirror, while Rowley, with a mixture of pride and anxiety which I could well understand, laid out his razors.

'Hey, Rowley?' I asked, not quite resigned to go under fire with such an inexperienced commander. 'It's all right, is it? You feel pretty sure of your weapons?'

'Yes, my lord,' he replied. 'It's all right, I assure your lordship.'

'I beg your pardon, Mr. Rowley, but for the sake of shortness, would you mind not belording me in private?' said I. 'It will do very well if you call me Mr. Anne. It is the way of my country, as I dare say you know.'

Mr. Rowley looked blank.

'But you're just as much a Viscount as Mr. Powl's, are you not?' he said.

'As Mr. Powl's Viscount?' said I, laughing. 'Oh, keep your mind easy, Mr. Rowley's is every bit as good. Only, you see, as I am of the younger line, I bear my Christian name along with the title. Alain is the *Viscount*; I am the *Viscount Anne*. And in giving me the name of Mr. Anne, I assure you you will be quite regular.'

'Yes, Mr. Anne,' said the docile youth. 'But about the shaving, sir, you need be under no alarm. Mr. Powl says I 'ave excellent dispositions.'

'Mr. Powl?' said I. 'That doesn't seem to me very like a French name.'

'No, sir, indeed, my lord,' said he, with a burst of confidence. 'No, indeed, Mr. Anne, and it do not surely. I should say now, it was more like Mr. Pole.'

'And Mr. Powl is the Viscount's man?'

'Yes, Mr. Anne,' said he. 'He 'ave a hard billet, he do. The Viscount is a very particular gentleman. I don't think as you'll be, Mr. Anne?' he added, with a confidential smile in the mirror.

He was about sixteen, well set up, with a pleasant, merry, freckled face, and a pair of dancing eyes. There was an air at once deprecatory and insinuating about the rascal that I thought I recognised. There came to me from my own boyhood memories of certain passionate admirations long passed away, and the objects of them long ago discredited or dead. I remembered how anxious I had been to serve those fleeting heroes, how readily I told myself I would have died for *them*, how much greater and handsomer than life they had appeared. And looking in the mirror, it seemed to me that I read the face of Rowley, like an echo or a ghost, by the light of my own youth. I have always contended (somewhat against the opinion of my friends) that I am first of all an economist; and the last thing that I would care to throw away is that very valuable piece of property—a boy's hero-worship.

'Why,' said I, 'you shave like an angel, Mr. Rowley!'

'Thank you, my lord,' says he. 'Mr. Powl had no fear of me. You may be sure, sir, I should never 'ave had this berth if I 'adn't 'ave been up to Dick. We been expecting of you this month back. My eye! I never see such preparations. Every day the fires has been kep' up, the bed made, and all! As soon as it was known you were coming, sir, I got the appointment; and I've been up and down since then like a Jack-in-the-box. A wheel couldn't sound in the avenue but what I was at the window! I've had a many disappointments; but to-night, as soon as you stepped out of the shay, I knew it was my—it was you. Oh, you had been expected! Why, when I go down to supper, I'll be the 'ero of the servants' 'all: the 'ole of the staff is that curious!'

'Well,' said I, 'I hope you may be able to give a fair account of me—sober, steady, industrious, good-tempered, and with a first-rate character from my last place?'

He laughed an embarrassed laugh. 'Your hair curls beautiful,' he said, by way of changing the subject. 'The Viscount's the boy for curls, though; and the richness of it is, Mr. Powl tells me his don't curl no more than that much twine—by nature. Gettin' old, the Viscount is. He *'ave* gone the pace, 'aven't 'e, sir?'

'The fact is,' said I, 'that I know very little about him. Our family has been much divided, and I have been a soldier from a child.'

'A soldier, Mr. Anne, sir?' cried Rowley, with a sudden feverish animation. 'Was you ever wounded?'

It is contrary to my principles to discourage admiration for myself; and, slipping back the shoulder of the dressing-gown,

I silently exhibited the scar which I had received in Edinburgh Castle. He looked at it with awe.

'Ah, well!' he continued, 'there's where the difference comes in! It's in the training. The other Viscount have been horse-racing, and dicing, and carrying on all his life. All right enough, no doubt; but what I do say is, that it don't lead to nothink. Whereas——'

'Whereas Mr. Rowley's?' I put in.

'My Viscount?' said he. 'Well, sir, I *did* say it; and now that I've seen you, I say it again!'

I could not refrain from smiling at this outburst, and the rascal caught me in the mirror and smiled to me again.

'I'd say it again, Mr. Hanne,' he said. 'I know which side my bread's buttered. I know when a gen'leman's a gen'leman. Mr. Powl can go to Putney with his one! Beg your pardon, Mr. Anne, for being so familiar,' said he, blushing suddenly scarlet. 'I was especially warned against it by Mr. Powl.'

'Discipline before all,' said I. 'Follow your front-rank man.'

With that, we began to turn our attention to the clothes. I was amazed to find them fit so well: not *à la diable*, in the haphazard manner of a soldier's uniform or a ready-made suit; but with nicety, as a trained artist might rejoice to make them for a favourite subject.

''Tis extraordinary,' cried I: 'these things fit me perfectly.'

'Indeed, Mr. Anne, you two be very much of a shape,' said Rowley.

'Who? What two?' said I.

'The Viscount,' he said.

'Damnation! Have I the man's clothes on me, too?' cried I.

But Rowley hastened to reassure me. On the first word of my coming, the Count had put the matter of my wardrobe in the hands of his own and my cousin's tailors; and on the rumour of our resemblance, my clothes had been made to Alain's measure.

'But they were all made for you express, Mr. Anne. You may be certain the Count would never do nothing by 'alf: fires kep' burning; the finest of clothes ordered, I'm sure, and a body-servant being trained a-purpose.'

'Well,' said I, 'it's a good fire, and a good set-out of clothes; and what a valet, Mr. Rowley! And there's one thing to be said for my cousin—I mean for Mr. Powl's Viscount—he has a very fair figure.'

'Oh, don't you be took in, Mr. Anne,' quoth the faithless

Rowley : 'he has to be hyked into a pair of stays to get them things on !'

'Come, come, Mr. Rowley,' said I, 'this is telling tales out of school ! Do not you be deceived. The greatest men of antiquity, including Cæsar and Hannibal and Pope Joan, may have been very glad, at my time of life or Alain's, to follow his example. 'Tis a misfortune common to all ; and really,' said I, bowing to myself before the mirror like one who should dance the minuet, 'when the result is so successful as this, who would do anything but applaud ?'

My toilet concluded, I marched on to fresh surprises. My chamber, my new valet and my new clothes had been beyond hope : the dinner, the soup, the whole bill of fare was a revela-tion of the powers there are in man. I had not supposed it lay in the genius of any cook to create, out of common beef and mutton, things so different and dainty. The wine was of a piece, the doctor a most agreeable companion ; nor could I help reflecting on the prospect that all this wealth, comfort and handsome profusion might still very possibly become mine. Here were a change indeed, from the common soldier and the camp kettle, the prisoner and his prison rations, the fugitive and the horrors of the covered cart !

CHAPTER XVII

THE doctor had scarce finished his meal before he hastened
with an apology to attend upon his patient; and almost immediately after I was myself summoned and ushered up the great
staircase and along interminable corridors to the bedside of my
great-uncle the Count. You are to think that up to the present
moment I had not set eyes on this formidable personage, only
on the evidences of his wealth and kindness. You are to think
besides that I had heard him miscalled and abused from my
earliest childhood up. The first of the *émigrés* could never
expect a good word in the society in which my father moved.
Even yet the reports I received were of a doubtful nature;
even Romaine had drawn of him no very amiable portrait; and
as I was ushered into the room, it was a critical eye that I cast
on my great-uncle. He lay propped on pillows in a little cot
no greater than a camp-bed, not visibly breathing. He was
about eighty years of age, and looked it; not that his face was
much lined, but all the blood and colour seemed to have faded
from his body, and even his eyes, which last he kept usually
closed as though the light distressed him. There was an unspeakable degree of slyness in his expression, which kept me
ill at ease; he seemed to lie there with his arms folded, like a
spider waiting for prey. His speech was very deliberate and
courteous, but scarce louder than a sigh.

'I bid you welcome, *Monsieur le Vicomte Anne*,' said he, looking
at me hard with his pale eyes, but not moving on his pillows.
'I have sent for you, and I thank you for the obliging expedition
you have shown. It is my misfortune that I cannot rise to receive you. I trust you have been reasonably well entertained?'

'*Monsieur mon oncle*,' I said, bowing very low, 'I am come
at the summons of the head of my family.'

'It is well,' he said. 'Be seated. I should be glad to hear
some news—if that can be called news that is already twenty
years old—of how I have the pleasure to see you here.'

By the coldness of his address, not more than by the nature of the times that he bade me recall, I was plunged in melancholy. I felt myself surrounded as with deserts of friendlessness, and the delight of my welcome was turned to ashes in my mouth.

'That is soon told, *monseigneur*,' said I. 'I understand that I need tell you nothing of the end of my unhappy parents? It is only the story of the lost dog.'

'You are right. I am sufficiently informed of that deplorable affair; it is painful to me. My nephew, your father, was a man who would not be advised,' said he. 'Tell me, if you please, simply of yourself.'

'I am afraid I must run the risk of harrowing your sensibility in the beginning,' said I, with a bitter smile, 'because my story begins at the foot of the guillotine. When the list came out that night, and her name was there, I was already old enough, not in years but in sad experience, to understand the extent of my misfortune. She——' I paused. 'Enough that she arranged with a friend, Madame de Chasseradès, that she should take charge of me, and by the favour of our jailers I was suffered to remain in the shelter of the *Abbaye*. That was my only refuge; there was no corner of France that I could rest the sole of my foot upon except the prison. Monsieur le Comte, you are as well aware as I can be what kind of a life that was, and how swiftly death smote in that society. I did not wait long before the name of Madame de Chasseradès succeeded to that of my mother on the list. She passed me on to Madame de Noytot; she, in her turn, to Mademoiselle de Braye; and there were others. I was the one thing permanent; they were all transient as clouds; a day or two of their care, and then came the last farewell and—somewhere far off in that roaring Paris that surrounded us—the bloody scene. I was the cherished one, the last comfort, of these dying women. I have been in pitched fights, my lord, and I never knew such courage. It was all done smiling, in the tone of good society; *belle maman* was the name I was taught to give to each; and for a day or two the new "pretty mamma" would make much of me, show me off, teach me the minuet, and to say my prayers; and then, with a tender embrace, would go the way of her predecessors, smiling. There were some that wept too. There was a childhood! All the time Monsieur de Culemberg kept his eye on me, and would have had me out of the *Abbaye* and in his own protection, but my "pretty mammas" one after another resisted the idea. Where could I be safer? they argued; and what was to become of them without the darling

of the prison? Well, it was soon shown how safe I was! The
dreadful day of the massacre came; the prison was overrun;
none paid attention to me, not even the last of my "pretty
mammas," for she had met another fate. I was wandering
distracted, when I was found by some one in the interests of
Monsieur de Culemberg. I understand he was sent on purpose; I believe, in order to reach the interior of the prison, he
had set his hand to nameless barbarities: such was the price
paid for my worthless, whimpering little life! He gave me his
hand; it was wet, and mine was reddened; he led me unresisting. I remember but the one circumstance of my flight—
it was my last view of my last pretty mamma. Shall I describe
it to you?' I asked the Count, with a sudden fierceness.

'Avoid unpleasant details,' observed my great-uncle gently.

At these words a sudden peace fell upon me. I had been
angry with the man before; I had not sought to spare him;
and now, in a moment, I saw that there was nothing to spare.
Whether from natural heartlessness or extreme old age, the
soul was not at home; and my benefactor, who had kept the
fire lit in my room for a month past—my only relative except
Alain, whom I knew already to be a hired spy—had trodden
out the last sparks of hope and interest.

'Certainly,' said I; 'and, indeed, the day for them is nearly
over. I was taken to Monsieur de Culemberg's,—I presume,
sir, that you know the Abbé de Culemberg?'

He indicated assent without opening his eyes.

'He was a very brave and a very learned man——'

'And a very holy one,' said my uncle civilly.

'And a very holy one, as you observe,' I continued. 'He
did an infinity of good, and through all the Terror kept himself
from the guillotine. He brought me up, and gave me such
education as I have. It was in his house in the country at
Dammarie, near Melun, that I made the acquaintance of your
agent, Mr. Vicary, who lay there in hiding, only to fall a victim
at the last to a gang of *chauffeurs*.'

'That poor Mr. Vicary!' observed my uncle. 'He had been
many times in my interests to France, and this was his first
failure. *Quel charmant homme, n'est-ce pas?*'

'Infinitely so,' said I. 'But I would not willingly detain you
any further with a story, the details of which it must naturally
be more or less unpleasant for you to hear. Suffice it that, by
M. de Culemberg's own advice, I said farewell at eighteen to
that kind preceptor and his books, and entered the service of
France; and have since then carried arms in such a manner as
not to disgrace my family.'

'You narrate well; *vous avez la voix chaude,*' said my uncle, turning on his pillows as if to study me. 'I have a very good account of you by Monsieur de Mauséant, whom you helped in Spain. And you had some education from the Abbé de Culemberg, a man of a good house? Yes, you will do very well. You have a good manner and a handsome person, which hurts nothing. We are all handsome in the family; even I myself, I have had my successes, the memories of which still charm me. It is my intention, my nephew, to make of you my heir. I am not very well content with my other nephew, Monsieur le Vicomte: he has not been respectful, which is the flattery due to age. And there are other matters.'

I was half tempted to throw back in his face that inheritance so coldly offered. At the same time I had to consider that he was an old man, and, after all, my relation; and that I was a poor one, in considerable straits, with a hope at heart which that inheritance might yet enable me to realise. Nor could I forget that, however icy his manners, he had behaved to me from the first with the extreme of liberality and—I was about to write, kindness, but the word, in that connection, would not come. I really owed the man some measure of gratitude, which it would be an ill manner to repay if I were to insult him on his deathbed.

'Your will, monsieur, must ever be my rule,' said I, bowing.

'You have wit, *monsieur mon neveu,*' said he, 'the best wit— the wit of silence. Many might have deafened me with their gratitude. Gratitude!' he repeated, with a peculiar intonation, and lay and smiled to himself. 'But to approach what is more important. As a prisoner of war, will it be possible for you to be served heir to English estates? I have no idea: long as I have dwelt in England, I have never studied what they call their laws. On the other hand, how if Romaine should come too late? I have two pieces of business to be transacted—to die, and to make my will; and, however desirous I may be to serve you, I cannot postpone the first in favour of the second beyond a very few hours.'

'Well, sir, I must then contrive to be doing as I did before,' said I.

'Not so,' said the Count. 'I have an alternative. I have just drawn my balance at my banker's, a considerable sum, and I am now to place it in your hands. It will be so much for you and so much less——' he paused, and smiled with an air of malignity that surprised me. 'But it is necessary it should be done before witnesses. *Monsieur le Vicomte* is of a particular disposition, and an unwitnessed donation may very easily be twisted into a theft.'

He touched a bell, which was answered by a man having the appearance of a confidential valet. To him he gave a key.

'Bring me the despatch-box that came yesterday, La Ferrière,' said he. 'You will at the same time present my compliments to Dr. Hunter and M. l'Abbé, and request them to step for a few moments to my room.'

The despatch-box proved to be rather a bulky piece of baggage, covered with Russia leather. Before the doctor and an excellent old smiling priest it was passed over into my hands with a very clear statement of the disposer's wishes; immediately after which, though the witnesses remained behind to draw up and sign a joint note of the transaction, Monsieur de Kéroual dismissed me to my own room, La Ferrière following with the invaluable box.

At my chamber door I took it from him with thanks, and entered alone. Everything had been already disposed for the night, the curtains drawn and the fire trimmed; and Rowley was still busy with my bedclothes. He turned round as I entered with a look of welcome that did my heart good. Indeed, I had never a much greater need of human sympathy, however trivial, than at that moment when I held a fortune in my arms. In my uncle's room I had breathed the very atmosphere of disenchantment. He had gorged my pockets; he had starved every dignified or affectionate sentiment of a man. I had received so chilling an impression of age and experience that the mere look of youth drew me to confide in Rowley: he was only a boy, his heart must beat yet, he must still retain some innocence and natural feelings, he could blurt out follies with his mouth, he was not a machine to utter perfect speech! At the same time, I was beginning to outgrow the painful impressions of my interview; my spirits were beginning to revive; and at the jolly, empty looks of Mr. Rowley, as he ran forward to relieve me of the box, St. Ives became himself again.

'Now, Rowley, don't be in a hurry,' said I. 'This is a momentous juncture. Man and boy, you have been in my service about three hours. You must already have observed that I am a gentleman of a somewhat morose disposition, and there is nothing that I more dislike than the smallest appearance of familiarity. Mr. Pole or Mr. Powl, probably in the spirit of prophecy, warned you against this danger.'

'Yes, Mr. Anne,' said Rowley blankly.

'Now there has just arisen one of those rare cases, in which I am willing to depart from my principles. My uncle has given me a box—what you would call a Christmas box. I don't know what's in it, and no more do you : perhaps I am an April fool, or perhaps I am already enormously wealthy; there might be five hundred pounds in this apparently harmless receptacle!'

'Lord, Mr. Anne!' cried Rowley.

'Now, Rowley, hold up your right hand and repeat the words of the oath after me,' said I, laying the despatch-box on the table. 'Strike me blue if I ever disclose to Mr. Powl, or Mr. Powl's Viscount, or anything that is Mr. Powl's, not to mention Mr. Dawson and the doctor, the treasures of the following despatch-box; and strike me sky-blue scarlet if I do not continually maintain, uphold, love, honour and obey, serve, and follow to the four corners of the earth and the waters that are under the earth, the hereinafter before-mentioned (only that I find I have neglected to mention him) Viscount Anne de Kéroual de St.-Yves, commonly known as Mr. Rowley's Viscount. So be it. Amen.'

He took the oath with the same exaggerated seriousness as I gave it to him.

'Now,' said I. 'Here is the key for you; I will hold the lid with both hands in the meanwhile.' He turned the key. 'Bring up all the candles in the room, and range them alongside. What is it to be? A live gorgon, a Jack-in-the-box, or a spring that fires a pistol? On your knees, sir, before the prodigy!'

So saying, I turned the despatch-box upside down upon the table. At sight of the heap of bank paper and gold that lay in front of us, between the candles, or rolled upon the floor alongside, I stood astonished.

'O Lord!' cried Mr. Rowley; 'oh Lordy, Lordy, Lord!' and he scrambled after the fallen guineas. 'O my, Mr. Anne! what a sight o' money! Why, it's like a blessed story-book. It's like the Forty Thieves.'

'Now, Rowley, let's be cool, let's be businesslike,' said I. 'Riches are deceitful, particularly when you haven't counted them; and the first thing we have to do is to arrive at the amount of my—let me say, modest competency. If I'm not mistaken, I have enough here to keep you in gold buttons all the rest of your life. You collect the gold, and I'll take the paper.'

Accordingly, down we sat together on the hearthrug, and for some time there was no sound but the creasing of bills and the jingling of guineas, broken occasionally by the exulting exclamations of Rowley. The arithmetical operation on which we were embarked took long, and it might have been tedious to others; not to me nor to my helper.

'Ten thousand pounds!' I announced at last.

'Ten thousand!' echoed Mr. Rowley.

And we gazed upon each other.

The greatness of this fortune took my breath away.   With that sum in my hands, I need fear no enemies.   People are arrested, in nine cases out of ten, not because the police are astute, but because they themselves run short of money; and I had here before me in the despatch-box a succession of devices and disguises that insured my liberty.   Not only so; but, as I felt with a sudden and overpowering thrill, with ten thousand pounds in my hands I was become an eligible suitor.   What advances I had made in the past, as a private soldier in a military prison, or a fugitive by the wayside, could only be qualified or, indeed, excused as acts of desperation.   And now, I might come in by the front door; I might approach the dragon with a lawyer at my elbow, and rich settlements to offer.   The poor French prisoner, Champdivers, might be in a perpetual danger of arrest; but the rich travelling Englishman, St.-Ives, in his post-chaise, with his despatch-box by his side, could smile at fate and laugh at locksmiths.   I repeated the proverb, exulting, *Love laughs at locksmiths*!   In a moment, by the mere coming of this money, my love had become possible— it had come near, it was under my hand—and it may be by one of the curiosities of human nature, but it burned that instant brighter.

'Rowley,' said I, 'your Viscount is a made man.'

'Why, we both are, sir,' said Rowley.

'Yes, both,' said I; 'and you shall dance at the wedding; and I flung at his head a bundle of bank notes, and had just followed it up with a handful of guineas, when the door opened, and Mr. Romaine appeared upon the threshold.

CHAPTER XVIII

MR. ROMAINE CALLS ME NAMES

FEELING very much of a fool to be thus taken by surprise, I scrambled to my feet and hastened to make my visitor welcome. He did not refuse me his hand; but he gave it with a coldness and distance for which I was quite unprepared, and his countenance, as he looked on me, was marked in a strong degree with concern and severity.

'So, sir, I find you here?' said he, in tones of little encouragement. 'Is that you, George? You can run away; I have business with your master.'

He showed Rowley out, and locked the door behind him. Then he sat down in an armchair on one side of the fire, and looked at me with uncompromising sternness.

'I am hesitating how to begin,' said he. 'In this singular labyrinth of blunders and difficulties that you have prepared for us, I am positively hesitating where to begin. It will perhaps be best that you should read, first of all, this paragraph.' And he handed over to me a newspaper.

The paragraph in question was brief. It announced the recapture of one of the prisoners recently escaped from Edinburgh Castle; gave his name, Clausel, and added that he had entered into the particulars of the recent revolting murder in the Castle, and denounced the murderer :—

'It is a common soldier called Champdivers, who had himself escaped, and is in all probability involved in the common fate of his comrades. In spite of the activity along all the Forth and the East Coast, nothing has yet been seen of the sloop which these desperadoes seized at Grangemouth, and it is now almost certain that they have found a watery grave.'

At the reading of this paragraph, my heart turned over. In a moment I saw my castle in the air ruined; myself changed from a mere military fugitive into a hunted murderer, fleeing from the gallows; my love, which had a moment since appeared so near to me, blotted from the field of possibility. Despair, which was my first sentiment, did not, however, endure for more than a moment. I saw that my companions had indeed succeeded in their unlikely design; and that I was supposed to have accompanied and perished along with them by shipwreck —a most probable ending to their enterprise. If they thought me at the bottom of the North Sea, I need not fear much vigilance on the streets of Edinburgh. Champdivers was wanted: what was to connect him with St. Ives? Major Chevenix would recognise me if he met me; that was beyond bargaining: he had seen me so often, his interest had been kindled to so high a point, that I could hope to deceive him by no stratagem of disguise. Well, even so; he would have a competition of testimony before him: he knew Clausel, he knew me, and I was sure he would decide for honour. At the same time, the image of Flora shot up in my mind's eye with such a radiancy as fairly overwhelmed all other considerations; the blood sprang to every corner of my body, and I vowed I would see and win her, if it cost my neck.

'Very annoying, no doubt,' said I, as I returned the paper to Mr. Romaine.

'Is annoying your word for it?' said he.

'Exasperating, if you like,' I admitted.

'And true?' he inquired.

'Well, true in a sense,' said I. 'But perhaps I had better answer that question by putting you in possession of the facts?'

'I think so, indeed,' said he.

I narrated to him as much as seemed necessary of the quarrel, the duel, the death of Goguelat, and the character of Clausel. He heard me through in a forbidding silence, nor did he at all betray the nature of his sentiments, except that, at the episode of the scissors, I could observe his mulberry face to turn three shades paler.

'I suppose I may believe you?' said he, when I had done.

'Or else conclude this interview,' said I.

'Can you not understand that we are here discussing matters of the gravest import? Can you not understand that I feel myself weighed with a load of responsibility on your account— that you should take this occasion to air your fire-eating manners against your own attorney? There are serious hours in life, Mr. Anne,' he said severely. 'A capital charge, and that of a very brutal character and with singularly unpleasant details; the presence of the man Clausel, who (according to your account of it) is actuated by sentiments of real malignity, and prepared to swear black white; all the other witnesses scattered and perhaps drowned at sea; the natural prejudice against a Frenchman and a runaway prisoner : this makes a serious total for your lawyer to consider, and is by no means lessened by the incurable folly and levity of your own disposition.'

'I beg your pardon!' said I.

'Oh, my expressions have been selected with scrupulous accuracy,' he replied. 'How did I find you, sir, when I came to announce this catastrophe? You were sitting on the hearthrug playing, like a silly baby, with a servant, were you not, and the floor all scattered with gold and bank paper? There was a tableau for you! It was I who came, and you were lucky in that. It might have been any one—your cousin as well as another.'

'You have me there, sir,' I admitted. 'I had neglected all precautions, and you do right to be angry. *Apropos*, Mr. Romaine, how did you come yourself, and how long have you been in the house?' I added, surprised, on the retrospect, not to have heard him arrive.

'I drove up in a chaise and pair,' he returned. 'Any one might have heard me. But you were not listening, I suppose? being so extremely at your ease in the very house of your enemy, and under a capital charge! And I have been long enough here to do your business for you. Ah, yes, I did it, God forgive me!—did it before I so much as asked you the explanation of the paragraph. For some time back the will has been prepared; now it is signed; and your uncle has heard nothing of your recent piece of activity. Why? Well, I had no fancy to bother him on his death-bed : you might be innocent; and at bottom I preferred the murderer to the spy.'

No doubt of it but the man played a friendly part; no doubt also that, in his ill-temper and anxiety, he expressed himself unpalatably.

'You will perhaps find me over delicate,' said I. 'There is a word you employed——'

'I employ the words of my brief, sir,' he cried, striking with his hand on the newspaper. 'It is there in six letters. And do not be so certain—you have not stood your trial yet. It is an ugly affair, a fishy business. It is highly disagreeable. I would give my hand off—I mean I would give a hundred pound down, to have nothing to do with it. And, situated as we are, we must at once take action. There is here no choice. You must at once quit this country, and get to France, or Holland, or, indeed, to Madagascar.'

'There may be two words to that,' said I.

'Not so much as one syllable!' he retorted. 'Here is no

room for argument. The case is nakedly plain. In the disgusting position in which you have found means to place yourself, all that is to be hoped for is delay. A time may come when we shall be able to do better. It cannot be now: now it would be the gibbet.'

'You labour under a false impression, Mr. Romaine,' said I. 'I have no impatience to figure in the dock. I am even as anxious as yourself to postpone my first appearance there. On the other hand, I have not the slightest intention of leaving this country, where I please myself extremely. I have a good address, a ready tongue, an English accent that passes, and, thanks to the generosity of my uncle, as much money as I want. It would be hard indeed if, with all these advantages, Mr. St. Ives should not be able to live quietly in a private lodging, while the authorities amuse themselves by looking for Champdivers. You forget, there is no connection between these two personages.'

'And you forget your cousin,' retorted Romaine. 'There is the link. There is the tongue of the buckle. He knows you are Champdivers.' He put up his hand as if to listen. 'And, for a wager, here he is himself!' he exclaimed.

As when a tailor takes a piece of goods upon his counter, and rends it across, there came to our ears from the avenue the long tearing sound of a chaise and four approaching at the top speed of the horses. And, looking out between the curtains, we beheld the lamps skimming on the smooth ascent.

'Ay,' said Romaine, wiping the window-pane that he might see more clearly. 'Ay, that is he by the driving! So he squanders money along the king's highway, the triple idiot! gorging every man he meets with gold for the pleasure of arriving—where? Ah, yes, where but a debtor's jail, if not a criminal prison!'

'Is he that kind of a man?' I said, staring on these lamps as though I could decipher in them the secret of my cousin's character.

'You will find him a dangerous kind,' answered the lawyer. 'For you, these are the lights on a lee shore! I find I fall in a muse when I consider of him; what a formidable being he once was, and what a personable! and how near he draws to the moment that must break him utterly! we none of us like him here; we hate him, rather; and yet I have a sense—I don't think at my time of life it can be pity—but a reluctance rather, to break anything so big and figurative, as though he were a big porcelain pot or a big picture of high price. Ay, there is what I was waiting for!' he cried, as the lights of a second chaise swam in sight. 'It is he beyond a doubt. The first was the signature and the next the flourish. Two chaises, the second following with the baggage, which is always copious and ponderous, and one of his valets: he cannot go a step without a valet.'

'I hear you repeat the word big,' said I. 'But it cannot be that he is anything out of the way in stature.'

'No,' said the attorney. 'About your height, as I guessed for the tailors, and I see nothing wrong with the result. But, somehow, he commands an atmosphere; he has a spacious manner; and he has kept up, all through life, such a volume of racket about his personality, with his chaises and his racers and his dicings, and I know not what—that somehow he imposes! It seems, when the farce is done, and he locked in Fleet prison—and nobody left but Buonaparté and Lord Wellington and the Hetman Platoff to make a work about—the world will be in a comparison quite tranquil. But this is beside the mark,' he added, with an effort, turning again from the window. 'We are now under fire, Mr. Anne, as you soldiers would say, and it is high time we should prepare to go into action. He must not see you; that would be fatal. All that he knows at present is that you resemble him, and that is much more than enough. If it were possible, it would be well he should not know you were in the house.'

'Quite impossible, depend upon it,' said I. 'Some of the servants are directly in his interests, perhaps in his pay: Dawson, for an example.'

'My own idea!' cried Romaine. 'And at least,' he added, as the first of the chaises drew up with a dash in front of the portico, 'it is now too late. Here he is.'

We stood listening, with a strange anxiety, to the various noises that awoke in the silent house: the sound of doors opening and closing, the sound of feet near at hand and farther off. It was plain the arrival of my cousin was a matter of moment, almost of parade, to the household. And suddenly, out of this confused and distant bustle, a rapid and light tread became distinguishable. We heard it come upstairs, draw near along the corridor, pause at the door, and a stealthy and hasty rapping succeeded.

'Mr. Anne—Mr. Anne, sir! Let me in!' said the voice of Rowley.

We admitted the lad, and locked the door again behind him.

'It's *him*, sir,' he panted. 'He've come.'

'You mean the Viscount?' said I. 'So we supposed. But

come, Rowley—out with the rest of it! You have more to tell us, or your face belies you!'

'Mr. Anne, I do,' he said. 'Mr. Romaine, sir, you're a friend of his, ain't you?'

'Yes, George, I am a friend of his,' said Romaine, and, to my great surprise, laid his hand upon my shoulder.

'Well, it's this way,' said Rowley—'Mr. Powl have been at me! It's to play the spy! I thought he was at it from the first! From the first I see what he was after—coming round and round, and hinting things! But to-night he outs with it plump! I'm to let him hear all what you're to do beforehand, he says; and he gave me this for an arnest'—holding up half a guinea; 'and I took it, so I did! Strike me sky-blue scarlet?' says he, adducing the words of the mock oath; and he looked askance at me as he did so.

'I saw that he had forgotten himself, and that he knew it. The expression of his eye changed almost in the passing of the glance from the significant to the appealing—from the look of an accomplice to that of a culprit; and from that moment he became the model of a well-drilled valet.

'Sky-blue scarlet?' repeated the lawyer. 'Is the fool delirious?'

'No,' said I; 'he is only reminding me of something.'

'Well—and I believe the fellow will be faithful,' said Romaine. 'So you are a friend of Mr. Anne's too?' he added to Rowley.

'If you please, sir,' said Rowley.

''Tis something sudden,' observed Romaine; 'but it may be genuine enough. I believe him to be honest. He comes of honest people. Well, George Rowley, you might embrace some early opportunity to earn that half-guinea, by telling Mr. Powl that your master will not leave here till noon to-morrow, if he go even then. Tell him there are a hundred things to be done here, and a hundred more that can only be done properly at my office in Holborn. Come to think of it— we had better see to that first of all,' he went on, unlocking the door. 'Get hold of Powl, and see. And be quick back, and clear me up this mess.'

Mr. Rowley was no sooner gone than the lawyer took a pinch of snuff, and regarded me with somewhat of a more genial expression.

'Sir,' said he, 'it is very fortunate for you that your face is so strong a letter of recommendation. Here am I, a tough old practitioner, mixing myself up with your very distressing business; and here is this farmer's lad, who has the wit to take a bribe and the loyalty to come and tell you of it—all, I take it, on the strength of your appearance. I wish I could imagine how it would impress a jury !' says he.

'And how it would affect the hangman, sir ? ' I asked

' *Absit omen !* ' said Mr. Romaine devoutly.

We were just so far in our talk, when I heard a sound that brought my heart into my mouth : the sound of some one slyly trying the handle of the door. It had been preceded by no audible footstep. Since the departure of Rowley our wing of the house had been entirely silent. And we had every right to suppose ourselves alone, and to conclude that the new-comer, whoever he might be, was come on a clandestine, if not a hostile, errand.

' Who is there ? ' asked Romaine.

' It's only me, sir,' said the soft voice of Dawson. ' It's the Viscount, sir. He is very desirous to speak with you on business.'

' Tell him I shall come shortly, Dawson,' said the lawyer. ' I am at present engaged.'

' Thank you, sir ! ' said Dawson.

And we heard his feet draw off slowly along the corridor.

' Yes,' said Mr. Romaine, speaking low, and maintaining the attitude of one intently listening, ' there is another foot. I cannot be deceived ! '

' I think there was indeed ! ' said I. ' And what troubles me —I am not sure that the other has gone entirely away. By the time it got the length of the head of the stair the tread was plainly single.'

' Ahem—blockaded ? ' asked the lawyer.

' A siege *en règle !* ' I exclaimed.

' Let us come farther from the door,' said Romaine, ' and reconsider this damnable position. Without doubt, Alain was this moment at the door. He hoped to enter and get a view of you, as if by accident. Baffled in this, has he stayed himself, or has he planted Dawson here by way of sentinel ? '

' Himself, beyond a doubt,' said I. ' And yet to what end ? He cannot think to pass the night there ! '

' If it were only possible to pay no heed ! ' said Mr. Romaine. ' But this is the accursed drawback of your position. We can do nothing openly. I must smuggle you out of this room and out of this house like seizable goods ; and how am I to set about it with a sentinel planted at your very door ? '

' There is no good in being agitated,' said I.

' None at all,' he acquiesced. ' And, come to think of it, it is droll enough that I should have been that very moment commenting on your personal appearance, when your cousin came upon this mission. I was saying, if you remember, that your face was as good or better than a letter of recommendation. I wonder if M. Alain would be like the rest of us—I wonder what he would think of it?'

Mr. Romaine was sitting in a chair by the fire with his back to the windows, and I was myself kneeling on the hearthrug and beginning mechanically to pick up the scattered bills, when a honeyed voice joined suddenly in our conversation.

'He thinks well of it, Mr. Romaine. He begs to join himself to that circle of admirers which you indicate to exist already.'

CHAPTER XIX

THE DEVIL AND ALL AT AMERSHAM PLACE

NEVER did two human creatures get to their feet with more alacrity than the lawyer and myself. We had locked and barred the main gates of the citadel; but unhappily we had left open the bath-room sally-port; and here we found the voice of the hostile trumpets sounding from within, and all our defences taken in reverse. I took but the time to whisper Mr. Romaine in the ear: 'Here is another tableau for you!' at which he looked at me a moment with a kind of pathos, as who should say, 'Don't hit a man when he's down.' Then I transferred my eyes to my enemy.

He had his hat on, a little on one side: it was a very tall hat, raked extremely, and had a narrow curling brim. His hair was all curled out in masses like an Italian mountebank—a most unpardonable fashion. He sported a huge tippeted overcoat of frieze, such as watchmen wear, only the inside was lined with costly furs, and he kept it half open to display the exquisite linen, the many-coloured waistcoat, and the profuse jewellery of watch-chains and brooches underneath. The leg and the ankle were turned to a miracle. It is out of the question that I should deny the resemblance altogether, since it has been remarked by so many different persons whom I cannot reasonably accuse of a conspiracy. As a matter of fact, I saw little of it and confessed to nothing. Certainly he was what some might call handsome, of a pictorial, exuberant style of beauty, all attitude, profile, and impudence: a man whom I could see in fancy parade on the grand stand at a race-meeting, or swagger in Piccadilly, staring down the women, and stared at himself with admiration by the coal-porters. Of his frame of mind at that moment his face offered a lively if an unconscious picture. He was lividly pale, and his lip was caught up in a smile that could almost be called a snarl, of a sheer, arid malignity that appalled me and yet put me on my mettle for the encounter. He looked me up and down, then bowed and took off his hat to me.

140

'My cousin, I presume?' he said.

'I understand I have that honour,' I replied.

'The honour is mine,' said he, and his voice shook as he said it.

'I should make you welcome, I believe,' said I.

'Why?' he inquired. 'This poor house has been my home for longer than I care to claim. That you should already take upon yourself the duties of host here is to be at unnecessary pains. Believe me, that part would be more becomingly mine. And, by the way, I must not fail to offer you my little compliment. It is a gratifying surprise to meet you in the dress of a gentleman, and to see'—with a circular look upon the scattered bills—'that your necessities have already been so liberally relieved.'

I bowed with a smile that was perhaps no less hateful than his own.

'There are so many necessities in this world,' said I. 'Charity has to choose. One gets relieved, and some other, no less indigent, perhaps indebted, must go wanting.'

'Malice is an engaging trait,' said he.

'And envy, I think?' was my reply.

He must have felt that he was not getting wholly the better of this passage at arms; perhaps even feared that he should lose command of his temper, which he reined in throughout the interview as with a red-hot curb, for he flung away from me at the word, and addressed the lawyer with insulting arrogance.

'Mr. Romaine,' he said, 'since when have you presumed to give orders in this house?'

'I am not prepared to admit that I have given any,' replied Romaine; 'certainly none that did not fall in the sphere of my responsibilities.'

'By whose orders, then, am I denied entrance to my uncle's room?' said my cousin.

'By the doctor's, sir,' replied Romaine; 'and I think even you will admit his faculty to give them.'

'Have a care, sir,' cried Alain. 'Do not be puffed up with your position. It is none so secure, Master Attorney. I should not wonder in the least if you were struck off the rolls for this night's work, and the next I should see of you were when I flung you alms at a pothouse door to mend your ragged elbows. The doctor's orders? But I believe I am not mistaken! You have to-night transacted business with the Count; and this needy young gentleman has enjoyed the privilege of still another interview, in which (as I am pleased to see) his dignity

has not prevented his doing very well for himself. I wonder
that you should care to prevaricate with me so idly.'

'I will confess so much,' said Mr. Romaine, 'if you call it
prevarication. The order in question emanated from the Count
himself. He does not wish to see you.'

'For which I must take the word of Mr. Daniel Romaine?'
asked Alain.

'In default of any better,' said Romaine.

There was an instantaneous convulsion in my cousin's face,
and I distinctly heard him gnash his teeth at this reply; but,
to my surprise, he resumed in tones of almost good humour:

'Come, Mr. Romaine, do not let us be petty!' He drew in
a chair and sat down. 'Understand you have stolen a march
upon me. You have introduced your soldier of Napoleon, and
(how, I cannot conceive) he has been apparently accepted with
favour. I ask no better proof than the funds with which I find
him literally surrounded—I presume in consequence of some
extravagance of joy at the first sight of so much money. The
odds are so far in your favour, but the match is not yet won.
Questions will arise of undue influence, of sequestration, and
the like: I have my witnesses ready. I tell it you cynically,
for you cannot profit by the knowledge; and, if the worst come
to the worst, I have good hopes of recovering my own and of
ruining you.'

'You do what you please,' answered Romaine; 'but I give
it you for a piece of good advice, you had best do nothing in
the matter. You will only make yourself ridiculous; you will
only squander money, of which you have none too much, and
reap public mortification.'

'Ah, but there you make the common mistake, Mr. Romaine!'
returned Alain. 'You despise your adversary. Consider, if
you please, how very disagreeable I could make myself, if I
chose. Consider the position of your *protégé* — an escaped
prisoner! But I play a great game. I condemn such petty
opportunities.'

At this Romaine and I exchanged a glance of triumph. It
seemed manifest that Alain had as yet received no word of
Clausel's recapture and denunciation. At the same moment
the lawyer, thus relieved of the instancy of his fear, changed
his tactics. With a great air of unconcern, he secured the
newspaper, which still lay open before him on the table.

'I think, Monsieur Alain, that you labour under some
illusion,' said he. 'Believe me, this is all beside the mark.
You seem to be pointing to some compromise. Nothing is
further from my views. You suspect me of an inclination to

trifle with you, to conceal how things are going. I cannot, on the other hand, be too early or too explicit in giving you information which concerns you (I must say) capitally. Your great-uncle has to-night cancelled his will, and made a new one in favour of your cousin Anne. Nay, and you shall hear it from his own lips, if you choose! I will take so much upon me,' said the lawyer, rising. 'Follow me, if you please, gentlemen.'

Mr. Romaine led the way out of the room so briskly, and was so briskly followed by Alain, that I had hard ado to get the remainder of the money replaced and the despatch-box locked, and to overtake them, even by running, ere they should be lost in that maze of corridors, my uncle's house. As it was, I went with a heart divided; and the thought of my treasure thus left unprotected, save by a paltry lid and lock that any one might break or pick open, put me in a perspiration whenever I had the time to remember it. The lawyer brought us to a room, begged us to be be seated while he should hold a consultation with the doctor, and, slipping out of another door, left Alain and myself closeted together.

Truly he had done nothing to ingratiate himself; his every word had been steeped in unfriendliness, envy, and that contempt which (as it is born of anger) it is possible to support without humiliation. On my part, I had been little more conciliating; and yet I began to be sorry for this man, hired spy as I knew him to be. It seemed to me less than decent that he should have been brought up in the expectation of this great inheritance, and now, at the eleventh hour, be tumbled forth out of the house door and left to himself, his poverty and his debts—those debts of which I had so ungallantly reminded him so short a time before. And we were scarce left alone ere I made haste to hang out a flag of truce.

'My cousin,' said I, 'trust me, you will not find me inclined to be your enemy.'

He paused in front of me—for he had not accepted the lawyer's invitation to be seated, but walked to and fro in the apartment—took a pinch of snuff, and looked at me while he was taking it with an air of much curiosity.

'Is it even so?' said he. 'Am I so far favoured by fortune as to have your pity? Infinitely obliged, my cousin Anne! But these sentiments are not always reciprocal, and I warn you that the day when I set my foot on your neck, the spine shall break. Are you acquainted with the properties of the spine?' he asked with an insolence beyond qualification.

It was too much. 'I am acquainted also with the properties of a pair of pistols,' said I, toising him.

'No, no, no!' says he, holding up his finger. 'I will take my revenge how and when I please. We are enough of the same family to understand each other, perhaps; and the reason why I have not had you arrested on your arrival, why I had not a picket of soldiers in the first clump of evergreens, to await and prevent your coming—I, who knew all, before whom that pettifogger, Romaine, has been conspiring in broad daylight to supplant me—is simply this: that I had not made up my mind how I was to take my revenge.'

At that moment he was interrupted by the tolling of a bell. As we stood surprised and listening, it was succeeded by the sound of many feet trooping up the stairs and shuffling by the door of our room. Both, I believe, had a great curiosity to set it open, which each, owing to the presence of the other, resisted; and we waited instead in silence, and without moving, until Romaine returned and bade us to my uncle's presence.

He led the way by a little crooked passage, which brought us out in the sick-room, and behind the bed. I believe I have forgotten to remark that the Count's chamber was of considerable dimensions. We beheld it now crowded with the servants and dependants of the house, from the doctor and the priest to Mr. Dawson and the housekeeper, from Dawson down to Rowley and the last footman in white calves, the last plump chambermaid in her clean gown and cap, and the last ostler in a stable waistcoat. This large congregation of persons (and I was surprised to see how large it was) had the appearance, for the most part, of being ill at ease and heartily bewildered, standing on one foot, gaping like zanies, and those who were in the corners nudging each other and grinning aside. My uncle, on the other hand, who was raised higher than I had yet seen him on his pillows, wore an air of really imposing gravity. No sooner had we appeared behind him, than he lifted his voice to a good loudness, and addressed the assemblage.

'I take you all to witness—can you hear me?—I take you all to witness that I recognise as my heir and representative this gentleman, whom most of you see for the first time, the Viscount Anne de St.-Yves, my nephew of the younger line. And I take you to witness at the same time that, for very good reasons known to myself, I have discarded and disinherited this other gentleman whom you all know, the Viscount de St.-Yves. I have also to explain the unusual trouble to which I have put you all—and, since your supper was not over, I fear I may even say annoyance. It has pleased M. Alain to make some threats of disputing my will, and to pretend that there are among your number certain estimable persons who may be trusted to swear as he shall direct them. It pleases me thus to put it out of his power and to stop the mouths of his false witnesses. I am infinitely obliged by your politeness, and I have the honour to wish you all a very good evening.'

As the servants, still greatly mystified, crowded out of the sickroom door, curtseying, pulling the forelock, scraping with the foot, and so on, according to their degree, I turned and stole a look at my cousin. He had borne this crushing public rebuke without change of countenance. He stood, now, very upright, with folded arms, and looking inscrutably at the roof of the apartment. ·I could not refuse him at that moment the tribute of my admiration. Still more so when, the last of the domestics having filed through the doorway and left us alone with my great-uncle and the lawyer, he took one step forward towards the bed, made a dignified reverence, and addressed the man who had just condemned him to ruin.

'My lord,' said he, 'you are pleased to treat me in a manner which my gratitude, and your state, equally forbid me to call in question. It will be only necessary for me to call your attention to the length of time in which I have been taught to regard myself as your heir. In that position, I judged it only loyal to permit myself a certain scale of expenditure. If I am now to be cut off with a shilling as the reward of twenty years of service, I shall be left not only a beggar, but a bankrupt.'

Whether from the fatigue of his recent exertion, or by a well-inspired ingenuity of hate, my uncle had once more closed his eyes; nor did he open them now. 'Not with a shilling,' he contented himself with replying; and there stole, as he said it, a sort of smile over his face, that flickered there conspicuously for the least moment of time, and then faded and left behind the old impenetrable mask of years, cunning, and fatigue. There could be no mistake: my uncle enjoyed the situation as he had enjoyed few things in the last quarter of a century. The fires of life scarce survived in that frail body; but hatred, like some immortal quality, was still erect and unabated.

Nevertheless my cousin persevered.

'I speak at a disadvantage,' he resumed. 'My supplanter, with perhaps more wisdom than delicacy, remains in the room,' and he cast a glance at me that might have withered an oak tree.

I was only too willing to withdraw, and Romaine showed as much alacrity to make way for my departure. But my uncle

was not to be moved.   In the same breath of a voice, and still
without opening his eyes, he bade me remain.

'It is well,' said Alain.   'I cannot then go on to remind you
of the twenty years that have passed over our heads in England,
and the services I may have rendered you in that time.   It
would be a position too odious.   Your lordship knows me too
well to suppose I could stoop to such ignominy.   I must leave
out all my defence—your lordship wills it so !   I do not know
what are my faults; I know only my punishment, and it is
greater than I have the courage to face.   My uncle, I implore
your pity : pardon me so far ; do not send me for life into a
debtors' jail—a pauper debtor.'

'*Chat et vieux, pardonnez ?*' said my uncle, quoting from La
Fontaine ; and then, opening a pale-blue eye full on Alain, he
delivered with some emphasis :

> ' La jeunesse se flatte et croit tout obtenir ;
> La vieillesse est impitoyable.'

The blood leaped darkly into Alain's face.   He turned to
Romaine and me, and his eyes flashed.

'It is your turn now,' he said.   'At least it shall be prison
for prison with the two viscounts.'

'Not so, Mr. Alain, by your leave,' said Romaine.   'There are
a few formalities to be considered first.'

But Alain was already striding towards the door.

'Stop a moment, stop a moment !' cried Romaine.   'Remember your own counsel not to despise an adversary.'

Alain turned.

'If I do not despise I hate you !' he cried, giving a loose to
his passion.   'Be warned of that, both of you.'

'I understand you to threaten Monsieur le Vicomte Anne,'
said the lawyer.   'Do you know, I would not do that.   I am
afraid, I am very much afraid, if you were to do as you propose,
you might drive me into extremes.'

'You have made me a beggar and a bankrupt,' said Alain.
'What extreme is left ?'

'I scarce like to put a name upon it in this company,' replied
Romaine.   'But there are worse things than even bankruptcy,
and worse places than a debtors' jail.'

The words were so significantly said that there went a visible
thrill through Alain; sudden as a sword-stroke, he fell pale again.

'I do not understand you,' said he.

'O yes, you do,' returned Romaine.   'I believe you understand me very well.   You must not suppose that all this time,
while you were so very busy, others were entirely idle.   You

must not fancy, because I am an Englishman, that I have not
the intelligence to pursue an inquiry. Great as is my regard
for the honour of your house, M. Alain de St.-Yves, if I hear of
you moving directly or indirectly in this matter, I shall do my
duty, let it cost what it will : that is, I shall communicate the
real name of the Buonapartist spy who signs his letters *Rue
Grégoire de Tours.*'

I confess my heart was already almost altogether on the side
of my insulted and unhappy cousin ; and if it had not been
before, it must have been so now, so horrid was the shock with
which he heard his infamy exposed. Speech was denied him ;
he carried his hand to his neckcloth ; he staggered ; I thought
he must have fallen. I ran to help him, and at that he revived,
recoiled before me, and stood there with arms stretched forth
as if to preserve himself from the outrage of my touch.

'Hands off!' he somehow managed to articulate.

'You will now, I hope,' pursued the lawyer, without any
change of voice, 'understand the position in which you are
placed, and how delicately it behoves you to conduct yourself.
Your arrest hangs, if I may so express myself, by a hair ; and as
you will be under the perpetual vigilance of myself and my
agents, you must look to it narrowly that you walk straight.
Upon the least dubiety, I will take action.' He snuffed, looking
critically at the tortured man. 'And now let me remind you
that your chaise is at the door. This interview is agitating to
his lordship—it cannot be agreeable for you—and I suggest that
it need not be further drawn out. It does not enter into the
views of your uncle, the Count, that you should again sleep
under this roof.'

As Alain turned and passed without a word or a sign from the
apartment, I instantly followed. I suppose I must be at bottom
possessed of some humanity ; at least, this accumulated torture,
this slow butchery of a man as by quarters of rock, had wholly
changed my sympathies. At that moment I loathed both my
uncle and the lawyer for their coldblooded cruelty.

Leaning over the banisters, I was but in time to hear his hasty
footsteps in that hall that had been crowded with servants to
honour his coming, and was now left empty against his friendless
departure. A moment later, and the echoes rang, and the air
whistled in my ears, as he slammed the door on his departing
footsteps. The fury of the concussion gave me (had one been
still wanted) a measure of the turmoil of his passions. In a
sense, I felt with him ; I felt how he would have gloried to slam
that door on my uncle, the lawyer, myself, and the whole crowd
of those who had been witnesses to his humiliation.

CHAPTER XX

No sooner was the house clear of my cousin than I began to reckon up, ruefully enough, the probable results of what had passed. Here were a number of pots broken, and it looked to me as if I should have to pay for all! Here had been this proud, mad beast goaded and baited both publicly and privately, till he could neither hear nor see nor reason; whereupon the gate had been set open, and he had been left free to go and contrive whatever vengeance he might find possible. I could not help thinking it was a pity that, whenever I myself was inclined to be upon my good behaviour, some friends of mine should always determine to play a piece of heroics and cast me for the hero—or the victim—which is very much the same. The first duty of heroics is to be of your own choosing. When they are not that, they are nothing. And I assure you, as I walked back to my own room, I was in no very complaisant humour: thought my uncle and Mr. Romaine to have played knuckle-bones with my life and prospects; cursed them for it roundly; had no wish more urgent than to avoid the pair of them; and was quite knocked out of time, as they say in the ring, to find myself confronted with the lawyer.

He stood on my hearthrug, leaning on the chimney-piece, with a gloomy, thoughtful brow, as I was pleased to see, and not in the least as though he were vain of the late proceedings.

'Well?' said I. 'You have done it now!'

'Is he gone?' he asked.

'He is gone,' said I. 'We shall have the devil to pay with him when he comes back.'

'You are right,' said the lawyer, 'and very little to pay him with but flams and fabrications, like to-night's.'

'To-night's?' I repeated.

'Ay, to-night's!' said he.

'To-night's *what*?' I cried.

'To-night's flams and fabrications.'

'God be good to me, sir,' said I, 'have I something more to admire in your conduct than ever *I* had suspected? You cannot think how you interest me! That it was severe, I knew; I had already chuckled over that. But that it should be false also! In what sense, dear sir?'

I believe I was extremely offensive as I put the question, but the lawyer paid no heed.

'False in all senses of the word,' he replied seriously. 'False in the sense that they were not true, and false in the sense that they were not real; false in the sense that I boasted, and in the sense that I lied. How can I arrest him? Your uncle burned the papers! I told you so—but doubtless you have forgotten—the day I first saw you in Edinburgh Castle. It was an act of generosity; I have seen many of these acts, and always regretted—always regretted! "That shall be his inheritance," he said, as the papers burned; he did not mean that it should have proved so rich a one. How rich, time will tell.'

'I beg your pardon a hundred thousand times, my dear sir, but it strikes me you have the impudence—in the circumstances, I may call it the indecency—to appear cast down?'

'It is true,' said he: 'I am. I am cast down. I am literally cast down. I feel myself quite helpless against your cousin.'

'Now, really!' I asked. 'Is this serious? And is it perhaps the reason why you have gorged the poor devil with every species of insult? and why you took such surprising pains to supply me with what I had so little need of—another enemy? That you were helpless against him? "Here is my last missile," say you; "my ammunition is quite exhausted: just wait till I get the last in—it will irritate, it cannot hurt him. There— you see!—he is furious now, and I am quite helpless. One more prod, another kick: now he is a mere lunatic! Stand behind me; I am quite helpless!" Mr. Romaine, I am asking myself as to the background or motive of this singular jest, and whether the name of it should not be called treachery?'

'I can scarce wonder,' said he. 'In truth it has been a singular business, and we are very fortunate to be out of it so well. Yet it was not treachery: no, no, Mr. Anne, it was not treachery; and if you will do me the favour to listen to me for the inside of a minute, I shall demonstrate the same to you beyond cavil.' He seemed to wake up to his ordinary briskness. 'You see the point?' he began. 'He had not yet read the newspaper, but who could tell when he might? He might have had that damned journal in his pocket, and how should we know? We were—I may say, we are—at the mercy of the merest twopenny accident.'

'Why, true,' said I : 'I had not thought of that.'

'I warrant you,' cried Romaine, 'you had supposed it was nothing to be the hero of an interesting notice in the journals ! You had supposed, as like as not, it was a form of secrecy ! But not so in the least. A part of England is already buzzing with the name of Champdivers ; a day or two more and the mail will have carried it everywhere : so wonderful a machine is this of ours for disseminating intelligence ! Think of it ! When my father was born——but that is another story. To return : we had here the elements of such a combustion as I dread to think of—your cousin and the journal. Let him but glance an eye upon that column of print, and where were we ? It is easy to ask ; not so easy to answer, my young friend. And let me tell you, this sheet is the Viscount's usual reading. It is my conviction he had it in his pocket.'

'I beg your pardon, sir,' said I. 'I have been unjust. I did not appreciate my danger.'

'I think you never do,' said he.

'But yet surely that public scene——' I began.

'It was madness. I quite agree with you,' Mr. Romaine interrupted. 'But it was your uncle's orders, Mr. Anne, and what could I do ? Tell him you were the murderer of Goguelat ? I think not.'

'No, sure !' said I. 'That would but have been to make the trouble thicker. We were certainly in a very ill posture.'

'You do not yet appreciate how grave it was,' he replied. 'It was necessary for you that your cousin should go, and go at once. You yourself had to leave to-night under cover of darkness, and how could you have done that with the Viscount in the next room ? He must go, then ; he must leave without delay. And that was the difficulty.'

'Pardon me, Mr. Romaine, but could not my uncle have bidden him go ?' I asked.

'Why, I see I must tell you that this is not so simple as it sounds,' he replied. 'You say this is your uncle's house, and so it is. But to all effects and purposes it is your cousin's also. He has rooms here ; has had them coming on for thirty years now, and they are filled with a prodigious accumulation of trash —stays, I dare say, and powder-puffs, and such effeminate idiocy —to which none could dispute his title, even suppose any one wanted to. We had a perfect right to bid him go, and he had a perfect right to reply, "Yes, I will go, but not without my stays and cravats. I must first get together the nine-hundred-and-ninety-nine chestsfull of insufferable rubbish, that I have spent the last thirty years collecting—and may very well spend the next thirty hours a-packing of." And what should we have said to that?'

'By way of repartee?' I asked. 'Two tall footmen and a pair of crabtree cudgels, I suggest.'

'The Lord deliver me from the wisdom of laymen!' cried Romaine. 'Put myself in the wrong at the beginning of a lawsuit? No, indeed! There was but one thing to do, and I did it, and burned my last cartridge in the doing of it. I stunned him. And it gave us three hours, by which we should make haste to profit; for if there is one thing sure, it is that he will be up to time again to-morrow in the morning.'

'Well,' said I, 'I own myself an idiot. Well do they say, *an old soldier, an old innocent!* For I guessed nothing of all this.'

'And, guessing it, have you the same objections to leave England?' he inquired.

'The same,' said I.

'It is indispensable,' he objected.

'And it cannot be,' I replied. 'Reason has nothing to say in the matter; and I must not let you squander any of yours. It will be enough to tell you this is an affair of the heart.'

'Is it even so?' quoth Romaine, nodding his head. 'And I might have been sure of it. Place them in a hospital, put them in a jail in yellow overalls, do what you will, young Jessamy finds young Jenny. O, have it your own way; I am too old a hand to argue with young gentlemen who choose to fancy themselves in love; I have too much experience, thank you. Only, be sure that you appreciate what you risk : the prison, the dock, the gallows, and the halter—terribly vulgar circumstances, my young friend ; grim, sordid, earnest; no poetry in that!'

'And there I am warned,' I returned gaily. 'No man could be warned more finely or with a greater eloquence. And I am of the same opinion still. Until I have again seen that lady, nothing shall induce me to quit Great Britain. I have besides——'

And here I came to a full stop. It was upon my tongue to have told him the story of the drovers, but at the first word of it my voice died in my throat. There might be a limit to the lawyer's toleration, I reflected. I had not been so long in Britain altogether ; for the most part of that time I had been by the heels in limbo in Edinburgh Castle ; and already I had confessed to killing one man with a pair of scissors ; and now I was to go on and plead guilty to having settled another with a holly stick ! A wave of discretion went over me as cold and as deep as the sea.

'In short, sir, this is a matter of feeling,' I concluded, 'and nothing will prevent my going to Edinburgh.'

If I had fired a pistol in his ear he could not have been more startled.

'To Edinburgh?' he repeated. 'Edinburgh? where the very paving-stones know you!'

'Then is the murder out!' said I. 'But, Mr. Romaine, is there not sometimes safety in boldness? Is it not a commonplace of strategy to get where the enemy least expects you? And where would he expect me less?'

'Faith, there is something in that, too!' cried the lawyer. 'Ay, certainly, a great deal in that. All the witnesses drowned but one, and he safe in prison; you yourself changed beyond recognition—let us hope—and walking the streets of the very town you have illustrated by your—well, your eccentricity! It is not badly combined, indeed!'

'You approve it, then?' said I.

'O, approve!' said he; 'there is no question of approval. There is only one course which I could approve, and that were to escape to France instanter.'

'You do not wholly disapprove, at least?' I substituted.

'Not wholly; and it would not matter if I did,' he replied. 'Go your own way; you are beyond argument. And I am not sure that you will run more danger by that course than by any other. Give the servants time to get to bed and fall asleep, then take a country cross-road and walk, as the rhyme has it, like blazes all night. In the morning take a chaise or take the mail at pleasure, and continue your journey with all the decorum and reserve of which you shall be found capable.'

'I am taking the picture in,' I said. 'Give me time. 'Tis the *tout ensemble* I must see: the whole as opposed to the details.'

'Mountebank!' he murmured.

'Yes, I have it now; and I see myself with a servant, and that servant is Rowley,' said I.

'So as to have one more link with your uncle?' suggested the lawyer. 'Very judicious!'

'And, pardon me, but that is what it is,' I exclaimed. 'Judicious is the word. I am not making a deception fit to last for thirty years; I do not found a palace in the living granite for the night. This is a shelter tent—a flying picture—seen, admired, and gone again in the wink of an eye. What is wanted, in short, is a *trompe-l'œil* that shall be good enough for twelve hours at an inn: is it not so?'

'It is, and the objection holds. Rowley is but another danger,' said Romaine.

'Rowley,' said I, 'will pass as a servant from a distance—

as a creature seen poised on the dicky of a bowling chaise. He will pass at hand as a smart, civil fellow one meets in the inn corridor, and looks back at, and asks, and is told, "Gentleman's servant in Number 4." He will pass, in fact, all round, except with his personal friends! My dear sir, pray what do you expect? Of course, if we meet my cousin, or if we meet anybody who took part in the judicious exhibition of this evening, we are lost; and who's denying it? To every disguise, however good and safe, there is always the weak point; you must always take (let us say—and to take a simile from your own waistcoat pocket) a snuff box-full of risk. You'll get it just as small with Rowley as with anybody else. And the long and short of it is, the lad's honest, he likes me, I trust him; he is my servant, or nobody.'

'He might not accept,' said Romaine.

'I bet you a thousand pounds he does!' cried I. 'But no matter; all you have to do is to send him out to-night on this cross-country business, and leave the thing to me. I tell you, he will be my servant, and I tell you, he will do well.'

I had crossed the room, and was already overhauling my wardrobe as I spoke.

'Well,' concluded the lawyer, with a shrug, 'one risk with another: *à la guerre comme à la guerre,* as you would say. Let the brat come and be useful, at least.' And he was about to ring the bell, when his eye was caught by my researches in the wardrobe. 'Do not fall in love with these coats, waistcoats, cravats, and other panoply and accoutrements by which you are now surrounded. You must not run the post as a dandy. It is not the fashion, even.'

'You are pleased to be facetious, sir,' said I; 'and not according to knowledge. These clothes are my life, they are my disguise; and since I can take but few of them, I were a fool indeed if I selected hastily! Will you understand, once and for all, what I am seeking? To be invisible, is the first point; the second, to be invisible in a post-chaise and with a servant. Can you not perceive the delicacy of the quest? Nothing must be too coarse, nothing too fine; *rien de voyant, rien qui détonne*; so that I may leave everywhere the inconspicuous image of a handsome young man of a good fortune travelling in proper style, whom the landlord will forget in twelve hours—and the chambermaid perhaps remember, God bless her! with a sigh. This is the very fine art of dress.'

'I have practised it with success for fifty years,' said Romaine, with a chuckle. 'A black suit and a clean shirt is my infallible recipe.'

'You surprise me; I did not think you would be shallow!' said I, lingering between two coats. 'Pray, Mr. Romaine, have I your head? or did you travel post and with a smartish servant?'

'Neither, I admit,' said he.

'Which change the whole problem,' I continued. 'I have to dress for a smartish servant and a Russia leather despatch-box.' That brought me to a stand. I came over and looked at the box with a moment's hesitation. 'Yes,' I resumed. 'Yes, and for the despatch-box! It looks moneyed and landed; it means I have a lawyer. It is an invaluable property. But I could have wished it to hold less money. The responsibility is crushing. Should I not do more wisely to take five hundred pounds, and intrust the remainder with you, Mr. Romaine?'

'If you are sure you will not want it,' answered Romaine.

'I am far from sure of that,' cried I. 'In the first place, as a philosopher. This is the first time I have been at the head of a large sum, and it is conceivable—who knows himself?—that I may make it fly. In the second place, as a fugitive. Who knows what I may need? The whole of it may be inadequate. But I can always write for more.'

'You do not understand,' he replied. 'I break off all communication with you here and now. You must give me a power of attorney ere you start to-night, and then be done with me trenchantly until better days.'

I believe I offered some objection.

'Think a little for once of me!' said Romaine. 'I must not have seen you before to-night. To-night we are to have had our only interview, and you are to have given me the power; and to-night I am to have lost sight of you again—I know not whither, you were upon business, it was none of my affairs to question you! And this, you are to remark, in the interests of your own safety much more than mine.'

'I am not even to write to you?' I said, a little bewildered.

'I believe I am cutting the last strand that connects you with common sense,' he replied. 'But that is the plain English of it. You are not even to write; and if you did, I would not answer.'

'A letter, however——' I began.

'Listen to me,' interrupted Romaine. 'So soon as your cousin reads the paragraph, what will he do? Put the police upon looking into my correspondence! So soon as you write to me, in short, you write to Bow Street; and if you will take my advice, you will date that letter from France.'

'The devil!' said I, for I began suddenly to see that this might put me out of the way of my business.

'What is it now?' says he.

'There will be more to be done, then, before we can part,' I answered.

'I give you the whole night,' said he. 'So long as you are off ere daybreak, I am content.'

'In short, Mr. Romaine,' said I, 'I have had so much benefit of your advice and services that I am loth to sever the connection, and would even ask a substitute. I would be obliged for a letter of introduction to one of your own cloth in Edinburgh —an old man for choice, very experienced, very respectable, and very secret. Could you favour me with such a letter?'

'Why, no,' said he. 'Certainly not. I will do no such thing, indeed.'

'It would be a great favour, sir,' I pleaded.

'It would be an unpardonable blunder,' he replied. 'What? Give you a letter of introduction? and when the police come, I suppose, I must forget the circumstance? No, indeed. Talk of it no more.'

'You seem to be always in the right,' said I. 'The letter would be out of the question, I quite see that. But the lawyer's name might very well have dropped from you in the way of conversation; having heard him mentioned, I might profit by the circumstance to introduce myself; and in this way my business would be the better done, and you not in the least compromised.'

'What is this business?' said Romaine.

'I have not said that I had any,' I replied. 'It might arise. This is only a possibility that I must keep in view.'

'Well,' said he, with a gesture of the hands, 'I mention Mr. Robbie; and let that be an end of it!—Or wait!' he added, 'I have it. Here is something that will serve you for an introduction, and cannot compromise me.' And he wrote his name and the Edinburgh lawyer's address on a piece of card and tossed it to me.

CHAPTER XXI

I BECOME THE OWNER OF A CLARET-COLOURED CHAISE

WHAT with packing, signing papers, and partaking of an excellent cold supper in the lawyer's room, it was past two in the morning before we were ready for the road. Romaine himself let us out of a window in a part of the house known to Rowley: it appears it served as a kind of postern to the servants' hall, by which (when they were in the mind for a clandestine evening) they would come regularly in and out; and I remember very well the vinegar aspect of the lawyer on the receipt of this piece of information—how he pursed his lips, jutted his eyebrows, and kept repeating, ' This must be seen to, indeed ! this shall be barred to-morrow in the morning !' In this preoccupation, I believe he took leave of me without observing it; our things were handed out; we heard the window shut behind us; and became instantly lost in a horrid intricacy of blackness and the shadow of woods.

A little wet snow kept sleepily falling, pausing, and falling again; it seemed perpetually beginning to snow and perpetually leaving off; and the darkness was intense. Time and again we walked into trees; time and again found ourselves adrift among garden borders or stuck like a ram in the thicket. Rowley had possessed himself of the matches, and he was neither to be terrified nor softened. ' No, I will not, Mr. Anne, sir,' he would reply. ' You know he tell me to wait till we were over the 'ill. It's only a little way now. Why, and I thought you was a soldier, too !' I was at least a very glad soldier when my valet consented at last to kindle a thieves' match. From this, we easily lit the lantern; and thenceforward, through a labyrinth of woodland paths, were conducted by its uneasy glimmer. Both booted and great-coated, with tall hats much of a shape, and laden with booty in the form of a despatch-box, a case of pistols, and two plump valises, I thought we had very much the look of a pair of brothers returning from the sack of Amersham Place.

We issued at last upon a country by-road where we might

walk abreast and without precaution. It was nine miles to Aylesbury, our immediate destination; by a watch, which formed part of my new outfit, it should be about half-past three in the morning; and as we did not choose to arrive before daylight, time could not be said to press. I gave the order to march at ease.

'Now, Rowley,' said I, 'so far so good. You have come, in the most obliging manner in the world, to carry these valises. The question is, what next? What are we to do at Aylesbury? or, more particularly, what are you? Thence, I go on a journey. Are you to accompany me?'

He gave a little chuckle. 'That's all settled already, Mr. Anne, sir,' he replied. 'Why, I've got my things here in the valise—a half a dozen shirts and what not; I'm all ready, sir: just you lead on: *you'll* see.'

'The devil you have!' said I. 'You made pretty sure of your welcome.'

'If you please, sir,' said Rowley.

He looked up at me, in the light of the lantern, with a boyish shyness and triumph that awoke my conscience. I could never let this innocent involve himself in the perils and difficulties that beset my course, without some hint of warning, which it was a matter of extreme delicacy to make plain enough and not too plain.

'No, no,' said I; 'you may think you have made a choice, but it was blindfold, and you must make it over again. The Count's service is a good one; what are you leaving it for? Are you not throwing away the substance for the shadow? No, do not answer me yet. You imagine that I am a prosperous nobleman, just declared my uncle's heir, on the threshold of the best of good fortune, and, from the point of view of a judicious servant, a jewel of a master to serve and stick to? Well, my boy, I am nothing of the kind, nothing of the kind.'

As I said the words, I came to a full stop and held up the lantern to his face. He stood before me, brilliantly illuminated on the background of impenetrable night and falling snow, stricken to stone between his double burden like an ass between two panniers, and gaping at me like a blunderbuss. I had never seen a face so predestined to be astonished, or so susceptible of rendering the emotion of surprise; and it tempted me as an open piano tempts the musician.

'Nothing of the sort, Rowley,' I continued, in a churchyard voice. 'These are appearances, petty appearances. I am in peril, homeless, hunted. I count scarce any one in England who is not my enemy. From this hour I drop my name, my title; I become nameless; my name is proscribed. My liberty, my life, hang by a hair. The destiny which you will accept, if you go forth with me, is to be tracked by spies, to hide yourself under a false name, to follow the desperate pretences and perhaps share the fate of a murderer with a price upon his head.'

His face had been hitherto beyond expectation, passing from one depth to another of tragic astonishment, and really worth paying to see; but at this it suddenly cleared. 'Oh, I ain't afraid!' he said; and then, choking into laughter, 'why, I see it from the first!'

I could have beaten him. But I had so grossly overshot the mark that I suppose it took me two good miles of road and half an hour of elocution to persuade him I had been in earnest. In the course of which I became so interested in demonstrating my present danger that I forgot all about my future safety, and not only told him the story of Goguelat, but threw in the business of the drovers as well, and ended by blurting out that I was a soldier of Napoleon's and a prisoner of war.

This was far from my views when I began; and it is a common complaint of me that I have a long tongue. I believe it is a fault beloved by fortune. Which of you considerate fellows would have done a thing at once so foolhardy and so wise as to make a confidant of a boy in his teens, and positively smelling of the nursery? And when had I cause to repent it? There is none so apt as a boy to be the adviser of any man in difficulties such as mine. To the beginnings of virile common sense he adds the last lights of the child's imagination; and he can fling himself into business with that superior earnestness that properly belongs to play. And Rowley was a boy made to my hand. He had a high sense of romance, and a secret cultus for all soldiers and criminals. His travelling library consisted of a chap-book life of Wallace and some sixpenny parts of the 'Old Bailey Sessions Papers' by Gurney the shorthand writer; and the choice depicts his character to a hair. You can imagine how his new prospects brightened on a boy of this disposition. To be the servant and companion of a fugitive, a soldier, and a murderer, rolled in one—to live by stratagems, disguises, and false names, in an atmosphere of midnight and mystery so thick that you could cut it with a knife—was really, I believe, more dear to him than his meals, though he was a great trencherman, and something of a glutton besides. For myself, as the peg by which all this romantic business hung, I was simply idolised from that moment; and he would rather

have sacrificed his hand than surrendered the privilege of
serving me.

We arranged the terms of our campaign, trudging amicably in
the snow, which now, with the approach of morning, began to
fall to purpose. I chose the name of Ramornie, I imagine from
its likeness to Romaine ; Rowley, from an irresistible conversion
of ideas, I dubbed Gammon. His distress was laughable to
witness : his own choice of an unassuming nickname had been
Claude Duval! We settled our procedure at the various inns
where we should alight, rehearsed our little manners like a
piece of drill until it seemed impossible we should ever be
taken unprepared ; and in all these dispositions, you may be
sure the despatch-box was not forgotten. Who was to pick it
up, who was to set it down, who was to remain beside it, who
was to sleep with it—there was no contingency omitted, all was
gone into with the thoroughness of a drill-sergeant on the one
hand and a child with a new plaything on the other.

'I say, wouldn't it look queer if you and me was to come to
the post-house with all this luggage ? ' said Rowley.

'I dare say.' I replied. 'But what else is to be done ? '

'Well, now, sir—you hear me,' says Rowley. 'I think it
would look more natural-like if you was to come to the post-
house alone, and with nothing in your 'ands—more like a
gentleman, you know. And you might say that your servant
and baggage was a-waiting for you up the road. I think I
could manage, somehow, to make a shift with all them dratted
things—leastways if you was to give me a 'and up with them at
the start.'

'And I would see you far enough before I allowed you to try,
Mr. Rowley ! ' I cried. 'Why, you would be quite defenceless !
A footpad that was an infant child could rob you. And I should
probably come driving by to find you in a ditch with your throat
cut. But there is something in your idea, for all that ; and I
propose we put it in execution no farther forward than the next
corner of a lane.'

Accordingly, instead of continuing to aim for Aylesbury, we
headed by cross-roads for some point to the northward of it,
whither I might assist Rowley with the baggage, and where
I might leave him to await my return in the post-chaise.

It was snowing to purpose, the country all white, and ourselves walking snowdrifts, when the first glimmer of the morning showed us an inn upon the highwayside. Some distance
off, under the shelter of a corner of the road and a clump of
trees, I loaded Rowley with the whole of our possessions, and
watched him till he staggered in safety into the doors of the

Green Dragon, which was the sign of the house. Thence I walked briskly into Aylesbury, rejoicing in my freedom and the causeless good spirits that belong to a snowy morning; though, to be sure, long before I had arrived the snow had again ceased to fall, and the eaves of Aylesbury were smoking in the level sun. There was an accumulation of gigs and chaises in the yard, and a great bustle going forward in the coffee-room and about the doors of the inn. At these evidences of so much travel on the road I was seized with a misgiving lest it should be impossible to get horses, and I should be detained in the precarious neighbourhood of my cousin. Hungry as I was, I made my way first of all to the postmaster, where he stood—a big, athletic, horsey-looking man, blowing into a key in the corner of the yard.

On my making my modest request, he awoke from his indifference into what seemed passion.

'A po'-shay and 'osses!' he cried. 'Do I look as if I 'ad a po'-shay and 'osses? Damn me, if I 'ave such a thing on the premises. I don't *make* 'osses and chaises—I *'ire* 'em. You might be God Almighty!' said he; and instantly, as if he had observed me for the first time, he broke off, and lowered his voice into the confidential. 'Why, now that I see you are a gentleman,' said he, 'I'll tell you what! If you like to *buy,* I have the article to fit you. Second-'and shay by Lycett, of London. Latest style; good as new. Superior fittin's, net on the roof, baggage platform, pistol 'olsters—the most com-plete and the most gen-teel turn-out I ever see! The 'ole for seventy-five pound! It's as good as givin' her away!'

'Do you propose I should trundle it myself, like a hawker's barrow?' said I. 'Why, my good man, if I had to stop here, anyway, I should prefer to buy a house and garden!'

'Come and look at her!' he cried; and, with the word, links his arm in mine and carries me to the outhouse where the chaise was on view.

It was just the sort of chaise that I had dreamed of for my purpose: eminently rich, inconspicuous, and genteel; for, though I thought the postmaster no great authority, I was bound to agree with him so far. The body was painted a dark claret, and the wheels an invisible green. The lamp and glasses were bright as silver; and the whole equipage had an air of privacy and reserve that seemed to repel inquiry and disarm suspicion. With a servant like Rowley, and a chaise like this, I felt that I could go from the Land's End to John o' Groat's House amid a population of bowing ostlers. And I suppose I betrayed in my manner the degree in which the bargain tempted me.

'Come,' cried the postmaster—'I'll make it seventy, to oblige a friend!'

'The point is: the horses,' said I.

'Well,' said he, consulting his watch, 'it's now gone the 'alf after eight. What time do you want her at the door?'

'Horses and all?' said I.

''Osses and all!' says he. 'One good turn deserves another. You give me seventy pound for the shay, and I'll 'oss it for you. I told you I didn't *make* 'osses; but I *can* make 'em, to oblige a friend.'

What would you have? It was not the wisest thing in the world to buy a chaise within a dozen miles of my uncle's house; but in this way I got my horses for the next stage. And by any other it appeared that I should have to wait. Accordingly I paid the money down—perhaps twenty pounds too much, though it was certainly a well-made and well-appointed vehicle —ordered it round in half an hour, and proceeded to refresh myself with breakfast.

The table to which I sat down occupied the recess of a bay-window, and commanded a view of the front of the inn, where I continued to be amused by the successive departures of travellers—the fussy and the offhand, the niggardly and the lavish— all exhibiting their different characters in that diagnostic moment of the farewell: some escorted to the stirrup or the chaise door by the chamberlain, the chambermaids and the waiters almost in a body, others moving off under a cloud, without human countenance. In the course of this I became interested in one for whom this ovation began to assume the proportions of a triumph; not only the under-servants, but the barmaid, the landlady, and my friend the postmaster himself, crowding about the steps to speed his departure. I was aware, at the same time, of a good deal of merriment, as though the traveller were a man of a ready wit, and not too dignified to air it in that society. I leaned forward with a lively curiosity; and the next moment I had blotted myself behind the teapot. The popular traveller had turned to wave a farewell; and behold! he was no other than my cousin Alain. It was a change of the sharpest from the angry, pallid man I had seen at Amersham Place. Ruddy to a fault, illuminated with vintages, crowned with his curls like Bacchus, he now stood before me for an instant, the perfect master of himself, smiling with airs of conscious popularity and insufferable condescension. He reminded me at once of a royal duke, or an actor turned a little elderly, and of a blatant bagman who should have been the illegitimate son of a gentleman. A moment after he was gliding noiselessly on the road to London.

I breathed again. I recognised, with heartfelt gratitude, how lucky I had been to go in by the stable-yard instead of the hostelry door, and what a fine occasion of meeting my cousin I had lost by the purchase of the claret-coloured chaise! The next moment I remembered that there was a waiter present. No doubt but he must have observed me when I crouched behind the breakfast equipage; no doubt but he must have commented on this unusual and undignified behaviour; and it was essential that I should do something to remove the impression.

'Waiter!' said I, 'that was the nephew of Count Carwell that just drove off, wasn't it?'

'Yes, sir: Viscount Carwell we calls him,' he replied.

'Ah, I thought as much,' said I. 'Well, well, damn all these Frenchmen, say I!'

'You may say so indeed, sir,' said the waiter. 'They ain't not to say in the same field with our 'ome-raised gentry.'

'Nasty tempers?' I suggested.

'Beas'ly temper, sir, the Viscount 'ave,' said the waiter with feeling. 'Why, no longer agone than this morning, he was sitting breakfasting and reading in his paper. I suppose, sir, he come on some pilitical information, or it might be about 'orses, but he raps his 'and upon the table sudden and calls for curaçoa. It gave me quite a turn, it did; he did it that sudden and 'ard. Now, sir, that may be manners in France, but hall I can say is, that I'm not used to it.'

'Reading the paper, was he?' said I. 'What paper, eh?'

'Here it is, sir,' exclaimed the waiter. 'Seems like as if he'd dropped it.'

And picking it off the floor he presented it to me.

I may say that I was quite prepared, that I already knew what to expect; but at sight of the cold print my heart stopped beating. There it was: the fulfilment of Romaine's apprehension was before me; the paper was laid open at the capture of Clausel. I felt as if I could take a little curaçoa myself, but on second thoughts called for brandy. It was badly wanted; and suddenly I observed the waiter's eye to sparkle, as it were, with some recognition; made certain he had remarked the resemblance between me and Alain; and became aware—as by a revelation—of the fool's part I had been playing. For I had now managed to put my identification beyond a doubt, if Alain should choose to make his inquiries at Aylesbury; and, as if that were not enough, I had added, at an expense of seventy pounds, a clue by which he might follow me through the length and breadth of England, in the shape of the claret-coloured chaise! That elegant equipage (which I began to regard as little better than a claret-coloured ante-room to the hangman's cart) coming presently to the door, I left my breakfast in the middle and departed; posting to the north as diligently as my cousin Alain was posting to the south, and putting my trust (such as it was) in an opposite direction and equal speed.

CHAPTER XXII

CHARACTER AND ACQUIREMENTS OF MR. ROWLEY

I AM not certain that I had ever really appreciated before that
hour the extreme peril of the adventure on which I was
embarked. The sight of my cousin, the look of his face—so
handsome, so jovial at the first sight, and branded with so
much malignity as you saw it on the second—with his hyper-
bolical curls in order, with his neckcloth tied as if for the con-
quests of love, setting forth (as I had no doubt in the world he
was doing) to clap the Bow Street runners on my trail, and
cover England with handbills, each dangerous as a loaded
musket, convinced me for the first time that the affair was no
less serious than death. I believe it came to a near touch
whether I should not turn the horses' heads at the next stage
and make directly for the coast. But I was now in the position
of a man who should have thrown his gage into the den of
lions; or, better still, like one who should have quarrelled
overnight under the influence of wine, and now, at daylight, in
a cold winter's morning, and humbly sober, must make good
his words. It is not that I thought any the less, or any the
less warmly, of Flora. But, as I smoked a grim segar that
morning in a corner of the chaise, no doubt I considered, in
the first place, that the letter-post had been invented, and
admitted privately to myself, in the second, that it would
have been highly possible to write her on a piece of paper,
seal it, and send it skimming by the mail, instead of going personally into these egregious dangers, and through a country
that I beheld crowded with gibbets and Bow Street officers.
As for Sim and Candlish, I doubt if they crossed my mind.

At the Green Dragon Rowley was waiting on the doorsteps
with the luggage, and really was bursting with unpalatable
conversation.

'Who do you think we've 'ad 'ere, sir?' he began breathlessly, as the chaise drove off. 'Red Breasts'; and he nodded
his head portentously.

164

'Red Breasts?' I repeated, for I stupidly did not understand at the moment an expression I had often heard.

'Ah!' said he. 'Red weskits. Runners. Bow Street runners. Two on 'em, and one was Lavender himself! I hear the other say quite plain, "Now, Mr. Lavender, *if* you're ready." They was breakfasting as nigh me as I am to that postboy. They're all right; they ain't after us. It's a forger; and I didn't send them off on a false scent—O no! I thought there was no use in having them over our way; so I give them "very valuable information," Mr. Lavender said, and tipped me a tizzy for myself; and they're off to Luton. They showed me the 'andcuffs, too—the other one did—and he clicked the dratted things on my wrist; and I tell you, I believe I nearly went off in a swound! There's something so beastly in the feel of them! Begging your pardon, Mr. Anne,' he added, with one of his delicious changes from the character of the confidential schoolboy into that of the trained, respectful servant.

Well, I must not be proud! I cannot say I found the subject of handcuffs to my fancy; and it was with more asperity than was needful that I reproved him for the slip about the name.

'Yes, Mr. Ramornie,' says he, touching his hat. 'Begging your pardon, Mr. Ramornie. But I've been very piticular, sir, up to now; and you may trust me to be very piticular in the future. It were only a slip, sir.'

'My good boy,' said I, with the most imposing severity, 'there must be no slips. Be so good as to remember that my life is at stake.'

I did not embrace the occasion of telling him how many I had made myself. It is my principle that an officer must never be wrong. I have seen two divisions beating their brains out for a fortnight against a worthless and quite impregnable castle in a pass: I knew we were only doing it for discipline, because the General had said so at first, and had not yet found any way out of his own words; and I highly admired his force of character, and throughout these operations thought my life exposed in a very good cause. With fools and children, which included Rowley, the necessity was even greater. I proposed to myself to be infallible; and even when he expressed some wonder at the purchase of the claret-coloured chaise, I put him promptly in his place. In our situation, I told him, everything had to be sacrificed to appearances; doubtless, in a hired chaise, we should have had more freedom, but look at the dignity! I was so positive, that I had sometimes almost convinced myself. Not for long, you may be certain! This detestable conveyance

always appeared to me to be laden with Bow Street officers, and
to have a placard upon the back of it publishing my name and
crimes.   If I had paid seventy pounds to get the thing, I
should not have stuck at seven hundred to be safely rid of it.

And if the chaise was a danger, what an anxiety was the
despatch-box and its golden cargo!   I had never had a care
but to draw my pay and spend it; I had lived happily in the
regiment, as in my father's house, fed by the great Emperor's
commissariat as by ubiquitous doves of Elijah—or, my faith! if
anything went wrong with the commissariat, helping myself
with the best grace in the world from the next peasant!   And
now I began to feel at the same time the burthen of riches and
the fear of destitution.   There were ten thousand pounds in
the despatch-box, but I reckoned in French money, and had two
hundred and fifty thousand agonies; I kept it under my hand
all day, I dreamed of it at night.   In the inns, I was afraid to
go to dinner and afraid to go to sleep.   When I walked up a
hill I durst not leave the doors of the claret-coloured chaise.
Sometimes I would change the disposition of the funds : there
were days when I carried as much as five or six thousand
pounds on my own person, and only the residue continued to
voyage in the treasure-chest—days when I bulked all over
like my cousin, crackled to a touch with bank paper, and had
my pockets weighed to bursting-point with sovereigns.   And
there were other days when I wearied of the thing—or grew
ashamed of it—and put all the money back where it had come
from : there let it take its chance, like better people!   In short,
I set Rowley a poor example of consistency, and in philosophy,
none at all.

Little he cared!   All was one to him so long as he was
amused, and I never knew any one amused more easily.   He
was thrillingly interested in life, travel, and his own melodra-
matic position.   All day he would be looking from the chaise
windows with ebullitions of gratified curiosity, that were sometimes justified and sometimes not, and that (taken altogether)
it occasionally wearied me to be obliged to share.   I can look
at horses, and I can look at trees too, although not fond of it.
But why should I look at a lame horse, or a tree that was like
the letter Y?   What exhilaration could I feel in viewing a
cottage that was the same colour as 'the second from the
miller's' in some place where I had never been, and of which
I had not previously heard?   I am ashamed to complain, but
there were moments when my juvenile and confidential friend
weighed heavy on my hands.   His cackle was indeed almost
continuous, but it was never unamiable.   He showed an amiable

curiosity when he was asking questions; an amiable guileless-ness when he was conferring information. And both he did largely. I am in a position to write the biographies of Mr. Rowley, Mr. Rowley's father and mother, his Aunt Eliza, and the miller's dog; and nothing but pity for the reader, and some misgivings as to the law of copyright, prevail on me to withhold them.

A general design to mould himself upon my example became early apparent, and I had not the heart to check it. He began to mimic my carriage; he acquired, with servile accuracy, a little manner I had of shrugging the shoulders; and I may say it was by observing it in him that I first discovered it in myself. One day it came out by chance that I was of the Catholic religion. He became plunged in thought, at which I was gently glad. Then suddenly—

'Odd-rabbit it! I'll be Catholic too!' he broke out. 'You must teach me it, Mr. Anne—I mean, Ramornie.'

I dissuaded him: alleging that he would find me very imper-fectly informed as to the grounds and doctrines of the Church, and that, after all, in the matter of religions, it was a very poor idea to change. 'Of course, my Church is the best,' said I; 'but that is not the reason why I belong to it: I belong to it because it was the faith of my house. I wish to take my chances with my own people, and so should you. If it is a question of going to hell, go to hell like a gentleman with your ancestors.'

'Well, it wasn't that,' he admitted. 'I don't know that I was exactly thinking of hell. Then there's the inquisition, too. That's rather a cawker, you know.'

'And I don't believe you were thinking of anything in the world,' said I—which put a period to his respectable conversion.

He consoled himself by playing for awhile on a cheap flageolet, which was one of his diversions, and to which I owed many intervals of peace. When he first produced it, in the joints, from his pocket, he had the duplicity to ask me if I played upon it. I answered, no; and he put the instrument away with a sigh and the remark that he had thought I might. For some while he resisted the unspeakable temptation, his fingers visibly itching and twittering about his pocket, even his interest in the landscape and in sporadic anecdote entirely lost. Presently the pipe was in his hands again; he fitted, unfitted, refitted, and played upon it in dumb show for some time.

'I play it myself a little,' says he.

'Do you?' said I, and yawned.

And then he broke down.

'Mr. Ramornie, if you please, would it disturb you, sir, if I was to play a chune?' he pleaded. And from that hour, the tootling of the flageolet cheered our way.

He was particularly keen on the details of battles, single combats, incidents of scouting parties, and the like. These he would make haste to cap with some of the exploits of Wallace, the only hero with whom he had the least acquaintance. His enthusiasm was genuine and pretty. When he learned we were going to Scotland, 'Well, then,' he broke out, 'I'll see where Wallace lived!' And presently after, he fell to moralising. 'It's a strange thing, sir,' he began, 'that I seem somehow to have always the wrong sow by the ear. I'm English after all, and I glory in it. My eye! don't I, though! Let some of your Frenchies come over here to invade, and you'll see whether or not! Oh, yes, I'm English to the backbone, I am. And yet look at me! I got hold of this 'ere William Wallace and took to him right off; I never heard of such a man before! And then you came along, and I took to you. And both the two of you were my born enemies! I—I beg your pardon, Mr. Ramornie, but would you mind it very much if you didn't go for to do anything against England'—he brought the word out suddenly, like something hot—'when I was along of you?'

I was more affected than I can tell.

'Rowley,' I said, 'you need have no fear. By how much I love my own honour, by so much I will take care to protect yours. We are but fraternising at the outposts, as soldiers do. When the bugle calls, my boy, we must face each other, one for England, one for France, and may God defend the right!'

So I spoke at the moment; but for all my brave airs, the boy had wounded me in a vital quarter. His words continued to ring in my hearing. There was no remission all day of my remorseful thoughts; and that night (which we lay at Lichfield, I believe) there was no sleep for me in my bed. I put out the candle and lay down with a good resolution; and in a moment all was light about me like a theatre, and I saw myself upon the stage of it playing ignoble parts. I remembered France and my Emperor, now depending on the arbitrament of war, bent down, fighting on their knees and with their teeth against so many and such various assailants. And I burned with shame to be here in England, cherishing an English fortune, pursuing an English mistress, and not there, to handle a musket in my native fields, and to manure them with my body if I fell. I remembered that I belonged to France. All my fathers had fought for her, and some had died; the voice in my throat, the sight of my eyes, the tears that now sprang there, the whole man of me, was fashioned of French earth and born of a French mother; I had been tended and caressed by a succession of the daughters of France, the fairest, the most ill-starred; and I had fought and conquered shoulder to shoulder with her sons. A soldier, a noble, of the proudest and bravest race in Europe, it had been left to the prattle of a hobbledehoy lackey in an English chaise to recall me to the consciousness of duty.

When I saw how it was I did not lose time in indecision. The old classical conflict of love and honour being once fairly before me, it did not cost me a thought. I was a Saint-Yves de Kéroual; and I decided to strike off on the morrow for Wakefield and Burchell Fenn, and embark, as soon as it should be morally possible, for the succour of my downtrodden fatherland and my beleaguered Emperor. Pursuant on this resolve, I leaped from bed, made a light, and as the watchman was crying half-past two in the dark streets of Lichfield, sat down to pen a letter of farewell to Flora. And then—whether it was the sudden chill of the night, whether it came by association of ideas from the remembrance of Swanston Cottage I know not, but there appeared before me—to the barking of sheep-dogs—a couple of snuffy and shambling figures, each wrapped in a plaid, each armed with a rude staff; and I was immediately bowed down to have forgotten them so long, and of late to have thought of them so cavalierly.

Sure enough there was my errand! As a private person I was neither French nor English; I was something else first: a loyal gentleman, an honest man. Sim and Candlish must not be left to pay the penalty of my unfortunate blow. They held my honour tacitly pledged to succour them; and it is a sort of stoical refinement entirely foreign to my nature to set the political obligation above the personal and private. If France fell in the interval for the lack of Anne de St.-Yves, fall she must! But I was both surprised and humiliated to have had so plain a duty bound upon me for so long—and for so long to have neglected and forgotten it. I think any brave man will understand me when I say that I went to bed and to sleep with a conscience very much relieved, and woke again in the morning with a light heart. The very danger of the enterprise reassured me: to save Sim and Candlish (suppose the worst to come to the worst) it would be necessary for me to declare myself in a court of justice, with consequences which I did not dare to dwell upon; it could never be said that I had chosen the cheap and the easy—only that in a very perplexing competition of duties I had risked my life for the most immediate.

We resumed the journey with more diligence : thenceforward posted day and night; did not halt beyond what was necessary for meals; and the postillions were excited by gratuities, after the habit of my cousin Alain. For twopence I could have gone farther and taken four horses; so extreme was my haste, running as I was before the terrors of an awakened conscience. But I feared to be conspicuous. Even as it was, we attracted only too much attention, with our pair and that white elephant, the seventy-pounds-worth of claret-coloured chaise.

Meanwhile I was ashamed to look Rowley in the face. The young shaver had contrived to put me wholly in the wrong ; he had cost me a night's rest and a severe and healthful humiliation; and I was grateful and embarrassed in his society. This would never do; it was contrary to all my ideas of discipline; if the officer has to blush before the private, or the master before the servant, nothing is left to hope for but discharge or death. I hit upon the idea of teaching him French; and accordingly, from Lichfield, I became the distracted master, and he the scholar—how shall I say? indefatigable, but uninspired. His interest never flagged. He would hear the same word twenty times with profound refreshment, mispronounce it in several different ways, and forget it again with magical celerity. Say it happened to be *stirrup*. 'No, I don't seem to remember that word, Mr. Anne,' he would say : 'it don't seem to stick to me, that word don't.' And then, when I had told it him again, '*Etrier !*' he would cry. 'To be sure ! I had it on the tip of my tongue. *Eterier !*' (going wrong already, as if by a fatal instinct). 'What will I remember it by, now ? Why, *interior,* to be sure ! I 'll remember it by its being something that ain't in the interior of a horse.' And when next I had occasion to ask him the French for stirrup, it was a toss-up whether he had forgotten all about it, or gave me *exterior* for an answer. He was never a hair discouraged. He seemed to consider that he was covering the ground at a normal rate. He came up smiling day after day. 'Now, sir, shall we do our French ?' he would say; and I would put questions, and elicit copious commentary and explanation, but never the shadow of an answer. My hands fell to my sides; I could have wept to hear him. When I reflected that he had as yet learned nothing, and what a vast deal more there was for him to learn, the period of these lessons seemed to unroll before me vast as eternity, and I saw myself a teacher of a hundred, and Rowley a pupil of ninety, still hammering on the rudiments! The wretched boy, I should say, was quite unspoiled by the inevitable familiarities of the journey. He turned out at each stage the pink of serving-lads, deft, civil, prompt, attentive, touching his hat like an automaton, raising the status of Mr. Ramornie in the eyes of all the inn by his smiling service, and seeming capable of anything in the world but the one thing I had chosen—learning French!

CHAPTER XXIII

THE ADVENTURE OF THE RUNAWAY COUPLE

THE country had for some time back been changing in character. By a thousand indications I could judge that I was again drawing near to Scotland. I saw it written in the face of the hills, in the growth of the trees, and in the glint of the waterbrooks that kept the high-road company. It might have occurred to me, also, that I was, at the same time, approaching a place of some fame in Britain—Gretna Green. Over these same leagues of road—which Rowley and I now traversed in the claret-coloured chaise, to the note of the flageolet and the French lesson—how many pairs of lovers had gone bowling northwards to the music of sixteen scampering horseshoes; and how many irate persons, parents, uncles, guardians, evicted rivals, had come tearing after, clapping the frequent red face to the chaise-window, lavishly shedding their gold about the post-houses, sedulously loading and re-loading, as they went, their avenging pistols! But I doubt if I had thought of it at all, before a wayside hazard swept me into the thick of an adventure of this nature; and I found myself playing providence with other people's lives, to my own admiration at the moment—and subsequently to my own brief but passionate regret.

At rather an ugly corner of an uphill reach I came on the wreck of a chaise lying on one side in the ditch, a man and a woman in animated discourse in the middle of the road, and the two postillions, each with his pair of horses, looking on and laughing from the saddle.

'Morning breezes! here's a smash!' cried Rowley, pocketing his flageolet in the middle of the *Tight Little Island*.

I was perhaps more conscious of the moral smash than the physical—more alive to broken hearts than to broken chaises; for, as plain as the sun at morning, there was a screw loose in this runaway match. It is always a bad sign when the lower classes laugh: their taste in humour is both poor and sinister; and for a man, running the posts with four horses, presumably

172

with open pockets, and in the company of the most entrancing little creature conceivable, to have come down so far as to be laughed at by his own postillions, was only to be explained on the double hypothesis, that he was a fool and no gentleman.

I have said they were man and woman. I should have said man and child. She was certainly not more than seventeen, pretty as an angel, just plump enough to damn a saint, and dressed in various shades of blue, from her stockings to her saucy cap, in a kind of taking gamut, the top note of which she flung me in a beam from her too appreciative eye. There was no doubt about the case: I saw it all. From a boarding-school, a black-board, a piano, and Clementi's *Sonatinas*, the child had made a rash adventure upon life in the company of a half-bred hawbuck; and she was already not only regretting it, but expressing her regret with point and pungency.

As I alighted they both paused with that unmistakable air of being interrupted in a scene. I uncovered to the lady and placed my services at their disposal.

It was the man who answered. 'There's no use in sham-ming, sir,' said he. 'This lady and I have run away, and her father's after us: road to Gretna, sir. And here have these nincompoops spilt us in the ditch and smashed the chaise!'

'Very provoking,' said I.

'I don't know when I've been so provoked!' cried he, with a glance down the road, of mortal terror.

'The father is no doubt very much incensed?' I pursued civilly.

'O God!' cried the hawbuck. 'In short, you see, we must get out of this. And I'll tell you what—it may seem cool, but necessity has no law—if you would lend us your chaise to the next post-house, it would be the very thing, sir.'

'I confess it seems cool,' I replied.

'What's that you say, sir?' he snapped.

'I was agreeing with you,' said I. 'Yes, it does seem cool; and what is more to the point, it seems unnecessary. This thing can be arranged in a more satisfactory manner otherwise, I think. You can doubtless ride?'

This opened a door on the matter of their previous dispute, and the fellow appeared life-sized in his true colours. 'That's what I've been telling her: that, damn her! she must ride!' he broke out. 'And if the gentleman's of the same mind, why, damme, you shall!'

As he said so, he made a snatch at her wrist, which she evaded with horror.

I stepped between them.

'No, sir,' said I; 'the lady shall not.'

He turned on me raging. 'And who are you to interfere?' he roared.

'There is here no question of who I am,' I replied. 'I may be the devil or the Archbishop of Canterbury for what you know, or need know. The point is that I can help you—it appears that nobody else can; and I will tell you how I propose to do it. I will give the lady a seat in my chaise, if you will return the compliment by allowing my servant to ride one of your horses.'

I thought he would have sprung at my throat.

'You have always the alternative before you: to wait here for the arrival of papa,' I added.

And that settled him. He cast another haggard look down the road, and capitulated.

'I am sure, sir, the lady is very much obliged to you,' he said, with an ill grace.

I gave her my hand; she mounted like a bird into the chaise; Rowley, grinning from ear to ear, closed the door behind us; the two impudent rascals of post-boys cheered and laughed aloud as we drove off; and my own postillion urged his horses at once into a rattling trot. It was plain I was supposed by all to have done a very dashing act, and ravished the bride from the ravisher.

In the meantime I stole a look at the little lady. She was in a state of pitiable discomposure, and her arms shook on her lap in her black lace mittens.

'Madam——' I began.

And she, in the same moment, finding her voice: 'O, what you must think of me!'

'Madam,' said I, 'what must any gentleman think when he sees youth, beauty and innocence in distress? I wish I could tell you that I was old enough to be your father; I think we must give that up,' I continued, with a smile. 'But I will tell you something about myself which ought to do as well, and to set that little heart at rest in my society. I am a lover. May I say it of myself—for I am not quite used to all the niceties of English—that I am a true lover? There is one whom I admire, adore, obey; she is no less good than she is beautiful; if she were here, she would take you to her arms: conceive that she has sent me—that she has said to me, "Go, be her knight!"'

'O, I know she must be sweet, I know she must be worthy of you!' cried the little lady. 'She would never forget female decorum—nor make the terrible *erratum* I've done!'

And at this she lifted up her voice and wept.

This did not forward matters: it was in vain that I begged

her to be more composed and to tell me a plain, consecutive
tale of her misadventures; but she continued instead to pour
forth the most extraordinary mixture of the correct school miss
and the poor untutored little piece of womanhood in a false
position—of engrafted pedantry and incoherent nature.

'I am certain it must have been judicial blindness,' she
sobbed. 'I can't think how I didn't see it, but I didn't; and
he isn't, is he? And then a curtain rose . . . O, what a
moment was that! But I knew at once that *you were*; you had
but to appear from your carriage, and I knew it. O, she must
be a fortunate young lady! And I have no fear with you, none
—a perfect confidence.'

'Madam,' said I, 'a gentleman.'

'That's what I mean—a gentleman,' she exclaimed. 'And
he—and that—*he* isn't. O, how shall I dare meet father!'
And disclosing to me her tear-stained face, and opening her
arms with a tragic gesture: 'And I am quite disgraced before
all the young ladies, my school-companions!' she added.

'O, not so bad as that!' I cried. 'Come, come, you exaggerate, my dear Miss ——? Excuse me if I am too familiar:
I have not yet heard your name.'

'My name is Dorothy Greensleeves, sir: why should I conceal it? I fear it will only serve to point an adage to future
generations, and I had meant so differently! There was no
young female in the county more emulous to be thought well
of than I. And what a fall was there! O, dear me, what a
wicked, piggish donkey of a girl I have made of myself, to be
sure! And there is no hope! O, Mr.——'

And at that she paused and asked my name.

I am not writing my eulogium for the Academy; I will
admit it was unpardonably imbecile, but I told it her. If you
had been there—and seen her, ravishingly pretty and little, a
baby in years and mind—and heard her talking like a book,
with so much of schoolroom propriety in her manner, with such
an innocent despair in the matter—you would probably have
told her yours. She repeated it after me.

'I shall pray for you all my life,' she said. 'Every night,
when I retire to rest, the last thing I shall do is to remember
you by name.'

Presently I succeeded in winning from her her tale, which
was much what I had anticipated: a tale of a schoolhouse, a
walled garden, a fruit-tree that concealed a bench, an impudent
raff posturing in church, an exchange of flowers and vows over
the garden wall, a silly schoolmate for a confidante, a chaise
and four, and the most immediate and perfect disenchantment

on the part of the little lady. 'And there is nothing to be done!' she wailed in conclusion. 'My error is irretrievable, I am quite forced to that conclusion. O, Monsieur de Saint-Yves! who would have thought that I could have been such a blind, wicked donkey!'

I should have said before—only that I really do not know when it came in—that we had been overtaken by the two post-boys, Rowley and Mr. Bellamy, which was the hawbuck's name, bestriding the four post-horses; and that these formed a sort of cavalry escort, riding now before, now behind the chaise, and Bellamy occasionally posturing at the window and obliging us with some of his conversation. He was so ill-received that I declare I was tempted to pity him, remembering from what a height he had fallen, and how few hours ago it was since the lady had herself fled to his arms, all blushes and ardour. Well, these great strokes of fortune usually befall the unworthy, and Bellamy was now the legitimate object of my commiseration and the ridicule of his own post-boys!

'Miss Dorothy,' said I, 'you wish to be delivered from this man?'

'O, if it were possible!' she cried. 'But not by violence.'

'Not in the least, ma'am,' I replied. 'The simplest thing in life. We are in a civilised country; the man's a male-factor——'

'O, never!' she cried. 'Do not even dream it! With all his faults, I know he is not *that*.'

'Anyway, he's in the wrong in this affair—on the wrong side of the law, call it what you please,' said I; and with that, our four horsemen having for the moment headed us by a consider-able interval, I hailed my post-boy and inquired who was the nearest magistrate and where he lived. Archdeacon Clitheroe, he told me, a prodigious dignitary, and one who lived but a lane or two back, and at the distance of only a mile or two out of the direct road. I showed him the king's medallion.

'Take the lady there, and at full gallop,' I cried.

'Right, sir! Mind yourself,' says the postillion.

And before I could have thought it possible, he had turned the carriage to the rightabout and we were galloping south.

Our outriders were quick to remark and imitate the manœuvre, and came flying after us with a vast deal of indis-criminate shouting; so that the fine, sober picture of a carriage and escort, that we had presented but a moment back, was transformed in the twinkling of an eye into the image of a noisy fox-chase. The two postillions and my own saucy rogue were, of course, disinterested actors in the comedy; they rode for the mere sport, keeping in a body, their mouths full of laughter, waving their hats as they came on, and crying (as the fancy struck them) 'Tally-ho!' 'Stop, thief!' 'A highwayman! A highwayman!' It was otherguess work with Bellamy. That gentleman no sooner observed our change of direction than he turned his horse with so much violence that the poor animal was almost cast upon its side, and launched her in immediate and desperate pursuit. As he approached I saw that his face was deadly white and that he carried a drawn pistol in his hand. I turned at once to the poor little bride that was to have been, and now was not to be; she, upon her side, deserting the other window, turned as if to meet me.

'O, O, don't let him kill me!' she screamed.

'Never fear,' I replied.

Her face was distorted with terror. Her hands took hold upon me with the instinctive clutch of an infant. The chaise gave a flying lurch, which took the feet from under me and tumbled us anyhow upon the seat. And almost in the same moment the head of Bellamy appeared in the window which Missy had left free for him.

Conceive the situation! The little lady and I were falling— or had just fallen—backward on the seat, and offered to the eye a somewhat ambiguous picture. The chaise was speeding at a furious pace, and with the most violent leaps and lurches, along the highway. Into this bounding receptacle Bellamy interjected his head, his pistol arm, and his pistol; and since his own horse was travelling still faster than the chaise, he must withdraw all of them again in the inside of the fraction of a minute. He did so, but he left the charge of the pistol behind him—whether by design or accident I shall never know, and I dare say he has forgotten! Probably he had only meant to threaten, in hopes of causing us to arrest our flight. In the same moment came the explosion and a pitiful cry from Missy; and my gentleman, making certain he had struck her, went down the road pursued by the furies, turned at the first corner, took a flying leap over the thorn hedge, and disappeared across country in the least possible time.

Rowley was ready and eager to pursue; but I withheld him, thinking we were excellently quit of Mr. Bellamy, at no more cost than a scratch on the forearm and a bullet-hole in the left-hand claret-coloured panel. And accordingly, but now at a more decent pace, we proceeded on our way to Archdeacon Clitheroe's. Missy's gratitude and admiration were aroused to a high pitch by this dramatic scene, and what she was pleased to call my wound. She must dress it for me with her handkerchief, a service which she rendered me even with tears. I could well have spared them, not loving on the whole to be made ridiculous, and the injury being in the nature of a cat's scratch. Indeed, I would have suggested for her kind care rather the cure of my coat-sleeve, which had suffered worse in the encounter; but I was too wise to risk the anti-climax. That she had been rescued by a hero, that the hero should have been wounded in the affray, and his wound bandaged with her handkerchief (which it could not even bloody), ministered incredibly to the recovery of her self-respect; and I could hear her relate the incident to 'the young ladies, my school-companions,' in the most approved manner of Mrs. Radcliffe! To have insisted on the torn coat-sleeve would have been unmannerly, if not inhuman.

Presently the residence of the archdeacon began to heave in sight. A chaise and four smoking horses stood by the steps, and made way for us on our approach; and even as we alighted there appeared from the interior of the house a tall ecclesiastic, and beside him a little, headstrong, ruddy man, in a towering passion, and brandishing over his head a roll of paper. At sight of him Miss Dorothy flung herself on her knees with the most moving adjurations, calling him father, assuring him she was wholly cured and entirely repentant of her disobedience, and entreating forgiveness; and I soon saw that she need fear no great severity from Mr. Greensleeves, who showed himself extra-ordinarily fond, loud, greedy of caresses and prodigal of tears.

To give myself a countenance, as well as to have all ready for the road when I should find occasion, I turned to quit scores with Bellamy's two postillions. They had not the least claim on me, but one of which they were quite ignorant—that I was a fugitive. It is the worst feature of that false position that every gratuity becomes a case of conscience. You must not leave behind you any one discontented nor any one grateful. But the whole business had been such a 'hurrah-boys' from the beginning, and had gone off in the fifth act so like a melodrama, in explosions, reconciliations, and the rape of a post-horse, that it was plainly impossible to keep it covered. It was plain it would have to be talked over in all the inn-kitchens for thirty miles about, and likely for six months to come. It only re-mained for me, therefore, to settle on that gratuity which should be least conspicuous—so large that nobody could grumble, so small that nobody would be tempted to boast. My decision was hastily and not wisely taken. The one fellow spat on his tip (so he called it) for luck; the other developing a sudden streak of piety, prayed God bless me with fervour.

It seemed a demonstration was brewing, and I determined to be off at once. Bidding my own post-boy and Rowley be in readiness for an immediate start, I reascended the terrace and presented myself, hat in hand, before Mr. Greensleeves and the archdeacon.

'You will excuse me, I trust,' said I. 'I think shame to interrupt this agreeable scene of family effusion, which I have been privileged in some small degree to bring about.'

And at these words the storm broke.

'Small degree! small degree, sir!' cries the father; 'that shall not pass, Mr. St. Eaves! If I've got my darling back, and none the worse for that vagabone rascal, I know whom I have to thank. Shake hands with me—up to the elbows, sir! A Frenchman you may be, but you're one of the right breed, by God! And, by God, sir, you may have anything you care to ask of me, down to Dolly's hand, by God!'

All this he roared out in a voice surprisingly powerful from so small a person. Every word was thus audible to the servants, who had followed them out of the house and now congregated about us on the terrace, as well as to Rowley and the five postillions on the gravel sweep below. The sentiments expressed were popular; some ass, whom the devil moved to be my enemy, proposed three cheers, and they were given with a will. To hear my own name resounding amid acclamations in the hills of Westmorland was flattering, perhaps; but it was inconvenient at a moment when (as I was morally persuaded) police handbills were already speeding after me at the rate of a hundred miles a day.

Nor was that the end of it. The archdeacon must present his compliments, and pressed upon me some of his West India sherry, and I was carried into a vastly fine library, where I was presented to his lady wife. While we were at sherry in the library, ale was handed round upon the terrace. Speeches were made, hands were shaken, Missy (at her father's request) kissed me farewell, and the whole party reaccompanied me to the terrace, where they stood waving hats and handkerchiefs, and crying farewells to all the echoes of the mountains until the chaise had disappeared.

The echoes of the mountains were engaged in saying to me privately: 'You fool, you have done it now!'

'They do seem to have got 'old of your name, Mr. Anne,' said Rowley. 'It weren't my fault this time.'

'It was one of those accidents that can never be foreseen,' said I, affecting a dignity that I was far from feeling. 'Some one recognised me.'

'Which on 'em, Mr. Anne?' said the rascal.

'That is a senseless question; it can make no difference who it was,' I returned.

'No, nor that it can't!' cried Rowley. 'I say, Mr. Anne, sir, it's what you would call a jolly mess, ain't it? looks like "clean bowled-out in the middle stump," don't it?'

'I fail to understand you, Rowley.'

'Well, what I mean is, what are we to do about this one?' pointing to the postillion in front of us, as he alternately hid and revealed his patched breeches to the trot of his horse. 'He see you get in this morning under Mr. Ramornie—I was very piticular to *Mr. Ramornie* you, if you remember, sir—and he see you get in again under Mr. Saint Eaves, and whatever's he going to see you get out under? that's what worries me, sir. It don't seem to me like as if the position was what you call *stratetegic*!'

'*Parrrbleu*! will you let me be!' I cried. 'I have to think; you cannot imagine how your constant idiotic prattle annoys me.'

'Beg pardon, Mr. Anne,' said he; and the next moment, 'You wouldn't like for us to do our French now, would you, Mr. Anne?'

'Certainly not,' said I. 'Play upon your flageolet.'

The which he did with what seemed to me to be irony.

Conscience doth make cowards of us all! I was so downcast by my pitiful mismanagement of the morning's business that I shrank from the eye of my own hired infant, and read offensive meanings into his idle tootling.

I took off my coat, and set to mending it, soldier-fashion, with a needle and thread. There is nothing more conducive to thought, above all in arduous circumstances; and as I sewed, I gradually gained a clearness upon my affairs. I must be done with the claret-coloured chaise at once. It should be sold at the next stage for what it would bring. Rowley and I must take back to the road on our four feet, and after a decent interval of trudging, get places on some coach for Edinburgh again under new names! So much trouble and toil, so much extra risk and expense and loss of time, and all for a slip of the tongue to a little lady in blue!

CHAPTER XXIV

THE INN-KEEPER OF KIRKBY-LONSDALE

I HAD hitherto conceived and partly carried out an ideal that was dear to my heart. Rowley and I descended from our claret-coloured chaise, a couple of correctly dressed, brisk, bright-eyed young fellows, like a pair of aristocratic mice; attending singly to our own affairs, communicating solely with each other, and that with the niceties and civilities of drill. We would pass through the little crowd before the door with high-bred preoccupation, inoffensively haughty, after the best English pattern; and disappear within, followed by the envy and admiration of the bystanders, a model master and servant, point-device in every part. It was a heavy thought to me, as we drew up before the inn at Kirkby-Lonsdale, that this scene was now to be enacted for the last time. Alas! and had I known it, it was to go off with so inferior a grace!

I had been injudiciously liberal to the post-boys of the chaise and four. My own post-boy, he of the patched breeches, now stood before me, his eyes glittering with greed, his hand advanced. It was plain he anticipated something extraordinary by way of a *pourboire*; and considering the marches and counter-marches by which I had extended the stage, the military character of our affairs with Mr. Bellamy, and the bad example I had set before him at the archdeacon's, something exceptional was certainly to be done. But these are always nice questions, to a foreigner above all: a shade too little will suggest niggardliness, a shilling too much smells of hush-money. Fresh from the scene at the archdeacon's, and flushed by the idea that I was now nearly done with the responsibilities of the claret-coloured chaise, I put into his hands five guineas; and the amount served only to waken his cupidity.

'O, come, sir, you ain't going to fob me off with this? Why, I seen fire at your side!' he cried.

It would never do to give him more; I felt I should become the fable of Kirkby-Lonsdale if I did; and I looked him in the face, sternly but still smiling, and addressed him with a voice of uncompromising firmness.

'If you do not like it, give it back,' said I.

He pocketed the guineas with the quickness of a conjurer, and, like a base-born cockney as he was, fell instantly to casting dirt.

''Ave your own way of it, Mr. Ramornie—leastways Mr. St. Eaves, or whatever your blessed name may be. Look 'ere'— turning for sympathy to the stable-boys—'this is a blessed business. Blessed 'ard, I calls it. 'Ere I takes up a blessed son of a pop-gun what calls hisself anything you care to mention, and turns out to be a blessed *mounseer* at the end of it! 'Ere 'ave I been drivin' of him up and down all day, a-carrying off of gals, a-shootin' of pistyils, and a-drinkin' of sherry and hale; and wot does he up and give me but a blank, blank, blanketing blank!'

The fellow's language had become too powerful for repro- duction, and I passed it by.

Meanwhile I observed Rowley fretting visibly at the bit; another moment, and he would have added a last touch of the ridiculous to our arrival by coming to his hands with the postillion.

'Rowley!' cried I reprovingly.

Strictly it should have been Gammon; but in the hurry of the moment, my fault (I can only hope) passed unperceived. At the same time I caught the eye of the postmaster. He was long and lean, and brown and bilious; he had the drooping nose of the humourist, and the quick attention of a man of parts. He read my embarrassment in a glance, stepped in- stantly forward, sent the post-boy to the rightabout with half a word, and was back next moment at my side.

'Dinner in a private room, sir? Very well. John, No. 4! What wine would you care to mention? Very well, sir. Will you please to order fresh horses? Not, sir? Very well.'

Each of these expressions was accompanied by something in the nature of a bow, and all were prefaced by something in the nature of a smile, which I could very well have done without. The man's politeness was from the teeth outwards; behind and within, I was conscious of a perpetual scrutiny: the scene at his doorstep, the random confidences of the post-boy, had not been thrown away on this observer; and it was under a strong fear of coming trouble that I was shown at last into my private room. I was in half a mind to have put off the whole business. But the truth is, now my name had got abroad, my fear of the mail that was coming, and the handbills it should contain, had waxed inordinately, and I felt I could never eat a meal in peace till I had severed my connection with the claret-coloured chaise.

Accordingly, as soon as I had done with dinner, I sent my compliments to the landlord and requested he should take a glass of wine with me. He came; we exchanged the necessary civilities, and presently I approached my business.

'By the bye,' said I, 'we had a brush down the road to-day. I dare say you may have heard of it?'

He nodded.

'And I was so unlucky as to get a pistol ball in the panel of my chaise,' I continued, 'which makes it simply useless to me. Do you know any one likely to buy?'

'I can well understand that,' said the landlord, 'I was looking at it just now; it's as good as ruined, is that chaise. General rule, people don't like chaises with bullet-holes.'

'Too much *Romance of the Forest*?' I suggested, recalling my little friend of the morning, and what I was sure had been her favourite reading—Mrs. Radcliffe's novels.

'Just so,' said he. 'They may be right, they may be wrong; I'm not the judge. But I suppose it's natural, after all, for respectable people to like things respectable about them; not bullet-holes, nor puddles of blood, nor men with aliases.'

I took a glass of wine and held it up to the light to show that my hand was steady.

'Yes,' said I, 'I suppose so.'

'You have papers, of course, showing you are the proper owner?' he inquired.

'There is the bill, stamped and receipted,' said I, tossing it across to him.

He looked at it.

'This all you have?' he asked.

'It is enough, at least,' said I. 'It shows you where I bought and what I paid for it.'

'Well, I don't know,' he said. 'You want some paper of identification.'

'To identify the chaise?' I inquired.

'Not at all: to identify *you*,' said he.

'My good sir, remember yourself!' said I. 'The title-deeds of my estate are in that despatch-box; but you do not seriously suppose that I should allow you to examine them?'

'Well, you see, this paper proves that some Mr. Ramornie paid seventy guineas for a chaise,' said the fellow. 'That's all well and good; but who's to prove to me that you are Mr. Ramornie?'

'Fellow!' cried I.

'O, fellow as much as you please!' said he. 'Fellow, with all my heart! That changes nothing. I am fellow, of course —obtrusive fellow, impudent fellow, if you like—but who are you? I hear of you with two names; I hear of you running away with young ladies, and getting cheered for a Frenchman, which seems odd; and one thing I will go bail for, that you were in a blue fright when the post-boy began to tell tales at my door. In short, sir, you may be a very good gentleman; but I don't know enough about you, and I'll trouble you for your papers, or to go before a magistrate. Take your choice; if I'm not fine enough, I hope the magistrates are.'

'My good man,' I stammered, for though I had found my voice, I could scarce be said to have recovered my wits, 'this is most unusual, most rude. Is it the custom in Westmorland that gentlemen should be insulted?'

'That depends,' said he. 'When it's suspected that gentlemen are spies it *is* the custom; and a good custom, too. No, no,' he broke out, perceiving me to make a movement. 'Both hands upon the table, my gentleman! I want no pistol balls in my chaise panels.'

'Surely, sir, you do me strange injustice!' said I, now the master of myself. 'You see me sitting here, a monument of tranquillity: pray may I help myself to wine without umbraging you?'

I took this attitude in sheer despair. I had no plan, no hope. The best I could imagine was to spin the business out some minutes longer, then capitulate. At least, I would not capitulate one moment too soon.

'Am I to take that for *no*?' he asked.

'Referring to your former obliging proposal?' said I. 'My good sir, you are to take it, as you say, for "No." Certainly I will not show you my deeds; certainly I will not rise from table and trundle out to see your magistrates. I have too much respect for my digestion, and too little curiosity in justices of the peace.'

He leaned forward, looked me nearly in the face, and reached out one hand to the bell-rope. 'See here, my fine fellow!' said he. 'Do you see that bell-rope? Let me tell you, there's a boy waiting below: one jingle, and he goes to fetch the constable.'

'Do you tell me so?' said I. 'Well, there's no accounting for tastes! I have a prejudice against the society of constables, but if it is your fancy to have one in for the dessert——' I shrugged my shoulders lightly. 'Really, you know,' I added, 'this is vastly entertaining. I assure you, I am looking on, with all the interest of a man of the world, at the development of your highly original character.'

He continued to study my face without speech, his hand still on the button of the bell-rope, his eyes in mine; this was the decisive heat. My face seemed to myself to dislimn under his gaze, my expression to change, the smile (with which I had begun) to degenerate into the grin of the man upon the rack. I was besides harassed with doubts. An innocent man, I argued, would have resented the fellow's impudence an hour ago; and by my continued endurance of the ordeal, I was simply signing and sealing my confession; in short, I had reached the end of my powers.

'Have you any objection to my putting my hands in my breeches pockets?' I inquired. 'Excuse me mentioning it, but you showed yourself so extremely nervous a moment back.'

My voice was not all I could have wished, but it sufficed. I could hear it tremble, but the landlord apparently could not. He turned away and drew a long breath, and you may be sure I was quick to follow his example.

'You're a cool hand at least, and that's the sort I like,' said he. 'Be you what you please, I'll deal square. I'll take the chaise for a hundred pound down, and throw the dinner in.'

'I beg your pardon,' I cried, wholly mystified by this form of words.

'You pay me a hundred down,' he repeated, 'and I'll take the chaise. It's very little more than it cost,' he added, with a grin, 'and you know you must get it off your hands somehow.'

I do not know when I have been better entertained than by this impudent proposal. It was broadly funny, and I suppose the least tempting offer in the world. For all that, it came very welcome, for it gave me the occasion to laugh. This I did with the most complete abandonment, till the tears ran down my cheeks; and ever and again, as the fit abated, I would get another view of the landlord's face, and go off into another paroxysm.

'You droll creature, you will be the death of me yet!' I cried, drying my eyes.

My friend was now wholly disconcerted; he knew not where to look, nor yet what to say; and began for the first time to conceive it possible he was mistaken.

'You seem rather to enjoy a laugh, sir,' said he.

'O, yes! I am quite an original,' I replied, and laughed again.

Presently, in a changed voice, he offered me twenty pounds for the chaise; I ran him up to twenty-five, and closed with the offer: indeed, I was glad to get anything; and if I haggled, it was not in the desire of gain, but with the view at any price of securing a safe retreat. For, although hostilities were suspended, he was yet far from satisfied ; and I could read his continued suspicions in the cloudy eye that still hovered about my face. At last they took shape in words.

'This is all very well,' says he : 'you carry it off well ; but for all that, I must do my duty.'

I had my strong effect in reserve ; it was to burn my ships with a vengeance! I rose. 'Leave the room,' said I. 'This is insufferable. Is the man mad ?' And then, as if already half-ashamed of my passion : 'I can take a joke as well as any one,' I added ; 'but this passes measure. Send my servant and the bill.'

When he had left me alone, I considered my own valour with amazement. I had insulted him ; I had sent him away alone ; now, if ever, he would take what was the only sensible resource, and fetch the constable. But there was something instinctively treacherous about the man which shrank from plain courses. And, with all his cleverness, he missed the occasion of fame. Rowley and I were suffered to walk out of his door, with all our baggage, on foot, with no destination named, except in the vague statement that we were come 'to view the lakes'; and my friend only watched our departure with his chin in his hand, still moodily irresolute.

I think this one of my great successes. I was exposed, unmasked, summoned to do a perfectly natural act, which must prove my doom and which I had not the slightest pretext for refusing. I kept my head, stuck to my guns, and, against all likelihood, here I was once more at liberty and in the king's highway. This was a strong lesson never to despair ; and, at the same time, how many hints to be cautious! and what a perplexed and dubious business the whole question of my escape now appeared ! That I should have risked perishing upon a trumpery question of a *pourboire*, depicted in lively colours the perils that perpetually surrounded us. Though, to be sure, the initial mistake had been committed before that ; and if I had not suffered myself to be drawn a little deep in confidences to the innocent Dolly, there need have been no tumble at the inn of Kirkby-Lonsdale. I took the lesson to heart, and promised myself in the future to be more reserved. It was none of my business to attend to broken chaises or shipwrecked travellers. I had my hands full of my own affairs ; and my best defence would be a little more natural selfishness and a trifle less imbecile good-nature.

CHAPTER XXV

I PASS over the next fifty or sixty leagues of our journey without comment. The reader must be growing weary of scenes of travel; and for my own part I have no cause to recall these particular miles with any pleasure. We were mainly occupied with attempts to obliterate our trail, which (as the result showed) were far from successful; for, on my cousin following, he was able to run me home with the least possible loss of time, following the claret-coloured chaise to Kirkby-Lonsdale, where I think the landlord must have wept to learn what he had missed, and tracing us thereafter to the doors of the coach-office in Edinburgh without a single check. Fortune did not favour me, and why should I recapitulate the details of futile precautions which deceived nobody, and wearisome arts which proved to be artless?

The day was drawing to an end when Mr. Rowley and I bowled into Edinburgh to the stirring sound of the guard's bugle and the clattering team. I was here upon my field of battle; on the scene of my former captivity, escape and exploits; and in the same city with my love. My heart expanded; I have rarely felt more of a hero. All down the Bridges I sat by the driver with my arms folded and my face set, unflinchingly meeting every eye, and prepared every moment for a cry of recognition. Hundreds of the population were in the habit of visiting the Castle, where it was my practice (before the days of Flora) to make myself conspicuous among the prisoners; and I think it an extraordinary thing that I should have encountered so few to recognise me. But doubtless a clean chin is a disguise in itself; and the change is great from a suit of sulphur-yellow to fine linen, a well-fitting mouse-coloured great-coat furred in black, a pair of tight trousers of fashionable cut, and a hat of inimitable curl. After all, it was more likely that I should have recognised our visitors, than that they should have identified the modish gentleman with the miserable prisoner in the Castle.

I was glad to set foot on the flagstones, and to escape from the crowd that had assembled to receive the mail. Here we were, with but little daylight before us, and that on Saturday afternoon, the eve of the famous Scottish Sabbath, adrift in the New Town of Edinburgh, and overladen with baggage. We carried it ourselves. I would not take a cab, nor so much as hire a porter, who might afterwards serve as a link between my lodgings and the mail, and connect me again with the claret-coloured chaise and Aylesbury. For I was resolved to break the chain of evidence for good, and to begin life afresh (so far as regards caution) with a new character. The first step was to find lodgings, and to find them quickly. This was the more needful as Mr. Rowley and I, in our smart clothes and with our cumbrous burthen, made a noticeable appearance in the streets at that time of the day and in that quarter of the town, which was largely given up to fine folk, bucks and dandies and young ladies, or respectable professional men on their way home to dinner.

On the north side of St. James' Square I was so happy as to spy a bill in a third-floor window. I was equally indifferent to cost and convenience in my choice of a lodging—'any port in a storm' was the principle on which I was prepared to act; and Rowley and I made at once for the common entrance and scaled the stair.

We were admitted by a very sour-looking female in bombazine. I gathered she had all her life been depressed by a series of bereavements, the last of which might very well have befallen her the day before; and I instinctively lowered my voice when I addressed her. She admitted she had rooms to let—even showed them to us—a sitting-room and bedroom in a *suite*, commanding a fine prospect to the Firth and Fifeshire, and in themselves well proportioned and comfortably furnished, with pictures on the wall, shells on the mantelpiece, and several books upon the table which I found afterwards to be all of a devotional character, and all presentation copies, 'to my Christian friend,' or 'to my devout acquaintance in the Lord, Bethiah McRankine.' Beyond this my 'Christian friend' could not be made to advance: no, not even to do that which seemed the most natural and pleasing thing in the world— I mean to name her price—but stood before us shaking her head, and at times mourning like the dove, the picture of depression and defence. She had a voice the most querulous I have ever heard, and with this she produced a whole regiment of difficulties and criticisms.

She could not promise an attendance.

'Well, madam,' said I, 'and what is my servant for?'

'Him?' she asked. 'Be gude to us! Is *he* your servant?'

'I am sorry, ma'am, he meets with your disapproval.'

'Na, I never said that. But he's young. He'll be a great breaker, I'm thinkin'. Ay! he'll be a great responsibeelity to ye, like. Does he attend to his releegion?'

'Yes, m'm,' returned Rowley, with admirable promptitude, and, immediately closing his eyes, as if from habit, repeated the following distich with more celerity than fervour:—

> 'Matthew, Mark, Luke and John,
> Bless the bed that I lie on!'

'Nhm!' said the lady, and maintained an awful silence.

'Well, ma'am,' said I, 'it seems we are never to hear the beginning of your terms, let alone the end of them. Come—a good movement! and let us be either off or on.'

She opened her lips slowly. 'Ony raferences?' she inquired, in a voice like a bell.

I opened my pocket-book and showed her a handful of bank bills. 'I think, madam, that these are unexceptionable,' said I.

'Ye'll be wantin' breakfast late?' was her reply.

'Madam, we want breakfast at whatever hour it suits you to give it, from four in the morning till four in the afternoon!' I cried. 'Only tell us your figure, if your mouth be large enough to let it out!'

'I couldnae give ye supper the nicht,' came the echo.

'We shall go out to supper, you incorrigible female!' I vowed, between laughter and tears. 'Here—this is going to end! I want you for a landlady—let me tell you that!—and I am going to have my way. You won't tell me what you charge? Very well; I will do without! I can trust you! You don't seem to know when you have a good lodger; but I know perfectly when I have an honest landlady! Rowley, unstrap the valises!'

Will it be credited? The monomaniac fell to rating me for my indiscretion! But the battle was over; these were her last guns, and more in the nature of a salute than of renewed hostilities. And presently she condescended on very moderate terms, and Rowley and I were able to escape in quest of supper. Much time had, however, been lost; the sun was long down, the lamps glimmered along the streets, and the voice of a watchman already resounded in the neighbouring Leith Road. On our first arrival I had observed a place of entertainment not far off, in a street behind the Register House. Thither we found our way, and sat down to a late dinner alone. But we had scarce given our orders before the door opened, and a tall young fellow entered with something of a lurch, looked about him, and approached the same table.

'Give you good evening, most grave and reverend seniors!' said he. 'Will you permit a wanderer, a pilgrim—the pilgrim of love, in short—to come to temporary anchor under your lee? I care not who knows it, but I have a passionate aversion from the bestial practice of solitary feeding!'

'You are welcome, sir,' said I, 'if I may take upon me so far to play the host in a public place.'

He looked startled, and fixed a hazy eye on me, as he sat down.

'Sir,' said he, 'you are a man not without some tincture of letters, I perceive! What shall we drink, sir?'

I mentioned I had already called for a pot of porter.

'A modest pot—the seasonable quencher?' said he. 'Well, I do not know but what I could look at a modest pot myself! I am, for the moment, in precarious health. Much study hath heated my brain, much walking wearied my—well, it seems to be more my eyes!'

'You have walked far, I dare say?' I suggested.

'Not so much far as often,' he replied. 'There is in this city—to which, I think, you are a stranger? Sir, to your very good health and our better acquaintance!—there is, in this city of Dunedin, a certain implication of streets which reflects the utmost credit on the designer and the publicans—at every hundred yards is seated the Judicious Tavern, so that persons of contemplative mind are secure, at moderate distances, of refreshment. I have been doing a trot in that favoured quarter, favoured by art and nature. A few chosen comrades—enemies of publicity and friends to wit and wine—obliged me with their society. "Along the cool, sequestered vale of Register Street we kept the uneven tenor of our way," sir.'

'It struck me, as you came in——' I began.

'O, don't make any bones about it!' he interrupted. 'Of course it struck you! and let me tell you I was devilish lucky not to strike myself. When I entered this apartment I shone "with all the pomp and prodigality of brandy and water," as the poet Gray has in another place expressed it. Powerful bard, Gray! but a niminy-piminy creature, afraid of a petticoat and a bottle—not a man, sir, not a man! Excuse me for being so troublesome, but what the devil have I done with my fork? Thank you, I am sure. *Temulentia, quoad me ipsum, brevis colligo est.* I sit and eat, sir, in a London fog. I should bring a link-boy to table with me; and I would too, if the little brutes were only washed! I intend to found a Philanthropical Society for Washing the Deserving Poor and Shaving Soldiers. I am pleased to observe that, although not of an unmilitary bearing, you are apparently shaved. In my calendar of the virtues shaving comes next to drinking. A gentleman may be a low-minded ruffian without sixpence, but he will always be close shaved. See me, with the eye of fancy, in the chill hours of the morning, say about a quarter to twelve, noon—see me awake! First thing of all, without one thought of the plausible but unsatisfactory small beer, or the healthful though insipid soda-water, I take the deadly razor in my vacillating grasp; I proceed to skate upon the margin of eternity. Stimulating thought! I bleed, perhaps, but with medicable wounds. The stubble reaped, I pass out of my chamber, calm but triumphant. To employ a hackneyed phrase, I would not call Lord Wellington my uncle! I, too, have dared, perhaps bled, before the imminent deadly shaving-table.'

In this manner the bombastic fellow continued to entertain me all through dinner, and by a common error of drunkards, because he had been extremely talkative himself, leaped to the conclusion that he had chanced on very genial company. He told me his name, his address; he begged we should meet again; finally he proposed that I should dine with him in the country at an early date.

'The dinner is official,' he explained. 'The office-bearers and Senatus of the University of Cramond—an educational institution in which I have the honour to be Professor of Nonsense—meet to do honour to our friend Icarus, at the old-established *howff*, Cramond Bridge. One place is vacant, fascinating stranger,—I offer it to you!'

'And who is your friend Icarus?' I asked.

'The aspiring son of Dædalus!' said he. 'Is it possible that you have never heard the name of Byfield?'

'Possible and true,' said I.

'And is fame so small a thing?' cried he. 'Byfield, sir, is an aëronaut. He apes the fame of a Lunardi, and is on the point of offering to the inhabitants—I beg your pardon, to the nobility and gentry of our neighbourhood—the spectacle of an ascension. As one of the gentry concerned I may be permitted to remark that I am unmoved. I care not a Tinker's Damn for his ascension. No more—I breathe it in your ear—does anybody else. The business is stale, sir, stale. Lunardi did it, and overdid it. A whimsical, fiddling, vain fellow, by all accounts—for I was at that time rocking in my cradle. But once was enough. If Lunardi went up and came down, there was the matter settled.

We prefer to grant the point. We do not want to see the experiment repeated *ad nauseam* by Byfield, and Brown, and Butler, and Brodie, and Bottomley. Ah! if they would go up and *not* come down again! But this is by the question. The University of Cramond delights to honour merit in the man, sir, rather than utility in the profession; and Byfield, though an ignorant dog, is a sound reliable drinker, and really not amiss over his cups. Under the radiance of the kindly jar partiality might even credit him with wit.'

It will be seen afterwards that this was more my business than I thought it at the time. Indeed, I was impatient to be gone. Even as my friend maundered ahead a squall burst, the jaws of the rain were opened against the coffee-house windows, and at that inclement signal I remembered I was due elsewhere.

CHAPTER XXVI

THE COTTAGE AT NIGHT

At the door I was nearly blown back by the unbridled violence of the squall, and Rowley and I must shout our parting words. All the way along Princes Street (whither my way led) the wind hunted me behind and screamed in my ears. The city was flushed with bucketfuls of rain that tasted salt from the neighbouring ocean. It seemed to darken and lighten again in the vicissitudes of the gusts. Now you would say the lamps had been blown out from end to end of the long thoroughfare ; now, in a lull, they would revive, re-multiply, shine again on the wet pavements, and make darkness sparingly visible.

By the time I had got to the corner of the Lothian Road there was a distinct improvement. For one thing, I had now my shoulder to the wind ; for a second, I came in the lee of my old prison-house, the Castle ; and, at any rate, the excessive fury of the blast was itself moderating. The thought of what errand I was on re-awoke within me, and I seemed to breast the rough weather with increasing ease. With such a destination, what mattered a little buffeting of wind or a sprinkle of cold water ? I recalled Flora's image, I took her in fancy to my arms, and my heart throbbed. And the next moment I had recognised the inanity of that fool's paradise. If I could spy her taper as she went to bed, I might count myself lucky.

I had about two leagues before me of a road mostly uphill, and now deep in mire. So soon as I was clear of the last street lamp, darkness received me—a darkness only pointed by the lights of occasional rustic farms, where the dogs howled with uplifted heads as I went by. The wind continued to decline : it had been but a squall, not a tempest. The rain, on the other hand, settled into a steady deluge, which had soon drenched me thoroughly. I continued to tramp forward in the night, contending with gloomy thoughts and accompanied by the dismal ululation of the dogs. What ailed them that they should have been thus wakeful, and perceived the small sound of my steps amid the general reverberation of the rain, was more than I could fancy. I remembered tales with which I had been entertained in childhood. I told myself some murderer was going by, and the brutes perceived upon him the faint smell of blood ; and the next moment, with a physical shock, I had applied the words to my own case !

Here was a dismal disposition for a lover. ' Was ever lady in this humour wooed ?' I asked myself, and came near turning back. It is never wise to risk a critical interview when your spirits are depressed, your clothes muddy, and your hands wet ! But the boisterous night was in itself favourable to my enterprise : now, or perhaps never, I might find some way to have an interview with Flora ; and if I had one interview (wet clothes, low spirits and all), I told myself there would certainly be another.

Arrived in the cottage-garden I found the circumstances mighty inclement. From the round holes in the shutters of the parlour, shafts of candle-light streamed forth ; elsewhere the darkness was complete. The trees, the thickets, were saturated ; the lower parts of the garden turned into a morass. At intervals, when the wind broke forth again, there passed overhead a wild coil of clashing branches ; and between whiles the whole enclosure continuously and stridently resounded with the rain. I advanced close to the window and contrived to read the face of my watch. It was half-past seven ; they would not retire before ten, they might not before midnight, and the prospect was unpleasant. In a lull of the wind I could hear from the inside the voice of Flora reading aloud ; the words of course inaudible—only a flow of undecipherable speech, quiet, cordial, colourless, more intimate and winning, more eloquent of her personality, but not less beautiful than song. And the next moment the clamour of a fresh squall broke out about the cottage ; the voice was drowned in its bellowing, and I was glad to retreat from my dangerous post.

For three egregious hours I must now suffer the elements to do their worst upon me, and continue to hold my ground in patience. I recalled the least fortunate of my services in the field : being out-sentry of the pickets in weather no less vile, sometimes unsuppered and with nothing to look forward to by way of breakfast but musket-balls ; and they seemed light in comparison. So strangely are we built : so much more strong is the love of woman than the mere love of life.

At last my patience was rewarded. The light disappeared from the parlour and reappeared a moment after in the room above. I was pretty well informed for the enterprise that lay before me. I knew the lair of the dragon—that which was just illuminated. I knew the bower of my Rosamond, and how excellently it was placed on the ground-level, round the flank of the cottage and out of earshot of her formidable aunt. Nothing was left but to apply my knowledge. I was then at the bottom of the garden, whether I had gone (Heaven save the mark!) for warmth, that I might walk to and fro unheard and keep myself from perishing. The night had fallen still, the wind ceased; the noise of the rain had much lightened, if it had not stopped, and was succeeded by the dripping of the garden trees. In the midst of this lull, and as I was already drawing near to the cottage, I was startled by the sound of a window-sash screaming in its channels; and a step or two beyond I became aware of a gush of light upon the darkness. It fell from Flora's window, which she had flung open on the night, and where she now sat, roseate and pensive, in the shine of two candles falling from behind, her tresses deeply embowering and shading her; the suspended comb still in one hand, the other idly clinging to the iron stanchions with which the window was barred.

Keeping to the turf, and favoured by the darkness of the night and the patter of the rain which was now returning, though without wind, I approached until I could almost have touched her. It seemed a grossness of which I was incapable to break up her reverie by speech. I stood and drank her in with my eyes; how the light made a glory in her hair, and (what I have always thought the most ravishing thing in nature) how the planes ran into each other, and were distinguished, and how the hues blended and varied, and were shaded off, between the cheek and neck. At first I was abashed: she wore her beauty like an immediate halo of refinement; she discouraged me like an angel, or what I suspect to be the next most discouraging, a modern lady. But as I continued to gaze, hope and life returned to me; I forgot my timidity, I forgot the sickening pack of wet clothes with which I stood burdened, I tingled with new blood.

Still unconscious of my presence, still gazing before her upon the illuminated image of the window, the straight shadows of the bars, the glinting of pebbles on the path, and the impenetrable night on the garden and the hills beyond it, she heaved a deep breath that struck upon my heart like an appeal.

'Why does Miss Gilchrist sigh?' I whispered. 'Does she recall absent friends?'

She turned her head swiftly in my direction; it was the only sign of surprise she deigned to make. At the same time I stepped into the light and bowed profoundly.

'You!' she said. 'Here?'

'Yes, I am here,' I replied. 'I have come very far, it may be a hundred and fifty leagues, to see you. I have waited all this night in your garden. Will Miss Gilchrist not offer her hand—to a friend in trouble?'

She extended it between the bars, and I dropped upon one knee on the wet path and kissed it twice. At the second it was withdrawn suddenly, methought with more of a start than she had hitherto displayed. I regained my former attitude, and we were both silent awhile. My timidity returned on me tenfold. I looked in her face for any signals of anger, and seeing her eyes to waver and fall aside from mine, augured that all was well.

'You must have been mad to come here!' she broke out. 'Of all places under heaven this is no place for you to come. And I was just thinking you were safe in France!'

'You were thinking of me!' I cried.

'Mr. St. Ives, you cannot understand your danger,' she replied. 'I am sure of it, and yet I cannot find it in my heart to tell you. O, be persuaded, and go!'

'I believe I know the worst. But I was never one to set an undue value on life, the life that we share with beasts. My university has been in the wars, not a famous place of education, but one where a man learns to carry his life in his hand as lightly as a glove, and for his lady or his honour to lay it as lightly down. You appeal to my fears, and you do wrong. I have come to Scotland with my eyes quite open to see you and to speak with you—it may be for the last time. With my eyes quite open, I say; and if I did not hesitate at the beginning do you think that I would draw back now?'

'You do not know!' she cried, with rising agitation. 'This country, even this garden, is death to you. They all believe it I am the only one that does not. If they hear you now, if they heard a whisper—I dread to think of it. O, go, go this instant. It is my prayer.'

'Dear lady, do not refuse me what I have come so far to seek; and remember that out of all the millions in England there is no other but yourself in whom I can dare confide. I have all the world against me; you are my only ally; and as I have to speak, you have to listen. All is true that they say of me, and all of it false at the same time. I did kill this man Goguelat—it was that you meant?'

She mutely signed to me that it was; she had become deadly pale.

'But I killed him in fair fight. Till then, I had never taken a life unless in battle, which is my trade. But I was grateful, I was on fire with gratitude, to one who had been good to me, who had been better to me than I could have dreamed of an angel, who had come into the darkness of my prison like sunrise. The man Goguelat insulted her. O, he had insulted *me* often, it was his favourite pastime, and he might insult me as he pleased—for who was I? But with that lady it was different. I could never forgive myself if I had let it pass. And we fought, and he fell, and I have no remorse.'

I waited anxiously for some reply. The worst was now out, and I knew that she had heard of it before; but it was impossible for me to go on with my narrative without some shadow of encouragement.

'You blame me?'

'No, not at all. It is a point I cannot speak on—I am only a girl. I am sure you were in the right: I have always said so —to Ronald. Not, of course, to my aunt. I am afraid I let her speak as she will. You must not think me a disloyal friend; and even with the Major—I did not tell you he had become quite a friend of ours—Major Chevenix, I mean—he has taken such a fancy to Ronald! It was he that brought the news to us of that hateful Clausel being captured, and all that he was saying. I was indignant with him. I said—I dare say I said too much—and I must say he was very good-natured. He said, " You and I, who are his friends, *know* that Champdivers is innocent. But what is the use of saying it?" All this was in the corner of the room, in what they call an aside. And then he said, " Give me a chance to speak to you in private, I have much to tell you." And he did. And told me just what you did—that it was an affair of honour, and no blame attached to you. O, I must say I like that Major Chevenix!'

At this I was seized with a great pang of jealousy. I remembered the first time that he had seen her, the interest that he seemed immediately to conceive; and I could not but admire the dog for the use he had been ingenious enough to make of our acquaintance in order to supplant me. All is fair in love and war. For all that, I was now no less anxious to do the speaking myself than I had been before to hear Flora. At least, I could keep clear of the hateful image of Major Chevenix. Accordingly I burst at once on the narrative of my adventures. It was the same as you have read, but briefer, and told with a very different purpose. Now every incident had a particular bearing, every by-way branched off to Rome—and that was Flora.

When I had begun to speak I had kneeled upon the gravel

withoutside the low window, rested my arms upon the sill, and lowered my voice to the most confidential whisper. Flora herself must kneel upon the other side, and this brought our heads upon a level with only the bars between us. So placed, so separated, it seemed that our proximity, and the continuous and low sounds of my pleading voice, worked progressively and powerfully on her heart, and perhaps not less so on my own. For these spells are double-edged. The silly birds may be charmed with the pipe of the fowler, which is but a tube of reeds. Not so with a bird of our own feather! As I went on, and my resolve strengthened, and my voice found new modulations, and our faces were drawn closer to the bars and to each other, not only she, but I, succumbed to the fascination, and were kindled by the charm. We make love, and thereby ourselves fall the deeper in it. It is with the heart only that one captures a heart.

'And now,' I continued, 'I will tell you what you can still do for me. I run a little risk just now, and you see for yourself how unavoidable it is for any man of honour. But if—but in case of the worst I do not choose to enrich either my enemies or the Prince Regent. I have here the bulk of what my uncle gave me. Eight thousand odd pounds. Will you take care of it for me? Do not think of it merely as money; take and keep it as a relic of your friend or some precious piece of him. I may have bitter need of it ere long. Do you know the old country story of the giant who gave his heart to his wife to keep for him, thinking it safer to repose on her loyalty than his own strength? Flora, I am the giant—a very little one: will you be the keeper of my life? It is my heart I offer you in this symbol. In the sight of God, if you will have it, I give you my name, I endow you with my money. If the worst come, if I may never hope to call you wife, let me at least think that you will use my uncle's legacy as my widow.'

'No, not that,' she said. 'Never that.'

'What then?' I said. 'What else, my angel? What are words to me? There is but one name that I care to know you by. Flora, my love!'

'Anne!' she said.

What sound is so full of music as one's own name uttered for the first time in the voice of her we love!

'My darling!' said I.

The jealous bars, set at the top and bottom in stone and lime, obstructed the rapture of the moment; but I took her to myself as wholly as they allowed. She did not shun my lips.

My arms were wound round her body, which yielded itself
generously to my embrace.   As we so remained, entwined and
yet severed, bruising our faces unconsciously on the cold bars,
the irony of the universe—or as I prefer to say, envy of some
of the gods—again stirred up the elements of that stormy night.
The wind blew again in the tree-tops ; a volley of cold sea-rain
deluged the garden, and, as the deuce would have it, a gutter
which had been hitherto choked up began suddenly to play
upon my head and shoulders with the vivacity of a fountain.
We parted with a shock ; I sprang to my feet, and she to hers,
as though we had been discovered.   A moment after, but now
both standing, we had again approached the window on either
side.

'Flora,' I said, 'this is but a poor offer I can make you.'

She took my hand in hers and clasped it to her bosom.

'Rich enough for a queen!' she said, with a lift in her
breathing that was more eloquent than words.   'Anne, my
brave Anne ! I would be glad to be your maidservant; I could
envy that boy Rowley.   But, no !' she broke off, 'I envy no
one—I need not—I am yours.'

'Mine,' said I, 'for ever !   By this and this, mine !'

'All of me,' she repeated.   'Altogether, and for ever !'

And if the god were envious, he must have seen with mortification how little he could do to mar the happiness of
mortals.   I stood in a mere waterspout ; she herself was wet,
not from my embrace only, but from the splashing of the
storm.   The candles had guttered out ; we were in darkness.
I could scarce see anything but the shining of her eyes in the
dark room.   To her I must have appeared as a silhouette,
haloed by rain and the spouting of the ancient Gothic gutter
above my head.

Presently we became more calm and confidential ; and when
that squall, which proved to be the last of the storm, had blown
by, fell into a talk of ways and means.   It seemed she knew
Mr. Robbie, to whom I had been so slenderly accredited by
Romaine—was even invited to his house for the evening of
Monday, and gave me a sketch of the old gentleman's character,
which implied a great deal of penetration in herself, and proved
of great use to me in the immediate sequel.   It seemed he
was an enthusiastic antiquary, and in particular a fanatic of
heraldry.   I heard it with delight, for I was myself, thanks to
M. de Culemberg, fairly grounded in that science, and
acquainted with the blazons of most families of note in Europe.
And I had made up my mind—even as she spoke, it was my
fixed determination, though I was a hundred miles from saying

it—to meet Flora on Monday night as a fellow-guest in Mr. Robbie's house.

I gave her my money—it was, of course, only paper I had brought. I gave it her, to be her marriage-portion, I declared.

' Not so bad a marriage-portion for a private soldier,' I told her, laughing, as I passed it through the bars.

' O, Anne, and where am I to keep it?' she cried. ' If my aunt should find it! What would I say!'

' Next your heart,' I suggested.

' Then you will always be near your treasure,' she cried, ' for you are always there!'

We were interrupted by a sudden clearness that fell upon the night. The clouds dispersed; the stars shone in every part of the heavens; and, consulting my watch, I was startled to find it already hard on five in the morning.

CHAPTER XXVII

THE SABBATH DAY

IT was indeed high time I should be gone from Swanston; but what I was to do in the meanwhile was another question. Rowley had received his orders last night: he was to say that I had met a friend, and Mrs. McRankine was not to expect me before morning. A good enough tale in itself; but the dreadful pickle I was in made it out of the question. I could not go home till I had found harbourage, a fire to dry my clothes at, and a bed where I might lie till they were ready.

Fortune favoured me again. I had scarce got to the top of the first hill when I spied a light on my left, about a furlong away. It might be a case of sickness; what else it was likely to be—in so rustic a neighbourhood, and at such an ungodly time of the morning—was beyond my fancy. A faint sound of singing became audible, and gradually swelled as I drew near, until at last I could make out the words, which were singularly appropriate both to the hour and to the condition of the singers. 'The cock may craw, the day may daw,' they sang; and sang it with such laxity both in time and tune, and such sentimental complaisance in the expression, as assured me they had got far into the third bottle at least.

I found a plain rustic cottage by the wayside, of the sort called double, with a signboard over the door; and, the lights within streaming forth and somewhat mitigating the darkness of the morning, I was enabled to decipher the inscription: 'The Hunters' Tryst, by Alexander Hendry. Porter, Ales, and British Spirits. Beds.'

My first knock put a period to the music, and a voice challenged tipsily from within.

'Who goes there?' it said; and I replied, 'A lawful traveller.'

Immediately after, the door was unbarred by a company of the tallest lads my eyes had ever rested on, all astonishingly drunk and very decently dressed, and one (who was perhaps the drunkest of the lot) carrying a tallow candle, from which he impartially bedewed the clothes of the whole company. As soon as I saw them I could not help smiling to myself to remember the anxiety with which I had approached. They received me and my hastily-concocted story, that I had been walking from Peebles and had lost my way, with incoherent benignity; jostled me among them into the room where they had been sitting, a plain hedgerow alehouse parlour, with a roaring fire in the chimney and a prodigious number of empty bottles on the floor; and informed me that I was made, by this reception, a temporary member of the *Six-Feet-High Club,* an athletic society of young men in a good station, who made of the Hunters' Tryst a frequent resort. They told me I had intruded on an 'all-night sitting,' following upon an 'all-day Saturday tramp' of forty miles; and that the members would all be up and 'as right as ninepence' for the noonday service at some neighbouring church—Collingwood, if memory serves me right. At this I could have laughed, but the moment seemed ill-chosen. For, though six feet was their standard, they all exceeded that measurement considerably; and I tasted again some of the sensations of childhood, as I looked up to all these lads from a lower plane, and wondered what they would do next. But the Six-Footers, if they were very drunk, proved no less kind. The landlord and servants of the Hunters' Tryst were in bed and asleep long ago. Whether by natural gift or acquired habit they could suffer pandemonium to reign all over the house, and yet lie ranked in the kitchen like Egyptian mummies, only that the sound of their snoring rose and fell ceaselessly like the drone of a bagpipe. Here the Six-Footers invaded them — in their citadel, so to speak; counted the bunks and the sleepers; proposed to put me in bed to one of the lasses, proposed to have one of the lasses out to make room for me, fell over chairs, and made noise enough to waken the dead: the whole illuminated by the same young torch-bearer, but now with two candles, and rapidly beginning to look like a man in a snowstorm. At last a bed was found for me, my clothes were hung out to dry before the parlour fire, and I was mercifully left to my repose.

I awoke about nine with the sun shining in my eyes. The landlord came at my summons, brought me my clothes dried and decently brushed, and gave me the good news that the Six-Feet-High Club were all abed and sleeping off their excesses. Where they were bestowed was a puzzle to me until (as I was strolling about the garden patch waiting for breakfast) I came on a barn door, and, looking in, saw all the red faces

mixed in the straw like plums in a cake.   Quoth the stalwart
maid who brought me my porridge and bade me 'eat them while
they were hot,' 'Ay, they were a' on the ran-dan last nicht!
Hout! they 're fine lads, and they 'll be nane the waur of it.
Forby Farbes's coat· I dinna see wha 's to get the creish off
that!' she added, with a sigh; in which, identifying Forbes as
the torch-bearer, I mentally joined.

It was a brave morning when I took the road; the sun shone,
spring seemed in the air, it smelt like April or May, and some
over-venturous birds sang in the coppices as I went by.   I had
plenty to think of, plenty to be grateful for, that gallant
morning; and yet I had a twitter at my heart.   To enter the
city by daylight might be compared to marching on a battery;
every face that I confronted would threaten me like the
muzzle of a gun; and it came into my head suddenly with how
much better a countenance I should be able to do it if I could
but improvise a companion.   Hard by Merchiston I was so
fortunate as to observe a bulky gentleman in broadcloth and
gaiters, stooping with his head almost between his knees, before
a stone wall.   Seizing occasion by the forelock, I drew up as I
came alongside and inquired what he had found to interest him.

He turned upon me a countenance not much less broad than
his back.

'Why, sir,' he replied, 'I was even marvelling at my own
indefeasible stupeedity: that I should walk this way every week
of my life, weather permitting, and should never before have
notticed that stone,' touching it at the same time with a goodly
oak staff.

I followed the indication.   The stone, which had been built
sideways into the wall, offered traces of heraldic sculpture.   At
once there came a wild idea into my mind: his appearance
tallied with Flora's description of Mr. Robbie; a knowledge of
heraldry would go far to clinch the proof; and what could be
more desirable than to scrape an informal acquaintance with the
man whom I must approach next day with my tale of the
drovers, and whom I yet wished to please?   I ·stooped in
turn.

'A chevron,' I said; 'on a chief three mullets?   Looks like
Douglas, does it not?'

'Yes, sir, it does; you are right,' said he: 'it *does* look like
Douglas; though, without the tinctures, and the whole thing
being so battered and broken up, who shall venture an opinion?
But allow me to be more personal, sir.   In these degenerate
days I am astonished you should display so much proficiency.'

'O, I was well grounded in my youth by an old gentleman, a

friend of my family, and I may say my guardian,' said I ; 'but I have forgotten it since. God forbid I should delude you into thinking me a herald, sir ! I am only an ungrammatical amateur.'

'And a little modesty does no harm even in a herald,' says my new acquaintance graciously.

In short, we fell together on our onward way, and maintained very amicable discourse along what remained of the country road, past the suburbs, and on into the streets of the New Town, which was as deserted and silent as a city of the dead. The shops were closed, no vehicle ran, cats sported in the midst of the sunny causeway ; and our steps and voices re-echoed from the quiet houses. It was the high-water, full and strange, of that weekly trance to which the city of Edinburgh is subjected : the apotheosis of the *Sawbath* ; and I confess the spectacle wanted not grandeur, however much it may have lacked cheerfulness. There are few religious ceremonies more imposing. As we thus walked and talked in a public seclusion the bells broke out ringing through all the bounds of the city, and the streets began immediately to be thronged with decent church-goers.

'Ah !' said my companion, 'there are the bells ! Now, sir, as you are a stranger I must offer you the hospitality of my pew. I do not know whether you are at all used with our Scottish form ; but in case you are not I will find your places for you ; and Dr. Henry Gray, of St. Mary's (under whom I sit), is as good a preacher as we have to show you.'

This put me in a quandary. It was a degree of risk I was scarce prepared for. Dozens of people, who might pass me by in the street with no more than a second look, would go on from the second to the third, and from that to a final recognition, if I were set before them, immobilised in a pew, during the whole time of service. An unlucky turn of the head would suffice to arrest their attention. 'Who is that ?' they would think : 'surely I should know him !' and, a church being the place in all the world where one has least to think of, it was ten to one they would end by remembering me before the benediction. However, my mind was made up : I thanked my obliging friend, and placed myself at his disposal.

Our way now led us into the north-east quarter of the town, among pleasant new faubourgs, to a decent new church of a good size, where I was soon seated by the side of my good Samaritan, and looked upon by a whole congregation of menacing faces. At first the possibility of danger kept me awake ; but by the time I had assured myself there was none to be apprehended, and the service was not in the least likely to be enlivened by the arrest of a French spy, I had to resign myself to the task of listening to Dr. Henry Gray.

As we moved out, after this ordeal was over, my friend was at once surrounded and claimed by his acquaintances of the congregation; and I was rejoiced to hear him addressed by the expected name of Robbie.

So soon as we were clear of the crowd—' Mr. Robbie ? ' said I, bowing.

' The very same, sir,' said he.

' If I mistake not, a lawyer ? '

' A writer to His Majesty's Signet, at your service.'

' It seems we were predestined to be acquaintances ! ' I exclaimed. ' I have here a card in my pocket intended for you. It is from my family lawyer. It was his last word, as I was leaving, to ask to be remembered kindly, and to trust you would pass over so informal an introduction.'

And I offered him the card.

' Ay, ay, my old friend Daniel ! ' says he, looking on the card. ' And how does my old friend Daniel ? '

I gave a favourable view of Mr. Romaine's health.

' Well, this is certainly a whimsical incident,' he continued. ' And since we are thus met already—and so much to my advantage !—the simplest thing will be to prosecute the acquaintance instantly. Let me propose a snack between sermons, a bottle of my particular green seal—and when nobody is looking we can talk blazons, Mr. Ducie ! '—which was the name I then used and had already incidentally mentioned, in the vain hope of provoking a return in kind.

' I beg your pardon, sir : do I understand you to invite me to your house ? ' said I.

' That was the idea I was trying to convey,' said he. ' We have the name of hospitable people up here, and I would like you to try mine.'

' Mr. Robbie, I shall hope to try it some day, but not yet,' I replied. ' I hope you will not misunderstand me. My business, which brings me to your city, is of a peculiar kind. Till you shall have heard it, and, indeed, till its issue is known, I should feel as if I had stolen your invitation.'

' Well, well,' said he, a little sobered, ' it must be as you wish, though you would hardly speak otherwise if you had committed homicide ! Mine is the loss. I must eat alone ; a very pernicious thing for a person of my habit of body, content myself with a pint of skinking claret, and meditate the discourse. But about this business of yours : if it is so particular as all that, it will doubtless admit of no delay.'

'I must confess, sir, it presses,' I acknowledged.

'Then, let us say to-morrow at half-past eight in the morning,' said he; 'and I hope, when your mind is at rest (and it does you much honour to take it as you do), that you will sit down with me to the postponed meal, not forgetting the bottle. You have my address?' he added, and gave it me—which was the only thing I wanted.

At last, at the level of York Place, we parted with mutual civilities, and I was free to pursue my way, through the mobs of people returning from church, to my lodgings in St. James' Square.

Almost at the house door whom should I overtake but my landlady in a dress of gorgeous severity, and dragging a prize in her wake : no less than Rowley, with the cockade in his hat, and a smart pair of tops to his boots! When I said he was in the lady's wake I spoke but in metaphor. As a matter of fact he was squiring her, with the utmost dignity, on his arm; and I followed them up the stairs, smiling to myself.

Both were quick to salute me as soon as I was perceived, and Mrs. McRankine inquired where I had been. I told her boastfully, giving her the name of the church and the divine, and ignorantly supposing I should have gained caste. But she soon opened my eyes. In the roots of the Scottish character there are knots and contortions that not only no stranger can understand, but no stranger can follow; he walks among explosives; and his best course is to throw himself upon their mercy—'Just as I am, without one plea,' a citation from one of the lady's favourite hymns.

The sound she made was unmistakable in meaning, though it was impossible to be written down ; and I at once executed the manœuvre I have recommended.

'You must remember I am a perfect stranger in your city,' said I. 'If I have done wrong, it was in mere ignorance, my dear lady ; and this afternoon, if you will be so good as to take me, I shall accompany *you*.'

But she was not to be pacified at the moment, and departed to her own quarters murmuring.

'Well, Rowley,' said I ; 'and have you been to church?'

'If you please, sir,' he said.

'Well, you have not been any less unlucky than I have,' I returned. 'And how did you get on with the Scottish form?'

'Well, sir, it was pretty 'ard, the form was, and reether narrow,' he replied. 'I don't know w'y it is, but it seems to me like as if things were a good bit changed since William Wallace! That was a main queer church she took me to, Mr. Anne! I don't know as I could have sat it out, if she 'adn't 'a' give me peppermints. She ain't a bad one at bottom, the old girl; she do pounce a bit, and she do worry, but, law bless you, Mr. Anne, it ain't nothink really—she don't *mean* it. W'y, she was down on me like a 'undredweight of bricks this morning. You see, last night she 'ad me in to supper, and, I beg your pardon, sir, but I took the freedom of playing her a chune or two. She didn't mind a bit; so this morning I began to play to myself, and she flounced in, and flew up, and carried on no end about Sunday!'

'You see, Rowley,' said I, 'they 're all mad up here, and you have to humour them. See and don't quarrel with Mrs. McRankine; and, above all, don't argue with her, or you 'll get the worst of it. Whatever she says, touch your forelock and say, "If you please!" or "I beg pardon, ma'am." And let me tell you one thing: I am sorry, but you have to go to church with her again this afternoon. That's duty, my boy!'

As I had foreseen, the bells had scarce begun before Mrs. McRankine presented herself to be our escort, upon which I sprang up with readiness and offered her my arm. Rowley followed behind. I was beginning to grow accustomed to the risks of my stay in Edinburgh, and it even amused me to confront a new churchful. I confess the amusement did not last until the end; for if Dr. Gray were long, Mr. McCraw was not only longer, but more incoherent, and the matter of his sermon (which was a direct attack, apparently, on all the Churches of the world, my own among the number), where it had not the tonic quality of personal insult, rather inclined me to slumber. But I braced myself for my life, kept up Rowley with the end of a pin, and came through it awake, but no more.

Bethiah was quite conquered by this 'mark of grace,' though, I am afraid, she was also moved by more worldly considerations. The first is, the lady had not the least objection to go to church on the arm of an elegantly dressed young gentleman, and be followed by a spruce servant with a cockade in his hat. I could see it by the way she took possession of us, found us the places in the Bible, whispered to me the name of the minister, passed us lozenges, which I (for my part) handed on to Rowley, and at each fresh attention stole a little glance about the church to make sure she was observed. Rowley was a pretty boy; you will pardon me if I also remembered that I was a favourable-looking young man. When we grow elderly, how the room brightens, and begins to look as it ought to look, on the entrance of youth, grace, health, and comeliness! You do not want them for yourself, perhaps not even for your son, but you look on smiling; and when you recall their images—again, it is with a smile. I defy you to see or think of them and not smile with an infinite and intimate, but quite impersonal, pleasure. Well, either I know nothing of women, or that was the case with Bethiah McRankine. She had been to church with a cockade behind her, on the one hand; on the other, her house was brightened by the presence of a pair of good-looking young fellows of the other sex, who were always pleased and deferential in her society and accepted her views as final.

These were sentiments to be encouraged; and, on the way home from church—if church it could be called—I adopted a most insidious device to magnify her interest. I took her into the confidence, that is, of my love affair, and I had no sooner mentioned a young lady with whom my affections were engaged than she turned upon me a face of awful gravity.

'Is she bonny?' she inquired.

I gave her full assurances upon that.

'To what denoamination does she beloang?' came next, and was so unexpected as almost to deprive me of breath.

'Upon my word, ma'am, I have never inquired,' cried I; 'I only know that she is a heartfelt Christian, and that is enough.'

'Ay!' she sighed, 'if she has the root of the maitter! There's a remnant practically in most of the denoaminations. There's some in the McGlashanites, and some in the Glassites, and mony in the McMillanites, and there's a leeven even in the Estayblishment.'

'I have known some very good Papists even, if you go to that,' said I.

'Mr. Ducie, think shame to yoursel'!' she cried.

'Why, my dear madam! I only——' I began.

'You shouldnae jest in sairious maitters,' she interrupted.

On the whole, she entered into what I chose to tell her of our idyll with avidity, like a cat licking her whiskers over a dish of cream; and, strange to say—and so expansive a passion is that of love!—that I derived a perhaps equal satisfaction from confiding in that breast of iron. It made an immediate bond: from that hour we seemed to be welded into a family-party; and I had little difficulty in persuading her to join us and to preside over our tea-table. Surely there was never so ill-matched a trio as Rowley, Mrs. McRankine, and the Viscount Anne! But I am of the Apostle's way, with a difference: all things to all women! When I cannot please a woman, hang me in my cravat!

CHAPTER XXVIII

By half-past eight o'clock on the next morning, I was ringing the bell of the lawyer's office in Castle Street, where I found him ensconced at a business table, in a room surrounded by several tiers of green tin cases. He greeted me like an old friend.

'Come away, sir, come away!' said he. 'Here is the dentist ready for you, and I think I can promise you that the operation will be practically painless.'

'I am not so sure of that, Mr. Robbie,' I replied, as I shook hands with him. 'But at least there shall be no time lost with me.'

I had to confess to having gone a-roving with a pair of drovers and their cattle, to having used a false name, to having murdered or half-murdered a fellow-creature in a scuffle on the moors, and to having suffered a couple of quite innocent men to lie some time in prison on a charge from which I could have immediately freed them. All this I gave him first of all, to be done with the worst of it; and all this he took with gravity, but without the least appearance of surprise.

'Now, sir,' I continued, 'I expect to have to pay for my unhappy frolic, but I would like very well if it could be managed without my personal appearance or even the mention of my real name. I had so much wisdom as to sail under false colours in this foolish jaunt of mine; my family would be extremely concerned if they had wind of it; but at the same time, if the case of this Faa has terminated fatally, and there are proceedings against Sim and Candlish, I am not going to stand by and see them vexed, far less punished; and I authorise you to give me up for trial if you think that best—or, if you think it unnecessary, in the meanwhile to make preparations for their defence. I hope, sir, that I am as little anxious to be Quixotic, as I am determined to be just.'

'Very fairly spoken,' said Mr. Robbie. 'It is not much in my line, as doubtless your friend, Mr. Romaine, will have told you. I rarely mix myself up with anything on the criminal side, or approaching it. However, for a young gentleman like you, I may stretch a point, and I dare say I may be able to accomplish more than perhaps another. I will go at once to the Procurator Fiscal's office and inquire.'

'Wait a moment, Mr. Robbie,' said I. 'You forget the chapter of expenses. I had thought, for a beginning, of placing a thousand pounds in your hands.'

'My dear sir, you will kindly wait until I render you my bill,' said Mr. Robbie severely.'

'It seemed to me,' I protested, 'that coming to you almost as a stranger, and placing in your hands a piece of business so contrary to your habits, some substantial guarantee of my good faith——'

'Not the way that we do business in Scotland, sir,' he interrupted, with an air of closing the dispute.

'And yet, Mr. Robbie,' I continued, 'I must ask you to allow me to proceed. I do not merely refer to the expenses of the case. I have my eye besides on Sim and Candlish. They are thoroughly deserving fellows; they have been subjected through me to a considerable term of imprisonment; and I suggest, sir, that you should not spare money for their indemnification. This will explain,' I added smiling, 'my offer of the thousand pounds. It was in the nature of a measure by which you should judge the scale on which I can afford to have this business carried through.'

'I take you perfectly, Mr. Ducie,' said he. 'But the sooner I am off, the better this affair is like to be guided. My clerk will show you into the waiting-room and give you the day's *Caledonian Mercury* and the last *Register* to amuse yourself with in the interval.'

I believe Mr. Robbie was at least three hours gone. I saw him descend from a cab at the door, and almost immediately after I was shown again into his study, where the solemnity of his manner led me to augur the worst. For some time he had the inhumanity to read me a lecture as to the incredible silliness, 'not to say immorality,' of my behaviour. 'I have the satisfaction in telling you my opinion, because it appears that you are going to get off scot free,' he continued, where, indeed, I thought he might have begun.

'The man, Faa, has been dischairged cured; and the two men, Sim and Candlish, would have been leeberated long ago, if it had not been for their extraordinary loyalty to yourself, Mr. Ducie—or Mr. St. Ivey, as I believe I should now call you. Never a word would either of the two old fools volunteer that in any manner pointed at the existence of such a person; and when they were confronted with Faa's version of the affair, they gave accounts so entirely discrepant with their own former declarations, as well as with each other, that the Fiscal was quite nonplussed, and imaigined there was something behind it. You may believe I soon laughed him out of that! And I had the satisfaction of seeing your two friends set free, and very glad to be on the causeway again.'

'Oh, sir,' I cried, 'you should have brought them here.'

'No instructions, Mr. Ducie!' said he. 'How did I know you wished to renew an acquaintance which you had just terminated so fortunately? And, indeed, to be frank with you, I should have set my face against it, if you had! Let them go! They are paid and contented, and have the highest possible opinion of Mr. St. Ivey! When I gave them fifty pounds apiece—which was rather more than enough, Mr. Ducie, whatever you may think—the man Sim, who has the only tongue of the party, struck his staff on the ground. "Weel," says he, "I aye said he was a gentleman!" "Man, Sim," said I, "that was just what Mr. St. Ivey said of yourself!"'

'So it was a case of "Compliments fly when gentlefolk meet."'

'No, no, Mr. Ducie, man Sim and man Candlish are gone out of your life, and a good riddance! They are fine fellows in their way, but no proper associates for the like of yourself; and do you finally agree to be done with all eccentricity—take up with no more drovers, or rovers, or tinkers, but enjoy the naitural pleesures for which your age, your wealth, your intelligence, and (if I may be allowed to say it) your appearance so completely fit you. And the first of these,' quoth he, looking at his watch, 'will be to step through to my dining-room and share a bachelor's luncheon.'

Over the meal, which was good, Mr. Robbie continued to develop the same theme. 'You're, no doubt, what they call a dancing-man?' said he. 'Well, on Thursday night there is the Assembly Ball. You must certainly go there, and you must permit me besides to do the honours of the ceety and send you a ticket. I am a thorough believer in a young man being a young man—but no more drovers or rovers, if you love me! Talking of which puts me in mind that you may be short of partners at the Assembly—oh, I have been young myself!— and if ye care to come to anything so portentiously tedious as a tea-party at the house of a bachelor lawyer, consisting mainly of his nieces and nephews, and his grand-nieces and grand-

nephews, and his wards, and generally the whole clan of the
descendants of his clients, you might drop in to-night towards
seven o'clock. I think I can show you one or two that are
worth looking at, and you can dance with them later on at the
Assembly.'

He proceeded to give me a sketch of one or two eligible
young ladies whom I might expect to meet. 'And then there's
my parteecular friend, Miss Flora,' said he. 'But I'll make no
attempt of a description. You shall see her for yourself.'

It will be readily supposed that I accepted his invitation;
and returned home to make a toilette worthy of her I was to
meet and the good news of which I was the bearer. The
toilette, I have reason to believe, was a success. Mr. Rowley
dismissed me with a farewell: 'Crikey! Mr. Anne, but you do
look prime!' Even the stony Bethiah was—how shall I say?
—dazzled, but scandalised, by my appearance; and while, of
course, she deplored the vanity that led to it, she could not
wholly prevent herself from admiring the result.

'Ay, Mr. Ducie, this is a poor employment for a wayfaring
Christian man!' she said. 'Wi' Christ despised and rejectit in
all pairts of the world, and the flag of the Covenant flung doon,
you will be muckle better on your knees! However, I'll have
to confess that it sets you weel. And if it's the lassie ye're
gaun to see the nicht, I suppose I'll just have to excuse ye!
Bairns maun be bairns!' she said, with a sigh. 'I mind when
Mr. McRankine came courtin', and that's lang by-gane—I mind
I had a green gown, passementit, that was thocht to become me
to admiration. I was nae just exactly what ye would ca' bonny;
but I was pale, penetratin', and interestin'.' And she leaned
over the stair-rail with a candle to watch my descent as long as
it should be possible.

It was but a little party at Mr. Robbie's—by which, I do not
so much mean that there were few people, for the rooms were
crowded, as that there was very little attempted to entertain
them. In one apartment there were tables set out, where the
elders were solemnly engaged upon whist; in the other and
larger one, a great number of youth of both sexes entertained
themselves languidly, the ladies sitting upon chairs to be
courted, the gentlemen standing about in various attitudes of
insinuation or indifference. Conversation appeared the sole
resource, except in so far as it was modified by a number of
keepsakes and annuals which lay dispersed upon the tables, and
of which the young beaux displayed the illustrations to the
ladies. Mr. Robbie himself was customarily in the card-room;
only now and again, when he cut out, he made an incursion

among the young folks, and rolled about jovially from one to another, the very picture of the general uncle.

It chanced that Flora had met Mr. Robbie in the course of the afternoon. 'Now, Miss Flora,' he had said, 'come early, for I have a Phœnix to show you—one Mr. Ducie, a new client of mine that, I vow, I have fallen in love with'; and he was so good as to add a word or two on my appearance, from which Flora conceived a suspicion of the truth. She had come to the party, in consequence, on the knife-edge of anticipation and alarm; had chosen a place by the door, where I found her, on my arrival, surrounded by a posse of vapid youths; and, when I drew near, sprang up to meet me in the most natural manner in the world, and, obviously, with a prepared form of words.

'How do you do, Mr. Ducie?' she said. 'It is quite an age since I have seen you!'

'I have much to tell you, Miss Gilchrist,' I replied. 'May I sit down?'

For the artful girl, by sitting near the door, and the judicious use of her shawl, had contrived to keep a chair empty by her side.

She made room for me, as a matter of course, and the youths had the discretion to melt before us. As soon as I was once seated her fan flew out, and she whispered behind it:

'Are you mad?'

'Madly in love,' I replied; 'but in no other sense.'

'I have no patience! You cannot understand what I am suffering!' she said. 'What are you to say to Ronald, to Major Chevenix, to my aunt?'

'Your aunt?' I cried, with a start. '*Peccavi!* is she here?'

'She is in the card-room at whist,' said Flora.

'Where she will probably stay all the evening?' I suggested.

'She may,' she admitted; 'she generally does!'

'Well, then, I must avoid the card-room,' said I, 'which is very much what I had counted upon doing. I did not come here to play cards, but to contemplate a certain young lady to my heart's content—if it can ever be contented!—and to tell her some good news.'

'But there are still Ronald and the Major!' she persisted. 'They are not card-room fixtures! Ronald will be coming and going. And as for Mr. Chevenix, he——'

'Always sits with Miss Flora?' I interrupted. 'And they talk of poor St. Ives? I had gathered as much, my dear; and Mr. Ducie has come to prevent it! But pray dismiss these fears! I mind no one but your aunt.'

'Why my aunt?'

'Because your aunt is a lady, my dear, and a very clever lady, and, like all clever ladies, a very rash lady,' said I. 'You can never count upon them, unless you are sure of getting them in a corner, as I have got you, and talking them over rationally, as I am just engaged on with yourself! It would be quite the same to your aunt to make the worst kind of a scandal, with an equal indifference to my danger and to the feelings of our good host!'

'Well,' she said, 'and what of Ronald, then? Do you think *he* is above making a scandal? You must know him very little!'

'On the other hand, it is my pretension that I know him very well!' I replied. 'I must speak to Ronald first—not Ronald to me—that is all!'

'Then, please, go and speak to him at once!' she pleaded. 'He is there—do you see?—at the upper end of the room, talking to that girl in pink.'

'And so lose this seat before I have told you my good news?' I exclaimed. 'Catch me! And, besides, my dear one, think a little of me and my good news! I thought the bearer of good news was always welcome! I hoped he might be a little welcome for himself! Consider! I have but one friend; and let me stay by her! And there is only one thing I care to hear; and let me hear it!'

'Oh, Anne,' she sighed, 'if I did not love you, why should I be so uneasy? I am turned into a coward, dear! Think, if it were the other way round—if you were quite safe and I was in, oh, such danger!'

She had no sooner said it than I was convicted of being a dullard. 'God forgive me, dear!' I made haste to reply, 'I never saw before that there were two sides to this!' And I told her my tale as briefly as I could, and rose to seek Ronald. 'You see, my dear, you are obeyed,' I said.

She gave me a look that was a reward in itself; and as I turned away from her, with a strong sense of turning away from the sun, I carried that look in my bosom like a caress. The girl in pink was an arch, ogling person, with a good deal of eyes and teeth, and a great play of shoulders and rattle of conversation. There could be no doubt, from Mr. Ronald's attitude, that he worshipped the very chair she sat on. But I was quite ruthless. I laid my hand on his shoulder, as he was stooping over her like a hen over a chicken.

'Excuse me for one moment, Mr. Gilchrist!' said I.

He started and span about in answer to my touch, and exhibited a face of inarticulate wonder.

'Yes!' I continued, 'it is even myself! Pardon me for interrupting so agreeable a *tête-à-tête*, but you know, my good fellow, we owe a first duty to Mr. Robbie. It would never do to risk making a scene in the man's drawing-room; so the first thing I had to attend to was to have you warned. The name I go by is Ducie, too, in case of accidents.'

'I—I say, you know!' cried Ronald. 'Deuce take it, what are you doing here?'

'Hush, hush!' said I. 'Not the place, my dear fellow—not the place. Come to my rooms, if you like, to-night after the party, or to-morrow in the morning, and we can talk it out over a segar. But here, you know, it really won't do at all.'

Before he could collect his mind for an answer, I had given him my address in St. James Square, and had again mingled with the crowd. Alas! I was not fated to get back to Flora so easily! Mr. Robbie was in the path: he was insatiably loquacious; and as he continued to palaver I watched the insipid youths gather again about my idol, and cursed my fate and my host. He remembered suddenly that I was to attend the Assembly Ball on Thursday, and had only attended to-night by way of a preparative. This put it into his head to present me to another young lady; but I managed this interview with so much art that, while I was scrupulously polite and even cordial to the fair one, I contrived to keep Robbie beside me all the time and to leave along with him when the ordeal was over. We were just walking away arm in arm, when I spied my friend the Major approaching, stiff as a ramrod and, as usual, obtrusively clean.

'Oh! there's a man I want to know,' said I, taking the bull by the horns. 'Won't you introduce me to Major Chevenix?'

'At a word, my dear fellow,' said Robbie; and 'Major!' he cried, 'come here and let me present to you my friend Mr. Ducie, who desires the honour of your acquaintance.'

The Major flushed visibly, but otherwise preserved his composure. He bowed very low. 'I'm not very sure,' he said: 'I have an idea we have met before?'

'Informally,' I said, returning his bow; 'and I have long looked forward to the pleasure of regularising our acquaintance.'

'You are very good, Mr. Ducie,' he returned. 'Perhaps you could aid my memory a little? Where was it that I had the pleasure?'

'Oh, that would be telling tales out of school,' said I, with a laugh, 'and before my lawyer, too!'

'I'll wager,' broke in Mr. Robbie, 'that, when you knew my

client, Chevenix—the past of our friend Mr. Ducie is an obscure chapter full of horrid secrets—I'll wager, now, you knew him as St. Ivey,' says he, nudging me violently.

' I think not, sir,' said the Major, with pinched lips.

' Well, I wish he may prove all right!' continued the lawyer, with certainly the worst-inspired jocularity in the world. ' I know nothing by him! He may be a swell mobsman for me with his aliases. You must put your memory on the rack, Major, and when ye've remembered when and where ye met him, be sure ye tell me.'

' I will not fail, sir,' said Chevenix.

' Seek to him!' cried Robbie, waving his hand as he departed.

The Major, as soon as we were alone, turned upon me his impassive countenance.

' Well,' he said, ' you have courage.'

' It is undoubted as your honour, sir,' I returned, bowing.

' Did you expect to meet me, may I ask?' said he.

' You saw, at least, that I courted the presentation,' said I.

' And you were not afraid?' said Chevenix.

' I was perfectly at ease. I knew I was dealing with a gentleman. Be that your epitaph.'

' Well, there are some other people looking for you,' he said, ' who will make no bones about the point of honour. The police, my dear sir, are simply agog about you.'

' And I think that that was coarse,' said I.

' You have seen Miss Gilchrist?' he inquired, changing the subject.

' With whom, I am led to understand, we are on a footing of rivalry?' I asked. ' Yes, I have seen her.'

' And I was just seeking her,' he replied.

I was conscious of a certain thrill of temper; so, I suppose, was he. We looked each other up and down.

' The situation is original,' he resumed.

' Quite,' said I. ' But let me tell you frankly you are blowing a cold coal. I owe you so much for your kindness to the prisoner Champdivers.'

' Meaning that the lady's affections are more advantageously disposed of?' he asked, with a sneer. ' Thank you, I am sure. And, since you have given me a lead, just hear a word of good advice in your turn. Is it fair, is it delicate, is it like a gentleman, to compromise the young lady by attentions which (as you know very well) can come to nothing?'

I was utterly unable to find words in answer.

' Excuse me if I cut this interview short,' he went on. ' It seems to me doomed to come to nothing, and there is more attractive metal.'

'Yes,' I replied, 'as you say, it cannot amount to much. You are impotent, bound hand and foot in honour. You know me to be a man falsely accused, and even if you did not know it, from your position as my rival you have only the choice to stand quite still or to be infamous.'

'I would not say that,' he returned, with another change of colour. 'I may hear it once too often.'

With which he moved off straight for where Flora was sitting amidst her court of vapid youths, and I had no choice but to follow him, a bad second, and reading myself, as I went, a sharp lesson on the command of temper.

It is a strange thing how young men in their teens go down at the mere wind of the coming of men of twenty-five and upwards! The vapid ones fled without thought of resistance before the Major and me; a few dallied awhile in the neighbourhood—so to speak, with their fingers in their mouths—but presently these also followed the rout, and we remained face to face before Flora. There was a draught in that corner by the door; she had thrown her pelisse over her bare arms and neck, and the dark fur of the trimming set them off. She shone by contrast; the light played on her smooth skin to admiration, and the colour changed in her excited face. For the least fraction of a second she looked from one to the other of her pair of rival swains, and seemed to hesitate. Then she addressed Chevenix :—

'You are coming to the Assembly, of course, Major Chevenix?' said she.

'I fear not; I fear I shall be otherwise engaged,' he replied. 'Even the pleasure of dancing with you, Miss Flora, must give way to duty.'

For awhile the talk ran harmlessly on the weather, and then branched off towards the war. It seemed to be by no one's fault; it was in the air, and had to come.

'Good news from the scene of operations,' said the Major.

'Good news while it lasts,' I said. 'But will Miss Gilchrist tell us her private thought upon the war? In her admiration for the victors, does not there mingle some pity for the vanquished?'

'Indeed, sir,' she said, with animation, 'only too much of it! War is a subject that I do not think should be talked of to a girl. I am, I have to be—what do you call it?—a non-combatant? And to remind me of what others have to do and suffer : no, it is not fair!'

'Miss Gilchrist has the tender female heart,' said Chevenix.

'Do not be too sure of that!' she cried. 'I would love to be allowed to fight myself!'

'On which side?' I asked.

'Can you ask?' she exclaimed. 'I am a Scottish girl!'

'She is a Scottish girl!' repeated the Major, looking at me. 'And no one grudges you her pity!'

'And I glory in every grain of it she has to spare,' said I. 'Pity is akin to love.'

'Well, and let us put that question to Miss Gilchrist. It is for her to decide, and for us to bow to the decision. Is pity, Miss Flora, or is admiration, nearest love?'

'Oh, come,' said I, 'let us be more concrete. Lay before the lady a complete case: describe your man, then I'll describe *mine*, and Miss Flora shall decide.'

'I think I see your meaning,' said he, 'and I'll try. You think that pity—and the kindred sentiments—have the greatest power upon the heart. I think more nobly of women. To my view, the man they love will first of all command their respect; he will be steadfast—proud, if you please; dry, possibly—but of all things steadfast. They will look at him in doubt; at last they will see that stern face which he presents to all the rest of the world soften to them alone. First, trust, I say. It is so that a woman loves who is worthy of heroes.'

'Your man is very ambitious, sir,' said I, 'and very much of a hero! Mine is a humbler, and, I would fain think, a more human dog. He is one with no particular trust in himself, with no superior steadfastness to be admired for, who sees a lady's face, who hears her voice, and, without any phrase about the matter, falls in love. What does he ask for, then, but pity?—pity for his weakness, pity for his love, which is his life. You would make women always the inferiors, gaping up at your imaginary lover; he, like a marble statue, with his nose in the air! But God has been wiser than you; and the most steadfast of your heroes may prove human, after all. We appeal to the queen for judgment,' I added, turning and bowing before Flora.

'And how shall the queen judge?' she asked. 'I must give you an answer that is no answer at all. "The wind bloweth where it listeth": she goes where her heart goes.'

Her face flushed as she said it; mine also, for I read in it a declaration, and my heart swelled for joy. But Chevenix grew pale.

'You make of life a very dreadful kind of lottery, ma'am,' said he. 'But I will not despair. Honest and unornamental is still my choice.'

And I must say he looked extremely handsome and very amusingly like the marble statue with its nose in the air to which I had compared him.

'I cannot imagine how we got upon this subject,' said Flora.

'Madame, it was through the war,' replied Chevenix.

'All roads lead to Rome,' I commented. 'What else would you expect Mr. Chevenix and myself to talk of?'

About this time I was conscious of a certain bustle and movement in the room behind me, but did not pay to it that degree of attention which perhaps would have been wise. There came a certain change in Flora's face; she signalled repeatedly with her fan; her eyes appealed to me obsequiously; there could be no doubt that she wanted something—as well as I could make out, that I should go away and leave the field clear for my rival, which I had not the least idea of doing. At last she rose from her chair with impatience.

'I think it time you were saying good-night, Mr Ducie!' she said.

I could not in the least see why, and said so.

Whereupon she gave me this appalling answer, 'My aunt is coming out of the card-room.'

In less time than it takes to tell, I had made my bow and my escape. Looking back from the doorway, I was privileged to see, for a moment, the august profile and gold eyeglasses of Miss Gilchrist issuing from the card-room; and the sight lent me wings. I stood not on the order of my going; and a moment after, I was on the pavement of Castle Street, and the lighted windows shone down on me, and were crossed by ironical shadows of those who had remained behind.

CHAPTER XXIX

EVENTS OF TUESDAY : THE TOILS CLOSING

This day began with a surprise. I found a letter on my break-fast-table addressed to Edward Ducie, Esquire ; and at first I was startled beyond measure. 'Conscience doth make cowards of us all!' When I had opened it, it proved to be only a note from the lawyer, enclosing a card for the Assembly Ball on Thursday evening. Shortly after, as I was composing my mind with a segar at one of the windows of the sitting-room, and Rowley, having finished the light share of work that fell to him, sat not far off tootling with great spirit and a marked preference for the upper octave, Ronald was suddenly shown in. I got him a segar, drew in a chair to the side of the fire, and installed him there—I was going to say, at his ease, but no expression could be farther from the truth. He was plainly on pins and needles, did not know whether to take or to refuse the segar, and, after he had taken it, did not know whether to light or to return it. I saw he had something to say ; I did not think it was his own something ; and I was ready to offer a large bet it was really something of Major Chevenix's.

'Well, and so here you are!' I observed, with pointless cor-diality, for I was bound I should do nothing to help him out. If he were, indeed, here running errands for my rival, he might have a fair field, but certainly no favour.

'The fact is,' he began, 'I would rather see you alone.'

'Why, certainly,' I replied. 'Rowley, you can step into the bedroom. My dear fellow,' I continued, 'this sounds serious. Nothing wrong, I trust.'

'Well, I'll be quite honest,' said he. 'I *am* a good deal bothered.'

'And I bet I know why!' I exclaimed. 'And I bet I can put you to rights, too!'

'What do you mean!' he asked.

'You must be hard up,' said I, 'and all I can say is, you've come to the right place. If you have the least use for a hundred pounds, or any such trifling sum as that, please mention it. It's here, quite at your service.'

'I am sure it is most kind of you,' said Ronald, 'and the truth is, though I can't think how you guessed it, that I really *am* a little behind board. But I haven't come to talk about that.'

'No, I dare say!' cried I. 'Not worth talking about!' But remember, Ronald, you and I are on different sides of the business. Remember that you did me one of those services that make men friends for ever. And since I have had the fortune to come into a fair share of money, just oblige me, and consider so much of it as your own.'

'No,' he said, 'I couldn't take it; I couldn't, really. Besides, the fact is, I've come on a very different matter. It's about my sister, St. Ives,' and he shook his head menacingly at me.

'You're quite sure?' I persisted. 'It's here, at your service —up to five hundred pounds, if you like. Well, all right; only remember where it is, when you do want it.'

'Oh, please let me alone!' cried Ronald: 'I've come to say something unpleasant; and how on earth can I do it, if you don't give a fellow a chance? It's about my sister, as I said. You can see for yourself that it can't be allowed to go on. It's compromising; it don't lead to anything; and you're not the kind of man (you must feel it yourself) that I can allow my female relatives to have anything to do with. I hate saying this, St. Ives; it looks like hitting a man when he's down, you know; and I told the Major I very much disliked it from the first. However, it had to be said; and now it has been, and, between gentlemen, it shouldn't be necessary to refer to it again.'

'It's compromising; it doesn't lead to anything; not the kind of man,' I repeated thoughtfully. 'Yes, I believe I understand, and shall make haste to put myself *en règle*.' I stood up, and laid my segar down. 'Mr. Gilchrist,' said I, with a bow, 'in answer to your very natural observations, I beg to offer myself as a suitor for your sister's hand. I am a man of title, of which we think lightly in France, but of ancient lineage, which is everywhere prized. I can display thirty-two quarterings without a blot. My expectations are certainly above the average: I believe my uncle's income averages about thirty thousand pounds, though I admit I was not careful to inform myself. Put it anywhere between fifteen and fifty thousand; it is certainly not less.'

'All this is very easy to say,' said Ronald, with a pitying smile. 'Unfortunately, these things are in the air.'

'Pardon me,—in Buckinghamshire,' said I, smiling.

'Well, what I mean is, my dear St. Ives, that you *can't prove*

them,' he continued. 'They might just as well not be: do you
follow me? You can't bring us any third party to back you up.'

'Oh, come!' cried I, springing up and hurrying to the table.
'You must excuse me!' I wrote Romaine's address. 'There
is my reference, Mr. Gilchrist. Until you have written to him,
and received his negative answer, I have a right to be treated,
and I shall see that you treat me, as a gentleman.'

He was brought up with a round turn at that.

'I beg your pardon, St. Ives,' said he. 'Believe me, I had
no wish to be offensive. But there's the difficulty of this
affair; I can't make any of my points without offence! You
must excuse me, it's not my fault. But, at any rate, you must
see for yourself this proposal of marriage is—is merely impossible, my dear fellow. It's nonsense! Our countries are at
war; you are a prisoner.'

'My ancestor of the time of the Ligue,' I replied, 'married
a Huguenot lady out of the Saintonge, riding two hundred
miles through an enemy's country to bring off his bride; and
it was a happy marriage.'

'Well!' he began; and then looked down into the fire, and
became silent.

'Well?' I asked.

'Well, there's this business of—Goguelat,' said he, still
looking at the coals in the grate.

'What!' I exclaimed, starting in my chair. 'What's that
you say?'

'This business about Goguelat,' he repeated.

'Ronald,' said I, 'this is not your doing. These are not your
own words. I know where they came from: a coward put them
in your mouth.'

'St. Ives!' he cried, 'why do you make it so hard for me?
and where's the use of insulting other people? The plain
English is, that I can't hear of any proposal of marriage from
a man under a charge like that. You must see it for yourself,
man! It's the most absurd thing I ever heard of! And you
go on forcing me to argue with you, too!'

'Because I have had an affair of honour which terminated
unhappily, you—a young soldier, or next-door to it—refuse my
offer? Do I understand you aright?' said I.

'My dear fellow!' he wailed, 'of course you can twist my
words, if you like. You *say* it was an affair of honour. Well,
I can't, of course, tell you that—I can't—— I mean, you must
see that that's just the point! Was it? I don't know.'

'I have the honour to inform you,' said I.

'Well, other people say the reverse, you see!'

'They lie, Ronald, and I will prove it in time.'

'The short and the long of it is, that any man who is so unfortunate as to have such things said about him is not the man to be my brother-in-law!' he cried.

'Do you know who will be my first witness at the court? Arthur Chevenix!' said I.

'I don't care!' he cried, rising from his chair and beginning to pace outrageously about the room. 'What do you mean, St. Ives? What is this about? It's like a dream, I declare! You made an offer, and I have refused it. I don't like it, I don't want it; and whatever I did, or didn't, wouldn't matter —my aunt wouldn't hear of it anyway! Can't you take your answer, man?'

'You must remember, Ronald, that we are playing with edged tools,' said I. 'An offer of marriage is a delicate subject to handle. You have refused, and you have justified your refusal by several statements: first, that I was an impostor; second, that our countries were at war; and third—— No, I will speak,' said I; 'you can answer when I have done,—and third, that I had dishonourably killed—or was said to have done so—the man Goguelat. Now, my dear fellow, these are very awkward grounds to be taking. From any one else's lips I need scarce tell you how I should resent them; but my hands are tied. I have so much gratitude to you, without talking of the love I bear your sister, that you insult me, when you do so, under the cover of a complete impunity. I must feel the pain —and I do feel it acutely—I can do nothing to protect myself.'

He had been anxious enough to interrupt me in the beginning; but now, and after I had ceased, he stood a long while silent.

'St. Ives,' he said at last, 'I think I had better go away. This has been very irritating. I never at all meant to say any-of the kind, and I apologise to you. I have all the esteem for you that one gentleman should have for another. I only meant to tell you—to show you what had influenced my mind; and that, in short, the thing was impossible. One thing you may be quite sure of: *I* shall do nothing against you. Will you shake hands before I go away?' he blurted out.

'Yes,' said I, 'I agree with you—the interview has been irritating. Let bygones be bygones. Good-bye, Ronald.'

'Good-bye, St. Ives!' he returned. 'I'm heartily sorry.'

And with that he was gone.

The windows of my own sitting-room looked towards the north; but the entrance passage drew its light from the direction of the square. Hence I was able to observe Ronald's departure, his very disheartened gait, and the fact that he was joined, about half-way, by no less a man than Major Chevenix. At this, I could scarce keep from smiling; so unpalatable an interview must be before the pair of them, and I could hear their voices, clashing like crossed swords, in that eternal antiphony of 'I told you,' and 'I told you not.' Without doubt, they had gained very little by their visit; but then I had gained less than nothing, and had been bitterly dispirited into the bargain. Ronald had stuck to his guns and refused me to the last. It was no news; but, on the other hand, it could not be contorted into good news. I was now certain that during my temporary absence in France, all irons would be put into the fire, and the world turned upside down, to make Flora disown the obtrusive Frenchman and accept Chevenix. Without doubt she would resist these instances: but the thought of them did not please me, and I felt she should be warned and prepared for the battle.

It was no use to try and see her now, but I promised myself early that evening to return to Swanston. In the meantime I had to make all my preparations, and look the coming journey in the face. Here in Edinburgh I was within four miles of the sea, yet the business of approaching random fishermen with my hat in the one hand and a knife in the other, appeared so desperate, that I saw nothing for it but to retrace my steps over the northern counties, and knock a second time at the doors of Birchell Fenn. To do this, money would be necessary; and after leaving my paper in the hands of Flora I had still a balance of about fifteen hundred pounds. Or rather I may say I had them and I had them not; for after my luncheon with Mr. Robbie I had placed the amount, all but thirty pounds of change, in a bank in George Street, on a deposit receipt in the name of Mr. Rowley. This I had designed to be my gift to him, in case I must suddenly depart. But now, thinking better of the arrangement, I despatched my little man, cockade and all, to lift the fifteen hundred.

He was not long gone, and returned with a flushed face, and the deposit receipt still in his hand.

'No go, Mr. Anne,' says he.

'How's that?' I inquired,

'Well, sir, I found the place all right, and no mistake,' said he. 'But I tell you what gave me a blue fright! There was a customer standing by the door, and I reckonised him! Who do you think it was, Mr. Anne? W'y, that same Red-Breast—him I had breakfast with near Aylesbury.'

'You are sure you are not mistaken?' I asked.

'Certain sure,' he replied. 'Not Mr. Lavender, I don't mean, sir; I mean the other party. "Wot's he doing here?' says I. "It don't look right."'

'Not by any means,' I agreed.

I walked to and fro in the apartment reflecting. This particular Bow Street runner might be here by accident; but it was to imagine a singular play of coincidence that he, who had met Rowley and spoken with him in the 'Green Dragon,' hard by Aylesbury, should be now in Scotland, where he could have no legitimate business, and by the doors of the bank where Rowley kept his account.

'Rowley,' said I, 'he didn't see you, did he?'

'Never a fear,' quoth Rowley. 'W'y Mr. Anne, sir, if he 'ad, you wouldn't have seen *me* any more! I ain't a hass, sir!'

'Well, my boy, you can put that receipt in your pocket. You'll have no more use for it till you're quite clear of me. Don't lose it, though; it's your share of the Christmas-box: fifteen hundred pounds all for yourself.'

'Begging your pardon, Mr. Anne, sir, but wot for!' said Rowley.

'To set up a public-house upon,' said I.

'If you'll excuse me, sir, I ain't got any call to set up a public-house, sir,' he replied stoutly. 'And I tell you wot, sir, it seems to me I'm reether young for the billet. I'm your body servant, Mr. Anne, or else I'm nothink.'

'Well Rowley,' I said, 'I'll tell you what it's for. It's for the good service you have done me, of which I don't care—and don't dare—to speak. It's for your loyalty and cheerfulness, my dear boy. I had meant it for you; but to tell you the truth, it's past mending now—it has to be yours. Since that man is waiting by the bank, the money can't be touched until I'm gone.

'Until you're gone, sir?' re-echoed Rowley. 'You don't go anywheres without me, I can tell you that, Mr. Anne, sir!'

'Yes, my boy,' said I, 'we are going to part very soon now; probably to-morrow. And it's for my sake, Rowley! Depend upon it, if there was any reason at all for that Bow Street man being at the bank, he was not there to look out for *you*. How they could have found out about the account so early is more than I can fathom; some strange coincidence must have played me false! But there the fact is; and Rowley, I'll not only have to say farewell to you presently, I'll have to ask you to stay indoors until I can say it. Remember, my boy, it's only so that you can serve me now.'

'W'y, sir, you say the word, and of course I'll do it!' he

cried. '"Nothink by 'alves," is my motto! I'm your man, through thick and thin, live or die, I am!'

In the meantime there was nothing to be done till towards sunset. My only chance now was to come again as quickly as possible to speech of Flora, who was my only practicable banker; and not before evening was it worth while to think of that. I might compose myself as well as I was able over the *Caledonian Mercury*, with its ill news of the campaign of France and belated documents about the retreat from Russia; and, as I sat there by the fire, I was sometimes all awake with anger and mortification at what I was reading, and sometimes again I would be three parts asleep as I dozed over the barren items of home intelligence. 'Lately arrived'—this is what I suddenly stumbled on—'at Dumbreck's Hotel, the Viscount of Saint-Yves.'

'Rowley,' said I.

'If you please, Mr. Anne, sir,' answered the obsequious, lowering his pipe.

'Come and look at this, my boy,' said I, holding out the paper.

'My crikey!' said he. 'That's 'im, sir, sure enough!'

'Sure enough, Rowley,' said I. 'He's on the trail. He has fairly caught up with us. He and this Bow Street man have come together, I would swear. And now here is the whole field, quarry, hounds and hunters, all together in this city of Edinburgh.'

'And wot are you goin' to do now, sir? Tell you wot, let me take it in 'and, please! Gimme a minute, and I'll disguise myself, and go out to this Dum—to this hotel, leastways, sir—and see wot he's up to. You put your trust in me, Mr. Anne: I'm fly, don't you make no mistake about it. I'm all a-growing and a-blowing, I am.'

'Not one foot of you,' said I. 'You are a prisoner, Rowley, and make up your mind to that. So am I, or next door to it. I showed it you for a caution; if you go on the streets, it spells death to me, Rowley.'

'If you please, sir,' says Rowley.

'Come to think of it,' I continued, 'you must take a cold, or something. No good of awakening Mrs. McRankine's suspicions.'

'A cold?' he cried, recovering immediately from his depression. 'I can do it, Mr. Anne.'

And he proceeded to sneeze and cough and blow his nose, till I could not restrain myself from smiling.

'Oh, I tell you, I know a lot of them dodges,' he observed proudly.

'Well, they come in very handy,' said I.

'I'd better go at once and show it to the old gal, 'adn't I?' he asked.

I told him, by all means; and he was gone upon the instant, gleeful as though to a game of football.

'I took up the paper and read carelessly on, my thoughts engaged with my immediate danger, till I struck on the next paragraph :—

'In connection with the recent horrid murder in the Castle, we are desired to make public the following intelligence. The soldier, Champdivers, is supposed to be in the neighbourhood of this city. He is about the middle height or rather under, of a pleasing appearance and highly genteel address. When last heard of he wore a fashionable suit of pearl-grey, and boots with fawn-coloured tops. He is accompanied by a servant about sixteen years of age, speaks English without any accent, and passed under the *alias* of Ramornie. A reward is offered for his apprehension.'

In a moment I was in the next room, stripping from me the pearl-coloured suit!

I confess I was now a good deal agitated. It is difficult to watch the toils closing slowly and surely about you, and to retain your composure; and I was glad that Rowley was not present to spy on my confusion. I was flushed, my breath came thick; I cannot remember a time when I was more put out.

And yet I must wait and do nothing, and partake of my meals, and entertain the ever-garrulous Rowley, as though I were entirely my own man. And if I did not require to entertain Mrs. McRankine also, that was but another drop of bitterness in my cup! For what ailed my landlady, that she should hold herself so severely aloof, that she should refuse conversation, that her eyes should be reddened, that I should so continually hear the voice of her private supplications sounding through the house? I was much deceived, or she had read the insidious paragraph and recognised the comminated pearl-grey suit. I remember now a certain air with which she had laid the paper on my table, and a certain sniff, between sympathy and defiance, with which she had announced it: 'There's your *Mercury* for ye!'

In this direction, at least, I saw no pressing danger; her tragic countenance betokened agitation; it was plain she was wrestling with her conscience, and the battle still hung dubious. The question of what to do troubled me extremely. I could not venture to touch such an intricate and mysterious piece of machinery as my landlady's spiritual nature; it might go off at a word, and in any direction, like a badly-made firework. And while I praised myself extremely for my wisdom in the past, that I had made so much a friend of her, I was all abroad as to my conduct in the present. There seemed an equal danger in pressing and in neglecting the accustomed marks of familiarity. The one extreme looked like impudence, and might annoy; the other was a practical confession of guilt. Altogether, it was a good hour for me when the dusk began to fall in earnest on the streets of Edinburgh, and the voice of an early watchman bade me set forth.

I reached the neighbourhood of the cottage before seven; and as I breasted the steep ascent which leads to the garden wall, I was struck with surprise to hear a dog. Dogs I had heard before, but only from the hamlet on the hillside above. Now, this dog was in the garden itself, where it roared aloud in paroxysms of fury, and I could hear it leaping and straining on the chain. I waited some while, until the brute's fit of passion had roared itself out. Then, with the utmost precaution, I drew near again, and finally approached the garden wall. So soon as I had clapped my head above the level, however, the barking broke forth again with redoubled energy. Almost at the same time, the door of the cottage opened, and Ronald and the Major appeared upon the threshold with a lantern. As they so stood, they were almost immediately below me, strongly illuminated, and within easy earshot. The Major pacified the dog, who took instead to low, uneasy growling intermingled with occasional yelps.

'Good thing I brought Towzer!' said Chevenix.

'Damn him, I wonder where he is!' said Ronald; and he moved the lantern up and down, and turned the night into a shifting puzzle-work of gleam and shadow. 'I think I'll make a sally.'

'I don't think you will,' replied Chevenix. 'When I agreed to come out here and do sentry-go, it was on one condition, Master Ronald: don't you forget that! Military discipline, my boy!· Our beat is this path close about the house. Down, Towzer! good boy, good boy—gently, then!' he went on, caressing his confounded monster.

'To think! The beggar may be hearing us this minute!' cried Ronald.'

'Nothing more probable,' said the Major. 'You there, St. Ives?' he added, in a distinct but guarded voice. 'I only want to tell you, you had better go home. Mr. Gilchrist and I take watch and watch.'

The game was up. '*Beaucoup de plaisir!*' I replied, in the

same tones. '*Il fait un peu froid pour veiller; gardez-vous des engelures!*'

I suppose it was done in a moment of ungovernable rage; but in spite of the excellent advice he had given to Ronald the moment before, Chevenix slipped the chain, and the dog sprang, straight as an arrow, up the bank. I stepped back, picked up a stone of about twelve pounds weight, and stood ready. With a bound the beast landed on the cope-stone of the wall; and, almost in the same instant, my missile caught him fair in the face. He gave a stifled cry, went tumbling back where he had come from, and I could hear the twelve-pounder accompany him in his fall. Chevenix, at the same moment, broke out in a roaring voice: 'The hell-hound! If he's killed my dog!' and I judged, upon all grounds, it was as well to be off

CHAPTER XXX

I AWOKE to much diffidence, even to a feeling that might be called the beginnings of panic, and lay for hours in my bed considering the situation. Seek where I pleased, there was nothing to encourage me and plenty to appal. They kept a close watch about the cottage; they had a beast of a watch-dog —at least, unless I had settled it; and if I had, I knew its bereaved master would only watch the more indefatigably for the loss. In the pardonable ostentation of love I had given all the money I could spare to Flora; I had thought it glorious that the hunted exile should come down, like Jupiter, in a shower of gold, and pour thousands in the lap of the beloved. Then I had in an hour of arrant folly buried what remained to me in a bank in George Street. And now I must get back the one or the other; and which? and how?

As I tossed in my bed, I could see three possible courses, all extremely perilous. First, Rowley might have been mistaken; the bank might not be watched; it might still be possible for him to draw the money on the deposit receipt. Second, I might apply again to Robbie. Or, third, I might dare everything, go to the Assembly Ball, and speak with Flora under the eyes of all Edinburgh. This last alternative, involving as it did the most horrid risks, and the delay of forty-eight hours, I did but glance at with an averted head, and turned again to the consideration of the others. It was the likeliest thing in the world that Robbie had been warned to have no more to do with me. The whole policy of the Gilchrists was in the hands of Chevenix; and I thought this was a precaution so elementary that he was certain to have taken it. If he had not, of course I was all right: Robbie would manage to communicate with Flora; and by four o'clock I might be on the south road and, I was going to say, a free man. Lastly, I must assure myself with my own eyes whether the bank in George Street were beleaguered.

I called to Rowley and questioned him tightly as to the appearance of the Bow Street officer.

230

'What sort of looking man is he, Rowley?' I asked, as I began to dress.

'Wot sort of a looking man he is?' repeated Rowley. 'Well, I don't very well know wot you would say, Mr. Anne. He ain't a beauty, any'ow.'

'Is he tall?'

'Tall? Well, no, I shouldn't say *tall*, Mr. Anne.'

'Well, then, is he short?'

'Short? No, I don't think I would say he was what you would call *short*. No, not piticular short, sir.'

'Then, I suppose, he must be about the middle height?'

'Well, you might say it, sir; but not remarkable so.'

I smothered an oath.

'Is he clean-shaved?' I tried him again.

'Clean-shaved?' he repeated, with the same air of anxious candour.

'Good heaven, man, don't repeat my words like a parrot!' I cried. 'Tell me what the man was like: it is of the first importance that I should be able to recognise him.'

'I'm trying to, Mr. Anne. But *clean-shaved*? I don't seem to rightly get hold of that p'int. Sometimes it might appear to me like as if he was; and sometimes like as if he wasn't. No, it wouldn't surprise me now if you was to tell me he 'ad a bit o' whisker.'

'Was the man red-faced?' I roared, dwelling on each syllable.

'I don't think you need go for to get cross about it, Mr. Anne!' said he. 'I'm tellin' you every blessed thing I see! Red-faced? Well, no, not as you would remark upon.'

A dreadful calm fell upon me.

'Was he anywise pale?' I asked.

'Well, it don't seem to me as though he were. But I tell you truly, I didn't take much heed to that.'

'Did he look like a drinking man?'

'Well, no. If you please, sir, he looked more like an eating one.'

'Oh, he was stout, was he?'

'No, sir. I couldn't go so far as that. No, he wasn't not to say *stout*. If anything, lean rather.'

I need not go on with the infuriating interview. It ended as it began, except that Rowley was in tears, and that I had acquired one fact. The man was drawn for me as being of any height you like to mention, and of any degree of corpulence or leanness; clean-shaved or not, as the case might be; the colour of his hair Rowley 'could not take it upon himself to put a name on'; that of his eyes he thought to have been blue—nay, it was the one point on which he attained to a kind of tearful certainty. 'I'll take my davy on it,' he asseverated. They proved to have been as black as sloes, very little and very near together. So much for the evidence of the artless! And the fact, or rather the facts, acquired? Well, they had to do not with the person but with his clothing. The man wore knee-breeches and white stockings; his coat was 'some kind of a lightish colour—or betwixt that and dark'; and he wore a 'mole-skin weskit.' As if this were not enough, he presently haled me from my breakfast in a prodigious flutter, and showed me an honest and rather venerable citizen passing in the Square.

'That's *him*, sir,' he cried, 'the very moral of him! Well, this one is better dressed, and p'r'aps a trifler taller; and in the face he don't favour him noways at all, sir. No, not when I come to look again, 'e don't seem to favour him noways.'

'Jackass!' said I, and I think the greatest stickler for manners will admit the epithet to have been justified.

Meanwhile the appearance of my landlady added a great load of anxiety to what I already suffered. It was plain that she had not slept; equally plain that she had wept copiously. She sighed, she groaned, she drew in her breath, she shook her head, as she waited on table. In short, she seemed in so precarious a state, like a petard three times charged with hysteria, that I did not dare to address her; and stole out of the house on tiptoe, and actually ran downstairs, in the fear that she might call me back. It was plain that this degree of tension could not last long.

It was my first care to go to George Street, which I reached (by good luck) as a boy was taking down the bank shutters. A man was conversing with him; he had white stockings and a moleskin waistcoat, and was as ill-looking a rogue as you would want to see in a day's journey. This seemed to agree fairly well with Rowley's *signalement*: he had declared emphatically (if you remember), and had stuck to it besides, that the companion of the great Lavender was no beauty.

Thence I made my way to Mr. Robbie's, where I rang the bell. A servant answered the summons, and told me the lawyer was engaged, as I had half expected.

'Wha shall I say was callin'?' she pursued; and when I had told her 'Mr. Ducie,' 'I think this'll be for you, then?' she added, and handed me a letter from the hall table. It ran:

'DEAR MR. DUCIE,
    'My single advice to you is to leave *quam primum* for the South.   Yours, T. ROBBIE.'

That was short and sweet. It emphatically extinguished hope in one direction. No more was to be gotten of Robbie; and I wondered, from my heart, how much had been told him. Not too much, I hoped, for I liked the lawyer who had thus deserted me, and I placed a certain reliance in the discretion of Chevenix. He would not be merciful; on the other hand, I did not think he would be cruel without cause.

It was my next affair to go back along George Street, and assure myself whether the man in the moleskin vest was still on guard. There was no sign of him on the pavement. Spying the door of a common stair nearly opposite the bank, I took it in my head that this would be a good point of observation, crossed the street, entered with a businesslike air and fell immediately against the man in the moleskin vest. I stopped and apologised to him; he replied in an unmistakable English accent, thus putting the matter almost beyond doubt. After this encounter I must, of course, ascend to the top story, ring the bell of a suite of apartments, inquire for Mr. Vavasour, learn (with no great surprise) that he did not live there, come down again and, again politely saluting the man from Bow Street, make my escape at last into the street.

I was now driven back upon the Assembly Ball. Robbie had failed me. The bank was watched; it would never do to risk Rowley in that neighbourhood. All I could do was to wait until the morrow evening, and present myself at the Assembly, let it end as it might. But I must say I came to this decision with a good deal of genuine fright; and here I came for the first time to one of those places where my courage stuck. I do not mean that my courage boggled and made a bit of a bother over it, as it did over the escape from the Castle; I mean, stuck, like a stopped watch or a dead man. Certainly I would go to the ball; certainly I must see this morning about my clothes. That was all decided. But the most of the shops were on the other side of the valley, in the Old Town; and it was now my strange discovery that I was physically unable to cross the North Bridge! It was as though a precipice had stood between us, or the deep sea had intervened. Nearer to the Castle my legs refused to bear me.

I told myself this was mere superstition; I made wagers with myself—and gained them; I went down on the esplanade of Princes Street, walked and stood there, alone and conspicuous, looking across the garden at the old grey bastions of the fortress, where all these troubles had begun. I cocked my hat, set my hand on my hip, and swaggered on the pavement, confronting detection. And I found I could do all this with a sense of exhilaration that was not unpleasing, and with a certain *crânerie* of manner that raised me in my own esteem. And yet there was one thing I could not bring my mind to face up to, or my limbs to execute; and that was to cross the valley into the Old Town. It seemed to me I must be arrested immediately if I had done so; I must go straight into the twilight of a prison cell, and pass straight thence to the gross and final embraces of the nightcap and the halter. And yet it was from no reasoned fear of the consequences that I could not go. I was unable. My horse baulked, and there was an end!

My nerve was gone: here was a discovery for a man in such imminent peril, set down to so desperate a game, which I could only hope to win by continual luck and unflagging effrontery! The strain had been too long continued, and my nerve was gone. I fell into what they call panic fear, as I have seen soldiers do on the alarm of a night attack, and turned out of Princes Street at random as though the devil were at my heels. In St. Andrew Square, I remember vaguely hearing some one call out. I paid no heed, but pressed on blindly. A moment after, a hand fell heavily on my shoulder, and I thought I had fainted. Certainly the world went black about me for some seconds; and when that spasm passed I found myself standing face to face with the 'cheerful extravagant,' in what sort of disarray I really dare not imagine, dead white at least, shaking like an aspen, and mowing at the man with speechless lips. And this was the soldier of Napoleon, and the gentleman who intended going next night to an Assembly Ball! I am the more particular in telling of my breakdown, because it was my only experience of the sort; and it is a good tale for officers. I will allow no man to call me coward; I have made my proofs; few men more. And yet I (come of the best blood in France and inured to danger from a child) did, for some ten or twenty minutes, make this hideous exhibition of myself on the streets of the New Town of Edinburgh.

With my first available breath I begged his pardon. I was of an extremely nervous disposition, recently increased by late hours; I could not bear the slightest start.

He seemed much concerned. 'You must be in a devil of a state!' said he; 'though of course it was my fault—damnably silly, vulgar sort of thing to do! A thousand apologies! But you really must be run down; you should consult a medico. My dear sir, a hair of the dog that bit you is clearly indicated. A touch of Blue Ruin, now? Or, come: it's early, but is man the slave of hours? what do you say to a chop and a bottle in Dumbreck's Hotel?'

I refused all false comfort; but when he went on to remind me that this was the day when the University of Cramond met; and to propose a five-mile walk into the country and a dinner in the company of young asses like himself, I began to think otherwise. I had to wait until to-morrow evening, at any rate; this might serve as well as anything else to bridge the dreary hours. The country was the very place for me: and walking is an excellent sedative for the nerves. Remembering poor Rowley, feigning a cold in our lodgings and immediately under the guns of the formidable and now doubtful Bethiah, I asked if I might bring my servant. 'Poor devil! it is dull for him,' I explained.

'The merciful man is merciful to his ass,' observed my sententious friend. 'Bring him by all means!

"The harp, his sole remaining joy,
    Was carried by an orphan boy;"

and I have no doubt the orphan boy can get some cold victuals in the kitchen, while the Senatus dines.'

Accordingly, being now quite recovered from my unmanly condition, except that nothing could yet induce me to cross the North Bridge, I arranged for my ball dress at a shop in Leith Street, where I was not served ill, cut out Rowley from his seclusion, and was ready along with him at the trysting-place, the corner of Duke Street and York Place, by a little after two. The University was represented in force: eleven persons, including ourselves, Byfield the aëronaut, and the tall lad, Forbes, whom I had met on the Sunday morning, bedewed with tallow, at the 'Hunters' Rest.' I was introduced; and we set off by way of Newhaven and the sea beach; at first through pleasant country roads, and afterwards along a succession of bays of a fairylike prettiness, to our destination—Cramond on the Almond—a little hamlet on a little river, embowered in woods, and looking forth over a great flat of quicksand to where a little islet stood planted in the sea. It was miniature scenery, but charming of its kind. The air of this good February afternoon was bracing, but not cold. All the way my companions were skylarking, jesting and making puns, and I felt as if a load had been taken off my lungs and spirits, and skylarked with the best of them.

Byfield I observed, because I had heard of him before, and seen his advertisements, not at all because I was disposed to feel interest in the man. He was dark and bilious and very silent; frigid in his manners, but burning internally with a great fire of excitement; and he was so good as to bestow a good deal of his company and conversation (such as it was) upon myself, who was not in the least grateful. If I had known how I was to be connected with him in the immediate future, I might have taken more pains.

In the hamlet of Cramond there is a hostelry of no very promising appearance, and here a room had been prepared for us, and we sat down to table.

'Here you will find no guttling or gormandising, no turtle or nightingales' tongues,' said the extravagant, whose name, by the way, was Dalmahoy. 'The device, sir, of the University of Cramond is Plain Living and High Drinking.'

Grace was said by the Professor of Divinity, in a macaronic Latin, which I could by no means follow, only I could hear it rhymed, and I guessed it to be more witty than reverent. After which the *Senatus Academicus* sat down to rough plenty in the shape of rizzar'd haddocks and mustard, a sheep's head, a haggis, and other delicacies of Scotland. The dinner was washed down with brown stout in bottle, and as soon as the cloth was removed, glasses, boiling water, sugar, and whisky were set out for the manufacture of toddy. I played a good knife and fork, did not shun the bowl, and took part, so far as I was able, in the continual fire of pleasantry with which the meal was seasoned. Greatly daring, I ventured, before all these Scotsmen, to tell Sim's Tale of Tweedie's dog; and I was held to have done such extraordinary justice to the dialect, 'for a Southron,' that I was immediately voted into the Chair of Scots, and became, from that moment, a full member of the University of Cramond. A little after, I found myself entertaining them with a song; and a little after—perhaps a little in consequence—it occurred to me that I had had enough, and would be very well inspired to take French leave. It was not difficult to manage, for it was nobody's business to observe my movements, and conviviality had banished suspicion.

I got easily forth of the chamber, which reverberated with the voices of these merry and learned gentlemen, and breathed a long breath. I had passed an agreeable afternoon and evening, and I had apparently escaped scot free. Alas! when I looked into the kitchen, there was my monkey, drunk as a lord, toppling on the edge of the dresser, and performing on the flageolet to an audience of the house lasses and some neighbouring ploughmen.

I routed him promptly from his perch, stuck his hat on, put his instrument in his pocket, and set off with him for Edinburgh.

His limbs were of paper, his mind quite in abeyance; I must uphold and guide him, prevent his frantic dives, and set him continually on his legs again. At first he sang wildly, with occasional outbursts of causeless laughter. Gradually an inarticulate melancholy succeeded; he wept gently at times; would stop in the middle of the road, say firmly 'No, no, no,' and then fall on his back: or else address me solemnly as 'M'lord' and fall on his face by way of variety. I am afraid I was not always so gentle with the little pig as I might have been, but really the position was unbearable. We made no headway at all, and I suppose we were scarce gotten a mile away from Cramond, when the whole *Senatus Academicus* was heard hailing, and doubling the pace to overtake us.

Some of them were fairly presentable; and they were all Christian martyrs compared to Rowley; but they were in a frolicsome and rollicking humour that promised danger as we approached the town. They sang songs, they ran races, they fenced with their walking-sticks and umbrellas; and, in spite of this violent exercise, the fun grew only the more extravagant with the miles they traversed. Their drunkenness was deep-seated and permanent, like fire in a peat; or rather—to be quite just to them—it was not so much to be called drunkenness at all, as the effect of youth and high spirits—a fine night, and the night young, a good road under foot, and the world before you!

I had left them once somewhat unceremoniously; I could not attempt it a second time; and, burthened as I was with Mr. Rowley, I was really glad of assistance. But I saw the lamps of Edinburgh draw near on their hill-top with a good deal of uneasiness, which increased, after we had entered the lighted streets, to positive alarm. All the passers-by were addressed, some of them by name. A worthy man was stopped by Forbes. 'Sir,' said he, 'in the name of the Senatus of the University of Cramond, I confer upon you the degree of LL.D.,' and with the words he bonneted him. Conceive the predicament of St. Ives, committed to the society of these outrageous youths, in a town where the police and his cousin were both looking for him! So far, we had pursued our way unmolested, although raising a clamour fit to wake the dead; but at last, in Abercromby Place, I believe—at least it was a crescent of highly respectable houses fronting on a garden—Byfield and I, having fallen somewhat in the rear with Rowley, came to a simultaneous halt. Our ruffians were beginning to wrench off bells and door-plates!

'Oh, I say!' says Byfield, 'this is too much of a good thing! Confound it, I'm a respectable man—a public character, by George! I can't afford afford to get taken up by the police.'

'My own case exactly,' said I.

'Here, let's bilk them,' said he.

And we turned back and took our way down hill again.

It was none too soon: voices and alarm bells sounded; watchmen here and there began to spring their rattles; it was plain the University of Cramond would soon be at blows with the police of Edinburgh! Byfield and I, running the semi-inanimate Rowley before us, made good despatch, and did not stop till we were several streets away, and the hubbub was already softened by distance.

'Well, sir,' said he, 'we are well out of that! Did ever any one see such a pack of young barbarians?'

'We are properly punished, Mr. Byfield; we had no business there,' I replied.

'No, indeed, sir, you may well say that! Outrageous! And my ascension announced for Friday, you know!' cried the aeronaut. 'A pretty scandal! Byfield the aeronaut at the police-court! Tut-tut! Will you be able to get your rascal home, sir? Allow me to offer you my card. I am staying at Walker and Poole's Hotel, sir, where I should be pleased to see you.'

'The pleasure would be mutual, sir,' said I, 'but I must say my heart was not in my words, and as I watched Mr. Byfield departing I desired nothing less than to pursue the acquaintance.

One more ordeal remained for me to pass. I carried my senseless load upstairs to our lodging, and was admitted by the landlady in a tall white nightcap and with an expression singularly grim. She lighted us into the sitting-room; where, when I had seated Rowley in a chair, she dropped me a cast-iron courtesy. I smelt gunpowder on the woman. Her voice tottered with emotion.

'I give ye nottice, Mr. Ducie,' said she. 'Dacent folks' houses . . .'

And at that apparently temper cut off her utterance, and she took herself off without more words.

I looked about me at the room, the goggling Rowley, the extinguished fire; my mind reviewed the laughable incidents of the day and night; and I laughed out loud to myself—lonely and cheerless laughter! . . . .

CHAPTER XXXI

THE ASSEMBLY BALL

My sleep was fitful, and whether awake or asleep visions danced in my head. Snatches of flageolet and outbursts of song accompanied them. It must have been near dawn before I fell into a heavy slumber; and when I awoke there were no visions, but a sense that my brain had grown solid as a cannonball. The closed shutters did not adequately conceal the fact that it was broad daylight.

Gradually the events of the previous day took shape in my mind. Memory, hampered by the rolling of the cannonball, told me I had fled through the wide streets of the New Town, had walked on country roads and by the shore of the Firth of Forth, had dined at an inn at Cramond, and−. I heard Dalmahoy's voice: 'Plain Living and High Drinking.' Whisky, it seemed, had taken me to considerable heights, only to send me plummeting to the depths. The University of Cramond had provided a pleasing interval, but had not banished the peril of my situation. I was still a hunted man, only now a hunted man with a throbbing head. I reflected weakly that Chance and Circumstance appeared to have withdrawn their favours.

I left my bed with considerable caution and opened the shutters; daylight did not soothe my disordered nerves. Rowley, I thought, might provide some comfort. I caught sight of myself in the glass, and did not like what I saw. The transformation of that sad-looking, bleary-eyed mortal in a nightshirt into someone worthy of name and fortune would take some care. It was late: Rowley should have shown himself; but then I remembered my last sight of Rowley, head in hands in front of the cold hearth, and the unrelenting Mrs. McRankine in attendance, and understood that today the vicomte was likely to be without the assistance of his body-servant.

The realisation did not improve my humour. Servant or no servant, I had a pressing need of hot water, so I put my head round the door of my room and shouted for Rowley. It was a means of venting my ill-temper, however unlikely to produce a response. In the silence that followed I went to the window and looked out onto the strip of garden and the lane behind. There at the end of the lane where it opened onto the square was a man idling against a wall. He may have been innocence itself, but the sight struck a chill into me that did wonders for my head. I strode back across the room, and bawled again for Rowley as I pulled open the door—and found myself face to face with my substantial and steely landlady, bearing before her a large tray, on which there was a teapot and a dish of bannocks. Without a word she marched past me and set the tray down.

'Hot water, Mrs. McRankine?' I ventured with hesitation, remembering my nightshirt.

'Are ye requiring hot water, sir?' she responded, with heavy emphasis, looking beyond me to the corner of the room as if she had noticed some item of furnishing that had not been there before.

'If you would be so good,' said I, humbly, and added, 'Rowley, Mrs. McRankine? How is the lad?

'None the better for your example,' she said loftily.

'I apologise, on his behalf and mine.'

'His behalf! Where you took him last night I am no' speiring. But there are those who say they are gentlemen who should know better.'

Her arms were folded fiercely across her bosom, and she shot a look directly at me and away again with a face that would have turned vintage burgundy to vinegar.

'I think we would both be more comfortable if I were dressed, Mrs. McRankine. Hot water—?' I enquired again in what I intended as tones of honeyed smoothness.

Her compressed mouth relaxed a little, I fancied. She left the room, and within a few moments was back with a can of hot water which she set down with a force that showered the wash stand. I carried out my toilet thoughtfully and with difficulty. There seemed a lack of smooth communication between my hands and my brain, nor was my situation helped by observing, each time I passed the window, that gentleman propped against the wall and examining his fingernails.

I was arranging my shirt cuffs, which looked less than fresh, when there was a heavy knock and the door opened slowly: it was Rowley. He stood on the threshold and gazed fixedly at the floor.

'Well, Mr. Rowley.'

He slowly raised a pale and tragic face. 'Mr. Anne, sir, I didn't mean it, Mr. Anne, sir. I ain't used to it, and that's the truth. Not to toddy, sir. I ain't never had that much before, sir.'

'So much is obvious,' said I coolly, 'and I trust you will avoid doing so again.' I was not disposed to let him off lightly.

'I'm sorry sir, I truly am, it won't happen again, sir, I swear.'

It occurred to me that his bloodshot eyes and uncombed hair reflected my own appearance of just a few minutes before. It occurred to me also that Rowley had entered the University of Cramond at my invitation and that perhaps Mrs. McRankine was right. I relented, and enquired after his state of health.

'I ain't half got a head, sir,' he said eagerly, seizing at the hint of sympathy.

'In that case you are of little use to me. You had better get back to your bed and sleep it off.'

'I'm truly sorry, Mr. Anne—' But I cut him off. 'Rowley,' I yelled, 'Get out. Go to bed. Out of my sight.' And in an instant he was gone, and there was nothing to distract me from the presence lurking at the end of the lane. As I watched he shuffled his feet and blew on his hands, and pulled his hat down against the wind.

I considered what lay before me. It was the day of the Assembly Ball. It was a day that of a surety meant danger—I did not need the gentleman outside to remind me of that—but a day that also meant Flora, and the thought of her revived my flagging spirits. I nibbled at Mrs. McRankine's dry bannocks, and acknowledged her perspicacity; I could not have stomached anything more. The hours stretched before me, empty and unappetising; I was as much a prisoner as if I had been plucked up and set again on the castle ramparts. I paced my room fretfully, and was surprised by a sudden longing for the windy corners and unexpected vistas of the New Town. As long as it was daylight I could not venture out, that much was certain: only under the veil of darkness would it be safe to attempt escape.'Come, civil night'—but now, as if to spite me, the sunshine sparkled and the clouds streamed high in the sky.

My head gradually recovered its equilibrium, but my spirits did not. From the window of my sitting room I could see into the square. For a moment I thought my watchful friend had given up his vigil—but no, he was making a reconnaissance of the other side of the square. I read the *Mercury* of yesterday: it told me that the escaped prisoner Champdivers was still not apprehended. I experienced little reassurance in reading about my successful evasion of the authorities. I took up a position to the side of the window, and was in time to see my gentleman in conversation with another, who handed him something wrapped in paper which, from the gusto with which it was attacked I surmised to be a meat pie. It reminded me that I had tasted nothing that day but a few morsels of bannock, and the faint stirrings of hunger suggested that I was restored to humanity. Now the consumer of the meat pie was alone again, measuring his steps up and down the street with his hands in his pockets.

I enquired of Mrs. McRankine if some refreshment might be forthcoming, and she obliged with an ill grace. She only softened when

Rowley appeared later, a little ruffled and apprehensive but with colour in his cheeks. He opened his mouth and I read in the contraction of his brow another attempt at apology.

'Rowley,' said I, 'we will say no more about it. There is work to be done.'

He closed his mouth, but eyed my chop with interest.

'Mrs. McRankine, I think a little dry toast would not be detrimental to the lad's digestion.'

'I'm as right as rain, sir, honest I am. I could eat a breakfast, and a dinner, and—'

Mrs. McRankine's tender hand was on his shoulder and propelled him to the door. 'Toast,' she said decisively, 'and a glass of ale, mebbe.'

I was sure I detected the ghost of a grin on Rowley's face as they made their exit, and a hint of almost maternal warmth cross Mrs. McRankine's stony visage. Rowley was the difficulty: I could not abandon him; I might commit him to the care of Mr. Robbie, or enquire if there was a place for him at Swanston Cottage, but there was no time to make trial of these suggestions. In a few hours I would close the door on Mrs. McRankine's iron-ruled abode, very possibly never to return. I was still deliberating when the lady herself entered the room to retrieve the relics of my meal. The tray in her hands fortified her already formidable presence. Her bosom expanded with what was clearly the harbinger of speech.

'Mr. Ducie,' she began, in a voice that vibrated with prodigious resolution, 'I have made up my mind.'

'Do not fear, my good Mrs. McRankine. I will not be troubling you with my presence for very much longer.'

'It's the devil's work, I've no doubt,' said she, with rigid severity, 'and the sooner you take yourself off the better. But the boy; I've made up my mind. He's no' the brand of Satan he might seem. There's good in him, if ye ken whaur to look. He'd best stay wi' me.'

I had faced the havoc of the battlefield and not flinched under fire, but I could not have summoned the courage to argue with my landlady, even had I wished to.

'I have a debt to settle,' said I, 'and I'll add something for his keep.'

I had underestimated her.

'Keep!' she exploded. 'Keep! He'll keep himsel'. He'll do to run up and doon the stair, and for the messages, and he can see to the fires—'

'He has a healthy appetite,' I interposed, thinking of the dry toast. 'He's still growing.'

'Aye, he is that, and growing wild, if gentlemen get their way. He'll get guid plain victuals, Mr. Ducie, but his thirst—that's anither matter.'

'I am confident, Mrs. McRankine, that in your tender care he'll have little opportunity to go astray.'

Still brandishing the tray she turned to the door, muttering as she went something concerning the disguises of the devil. It reminded me that I had yet to inspect my ball suit, which had been delivered the day before in my absence. An examination might serve to hurry on the hours of the afternoon. Mrs. McRankine had hung it in the press in my bedroom, whither I now repaired. My Leith Street tailor had accomplished his task neatly, if not in the height of fashion. I had selected a pleasing combination of dove grey and deep blue, which I now regarded with some satisfaction. The lack of ostentation would, in the circumstances, serve me well; it would not do to draw too much attention to myself, and besides I had only to think of my cousin to be reminded that simplicity better became my position than extravagance. The Assembly Ball was not an occasion to be kenspeckle, to use a word I have since learned.

Outside the light was fading, and with it what warmth the winter sun had introduced. In the dusk I could not at first see the watcher in the square, until a movement attracted my attention. He had retreated into a doorway, and was blowing and rubbing his hands. I wondered he did not summon his fellows, knock on Mrs. McRankine's door, and make an end of it. It seemed he could not be sure of my presence; he had had a long, cold day of it on mere supposition. I had no inclination to reward him for his pains, and must deliberate on how I was to avoid this.

There was a back entrance, leading from Mrs. McRankine's kitchen into the walled garden. I would need to scale the wall in ball suit and dancing pumps, but it could be done. My plan was to skirt the square and make my way up North Bridge. I thought it wise not to inform the good Bethiah of my intentions, nor to enter into any explanations, but I would need Rowley's assistance. I summoned him, therefore, to help me dress, and as I equipped myself for the evening's entertainment sketched out my strategy.

'Crikey, Mr. Anne,' was his first response, 'in them togs!'

'Yes, Rowley,' I assured him, 'in these, as you are pleased to call them, togs, with the addition of a great-coat, for even within these four walls I can smell the coldness of the wind.'

'Sir, let me go with you, sir, I'll see you right. Between us we'll give them Red-breasts the slip.'

'No, Rowley. You may see me over the wall, and then you must return to the safe-keeping of the good Mrs. McRankine, who swears she'll feed you, body and soul, in return for which some small duties may be required.'

His protests were less vociferous than I had expected, but I had other things on my mind and did not wonder at the matter. I arranged my modest shirt frills and straightened my coat, and satisfied myself that the figure in the glass was up to the mark. Rowley removed a speck of dust from my sleeve and stepped back to view the ensemble. His good-natured, freckled face beamed.

'Lord, Mr. Anne, sir, you'll be the admiration of the ladies.'

I turned and gave him a bow, and his freckles were lost in a blush. I did not see fit to remark that there was only one lady whose approbation I cherished.

'Come, my good Rowley, we must assault the wall. Step out and see if the coast is clear. We can do without the lady of the house as witness to this adventure.'

Rowley darted to the door and opened it silently; a moment later he beckoned me to follow. We slipped down the stair in the dark. There was a sliver of light showing under the parlour door, and we tiptoed past and through into the back premises. The pots and pans in Mrs. McRankine's kitchen shone dimly as we crept to the back door. Rowley lifted the latch; the creak of the door could have awakened the dead, and we hurried out into the cold night. With Rowley's help I hoisted myself to the top of the wall. There was no-one about. I whispered my farewell to my faithful attendant.

'You'll come back, Mr. Anne, sir?' was the anxious reply.

'I'll be back, Rowley, for a certainty. I'm drawn by a magnet more powerful than volition.'

I looked down at his puzzled face, and dropped to the ground on the far side. I remembered another cold night, and a more perilous escape; and pulling my great-coat about me set off for the Assembly Ball.

A sleety rain began to fall as I made my brisk way up the North Bridge. I bent my head against the wind, and mercifully overcame my aversion for the Old Town: for the Ball was at Buccleuch Place, beyond the Bristo Port. Carriages overtook me, and I wondered if they, too, were destined for the Ball. I crossed the High Street, and blessed the darkness, which kept the looming walls of the castle from my sight. When I turned into Buccleuch Place there were lights and a caravan of carriages to show me where to go. A few evening wanderers had been drawn by the bustle at the entrance, and now stood and stared with dull interest as the guests arrived.

I had no wish to offer the opportunity for examination, and entered without a pause; and having entered, decided I could do without the extravagance of an announcement. I attached myself to the wake of two gentlemen who first left their coats with an attendant, in which I imitated them, and then made for the ballroom. On the presentation of their cards their names were announced in ringing tones and, taking advantage of the momentary confusion that attended the finish of a dance, I insinuated myself behind them. I was confident that I looked my part, and besides, I had my invitation in my pocket, and if challenged would produce it with a flourish.

Luck was at my elbow, for the moment at least. In the swirl of movement, as gentlemen escorted their partners to the chairs arranged around the walls, I was able to mingle, and gradually I edged my way to a corner where I could survey the scene. I needed time to look about me, for I was not at all sure what to expect, or how I should conduct myself; I was not familiar with the formal amusements of Edinburgh society. I scanned the assembled company, and recognised the young woman who had commanded Ronald's attentions at Mr. Robbie's. But the face I sought was not there.

The music struck up again. I kept my eyes on the entrance, but, although guests were arriving and names were bellowed, the name I strained to hear was not announced. I was not so oblivious of my surroundings as to be unaware of the glances I attracted and the murmurings amongst the young ladies. I began to feel foolish; then, just as I thought I might introduce myself to Ronald's acquaintance, I saw and heard the arrivals I was waiting for.

The name 'Gilchrist' rang across the room as if flutes and fiddles did not exist; and the name 'Chevenix' followed like an encore. Miss Gilchrist, regal in black, led the way. Flora came behind, on the arm of Chevenix, and I think a curse escaped me, for there was a sudden turning of heads in my direction. Mr. Robbie and Ronald brought up the rear. They skirted the dancers, and were unaware of my presence, although how Flora could not have felt the intensity of my gaze I do not know. I fancied there was some awkwardness in her step, and attributed it to the attentions of Chevenix. She was not comfortable, I explained to myself, with that obtrusively scrubbed and upright officer so close.

My heart and my head were in my feet, which took me inexorably to Flora; I could not have prevented them if Chevenix had flourished a sabre and ordered the repulse of my impetuous advance. I had eyes only for Flora, whose own eyes widened at my approach. I bowed, she blushed, Ronald spluttered, and the Major's hand went to his empty hip. Miss Gilchrist turned to stone; not a muscle moved. Mr. Robbie bustled to her side and muttered something I did not catch. I bowed; then I heard Mr. Robbie say, 'Madam, he is acting under my advice. Let me explain—,' and he drew her aside. I despatched silent thanks and turned to Flora, whose eloquent cheek paled and flushed and paled again. She disengaged one arm from Chevenix and I laid claim to the other. Chevenix looked thunderous but could not find his voice. Ronald shifted from one foot to the other and attempted speech. 'Now look here, St. Ives—'

'Ronald!' Flora's clear voice and reproachful look would surely have silenced a battalion. Ronald fell back, and his capitulation was an effective restraint on Chevenix. I seized my opportunity, and drew her gently away to the far side of the ballroom. Looking back we saw the four of them, like vessels run aground. As we watched Mr. Robbie piloted Miss Gilchrist in the direction of the card room, while Ronald and Chevenix, by the angry set of their shoulders, sent signals of pique and frustration across the room. Flora looked up at me: her eyes were clouded with anxiety, yet—I am sure I did not delude myself—the light of love danced there also.

'Anne, this is an appalling risk. Why are you here, of all places, where the whole of Edinburgh society can see you?'

'My dear,' said I, pressing her arm as warmly as I dared, 'I am here to see you.'

Her answering blush was a joy to behold, but nevertheless she frowned. 'It is far too dangerous; I fear you have been very foolish.'

'Yes, I have been foolish; not in coming here, for I swear I have had no choice, but in placing my money in a bank that is now being watched. To leave Scotland, I must have money, and I must leave Scotland. Money may not answer all, but it is, just now, much to the purpose. And so, my dearest Flora, my only course of action was to see you, for you are my only other banker. I try to reach you at Swanston, and what do I find? There is Chevenix on sentry go with an infernal beast called Towzer. I believe I may have sent Towzer to the land of his ferocious forefathers, but Chevenix is clearly not contemplating such a journey, and I am too much of a gentleman to provide him with the necessary passport. Dearest, do you have the money?'

She bit her lip, and turned to a chair set against the wall. She sat down, as if suddenly faint, and twisted her hands. When she looked up there were tears in her beautiful eyes and she shook her head.

'Until tonight I have kept the notes next to my heart, but I could not bring them to the ball. O Anne, I am sorry: they are in my room at Swanston, locked in my jewellery box.'

Tragedy was painted on her face; I bent closer to her. 'Well then,' said I, 'you will get them for me, and leave them somewhere safe. I'm sure it can be done. Even the vigilant Chevenix must sleep, and Towzer, I hope and trust, is no more. I'll get me to Swanston Cottage again, and this time won't be so easily turned away.'

'You must not come to the cottage, Anne. It cannot be long before the scent will lead your pursuers there. No, I will have to meet you, somewhere on the hill.'

Her eyes darkened as she considered, and I admired her the more, for her beauty and for her care for my safety.

'You must do nothing that will put you at risk,' I said urgently.

'The danger is small,' said she, with a little smile. 'My reputation, perhaps, is at hazard, but not my life. And besides, to do something of use, to do something for you, Anne, is what I most want in the world.'

She spoke with such grave simplicity I almost, there and then, threw caution aside and took her in my arms to show my gratitude; and perhaps would have done, if a commotion at the entrance to the ballroom had not attracted my attention. I saw and heard at the same time: my cousin, resplendent, dripping with frills, clouded, I am sure, with scent, and careful to hold himself aloof from the crowd, paused and surveyed the company while his name was trumpeted. I saw Ronald spin on his heel, examine this new Viscount of St. Ives with dropping jaw, and turn his eyes slowly back on me with a face of sheer bewilderment. Beside me Flora caught her breath.

Although minutes before the floor had swirled with dancers, the music had tailed away again and the dancers had, as if on purpose to expose us, drifted to the peripheries of the room. Alain took this opportunity to advance across the room, directing his eyeglass this way and that. Silently and without the flicker of an eyelid I watched his swaggering approach; it was clear that he was casting about for someone, and my guess that I was the object of his search put little to the hazard. I heard Flora whisper, 'There must be a back entrance,' but I was not going to run like a fox sprung from its lair. I kept my eyes steadily on Alain and waited for the inevitable moment when he would see me. When he did, he paused for the briefest of seconds, his lip forming a scornful curve—some might have thought it a smile. He steered his way towards us, but did not hurry his pace.

'This is an unexpected pleasure,' I said smoothly, 'I saw in the newspaper that you were gracing Edinburgh with your presence, but I would not have thought this to be the milieu you favoured.'

'You are right, my dear cousin,' he replied, looking about him with an intensification of disdain. 'But pressing business has brought me here. I was fortunate enough to discover that a kinsman I have urgent need to see was on the invitation list. And so I have sought him out. He is not so discriminating as I.' He smiled wolfishly, and allowed his gaze to linger on Flora, who returned his look with a little too much interest. 'Are you going to present me to the young lady?'

He bowed, without waiting for an introduction which I had no intention of providing. Flora inclined her head, and fury boiled in my breast, but of a sudden subsided. The music had struck up again and couples were beginning to take the floor. I tried to convey all my thoughts to Flora.

'Miss Gilchrist,' I said, 'will you dance?' And I appended to my question a mute prayer that she would not take it into her head to refuse me. She looked uncertain; I proffered my arm and addressed her with my eyes. At last she rose, and with another inclination towards my odious cousin laid her hand on my arm.

Once on the floor I had to convey my plan in as few words as possible, as we spun past each other.

'You must feign illness,' I breathed into her ear. 'Or an injury, though that would cast aspersions on my dancing. Do not ask why. You are feeling faint and must go home.'

Whether it was the music, or the movement of the dance, or Flora's graceful figure brushing me so close, I do not know, but there was courage and gaiety in my heart that laughed at danger; 'pleased with the danger, when the waves went high'—though when I faced the waves later in my adventure I could not have recalled that line with such confidence. Even when I saw Alain make his way to the entrance and consult with someone in the shadows, even when I looked the other way and recognised the moleskin waistcoat at the back of the room, even when I became aware of two gentlemen who were assuredly uninvited guests and clearly had no interest in the melée except in me, the surge of my spirits was not quelled.

At this juncture Flora stumbled, and I caught her, while the other dancers in our set eddied round us.

'My ankle,' she gasped with admirable effect. I led her, hobbling, to the side.

In a moment Ronald and Chevenix were beside her. I intimated that a glass of water was required, and Chevenix sped off to oblige, while Ronald hovered uncertainly.

'We must get your sister home,' said I.

Flora sat silent, with her lips pressed together, as if in pain.

'I think you should inform your aunt,' I went on, with deliberate emphasis. Ronald was not of the speediest in his apprehension, and showed some reluctance to leave his sister in my care; but Flora, blessed girl, came to my aid.

'Please, Ronald,' she murmured. 'Mr. St. Ives is right—I think I must go home.'

He could not hesitate then, and I took advantage of our few moments alone together to press Flora's hand and whisper, 'I will endeavour to accompany you. It may be the only way I can give these hounds the slip. Your aunt—will she hide the fox with her skirts, do you think, or ride with the whippers-in?'

There was no time for Flora to reply before Miss Gilchrist herself was sweeping towards us, Ronald and Mr. Robbie in her train. From the other side came Chevenix with a glass of water in his gloved hand. Miss Gilchrist regarded Flora with more scepticism than concern, and turned on me a severe look.

'The French style of dancing seems a trifle violent, Mosha,' said she, raising her eyeglass as Chevenix bent over Flora with the water. She sipped pathetically. 'Well, well, we'd better get you home. Ronald, the carriage, if you please, and Major, if you would be so good—', and she indicated with a gesture that allowed no miscomprehension that she required his assistance. He offered his arm. Robbie fussed behind, a little out of countenance; I helped Flora to her feet, and privately blessed her aunt for an angel. Thus we processed slowly to the entrance. Alain watched us; the uninvited guests, one of whom looked up from the study of his fingernails in a manner that was familiar, watched us; I dare say the gentleman in the moleskin waistcoat watched us, but I did not look behind to see. I counted on their reluctance to create a disturbance, and hoped they were relying on a discreet arrest on the street outside.

In the entrance hall there was some little commotion as coats and wraps were collected and dispersed; I stood a little apart. I was ready to take my cue from Miss Gilchrist, or if need be to direct my own play. Flora, her face a picture of pain endured without complaint, was proving a consummate actress. I forced myself to make no move as Chevenix tenderly arranged a shawl about my Flora's shoulders, and again I had to bring to mind that jealous indignation was not my part. Equipped for the cold night, Miss Gilchrist turned towards me.

'Mosha,' said she, with the slightest inclination of the head, 'you have been most attentive. Could I prevail upon your kindness a little longer—if you would step outside and see if Ronald has brought the carriage up—' This last she said with her voice a trifle raised.

I bowed and complied, although it meant turning my back on Chevenix who was now encouraging Flora to lean heavily on his arm. I slipped through the front door. A glance behind showed me Miss Gilchrist and Mr. Robbie arrange themselves expansively in the doorway, almost obscuring Alain's henchmen. The wind blew a flurry of sleet against me as I came down the steps, and the cobbles threw back an uncertain reflection of the street lamps. A carriage was approaching, and as it slowed the door opened and Ronald leapt out. The others had followed me down the steps. Flora was helped into the carriage first, both Ronald and Chevenix in attendance; and then Miss Gilchrist made a performance of her entry that brought a whispered 'brava' to my throat. She dropped her fan, called to the coachman to hold the horses still, and reproved Ronald for his clumsiness. In the midst of this small ferment I was

able to insinuate myself round to the other side of the carriage.
There were no bystanders at this late hour, and no one at all that I
could see to witness me silently open the carriage door and climb in
on my hands and knees as the wonderful Miss Gilchrist made her
entry on the near side. She paused to turn imperiously to Ronald.

'Instruct the coachman to make all speed, if you please Ronald.
You gentlemen may remain and enjoy yourselves.'

I crouched on the floor of the coach, and could have believed that
time had stopped. Then, of a sudden, all was action. With an unto-
ward briskness Miss Gilchrist settled herself in her seat, the door
was slammed shut, I heard Ronald's voice call out to the coachman,
and the carriage jolted forward. As the horses moved into a lively
trot I was aware of a disturbance behind us.

'Ah,' said Miss Gilchrist blithely, 'so they are not entirely blind. If
they were in my hire I'd be loath to part with a bawbee for their
services.'

She settled back with a sigh that smacked of satisfaction. Flora
had said nothing all this while. She was tantalisingly close, but I did
not dare to reach out my hand, or even speak.

'Mosha Viscount,' the old lady continued. 'Pray get off the floor
and take a seat like a gentleman. I do not care to share my carriage
with a man who behaves like a thief—or a murderer.'

'Madam—,' I began, and at the same time there was a little cry of
protest from Flora.

'It's ower late for explanations, Mosha. Mr. Robbie has informed
me: I trust I will not live to regret tonight's work.'

I began to reassure her, but she had more to say. 'Do not make the
mistake of thinking you are welcome at Swanston. I'll not have ye
in my house; I'll not have Runners and riffraff at my door. I'll gie ye
a hurl out of the city, sir, but thereafter you must make your own
way as best you can. Mr. Robbie tells me you're an innocent man;
but innocence in the eyes of the law may not be the same as innocence in the eyes of the world.'

'But aunt—,' Flora attempted, but she too was cut short.

'Flora, you have been foolish enough and caused trouble enough
for one evening. We must think of your health.'

In the darkness I felt rather than saw Flora blush, and I longed to
comfort and console her. Some moments passed with only the clat-
ter of wheels and hooves over the cobbles to break the silence. I
strained my ears for sounds of pursuit; at last, unable to tolerate
the suspense longer, I let down the window and looked back along
the road. All I could see were the shimmering street lights and the
dark windows of the houses on either side.

'Madam,' said I, pulling my head back out of the rain. 'I have no
wish to take advantage for longer than is forced upon me. I do not

think we are being followed. From now on my own legs can carry me.'

'We'll bring ye altogether out of the city,' she said in a voice that brooked no argument.

In another mile or two we had left the lights and the cobbles behind us. Without a word Miss Gilchrist banged on the carriage roof as a signal to stop; the horses slowed to a trot, then to a walk, then halted.

'Miss Gilchrist,' I said, 'I will always be grateful.' I could not look at Flora, but trusted she could feel all that I could not say. I opened the carriage door, and dropped to the ground.

'Anne—Mr. St. Ives—you cannot spend a winter's night with no protection. Take this plaid—' and taking the rug from her knee Flora bundled it into my arms; it was like the one that had served me well in my former walk to England. As she pressed it on me she contrived to touch my hand, and that brief contact warmed me as a plaid never could. I was still standing clutching it to my breast as the door banged shut and the carriage lurched forward. I was splashed by the turning wheels, but was changed to stone and could not step aside. How long I stood there I do not know; the lights and the sound of the carriage both vanished as I held the thought of Flora to me with the plaid. I was standing thus, oblivious of the icy rain, when I became aware of another sound, and in an instant I saw what a gift I made, alone at the roadside, to my cousin's vengeance. If he found me now it was not arrest that I should fear so much as execution.

I threw myself over the roadside dyke and lay face down in the wet grass. Minutes later came the sound of flagging hooves and blowing horses. Wherever I betook myself now I would have to stay clear of the road; and I deemed it a certainty that they would scarcely wait for daylight before knocking on the door of Swanston Cottage, and scouring the nearby countryside.

CHAPTER XXXII

A NIGHT OF TROUBLE

SILENCE returned to the roadway and cautiously I got to my feet. My dove grey and blue were smeared with mud, my dancing pumps full of water. I was in all probability less than an hour's walk from Swanston, yet never since I first set eyes on her had I felt so distant from Flora. The blood that had rushed through my veins so short a time ago slowed to a surly trickle, and all spirit was exhausted. Chance had raised my hopes only to dash them to the ground again; I was the plaything of fate, of the elements, with no shelter or comfort but a checked plaid, which at that moment seemed more fit for a sheep than a man.

As if to drive the point home a gust of wind found every chink in my insufficient covering and flung the rain in my face. Before me were the dark slopes of the Pentland Hills and a moon veiled with cloud. My only way south now lay across those hills, for the second time, and the prospect did not cheer me. Now I would not even have the unloquacious companionship of Sim and Candlish; and now I had not only the law at my heels but my cousin, whipped on by jealousy and greed. His sneering smile danced even now in my head, all the more furiously as I remembered my bold statement of intentions to Romaine, and I began to rehearse my reproaches that he had let me set off on such a harebrained enterprise. But would I, could I, not have turned my steps towards Edinburgh? Could I have resisted the enchantment of Flora and the eloquent hints of happiness I was sure I read in her eyes? I fixed my thoughts on her and on the dawn that would bring her. No, I could not wish myself out of that infernal night, if that was the price I had to pay for Flora. *Forsan et haec olim meminisse iuvabit.*

I began to pick my way across a field of rough pasture. I must have cut a fine figure, if there had been anyone to see me: my ruffles drooping in the rain, my face and incongruous costume bedaubed with mud, my shoes squelching at every step. I clambered over another dry stone dyke, making sure I kept at a distance from the road. My cousin's carriage might have pulled up anywhere, to rest the tired horses, or his men might now be importunately calling for entrance at Swanston Cottage, disregarding all respect for the hour or the ladies.

Above me half a moon lolled in the sky, and by its dim light I made out the shapes of trees. Some half an hour of trudging through mud and wet grass brought to view the glimmer of stone cottages. I recalled the hamlet of Swanston, and thought I had my bearings. To the right should be the roof that sheltered my Flora. I could not risk too close an approach to any habitation, so struck to the left, half fell into a rivulet of water, stumbled on stones, and dodged branches that I swear reached out to impede my progress. There was misery in every step I took, and it was with a blind instinct that I kept going, until at last I found myself under some tall pines which had dropped a carpet of needles on the ground that was soft and almost dry.

I sank down and pulled the plaid around me. There was some small shelter here from the wind and rain, and I stretched myself out with my head against a tree trunk. I think I could have wept, though whether from relief or wretchedness I cannot tell. And, to say the truth, whether the moisture on my cheek was salt tears or the rain even now I do not know. I ached with weariness; I might almost have wished to see my cousin stalking through the trees with a weapon in his hand, so we might then and there have made an end of it, one way or the other. But nothing came to disturb my fitful rest, unless it were my dreams. As I slept and woke by snatches the owl hunted through my visions of claret-coloured coaches beset by saffron-coated ruffians in dancing pumps. Rowley's freckled countenance appeared in a cloud of scented lace and a wreath of chains and ornaments. Miss Gilchrist, with a great ring of keys, patrolled the ramparts of Edinburgh Castle and called out the hour in stentorian tones. More than once I started half to my feet, sure it was morning and that I heard approaching footsteps, but just as I thought I saw the shape of Flora through the trees, I realised it was the moonlight playing tricks with my weakened imagination, and that the sound that had roused me was some tiny denizen of the night going about its business.

That I was light-headed in those half-waking moments I can believe. The cold and the rain, the low ebb of my spirits, the shivers that at intervals engulfed me, all combined to raise phantoms that mocked and taunted. At last I became aware of chirruped phrases from the waking birds. My limbs were so stiff they at first refused any instruction to move, and when at last I did struggle to my feet the pain when the blood began to flow again was excruciating. I took myself uncertainly to the edge of the trees and looked to the east. A delicate yellow light was spreading across the sky; I watched this wondrous dawn with a kind of vacancy of heart and mind, as if it were my last, or beyond my last, and I was no longer alive to understand it.

Some instinct urged me to keep moving, and I ventured a little way beyond the pines. I could see the village of Swanston and the mired track that led to the road beyond; I could see the fields I must have crossed and the stone dykes I had climbed. There was Swanston Cottage, within its sheltering ring of elms and beeches, with a thread of smoke rising from its chimney. Beyond, I could just make out, as the darkness faded, the Hunters' Tryst, with an answering pillar of smoke atop its chimney, and I was beset by a passionate longing for blazing logs and steaming toddy.

I began to make my way down the hillside and away from the cottages. With no clear intention in mind, yet with a need to keep moving, for if I did not exert my limbs I might remain permanently in the contortions of Laocoon, I knew only that I must not stray too far from Swanston. I prayed that Flora, or Miss Gilchrist even, might find a way to make contact with me. They would guess that I would be skulking nearby, but how they might get a message to me, or venture onto the hillside, I could not imagine.

My feet had taken me dangerously near the road, and I was brought up sharply by the sight of two country people, a woman with a shawl and a basket, and a man with a shepherd's staff, making their way briskly along. I slipped behind a tree and watched them go; they were soon followed by others, and I wondered idly what their destination was at such an early hour. Discretion determined that I should retreat up the hillside again, and I studied the road from my former vantage point. Clusters of people, in twos and threes, came along the road from the city, but they did not interest me. It was a carriage I was looking for, or some sign that Swanston Cottage was being watched.

By now hunger was gnawing relentlessly at my innards. I bethought me—I could not help it—of the little bow-windowed dining room of the cottage, and of eggs and game pie; and before I knew it, I was again at the edge of the abyss, looking down into a deep pool of black despair, and convinced that fate was my enemy. A wretched hopelessness took possession of me: although so close, I would never see Flora again; and the hunters were no doubt at that very moment preparing to spring the trap. If there are times when all seems to go well with a man, there are others when all goes ill; I felt I had lived half my life in the last twenty-four hours and that in that half lifetime fortune had entirely deserted me. But even as I was brooding thus I was edging towards Swanston Cottage, almost without being aware. I had sufficient presence of mind to approach with caution, yet it was madness even to draw near.

I crouched behind a whin bush on the slope above. The smoke still plumed thinly from the chimney. I thought of them all within; Ronald and Chevenix, no doubt, as well as the ladies. I thought of Miss Gilchrist with a silver teapot before her, and Ronald doing justice to a boyish appetite. It was no use: I could not for long stave off a vision of comestibles, and it was so commanding that I almost missed the movement of the cattle, which had all the while been clustered at the gate. Now the gate was open, and a slight female figure in rough country clothes was leading them to the byre, with a black and white collie bringing up the rear. Each of the half-dozen beasts made a sedate entry into the byre, and moments later the shawled figure came out again, with the collie at her heels, and I wondered that she should neglect the milking of her charges. She went to the back door and picked up a basket, and then to my surprise, came through another gate that led onto the hillside. She walked slowly, pausing often to look about her. Her shawl was drawn close over her head: she held her basket firmly to her side. She was half way up the slope before I recognised my Flora.

I held my breath and invoked all the fates I had just been cursing to send her to me. I did not dare to call out or even show myself, in case it proved a signal for a view halloo. In the event, it was the dog that found me. He came quartering up the hillside, his nose to the ground, his tail hoisted high in the breeze. He soon sniffed me out, and barked a message to his mistress, and all who chanced to be near, his tail wagging the while.

'Wattie!' she called. 'What is it, what have you found?'

Fortunately for Wattie he was an amiable beast, though for his mistress's sake I would not have harmed a hair of his hide, even with the memory of Towzer so fresh in my mind. When Flora was close enough I raised my hand carefully and assayed a reticent wave. At first she looked puzzled; then understanding suffused her face. But, wonderful girl, she came steadily on, calling to the dog, as if he were her only care. When she reached the whin bush she dropped to the ground beside me, and I embraced her, her rough clothes blending with my mired velvet.

'I almost did not know you,' said I.

'These are borrowed clothes. I wish I had been able to borrow clothes for you.' She looked piteously at me. 'But at least I have brought food, and this time I think my aunt will overlook any shortage at our own table. O Anne, I so much hoped I should find you on the hillside, and so much feared I should not.'

'We cannot stay here. Are our friends of last night about this early?'

'I have seen no one. My disguise is as much to shield me from Ronald and the Major as from your pursuers, for they consider me

compromised enough without seeking your company on the hill.
But they will soon discover I have gone, and will guess I have gone
in search of you. Dearest Anne, you must be so cold, and so
hungry!'

'Never mind that. A place of safety is the first desideratum. We
must not linger.' I had my eye on the cottage below us, expecting to
see at any moment the figures of Ronald and Chevenix bustling out
of the door.

Flora, meanwhile, was looking about her. 'Do you see the T
Wood—those trees on the hillside?' She pointed higher, and to the
left. 'And the course of the burn?'

I looked where she pointed, and saw not only the T-shaped stand
of trees and the burn, but the mist that had shrouded the summit of
the hill drifting downwards. I nodded, perceiving her meaning.

'The mist favours us. We should make our way singly to the trees.
I'll climb up to meet the mist, and come down the course of the
stream. It will be safe for you to take a more direct route. In that
dress and with your dog you will be taken at a distance for a dairy
lass in search of a stray beast.'

She smiled. 'That was my intention.'

'Go now,' I urged, 'as if Wattie had found a rabbit, not a man—
although, I swear, I feel more like a rabbit.'

Flora went on her way, from time to time casting an anxious
glance back in my direction, and the collie, who had watched us
with his ears pricked and his tongue lolling, escorted her on the
flank. I waited, and prayed for the mist to descend still further. I
counted to one hundred, then to one hundred again. At last, I
emerged from my inadequate hiding place and strolled casually up
the green slope. Within minutes I was in the clammy embrace of the
mist. I continued upwards, until I judged I was higher than the
wood Flora had pointed out, and then struck across to meet the
burn. There was an eerie silence, and I was almost in the stream
before I heard its cheerful rippling.

I followed the burn down, more than once missing my footing on
the bank and plunging into the water up to the knee. The mist
thinned as I descended: the trees appeared as shadowy emana-
tions, and then a shape rose to meet me, and we embraced again,
this time with rather more security, and with Wattie dancing attendance. Then Flora released herself from my arms and regarded me
with the tenderest concern.

'My poor Anne, you must eat. How I wish I had something to
warm you.'

'Dearest, you have warmed me more thoroughly than any fire.'

Her cheeks, already pink from the coldness of the air, deepened,
and she at once brought forth bannocks, cheese and milk from her

basket. We made a ghostly meal, sitting side by side in the creeping mist. When we had finished—and Flora insisted that I had the lion's share; I needed small persuasion—I wrapped my plaid around us both and laid my cheek, rough with a day's growth of beard, next to hers. For a few blissful moments we sat thus, and I wondered at myself, the Vicomte Anne de Saint-Yves, who had often boasted that he was carefree and heart-whole, wooing a daughter of the enemy of France on a rough hillside.

The interlude was brief, for the remembrance that I was a hunted man stalked our happiness. 'You are sure no-one saw you?' I enquired anxiously.

Flora shook her head, free now from the shawl that had covered it, with a few curls escaping which even in the mist-filled wood glinted with gold.

'I do not think so, but I cannot tell for sure. There were people on the road below, but they had no reason to take note of me. They were probably thinking only of Professor Byfield and his balloon ascension.'

'Byfield! Of course! That is the attraction. I wondered at so many people on the road at so early an hour. Well, well, so today sees his great attempt.'

Having found an explanation I thought no more about it. Every minute that we lingered was foolishness, and we both knew it; yet to take my leave and set my face to the south was almost more than I could bear. It was Flora who made the first move, gathering up the remnants of our feast then she took from the basket a little packet, which she placed in my hand.

'Do not go without these,' she said.

The delight of being with Flora had quite obliterated the object of my night's suffering. I looked up and our eyes met. I crushed the packet inside my coat and reached for both her hands. Above us the wind shook the branches, and through them I saw clear blue sky. The mist had retreated up the hill, where it still obscured the summit, but beyond it again was the blue of the sky. We got to our feet in silence; I could think of no words sufficient to the purpose. We might defer our parting for a little, but we both knew it had to come, as sure as fate.

'Will you see me on my way?'

She nodded. Before we left the shelter of the T Wood I took her in my arms once more. 'Whatever happens I will return for you,' I murmured. 'You must believe me.'

'I do,' was her soft reply, and I felt beneath the rough wool of her borrowed dress the quickened beat of her heart, and it was not in me to doubt that we would be reunited.

We came out onto the hillside. High clouds scudded across the sky, chased by a brisk east wind. The cry of the curlew mingled with the bleating of sheep, and I was almost reconciled to the prospect of life in this inhospitable land, which without Flora would have seemed bleak beyond measure.

'We go west, I fancy,' said I, surveying a pathless terrain scattered with whin bushes and fragments of the autumn's yellowed bracken.

'I think we must climb first,' was Flora's answer, 'and make our way along the ridge until we meet the drove road. It will be safer that way.'

There was a fickle warmth in the sun, and the hills seemed peaceful enough. I felt calmer now: the gentle presence of Flora had cast the fear of pursuit into the shadows. But I was concerned that, though the slopes seemed gentle, the climb would prove too steep for Flora. I remembered Sim and Candlish and the shaggy cattle on the top of Howden, and the grey hills rolling into the distance. With a rush all the events that followed crowded into my brain: I could not allow Flora to take her place with them.

'My dear,' I began, but got no further, for as I turned to her I saw beyond that the trickle of people making their way along the road towards the Hunters' Tryst had become a stream, and at the same instant there came into my view, stepping briskly up the path from Swanston, Ronald and Chevenix. I seized Flora's hand and we ran over the rough ground, Wattie keeping us delighted company, and scattering a half-dozen matted and indignant sheep as we went. But we had been seen, and our two pursuers at once diverged from the path to cut us off. We turned and began to climb but Flora was already out of breath and my legs were weak as water after the night's exertions. We came to a panting halt.

'Let me talk to them,' gasped Flora. 'Ronald is my brother—he would not wish to harm the man I love—and the Major—he is a gentleman—'

I found breath to expostulate. 'The Major is a confounded, interfering—'

Something in Flora's face prevented me from finishing the sentence, and besides it was too late. The Major and Ronald, red-faced but with the benefit of a good night's sleep and a hot breakfast, no doubt, were coming on us fast. I swung round to confront them, and had time to compose myself before they reached us. I own that although I summoned every shred of dignity to my aid I cannot have struck a very impressive figure. I saw the faces of the two gentlemen before me take in my bedraggled appearance, and also the unfamiliar apparel of Miss Flora. I was determined to spike their guns before they mounted their attack; I bowed.

'Good morning, gentlemen. A fine day for a balloon ascent: you are no doubt making your way to observe the spectacle. I understand Professor Byfield is an aeronaut of considerable experience. I had the honour of meeting him only the other day. I am sure he is worthy of your attention.'

Ronald was beyond words, or perhaps only beyond breath. It was Chevenix who replied.

'This is no time to jest,' he admonished. 'Miss Flora—'

At this point Ronald found his voice. 'Flora, what are you thinking of? In those clothes, with this man? Let us take you home.'

'But Ronald,' said Flora sweetly, 'I only wish to watch the ascension of Professor Byfield's balloon. It is a most important event in the history of science. I would not miss it for the world. Will you and the Major not accompany us?'

'Indeed,' said I, a jot put out for I suspected that Flora had contrived to take the wind out of my sails, 'indeed, we would be delighted to have your company.'

I took Flora's arm and we strolled on over the shoulder of the hill, for all the world like a married couple on an afternoon's ambulation. There below us, in a green hollow scooped out of a narrow glen, was Byfield's balloon. It was a choice spot, near enough the road and the Hunters' Tryst to attract attention, yet shielded from the worst of the wind. A crowd had assembled, and a band was playing in a rather desultory fashion, and some of the crowd were making in the direction of the Tryst, no doubt desirous of some refreshment. Ronald and the Major came up with us as we watched Byfield's *Lunardi* expand to magnificent proportions.

Chevenix began again. 'St. Ives, I beg you, think of Miss Flora's reputation. Your presence endangers her. Miss Flora, let Ronald take you home. You cannot, you must not, involve yourself further with this man, who may at any moment be arrested.'

'The Runners were at the door of Swanston Cottage not half an hour since,' added Ronald, somewhat dilatory, I thought, with this intelligence. 'They took the track beyond the Tryst. They are convinced you are somewhere on the hills, and propose now it is daylight to hunt you down. We guessed Flora would have taken the Caer Ketton path, but if your pursuers gain the summit you will be fully in view.'

Ronald spoke with a relish that did not please me, but I had no opportunity to reflect on this, for at that moment there was a cry from Flora, who pointed up the hill. We all turned. On the heights above, now entirely free of mist, two figures stood against the sky. We saw rather than heard the cry of recognition as they plunged towards us; their descent led them through a drift of scree, which slowed their progress.

'Anne, run!' exclaimed Flora, and: 'St. Ives, confound you, save your skin while you can,' escaped from the Major at the same time. Wattie the collie, busy on his own ploys some yards away, caught the excitement and began to bark. Ronald shifted from one foot to the other, and grew redder.

I watched my pursuers coolly. I was resigned to flight, yet reluctant to take to my heels. As I surveyed their approach a third figure appeared on the ridge; it was my cousin, leading from the rear. Looking about me I saw a fourth struggling up the slope from Swanston Cottage: I recognised the gentleman in the moleskin waistcoat.

'Go, dearest, go. My thoughts will never leave you.'

Even as she spoke I had bestowed on her a final kiss and torn myself away. A shout behind me told me my pursuers had me in their sights and were not far off. I paused to catch one more sight of Flora and to wave a last farewell. A flash of black and white crossed my vision, and as I pressed on a shout was transmuted to a howl of pain. Whin bushes tugged at my thin-stockinged legs and rabbit holes seemed to open before me on purpose to break a leg. I leapt a burn, sent a pair of grouse squawking upwards, and slithered on the wet grass. The raucous medley of the band accompanied my headlong flight into the midst of the assembled crowd.

I hoped that so theatrical an occasion would serve to explain my somewhat unorthodox appearance, and indeed, although there was some muttered resentment as I pushed through the crowd no-one took a great deal of notice of me. I glanced behind, and saw Moleskin Waistcoat leading the chase. Some yards behind was the scholar of the fingernails. The third was still being harried by the dog, who barked frantically and made sudden dashes at his calves. Away to the left, making a wide detour of the furious Wattie, was my cousin, panting—it pleased me to imagine how sorely—across the lower slopes.

Some heads turned at the barking of the dog, and it seemed to me that what was going on behind the crowd offered more entertainment than Byfield and his balloon, both of which were oddly, and to me disconcertingly, inert. I pushed on through the crowd; I could see Byfield now, fussing with the cables and giving orders to his assistants. I called out to him; he looked about him vaguely, and fondly caressed the side of the wicker car suspended beneath the straining *Lunardi*. Then, with a flourish to the inattentive crowd, he began to climb the rope ladder that hung over the side. I was relieved to see such signs of imminent departure. When he reached the top he gave another flourish and received in return a lukewarm cheer. He was pulling up the ladder behind him when I broke through the crowd, calling out to him again and signalling violently. As I ran across the last few yards of empty ground I heard him, clear as a bell, give the order to cut the rope.

'Byfield!' I cried, desperation lending wings to my voice.

On hearing his name he paused, the ladder still dangling in the air. I made a leap for it. I felt the *Lunardi* shudder as the ropes were cut, and at once she began to rise. At that moment Moleskin launched himself at my feet and I heard a shout, in the unmistakable tone of my cousin.

'One hundred guineas to the man who apprehends Champdivers the murderer!'

Moleskin hung like a limpet. Above me Byfield's face peered over the edge.

'Confound you, Ducie, have you no respect for science? Let go at once. I carry no passengers on this voyage.'

'One passenger, Byfield,' I gasped, 'surely you can accommodate one: I'll pay handsomely for your pains. But as for two—I share your sentiments entirely.' And I endeavoured to dislodge Moleskin with a kick, but he clung to my legs as if his life depended on it. It was understandable that he should because every second we were rising, though with the unexpected extra weight the ascent was slow. There we hung, the two of us, like links in a string of sausages, with Byfield's ireful countenance grimacing above.

We were now some ten feet off the ground, and would have been higher but for the wind blowing us towards the upward slope. With Moleskin fastened to me I could not climb the ladder, and my arms were likely to be pulled out of their sockets by his weight. My view beneath the wicker car showed blue sky, and the dark outline of the distant Castle, which I found the breath to curse as the source and fount of my predicament. Beyond, at the tail end of the castellated ridge of the Old Town, slumbered the twin humps of Arthur's Seat. It was curious that, even in my desperation, I took in these sights, and marvelled.

I assayed another movement of my legs to discourage my fellow traveller and was gratified by what seemed to be a loosening of his grip but he was not so easily dissuaded from my company, and hung on the faster. I looked up, and saw the glint of steel in Byfield's hand.

'Byfield! For God's sake, man, don't do it. You would not have a man's—two men's—blood on your hands.'

There was a wild look in his eyes, and an answering inspiration in my own.

'Byfield!' I called again, my voice rasping like a blunt razor, 'Byfield, give me the knife. I can save you and the *Lunardi* too.' I scarcely knew what I was saying, but grasped at words like a drowning man.

Byfield's hand was raised, but he hesitated.

'Reach it to me, man. I promise you, all will be saved.'

At last, with excruciating slowness, he leaned over the side of the car. He had the sense to hold the knife by the blade, so I could grasp the handle. 'I swear, Ducie,' he hissed above me, 'if you harm the *Lunardi* I shall have not only your blood but your hide.'

I took the knife in my left hand: I needed all the strength of my right to hang on. Moleskin turned his face, white and perspiring, upwards, and now saw the knife above him. I myself was almost blinded with drops of sweat as I clung to the ladder and held the knife inches above the fingers clutching my left leg.

'I have no wish to deprive you of your fingers,' I managed to get out; his face became, if it were possible, more drained of colour. 'let go, my friend. You will have a safe landing. The turf is soft below you.'

His grip slackened, and tightened again in frantic reflex. I encouraged him with a gentle pressure of the blade. The extremity of pain in my right arm almost drove consciousness from me, but somehow I succeeded in hanging on. I had drawn a little sketch of red upon the back of his hand; this time the fingers relaxed and slid down what remained of my silk stockings, and he fell. In my haste to lay hold of the ladder with my left hand I released the knife. I let out a sob, of mixed relief and pain, and scrabbled for a rung on which to rest my nerveless feet. Her load now lightened, the *Lunardi* began to climb more convincingly, and the ground receded. Below, Moleskin had landed in a heap on the grassy slope, had rolled a few yards, and was now sitting up and examining his limbs. Above me, Byfield looked less angry and more anxious. With infinite slowness, my head reeling and my legs scarcely doing my bidding, I climbed to safety, and tumbled, faint and exhausted, at Byfield's feet.

CHAPTER XXXIII

THE EAST WIND BLOWS

I FELT the shifting of the *Lunardi* in the wind, and thought of those below. At once I struggled to my feet, and steadied myself against the rim of the car. We were not yet a hundred feet in the air, and I saw the crowd, who had got more entertainment than they bargained for, and a little apart from the crowd a figure proclaimed my cousin by the elaborate curls and costume; he was shaking a miniature fist in our direction. As I watched he seemed of a sudden to fling himself upon the ground, like a howling child, and I fancied I could see his boots drum the turf in fury. His two henchmen stood a few yards distant, with a somewhat embarrassed air, I thought, and there was Moleskin, limping but whole, coming down the slope to join them.

We continued to climb gallantly. The upturned faces and multi-coloured garments became a blur. Then I caught sight of another group of figures on the shoulder of the hill, with a fragment of black and white beside them. It was Flora, with her brother and the Major, and the noble Wattie. Did I detect a salute, arms raised with a message of Godspeed? If I did not see it, my imagination painted it for me with vivid expression, and I was moved to the soul by those scraps of humanity on the broadening hill.

A consciousness of the narrowness of my escape began to flood over me, but as I bade farewell to one danger another jangled an alarm in my mind. The *Lunardi*, spreading blue and yellow above us, shuddered and trembled in the buffets of the wind. The fragile globe of cloth seemed hardly substantial enough to carry us; I was entrusting my safety to a frail and insubstantial craft. A gull wheeled close with a screeching cry. I thought how easy it would be to puncture our sustaining gas bag.

Byfield interrupted the tenor of my thoughts. 'Ducie,' he began, 'I believe an explanation is the least you owe me.'

'My dear Byfield,' replied I, 'I know it. My tale is long and tangled, and I will relate you the whole, if you have leisure to hear it. I am deeply indebted to you—', and I contrived to bow, although with

263

some difficulty as my head was still light and the space was small. 'But may I suggest we postpone the narration until we find ourselves in more comfortable circumstances? It is enough to say, you have saved my life, and I am eternally grateful.'

For a moment I thought he was going to protest at an implied criticism of the amenities offered by the *Lunardi*, but I went on before he could speak.

'Let me congratulate you on a most successful ascent. The view is magnificent; it is an experience I shall cherish.'

We were now several hundred feet above the earth. Fragments of white mist still lingered on the hilltops, but round about the countryside was lit by the sun. The grassy Pentland slopes were a warmer and brighter green than I had ever seen them; the dark ploughed fields looked neater and smoother than they ever can on the ground; the rivers wound a sparkling course to the Forth. There was the Almond, sliding through the trees to meet the Firth at Cramond, of blessed memory. Beyond, on the Firth itself, boats scudded in the breeze, and a ship at anchor at the Queen's Ferry was hoisting sail. Looking back I saw the smoking chimneys of the capital creating a camouflage for all the human business conducted there.

Beside me Byfield had a glass to his eye and shared my absorption. After a minute or two he passed me his telescope and I took a last look at the flank of Caer Ketton, where not so many hours before I had spent the coldest and wettest night of my life. Although Flora was now lost to my eye, I could just make out Swanston Cottage amidst its sheltering trees. I imagined Flora's return after her adventure, Miss Gilchrist's chill disapproval, the awkward mien of the two gentlemen who were deputed to protect her. Long afterwards Flora told me of her fears, of her horror at the balloon's ascent, of her struggle against the certain apprehension of imminent disaster. But faith, she assures me, prevailed, though I am bound to say that rarely has so much been demanded of that virtue.

My own was of a certainty put to the test. Byfield busied himself amongst his instruments, checked the cables, examined the barometer, put the glass to his eye, and so forth, in an incessant round of trivial duties. I was glad enough to be ignored. I watched with some amazement as he quietly went about his business; my earlier encounter with Byfield had suggested to me that his aeronautical ambitions were quite beyond the reach of reason, and I could not help reflecting now that *Lunardi* might have been more aptly christened *Lunatic*.

We were still gaining height, and each time the wind shook the little car I cast an unquiet look upwards, while Byfield did not seem to notice the disturbance. Now drifting cloud at times obscured our view, but I could see the Pentland Hills rolling away to the south-west, and on the other side the silvery Firth. Our direction must have been almost due west. As I grew more accustomed to this suspension in the air I began to enjoy a delicious sense of freedom. The brilliant blue of the sky, the translucent air around us, the earth spread out below for our delectation, here was enchantment indeed. Given time, I thought, I might even come to share Byfield's aeronautical enthusiasm. Byfield coughed beside me.

'I am beginning to think I might be a convert to the miracles of science,' said I, willing to be conciliatory.

'Confound it, Ducie,' was his spluttering reply, 'it won't do, you know, it won't do.'

'On the contrary, it does remarkably well,' I said, looking up at the *Lunardi's* expansive curves. 'I am lost in admiration.'

'I mean, *you* won't do, Ducie. I can't have you here. This is—was to be—a solo flight. And now the whole country knows where you are, and who you are too, although I do not have the pleasure of that intelligence. Confound it, Ducie, I am compromised, and compromised by a man I have reason to believe is dangerous. I would set you down, but where? And once on the ground, how do I rise again, without my apparatus?'

'My dear fellow, you would not wish to prejudice the success of your venture on my account. Let me make myself small in a corner, and do you proceed with your original intent. I admit I am a hunted man, but unjustly accused, I swear it. You helped me out of a devilish tight corner, and I am infinitely obliged. But it was desperation that drove me to the *Lunardi*, and to yourself, *deus ex machina* indeed, not a wish to share in the glory of your flight. My intention is not to seek public notice—in fact, the opposite. I had been happier if I had been able to slip quietly on board and stow myself away out of sight. But circumstances forced a ruder embarkation.'

I would have continued in this vein, in the belief that words might have a calming effect on my companion, but he interrupted me.

'I am a respectable man, Ducie, a man of my word. You have made an assault upon my honour—' His eyes burned with indignation.

'And I am an innocent man,' said I, 'and I assure you that when the true facts of the case are brought to light you will be applauded as a hero—and not just of an aeronautical adventure.'

My choice of words was not felicitous. Although at the word 'hero' his features brightened, at the qualification 'just' a prodigious frown reasserted itself.

'Just, Mr. Ducie, *just* an aeronautical adventure! This is the most ambitious balloon flight in North Britain since the ascents of Vincenzo Lunardi in '85. I was there, sir, as a young boy, when the magnificent Lunardi ascended from the grounds of Heriot's Hospital. I remember it, sir, as if it were yesterday; a sharp-featured young man, in a scarlet uniform with blue facings. He was much admired by the ladies. The flight lasted one hour and thirty-five minutes, Mr. Ducie, and the balloon came down near Ceres, in Fife. He received a hero's welcome, sir, a hero's welcome. The ladies of Cupar repaired his balloon. Edinburgh awarded him the freedom of the city.'

I endeavoured to remain attentive throughout this narration, and hoped that memories of childhood inspiration would distract him from my unwelcome presence. I smiled and murmured my admiration. Byfield was well into a description of Lunardi's second flight from Heriot's Hospital, which, it seemed, terminated in the Firth of Forth, where Lunardi was picked up by a fishing boat after some hours in the water. It was a prospect I did not relish, and I was relieved to see the broad estuary of the Forth receding to the east. We were moving steadily; with each mile that passed I felt safer from the ire of Byfield, and hoped that the adventures of the noble Lunardi might continue indefinitely. However, the tale could not be prolonged, for after a year or two the aeronaut abandoned Britain, and although he flew on the Continent he never achieved the same success.

'But there were others, no doubt,' I prompted Byfield. I would have done better to stay silent. Byfield turned his dark eyes on me once again. 'Ducie?' he questioned thoughtfully, 'Ducie?' I nodded. 'I believe,' he went on, 'that someone in the crowd called you by a name that was not Ducie.'

His remark hung in the ethereal silence, and he reached in a preoccupied manner for the valve-string. 'Something to do with fields,' he said.

I thought it best not to allow him to arrive there unaided; a little assistance might improve my standing. 'The name was Champdivers,' said I, casually, and noting that he did not remove his hand from the valve-string.

'Ah yes,' he said. 'Mosha Champdivers, the mur—'

'Certainly not. I killed the man in a fair duel.'

I thought I detected a faint spasm of nervousness cross his dark gaze, but he spoke with sour distrust. 'It is others you will have to persuade of that.'

'There are those, among them my own cousin, who have much to gain from fabricating my guilt. Mr. Byfield, I am innocent of murder, I swear it; any gentleman would have acted as I did—any gentleman *must* have acted as I did.'

'Innocence must be proved.'

'Man alive, you don't expect me to demonstrate it a thousand feet

above the earth. And besides, I believe the law puts another inter-
pretation on the burden of proof.'

He shook his head, and simultaneously pulled the valve-string.
'Let us give the law that opportunity,' said he. For a moment I
stared open-mouthed, and felt confoundedly foolish. The balloon
was already slipping downwards, and there was an unpleasant sensation in my vitals that was caused by more than our descent. At
last I found my voice.

'Mr. Byfield,' I said, patting my breast where the money was still
securely lodged, 'I mentioned I had means. Two hundred guineas is
yours if you land me in a place of safety. Justice is a fickle master,
and I would not want my life or your reputation to rest upon what
my lord had for breakfast. Have you ever seen a man hanged, Mr.
Byfield? It is an ugly business, and if the victim is innocent it is a
deal uglier.'

I saw the play of warring interests in his face, and continued.

'Three hundred guineas, Byfield, if we reach Ireland. We are
heading in a westerly direction, I believe? Consider the additional
reward in heaven, for the rescue of an innocent man unjustly
accused.' I patted my store of banknotes once again.

He still hesitated, opened his mouth, stammered a few words,
then closed it again. All this time we had been losing height, and
now I lost my patience.

'Come on, man, this is no time to dally. Time is one commodity we
are entirely without.' A glance over the side confirmed this; to our
right the contours of dark hills were taking on discernible features,
and I could identify cattle and sheep below us. Then a village
spread out under our eyes, and I could see into the gardens, and a
grey farmhouse, and a pair of horses at the plough. Byfield stood
before me, indecision etched upon his face.

'What must we do? Throw out some ballast?' I bent to lay hold of a
sack of sand that lay at my feet. At that moment the gods
befriended me, for a gust of wind caught and shook the car. Byfield
lost his balance and let go his hold on the valve-string. I seized the
bag and heaved it over the side; the balloon steadied, then shuddered, and began to rise. For good measure, I hoisted a second bag
of ballast into the void beneath us.

Byfield looked out of countenance, but not angry. Indeed, something like resignation seemed to settle on him, perhaps even relief
that events had been taken out of his hands. He straightened his
coat.

'Mr. Ducie,' said he, with admirable dignity, 'I have considered
your offer, and I accept it. It's a curst awkward position—'

'For a public character,' I put in affably.

'You fail to appreciate, Mr. Ducie, the difficulty—the *Lunardi* is my life, sir: I've staked my all on her success. The future lies in the air: a century hence Byfield's balloon and her contribution to the history of flight will be remembered.'

'Flight indeed,' I murmured, but not so loud as to interrupt his prophetic tangent.

'That is my conviction, sir. Byfield's balloon, inheritor of the brothers Montgolfier, of the ill-fated Tytler (a genius, sir, but a misguided one), the great Lunardi—'

'Assuredly,' said I, 'future generations will remember Byfield and forget Ducie—and the notorious Champdivers. Allow me the privilege of making a contribution to your success: four hundred guineas towards a future experiment.'

I counted out the notes.

'I admire a man with ambition. And a balloon, as you hint and I begin to discover, may alter the perspective of a man's ambitions. Here are the notes, four hundred, and on top of them I give you my word that you are not abetting a criminal.'

He accepted the notes with gravity, and tucked them into an inside pocket. I became aware of the cold; my hands had grown quite numb. My plaid I had abandoned as I fled across the hillside, but the experienced Byfield was well supplied with wraps, and I selected and donned an overcoat. We had regained the height we lost, and below us the central part of Scotland lay spread from firth to firth. To our right lay a silvery finger of loch, flanked by a mountain peak; beyond, more mountains, stretching northwards, snow-covered, and smoothed by distance. Little towns were linked by pale threads of highway. To people these little nodules of habitation defied the imagination; to picture a workshop, a mill, a weaver at his loom, a family at the hearth, was more than my mind could encompass. From so far above the earth had a strange, legendary nature.

That buffet from the wind heralded its revival, and we soared rapidly westward: it must have been the estuary of the Clyde that soon opened out before us. Even in my borrowed overcoat the chill reached my bones.

'If we continue in a westerly direction,' I said, 'we are likely to come down in the Atlantic ocean.' As if to emphasise the perils of the deep another blast of wind shook us. It did not deflect a sharp look from Byfield.

'I suppose you were hoping the wind would take us to France,' said he. 'But even if the current had been right a journey of that distance would be near to impossible. The *Lunardi* is unlikely to stay in the air for more than twenty hours. I had thought of Ireland; or we might aim to descend on one of the Hebridean islands. In the meantime, I suggest some refreshment.'

He made himself comfortable on a pile of rugs and lifted the lid of a wicker basket that was stowed beside them. Out of it came a pork pie and a bottle of wine of Bordeaux. I could have wished for the appearance of a sample of native distillation, to which I had grown partial, and must have betrayed my expectancy, for Byfield said drily, 'I arranged provisions for one.' He divided the pie, without further comment, and poured a generous measure of Bordeaux into the only tumbler, which he handed to me. I sat amongst the plaids, hardly wanting food, but of a sudden overcome with the need to sleep. I had scarcely emptied my glass before my drowsiness got the better of me and, dimly conscious of the strengthening wind, my eyelids drooped, and I slept.

I awoke suddenly, and lay blinking up at the sun, which had passed its meridian. The *Lunardi* quivered and shook, and there was a raucous note in the singing of the wind. Something, perhaps the sight of Byfield's white face, sent my stomach slipping like a bucket in a fathomless well. When I raised myself the wind forced my breath back down my throat. I shivered; it could have been the cold, but the dark ribbons of cloud that streamed below were reminders of the hostility of the elements. Byfield's hair and coat tails were thrashed by the wind, giving him the appearance of a desperate, predatory bird.

I closed my eyes again, and for an instant wished fervently that the oblivion of sleep would reclaim me. In my mind was the figure of Flora as I had last seen her, in miniature, against the hill's green slopes. But the temporary comfort of this vision was rudely blasted as the wind yet again rocked our frail craft and sent Byfield staggering against the side. Now my eyes were open wide: there were the ropes and swollen bladder of the balloon, infinitely smaller and more fragile than it had been when I had bounded towards its cheerful colours and promise of escape.

I struggled to my feet: the wind stung like a blow. Byfield leant towards me and bellowed something in my ear, but a gust snatched the words away. I ventured a look over the side, holding firmly to one of the cables. Below was a narrow tongue of land stretching into the sea, a deep blue-grey and flecked with white, like foam on the flanks of a straining horse. On the other side were islands, two of substantial size, with smaller fragments of land like outriders. The furthest island, to the north as I judged by the westering sun, was barren and mountainous, while the nearest, close to it, was patterned with green and fringed here and there with sand.

It seemed at first that the current would take us well south of the green island, and I wondered if anything but ocean lay beyond. Byfield, too, was staring westward, as if willing Atlantis to rise from the depths and appear before us. The sun was sinking now, and lit the breakers that crashed upon the shore; I could see the line of white, and fancied I could hear the roar above the wind.

I gripped Byfield by the shoulder. 'We must descend,' I shouted into his ear. 'Rather water within sight of land than the deep ocean.' Byfield's nod was, I thought, rather too grim to be of any comfort.

We were drawing parallel to the green island now, which was almost split in two by a deep inlet. Far to the south a greyish outline indicated more land: I did not think about this at the time but later I surmised that it was Ireland. But the wind sped us westward, though it blew in fits and starts, and to the west there was nothing, only the sun, a mocking, angry red, and dropping almost visibly.

Byfield had his hand upon the valve-string. The balloon shuddered and seemed to pause: had the wind veered? My knuckles were bloodless with their grip upon the side. The balloon was wrenched sideways, as if tugged by an unseen hand, and at the same time I felt our descent. Byfield stood, one hand grasping a cable, the other on the valve. A momentary lull in the wind enabled the car to regain its equilibrium.

'Hold tight. Mr. Ducie,' I heard Byfield shout, before another blast drowned his words. 'I trust you can swim. We are in for a ducking, I wager.'

The curious thing was that he sounded almost cheerful. I did not need his warning: we were rushing towards the sea and my stomach leapt into my throat. I could find no voice with which to reply; yet a series of images printed themselves on my mind so clearly that I cannot believe they will ever fade: a small boat tossing on the waves; a huddle of houses on the shore; the deep red of the horizon. Then with a sickening lurch we hit the water and I was drenched and blinded with spray. The wind was no less furious at sea level; it caught and drove the *Lunardi*, dragging the encumbering car after it. We could do nothing but hang on. I prayed and cursed in turn, unable to see where the wind was driving us, and helpless as a kitten. The sea rolled and tossed us merrily, and I persuaded myself I preferred the dangers of the air to those of the water.

Byfield, master of the sky, lay collapsed and grey-faced. The balloon loomed before us, now bouncing on the waves, now uplifted by the wind. Out of his natural element Byfield gasped like a netted fish, and I was no better. The sky darkened above us, and it was the presentiment of night that forced my limbs into movement and got me, staggering, to my feet. As I pulled myself up another wave crashed over us, and, though I would not have thought it possible for my garments to increase their degree of wateriness, I swear they became wetter. All around churned a boiling cauldron of a sea. As I clung unsteadily to the rim of the car a huge swell heaved us upwards, and I saw the sun sitting angrily on the edge of the horizon, and would have received with no surprise the information that it marked the edge of the earth, and that our little craft was inexorably bound to fall off.

I knew we could not be far from land, for we had seen the island spread below us. Our only hope lay in being picked up—but what madman would be out in this weather?—or in being driven ashore. Another swell bore us up, and this time I looked away from the setting sun. I saw that behind us loomed a dark rampart of cliffs, and I saw also the white foam at their base. Whatever our hopes for landfall, I was thankful that we were not being driven towards them.

I looked at Byfield, and remembered the claret. I rummaged and found the bottle, and regretted again that Byfield's foresight had not extended to whisky; but there also emerged from the basket a tin containing shortbread, and I became aware that half a pork pie was not a repast to sustain a man in conditions such as these. The sight of refreshments served to remind Byfield that blood still flowed in his veins, and he stirred. His half-closed eyes flickered, and a white hand reached out uncertainly to accept the measure I poured for him. Another hand clasped some shortbread; and so we reclined, with plaids pulled around us, and sipped our wine and munched our shortbread, tossed and tilted by the wind and waves: the strangest *al fresco* meal of my varied experience. We were thus engaged when I thought I caught a sound that could have been a voice above the hurdy-gurdy of the wind. I could see from the twitch of interest in Byfield's face that he had heard something too. Our eyes met. I took another swig of wine—I had the bottle, Byfield the glass, a distribution dictated by politeness as I had taken on the role of host—and took the trouble to replace the cork before again raising myself upright. At first I saw nothing; then a little boat, I supposed a fishing boat though it seemed scarce probable, appeared almost at eye level. I made out through the spray two figures. I leaned out as far as I dared, and a voice came again, but no words that I could understand. That hardly mattered: I waved vigorously. I shouted, I know not what, to Byfield who, moved by the excitement of my voice, came to life and in a moment was beside me.

Side by side, clutching the rim of the car, we bent towards the waves, indeed were nearly tipped out of our tossing bucket, and bawled across the gulf that separated us from the little boat. It danced sportively like a skittish horse: it was a miracle that it did not unseat its occupants. But we could see them clearly now, solid and steady, one tall and broad with a rope in his hand, the other smaller and more slender, doing his best against the wind with a pair of oars. With inexpressible slowness the gap narrowed. The large man was shouting again, but still the sounds would not form themselves into words we could make out, and as we drew closer it seemed to me that their strangeness was more than the distortions of the wind.

The smaller of the two was no more than a boy: how he held his own I cannot guess. Each inch gained seemed to be at the expense of a foot lost, yet now I could see the red hair of the man with the rope and moments later I could discern the pattern on his thick woollen guernsey. I was impatient for him to make the throw, but he bided his time, and I had to admire his skill, for he judged the moment nicely and it was only our clumsiness that rendered his first attempt unsuccessful. Byfield cried aloud as the rope's end slithered into the sea before either of us could grasp it. I cursed, but whether aloud or not I could not tell.

Our saviour with red hair seemed unperturbed, and pulled back the rope, the little fishing boat rearing and bucking the while, coiling it for another throw. Again he judged his moment; I saw the swing of his arm and simultaneously reached forward with both mine.

'Hold onto me,' I shouted to Byfield who, I am thankful to say, had the presence of mind to grasp my coat tails. This time I caught the rope, and with Byfield clinging like a monkey to a cable with one hand and my poor metamorphosed dove grey with the other, I secured the rope, awkwardly, with half-dead fingers, yet it served. When I looked over the edge again both men were rowing, now with the wind behind them, or they could have made no progress. We were a chariot pulled by an ill-matched pair, the balloon still swollen, but clumsy and erratic, and the fishing boat bobbing gamefully.

'The Lord be thanked,' breathed Byfield, beside me. But I wondered if his offering was premature for, grateful though I was for the presence of fellow human creatures, I considered their chances of reaching dry land little better than our own.

Yet it would have been churlish not to join Byfield in his gratitude, and I nodded vigorously. 'The Lord be thanked,' I echoed. It could do no harm, and I had rarely been more in need of divine assistance.

We made a striking picture, for anyone with the leisure to dwell on it: the magnificent *Lunardi* floundering like a bird that loses all its grace when not in flight, a boat that hardly looked big enough for a child to play pirates in, and a bucket-shaped receptacle containing two half-drowned specimens of humanity, one at least of whom would have given his last guinea to feel something under his feet that did not move. It was a spectacle whose singularity might have provoked laughter, yet I had not thought there could have been anyone for miles to witness it. But then I noticed the oarsmen had paused and were staring into the dusk; at the same instant Byfield exclaimed.

'A ship! Ducie, look behind you!'

I turned, and there, looming sombrely, was a fine brig, her masts black against the last faint colour of the sky, and her bow dipping as the sea broke against her. Here was rescue indeed, I thought, and the safety hitherto embodied in a puny fishing boat melted away. Our fickle attention was all turned to this new entrant on the scene, and if my face was half as expressive as Byfield's, relief was written on it in letters of fire.

We forgot the fishermen and strained eagerly for a sight of some of the brig's crew. There seemed at first to be no sign of life.

'Infernally quiet,' I shouted to Byfield, who like me was scanning the decks. 'You'd expect some activity on a ship in a gale.'

'She's not flying a flag,' shouted Byfield in reply.

Then I heard, faint but distinct above the roar of wind and sea, a cry, and the words this time were intelligible.

'Ahoy there,' came a voice in plain English. 'Ahoy there. Can we assist?'

We signalled in reply, though we could see no body to which to attach the voice. Then out of the corner of my eye I saw movement in the fishing boat, and when I turned there was the young lad on his feet, shouting against the wind through cupped hands. I was sure he would be toppled into the sea, but he maintained his footing. The voice from the brig came again, and I thought I heard the word 'pilot' and something that I realised later was 'Bowmore', but the word was not familiar to me then.

The brig and the fishing boat seemed to understand each other, for the smaller craft was now pulling towards the larger, though it seemed impossible that she would escape being dashed to fragments against the brig's steep sides. Still attached to the rope, we followed, and made an erratic approach to the dark ship. As the fishing boat drew near, the stillness of the brig erupted and shadowy figures moved about the deck. A rope ladder snaked over the side; the lad climbed first, then his companion, in his hand the end of the rope that maintained its umbilical connection with the *Lunardi*. When he reached the deck others assisted, and slowly what was left of Byfield's aeronautical adventure was pulled to safety: *quantum mutatus ab illo.*

Byfield insisted that I should be the first to scale the brig's side, almost more of an ordeal than we had already undergone, as she plunged and shuddered and the rope ladder swayed. But I was glad to see human faces above me and strong hands reach to receive me. Byfield paused for a last look at the *Lunardi*, which now lay alongside the ship like a harpooned whale. Seeing him below, steadying himself with a hand on the rope ladder, his face betraying more dejection than relief, I was moved to pity. Flesh and blood had survived, but it was unlikely that the gallant *Lunardi* would ever fly again, or that Byfield would embark on another adventure with such confidence and courage. Scarcely was he safely on deck when the rope was severed, and the *Lunardi* was left to continue her water-bound voyage untenanted.

CHAPTER XXXIV

THE TRUE BLOODED YANKEE

THERE was scarce time to feel the solid planks beneath our feet before we were encircled by brown-faced seamen. Two or three had pistols in their hands, and the look of those accustomed to their use. I had no disposition to be anything but conciliatory, under whatever flag our rescuers sailed, but I could not be sure of my companions. Byfield was fussing with his dress, no doubt in an attempt to restore his dignity as professor and man of science. The two fishermen were speaking together in low voices. I could not catch their words, but detected an intonation that seemed not to be English. Then it came upon me that their language must be Gaelic, and I cursed my slow brain and wondered if the weather of the past two days had left it irrevocably sodden.

I endeavoured to compose myself into an attitude of pleasant politeness, though I was wary of those pistols. Then my attention was caught by other voices, as some of the seamen exchanged comments. Their language was certainly English, yet it was like no English familiar to my ear, and I had encountered and learned to imitate many of its accents; a second moment of realisation came to me, and I turned to Byfield excitedly.

'My dear Byfield,' said I, in a hoarse whisper. 'We have had the good luck to be picked up by an American vessel, though what in God's name she is doing here is beyond guessing. She is a long way from home. She'll be no friend to England, nor to Scotland either—I wager it will do little good to invoke the Auld Alliance. Byfield, *mon brave*, you may forget you ever knew a Mr. Edward Ducie. It is time for Saint-Yves to become himself again.'

As I spoke the seamen parted to allow the passage of a tall man with a lean and pleasant face, whom I supposed was the master of the brig. He came towards us, in apparent friendliness, and shook each of us by the hand.

'Captain Oxnard, at your service.'

'Le Vicomte Anne de Keroual de Saint-Yves,' I replied, augmenting the handshake with a bow. Byfield did likewise, a little stiffly I

275

thought, and introduced himself as 'Professor Byfield, aeronaut and man of science.' The fishermen were not excluded from the welcome, though only the young lad spoke, which he did in clear but hesitant English.

'I am James Macallister,' said he, and though so youthful there was a dignity about him which I admired, 'and this is my uncle Neil Connell, miller of Ardnish. The boat is my uncle's boat. We were after the herring.'

Captain Oxnard looked thoughtful, though his amiable expression remained. 'So you were fishing,' he said. 'You must know these waters well.'

'Aye. My uncle knows every current, every rock and shoal.' The lad turned to the miller and said something in Gaelic, to which the miller nodded in reply.

Captain Oxnard clapped a hand on the boy's shoulder. 'That's my good fortune then, for I am in need of a pilot. Will your uncle, Mr. Connell, take us up the loch? We are short of provisions, and I am told Bowmore is a good anchorage.'

He smiled as he spoke, but I noticed a sudden change in the countenance of Neil Connell, who gripped his nephew by the arm and pulled him aside. Aha, I thought, the miller smells a rat; these Americans must be known. There was a stir of movement amongst the seamen and two of those with pistols slipped almost without a sound into a position behind the miller and the boy. Captain Oxnard looked a shade less friendly; the miller had spoken something urgently into the ear of the boy, who now stood biting his lip.

'I am in need of a pilot, my friends,' Oxnard repeated, this time with an unmistakable bluntness.

Young James drew himself up and gazed steadfastly at the captain. 'My uncle says he will not be piloting an enemy ship, sir.'

'An enemy ship? And what brings you to that conclusion?' asked Captain Oxnard mildly, but behind the boy a pistol was cocked and we all heard the sharp click.

'You will be American, I am thinking. There has been news of American privateers. There was talk in Bowmore of the *Daphne*, and the *Hope* out of Kirkwall, both taken by the Yankee.'

Captain Oxnard laughed, but there was no amusement reflected in the faces around him. 'Your uncle has a sharp eye and a sharp ear, for one who does not speak English. But I fear he is being over-scrupulous. I intend to anchor at Bowmore, to re-provision, and I need his help to do so. Keep them under guard,' he said, this last sharply. He turned away; his business with the miller was, for now, concluded, and he had other guests to attend to.

'And now for the aeronauts,' he said, his smile returning.

'We are allies, I believe,' I said quickly. 'I am from France, Captain, and Professor Byfield here is quite innocent of any military intention.'

He looked at us both with an interest touched, I fancied, with some scepticism. It was now quite dark, and the wind had dropped a little. A lamp had been lit, and swung with the motion of the waves, casting a fitful pool of light across our faces. As both he and Byfield remained silent I ventured another remark.

'You are a long way from home.'

'Indeed, sir, though we have a temporary one that is not so distant. We are twelve days out of Brest. We need fresh water and provisions.' He paused for a moment. 'And you, you are also in a place where I would not expect a Frenchman. How do you come to be boating in Loch Indaal?'

'I was participating in Professor Byfield's aeronautical experiment, though I acknowledge I had not planned the adventure.'

At this point Byfield, who had been gazing morosely over the side as the wind and waves carried the *Lunardi* away from the brig, turned, and said in a voice tinged with bitterness, 'No, indeed. It was, Captain Oxnard, intended as a solo flight, entirely in the interests of science. Mr. Ducie—I beg your pardon, Mr. St. Ives—became a passenger, quite by accident. Indeed, I—er—attempted to discourage him. I am, sir, I assure you, a respectable man, a man of some reputation, there are many who will vouch for that. I think I have about my person some cuttings from the press—' He began searching his pockets and at last produced a handful of sodden newsprint.

'My dear Mr. Byfield, pray do not concern yourself. I see you have a story to tell. May I suggest that you join me below? There I can offer you some refreshment, and you can relate your adventures.'

He turned to speak some words to one of the seamen whose style of dress indicated that he was an officer. They both cast a look in the direction of the miller and his nephew; I had no doubt that instructions were being given concerning the piloting of the brig up the loch. There was a moon now, and the wind was much calmer. I could just make out the murky bulk of the cliffs on the starboard side, and hoped the miller was as familiar with these waters as he claimed.

'Monsieur le Vicomte, Professor Byfield—' Captain Oxnard's voice reclaimed my attention. 'Welcome aboard the *True Blooded Yankee.*'

In his cabin, refreshed with good French brandy and a ration of salt pork with ship's biscuit which was rather less to my taste, I told my story, or as much of it as I deemed fitting for the captain's ears. Byfield likewise narrated how he had come to accept, with great reluctance, a passenger. Neither of us made mention of Champdivers the murderer; it did not seem politic.

'You are a courageous man, Professor Byfield,' said Captain Oxnard pleasantly, when Byfield had finished. 'Did you not fear an accident? And what was your intended destination?'

'Well, sir, as you must understand a balloon such as the *Lunardi* is at the mercy of the wind, but, although I knew I could not rely upon the weather, there was a brisk east wind, and I had hopes of crossing the Irish Sea. It has not been done before, sir; I would have been the first.'

'Ah, Ireland. Yes indeed. I have had hopes myself of making a visit there.'

'It was the high winds that forced us down. We are off the coast of the island of Islay, if my calculations are correct.'

The captain nodded. 'They are, sir, they are. Islay. A pleasant place, so I'm told. I hear they distil a fine liquor and I much look forward to tasting it. Ours will be a brief visit, but my intention is to linger long enough to visit the distillery at Bowmore.'

'I know little of the island,' Byfield said.

'A pity. I warrant our friends of the fishing boat will tell us no more than they have to. And you, sir,' he said, turning to me, 'I suppose you are no more familiar with the islands?'

'I have not had the pleasure of a visit, though I own if I had known Islay's reputation for whisky I might have made a point of it. Whisky is one of the few contributions Scotland has made to civilisation—indeed, I believe one may find more enlightenment in a glass of usquebaugh than in the great intellects of Edinburgh. Only the beauty of Scotland's women rivals the influence of her whisky.'

'Good whisky and beautiful women! I regret even more that, on this visit at least, there will be little time to enjoy either.'

The professor pursed his lips in disapproval at this conversation, but, I confess, I found Captain Oxnard's company agreeable, and relished the brandy and the thought of Flora. It was difficult to tell which was more calculated to make me feel light-headed. My clothes were drying on my back, and for the first time in what seemed like days I felt more like a man than a water-rat. As we were talking the *True Blooded Yankee* was moving slowly up the sea loch. There was a chart spread out on the captain's table, at which I contrived a casual glance; it showed the southern end of the loch opening wide into the sea and narrowing sharply half way up its length.

Captain Oxnard got to his feet with a smooth but deliberate movement. His face showed nothing but amiability, yet I was sure that nothing he said or did was without calculation. 'Gentlemen,' said he, 'if you have finished your brandy I think we will go on deck.'

We were not given a choice: it was made clear, with perfect politeness, that we were required to ascend. Yet the captain paused to take a great-coat from a hook, at the same time shouting for his first officer. He handed me the great-coat.

'You will have need of this, I think. Ah, Mr. Martin, be so good as to lend Professor Byfield here some protection against the cold.' This last was addressed to the officer, who quickly reappeared with a coat so large that it impeded Byfield's progress as he made his way on deck. But the covering was needed; we had removed our own sodden outer garments, and after the comfortable warmth of the cabin the winter's cold and damp threatened to penetrate to the bones.

On deck we found Neil Connell, the lad at his side as interpreter and two armed men close by, in the bow scanning the darkness. Just ahead, on the right, was the dark outline of a rocky point. I remembered it from the chart—it was there that the loch narrowed. It seemed to me we were coming in rather close, but I could only trust the pilot knew his job. In the dim glimmer of moonlight a pale curve of the shore indicated a sandy beach.

Captain Oxnard moved about his business, but we had not been left alone. A sandy-headed, heavy-browed ruffian with a pistol in his belt leaned nonchalantly against the rail just behind us. I fancied we were moving even closer inshore, and as that thought was idly in my mind I saw one of the guards bend forward and say something in the miller's ear. He turned with a start, and the boy, too, jumped back. The guard almost imperceptibly shook his head and raised a finger to his mouth as if to scratch his beard, and the miller put a hand on his nephew's arm and turned back to his task.

The vessel leaned to port, and the headland, which I learned later was called Laggan Point, was rounded. I wondered then if the miller had intended to run us aground, a suspicion that was confirmed when I joined him and his nephew at the rail, the lights of Bowmore before us, and the guard out of range of our voices.

'Mr. Connell,' said I. 'I understand your intentions, but I am thankful you were deterred. I have had enough salt water to pickle me like a herring in a barrel. The brig may be Yankee, but the safety of all of us lies in her seaworthiness.'

The miller said nothing, though I fancied he understood. The boy gave me an uneasy look, as if I were a sea creature a little out of the usual. He said, 'D'ye think my uncle would have sent her to the bottom? No, no. There are shoals at Laggan. She'd just have gone aground.'

'And what changed his mind?' I asked, in a tone of idle curiosity.

The boy dipped his head in the direction of the guard. 'An island man,' was the cryptic answer.

'But if your uncle meant no harm—'

'He knew. He spoke to my uncle: I heard it: 'more water on your mill, miller'—that's what he said.'

'There are Gaelic speakers on board?'

'Aye.'

'And how do you explain that?' I asked my uncommunicative friend.

'They'll have gone during the bad times, when there was little to eat, and it was either the fishing or the colonies. Gone to America, and not from choice.'

And now, I thought but did not speak aloud, seamen on a privateer raiding their own waters. I cast a covert look in the direction of the guard, who was now watching us with an attention that made me uncomfortable. I moved away. Ahead a little galaxy of lights proclaimed the harbourage. The plash of water as the brig moved slowly onward was soothing, and for some moments I was bathed in an unexpected peacefulness. I thought of Flora, who seemed worlds away, and saw her in the garden at Swanston, with a shawl about her and her cheek glowing. I heard her soft, compassionate voice. The unlikeliness of it all, of the whole misadventure, of Anne de Saint-Yves as a hunted man, of Flora's love, of a sudden exploded on me and dispelled the peace with the vehemence of grapeshot. I may have let escape an oath or two; I am certain I beat my hand upon the rail for I felt the bruises afterwards. At any rate, when I again became aware of the *True Blooded Yankee* and the lights of Bowmore growing nearer, there was the captain beside me, his lean and amiable face not a yard from mine.

'I understand they have built a fine new village here,' said he. 'It is a regrettable business. You and I are both slaves to the fortunes of war.'

'What do you mean, sir?' I asked. 'I understood you were in need of provisions. Violence should not be necessary.'

'I will do all I can to avoid loss of life; but I've heard tales of these islanders. We are at war, Monsieur le Vicomte. I must do my duty, and they, I do not doubt, will resist. It is what one would expect: the Scots have a certain reputation as fighters, I am sure you are aware. But I have it in mind to send a warning, and I'm looking for a volunteer.'

'You have a gallant crew,' said I drily.

'And I need every man of them.'

'It seems your generous impulse will go no further then.'

'Ah, my dear Viscount, I am carrying passengers whom I think I will ask to pay their passage.'

'You are intending that Byfield and I should be your messengers?'

He turned on me the full radiance of his genial smile. 'Just so.'

'Captain,' I said, 'I am in no position to refuse. But I am dependent on you and your vessel to carry me to safety. You understand the delicacy of my position. I must return to France: it is my only place of refuge. If we do as you ask—and I share your anxiety that lives should not be lost—how are we to regain the ship?'

'I have not overlooked your difficulties. The professor, I imagine, will have no great disquiet on that score. I am told there is a boat will take him to the mainland, if he can get himself to the other side of the island, to a place called Port Askaig. He'll be in no danger. Now you, sir, I own, may run some risk: but you are a soldier, and risk will not be new to you.'

'I have recently had all too intimate an acquaintance with risk,' I said, 'to have any wish for more. However, I am at your service. I see I have no choice. My only stipulation is that a way is found for me to rejoin the *True Blooded Yankee*, for which I own I have a growing affection.'

'Mr. Connell has done us good service. I intend to show my appreciation by putting him and his nephew ashore, when we are safely away from Bowmore. You are a man of initiative, monsieur. I think you could find your way to an appointed meeting place. I should be delighted to welcome you back on board the *True Blooded Yankee*, and to have the pleasure of your company to Brest.'

All this was spoken in the tone of one issuing an invitation to dine, and I replied in the same vein. 'Captain Oxnard, you do me too much honour.'

'I have been speaking with Connell, or rather with the young lad. It appears the mill is near the shore on the other side of this loch, two or three miles south of a village they call Port Sgioba. When you have delivered the warning to the good people of Bowmore, make your way there. If someone is willing to lend you a horse your journey will be speedier. Once my business is done I do not intend to linger.'

'How will I know the place?'

'I understand the road runs past a few cottages, that have their backs to a hillside. There is an old burial ground between the road and the sea, and one of the stone slabs is carved with the device of a sword. Follow the stream down to the mill. There will be a light in the window; the miller's wife always sets a light in the window to guide her husband home.'

We could now make out the silhouettes of ships in the Bowmore anchorage. Captain Oxnard moved away and issued orders in a low voice. I looked around for Byfield, and found him huddled in the generous wrappings of his borrowed coat.

'It seems we are going ashore,' I said.

He nodded gloomily.

'I understand there is a boat can take you to the mainland.'

He nodded again.

'Come, Byfield, there is no need to look so desolate. You will soon be on dry land, and on your way to the metropolis. You will doubtless find an eager audience there, waiting to hear the tale of your adventures with the villainous Champdivers.'

'I do not think you appreciate what it is to lose the summation of a life's work,' replied Byfield, in a voice weighty with sorrow and dignity. 'The *Lunardi* was the only child I had.'

'My dear Byfield, there will be another! I am looking forward to the day when I pick up my Paris newspaper and read that a second *Lunardi* has risen from the ashes of the first. The metaphor is not apt but the sentiment is. I have every confidence in you; and on your next flight you will not have an escaped convict as passenger.'

'That would be a cruelty of fortune I do not deserve to suffer twice.'

I clapped him on the shoulder, and at that moment our escort approached to conduct us to the boat. We moved almost silently through the water, as devilishly black as the now moonless sky above. The boat took us to a sheltered spot where the force of the waves was mollified by the angle of the shore. We waded the last few yards, and once beyond the reach of the tide turned to watch the retreat of the little vessel, I, at least, with a feeling almost of regret. Captain Oxnard and his crew seemed congenial company now that I found myself alone with Byfield on this unknown shore.

We began to stumble towards the lights, not many now, for the inhabitants of Bowmore had mostly long since retired to their beds. We came first to the curiously shaped buildings of the distillery, and then to a row of cottages. A light burned in one of them.

'Well,' I whispered to Byfield, 'the sooner the message is delivered the better for them and for us.'

I made a bold approach and rapped on the door. There was silence, then the sound of footsteps. A voice on the other side said something in Gaelic, which I took to be an enquiry as to our identity.

'The bearers of a message for the citizens of Bowmore,' said I with as much authority in my voice as I could muster.

The bolt was drawn and the door opened; in front of us stood a young man with a cruisie in his hand.

'A fine time for messages!' he said, holding the light up so as to get a better look at his visitors. 'Could it not wait till morning?'

'No, sir, it could not,' I replied. 'There is no time to be lost. Do not ask how we come by this intelligence, but there is a Yankee privateer out in the bay, and the captain plans to raid the village. At the very least we must get the women and children out of harm's way.

There is no time for questions, still less for answers. You must raise the alarm at once.'

'I have heard of these privateers. So it is to Bowmore they have come! They are bold, or desperate.' Even as he was speaking he had strapped an ancient sword to his waist and reached a musket from the wall. I had time to look about me; there were ledgers on the table, and a bottle of what I took to be the local spirit. There were papers covered in figures on a chair, and I guessed the young man's connection with the distillery.

With his musket in his hand he ran to the end of the row of cottages, pausing only to pound on each door and call out something in Gaelic. We followed at his heels, and came to the corner of a broad thoroughfare with houses on either side. It swept down towards the sea, where it appeared to plummet of a sudden into dark nothingness. Lights appeared and doors were flung open; one by one, hastily pulling their clothes about them, the inmates of the houses came out on to the street. Some of the women had young children in their arms. Above the babble of sounds I could hear the young man's voice, directing some to carry the warning up the street and others, it seemed, to collect what weapons they could find. A few moments later a church bell rang out, from somewhere at the landward end of the street, though in the darkness I could see nothing that looked like a church.

Within minutes the street, as quiet as the grave when Byfield and I had approached, was in a turmoil. Some of the men ran down to the shore, brandishing their primitive weapons, studying the bay for a sign of the Yankee menace. Byfield stuck to my side like a limpet, and his disquiet grew as we became aware of a heated conversation, and glances thrown in our direction. I would have to find a way of detaching myself from my faithful companion, and from the crowd also. Our friend of the ledgers seemed to cool the argument; by his gestures I guessed he was drawing attention to the need of getting the women and children to a place of safety. Shortly afterwards, a few of the men began to escort the little group up the broad street. A child cried; an old woman near to me set up a low keening, but moved on with the others. I watched them go, wrapped in plaids and shawls against the frosty night, two or three carrying torches which illuminated pale faces and anxious eyes.

Out of the darkness came the sound of trotting hooves. It was the minister on his pony, and I regarded the beast with unusual interest, for I was now thinking of my own safety. The minister dismounted carefully and spoke to the women, before continuing down the street on foot, leaving the pony untended.

'Byfield,' I said softly, 'I must wish you good fortune and bid you farewell. I am sure when the danger has passed one of these good people will show you the direction to Port Askaig.'

'My reputation,' he muttered, backing away from two men with muskets who brushed past him. 'This is too much. I am a respectable man, sir, a man of science—' Out of the corner of my eye I noted that the minister had joined those gathered at the bottom of the street; the pony ambled with its reins trailing. Byfield continued, 'Ducie, St. Ives, Champdivers, whatever name you choose, you cannot leave me here, without my *Lunardi—*'

But leave him I did, still lamenting his balloon with the anguish of a disappointed lover. I strolled across the street with my hands in my pockets. A youth passed me with a club in his hand, but gave me scarcely a glance, so intent was he on joining his comrades in arms. Beyond them, out in the anchorage, all was still. I ensconced myself in a doorway, within a yard of the pony, but the infuriating beast began to meander back the way he had come. I stalked him, dodging from doorway to doorway, sure that at any moment my erratic behaviour would be noticed, or the minister would detach himself from the cluster of men and retrieve his steed. I prayed then that Byfield would not take it into his head to follow; but he remained, rooted to the corner where I left him. I slipped from door to door; the pony now paused, now trotted a pace or two, now slowed to a tranquil walk. Each time I ventured to reach out for the trailing rein he tossed his head with uncharacteristic spirit, or decided at that moment to try out his paces.

We were nearly at the top of the street. Ahead I could just make out a curious round building, and approaching closer realised that this was the church. I was informed later that it had been built thus, without corners, so as to provide no hiding place for the devil. And indeed, if there was a touch of the devil in the beast I stalked it took its leave at this moment, for the pony had found a clump of yellowed grass hard by the church and was now cropping contentedly. I approached softly, picked up the reins, and with the double blandishment of the bridle and some words of French, which I believe to be a more persuasive language than English, at least to a horse, led it out of sight of the street. It was an unnecessary precaution; yet I did not wish to expose myself through any disturbance my newly acquired charger might choose to create. He stood placidly enough as I mounted; indeed, his placidity was such that it took several hard kicks to stir him into any action at all.

At a cautious walk we skirted the backs of the houses and regained the road beyond the harbour. The wind had dropped entirely, and it was a calm, clear night. I pulled up and listened: I heard the steady swish of the waves rippling on the shore, and the occasional snatch of sound from the men behind me. Out in the

loch all seemed quiet. I could make out the shapes of the nearer
vessels, but no movement disturbed the heavy mantle of the night.

I walked the pony half a mile or so, but even that required cease-
less encouragement. Then, of a sudden, my reluctant steed stopped
dead, and raised his head, snorting in alarm. I looked around to see
what could have startled him, and there out in the bay was a red
glow. As I watched another glow flared out, from a small yellow
point of light to an angry expanse of red. Then a third joined it. The
snorting pony rolled his eye and there was sweat on his shoulder.
Soon there were half a dozen cauldrons of flame, and a commotion
on the water as ships' crews sought the safety of their boats. I had
no doubt it was the work of the *True Blooded Yankee*; Captain
Oxnard must have had a change of heart, and decided to spare the
town but fire the ships. But if his work was done, I must make all
speed to the rendezvous. The captain had no particular affection
for me, nor any reason to await an errant Frenchman if he failed to
keep his appointment.

I clapped my heels to the pony's trembling sides, but it was fear
rather than chastisement that lent wings to his heels. I had scarce
thought such velocity was in him, but he kept up a lumbering canter for a mile or two, and although once I would have said that the
saddle was my true element I was glad there was no witness to my
far from elegant horsemanship. Truth to say, the pony had the
better of me, and I could only grip his untended mane and fasten my
legs to the shaggy belly. Thus we advanced, beating a tattoo
through the night, until gradually my steed slackened his pace, and
slowed first to a trot, then to a walk. The road had followed the
curve of the shore; out on the water the fires still blazed, and the
smell of charred wood was carried through the air. With so little
wind the brig's retreat down the loch would be slow; nevertheless,
she was my lifeline to France, and I could not risk letting her bid
farewell to Islay without me.

I urged the pony on, but now he would attempt nothing more
adventurous than a jog trot. At length I made out a huddle of
houses by the shore, and as we approached realised there were
people on the street, doubtless come out in alarm and now watching the fires in the loch. It would have been madness to ride on, a
stranger on the minister's horse, and for a moment I was baulked.
On my left was the shore, sand and shingle stretching to the water's
edge, eerily lit by the firy glow; to my right a black hillside, a terrain
of unknown hazards. I pondered for a while. Above the cloud had
parted and a myriad of stars winked and glittered, while the frost
bit at my finger ends. The pony stood still with his head drooping
nearly to the ground. If I took to the shore I could easily be seen; if I
took to the hillside I would have to say farewell to my charger.

Beyond the incandescent water I could make out lights; I was opposite Bowmore, and I guessed the village ahead to be that they called Port Sgioba. The miller lived not far beyond, yet across rough country it could take me hours to reach the mill.

Inspiration came to my aid once more. I shook the reins, plied my heels, and leaning forward murmured silken blandishments into the pony's ears, invoking the spirit of the Godolphin Arabian, with whom my island animal can have had little connection, but that is by the by. More to the purpose is the fact that it did not stir until I let out a trooper's yell, at which it leapt into a canter again.

We made our entry into Port Sgioba in considerable style. Men, women and children were on the pier, watching the flames and murmuring in alarm. At the sound of my approach they turned their attention to the road. I rode in amongst them and pulled my charger to a halt as children scattered to their mothers' skirts.

'Yankee raiders,' I shouted. 'They plan to fire Bowmore. Arm yourselves, and get the women and children to a place of safety.' I did not stop to discover if I had been understood, but added breathlessly, 'I must ride on,' and gestured south. I repeated my trooper's whoop and the signal had the desired effect. We lumbered on, and I did not look back to see how the good citizens of Port Sgioba had received my message.

The pony's sides were heaving and his shoulders flecked with foam. As soon as we were a safe distance from the village I slowed to a walk again, and gave his neck a pat. I had been well served, but caution was the watchword now. About a mile further on I slipped from the saddle, turned his head for home, and sent him off with a slap on the rump. If the people of Ardnish were abroad I did not wish to meet them.

There was rough scrubby ground now between me and the shore, and only the stars to guide me. When I came to two or three cottages on the right of the road I struck to the left, and stumbled through bog and dead bracken. A low wall loomed in front of me; I peered over it, and found a few windworn gravestones. This was the burial ground I had been told of; nearby were three curiously carved stone slabs. In the darkness I could just detect the design of a sword with scrolling decorations round about, and next to it what seemed to be the figure of an angel.

I found the little stream and followed it down towards the shore, as I had followed another stream on another night, since when had passed only a single dawning of the sun. It seemed like half a lifetime. Now I could hear the sea, and there in front of me was the mill itself, with a light in the window. I knocked softly at the door; at once a woman's voice replied, but I could not comprehend it. I knocked again; this time the door was opened, and there, holding a cruisie that gave out a smell of fish oil, was a handsome woman who showed no surprise at the stranger on the threshold.

She spoke to me in Gaelic; I shook my head.

'I have news of your husband,' I said. She clearly understood, and I made out the word 'Neil' in her reply.

'He is on his way,' I went on. 'I am to meet him on the shore.' I gestured towards the sea. She spoke again, volubly, and with a hint of temper in her voice; and pulling her shawl about her she came out into the night. I followed her along a narrow path that opened onto a cluster of rocks. We stood side by side staring out into the dark water, but her eyes were sharper than mine, for she exclaimed and pointed. Sure enough, I could just make out a shape of slightly denser blackness: it was the brig, and nearer to us, just beyond the swell of the breakers, were two small boats. The first came steadily on, though I was sure it would be dashed against the rocks; the second hung back. In between the rocks was a pool of quieter water and the first boat slid into this with practised ease. It could only be Connell at the helm, with his young nephew plying the oars. They brought the boat against a shelf of rock that served as a natural jetty, and made it fast. I could see them now, Neil Connell carrying something bulky on his back, and the boy.

We went to meet them. I judged by the tone of Mrs. Connell's greeting that she was not pleased at the lateness of the hour and the worry she had been caused, and was not allowing the opportunity for explanation. I spoke to the boy.

'I am pleased indeed to see you,' said I, with an attempt at joviality.

He did not seem to hear. 'They fired the ships, the bloody Yankee fired the ships,' were all his words, and he stared out into the black loch where in the distance a lambent glimmer showed where the ships still burned.

I bethought me of my own safety. The second boat still hovered beyond the rocks and the breakers, not daring to approach nearer. I saluted it with a wave. Connell said something to me, which I interpreted as meaning that it was for me to devise a means of reaching it. I looked at his boat, neatly tied up, and felt for my packet of bank notes. But his good wife had him by the arm, and the boy was shivering beside me; so I turned away without a word, and I warrant they were not sorry to see me go. I made my way to the furthest edge of the rocks and cast aside the captain's great-coat. There were still fifty yards between the rocks and the boat that awaited me; there was nothing for it but to take to the salt sea and swim.

CHAPTER XXXV

THE FINAL ACT

I REMEMBER the icy embrace of the water. I remember the buffet of the waves, and the dense profile of the boat, appearing and disappearing; but there follows a chasm in my memory. I suppose I was hauled on board the boat, and from there on to the brig. I suppose someone took me down below and laid me in a narrow bunk. I am told I slept, and woke, and raved, and slept again. I have the dimmest recollection of broth being put to my lips; I am sure I tasted rum. I think the captain stood near me and spoke; a picture lingers of the cook, a half-caste who later informed me he was from Jamaica and rejoiced in the name of Wallace, showing his gleaming teeth at my bedside. At any rate, what is a certainty is that for most of the days that followed I had only a tenebrous perception of the world around me, that I slept much, and when I began to see more clearly I had scarcely the strength to lift a hand to feel the growth of beard on my face.

It was Wallace who nursed me, who supported me with an arm around my shoulders as he fed me with thin soup in which floated unappetising lumps of salt pork. It was Wallace who brought me extra blankets when I tossed and shivered. It was Wallace who, when at last I set foot upon the heaving planks of the ship, took a firm hold of my elbow, and brought me grog to dispel the faintness that ensued. It was Wallace who informed me that the miller had been well rewarded for his trouble, and who exulted in the speed of the brig, which had outstripped all pursuit.

At last I made my first sortie on deck, blinking in the unaccustomed sunlight; then I made out the coast of France lying low and grey to port. We had rounded the island of Ushant, Captain Oxnard informed me, and were making our way to Brest. I watched the coast take firmer shape with a tumult of feelings. It seemed an epoch since I last set foot in my own country, since I had last spoken French to my own countrymen; an epoch since I had been able to walk with the unconcern of a free man. Yet I had no wish to linger in France; it was hardly a place of safety, as events sped the little emperor to his destiny, and my cousin, no doubt, would take advantage of changing circumstances to make his own return to his native country. And besides, my only thought was of Scotland, where I was branded with the name of murderer, but where Flora was waiting.

I need not detain the reader with an account of how I recovered my strength in an inn at Brest, and then made my way to Paris where my chief object was to bide my time until it was safe to return to Scotland. While in Paris I had no wish to attract notice, for I was sure Alain would soon be sniffing at my trail, and so I adopted the dress of a rather down-at-heel gentleman, and found obscure lodgings near the Quai St. Michel. Even so, as I moved about Paris, I sometimes felt a prickling sensation at the back of my neck, and turned in the expectation of encountering a pair of watchful eyes. Once or twice I caught a movement, as of someone slipping out of sight, but I could never be sure.

I avoided going out at night, for I knew how easy it would be, on the crowded and unsettled streets of Paris, to slide a knife between my ribs and leave me in the gutter, and I knew my cousin too well to believe that he would be deterred from stooping to such dishonourable means of removing me from his path. During this time of confusion the streets of Paris saw the settling of many an old score.

This need for caution and anonymity would have tried the patience of the holiest of saints. For me it was agony. I paced my meagre rooms as I waited for news that would mean I could set forth again. The war dragged on, but Napoleon's day was done, and I, a soldier of Napoleon, shed few tears. His triumph had been great, and I was proud to have played my part, even though the role had for some months confined me to a narrower stage than I would have wished; but I am no idealist, and if a romantic only in matters of love. It was not written that Napoleon should conquer the world, and my own future happiness lay in his rapid capitulation. When Paris fell I mingled with the crowds, out of curiosity, but never forgot that somewhere my cousin or his spies might be at a window or in a doorway.

As uncertainty eddied, and Paris changed her colours, I had little thought of her, or of the fate of France, or of my parents who had died. These were dreary weeks, unenlivened by any sense that I was witness to history changing course. How I passed them I can hardly tell, except that my mind ran often on the Pentland slopes, on Flora and that last farewell. I tortured myself with visions of Chevenix in the parlour at Swanston, and Flora's smile directed up at him. Why should she remember Anne, or think of him alone in Paris, when she could lean upon the arm of the Major, and stroll by the burn or linger in the garden? Ronald would be there, cleaving to

the company of Chevenix, as if such closeness would conjure up
the commission for which he longed. And Miss Gilchrist: there
were moments when I thought she favoured me, yet who could
blame her if she considered the reputable Major a more desirable
match for her niece?

Ah, what anguish, yet what consolation to envisage the bright
eyes of my beloved, and remember her sweet voice and her trembling promise! Then, at last, there came letters, first from Flora herself, telling me that Chevenix, the noble, inestimable Chevenix, had
come forward with the true account of the duel at the Castle, and
then from Robbie, equally reassuring, and last from Romaine, with
the news that my uncle's life had fled at last, and I now was rightful
proprietor of an estate in Buckinghamshire. I began to feel my sun
was rising again, and that only one dark cloud remained to obscure
a bright horizon.

Now I could return to Scotland, as a free man, and claim my bride.
I made arrangements to travel by barge down the Seine, and then to
take ship for Leith. I wrote in undisguised triumph to Flora, to
inform her when I would arrive. The weather smiled on us as we
slipped through the Channel; the air was stirred by balmy breezes,
and any memory of inclement winds and a hostile sea was banished
like a bad dream. I did briefly wonder where Captain Oxnard and
the *True Blooded Yankee* were now—it seemed scarcely likely he
would have lingered in Brest—and if the incomparable Wallace still
flashed his pearly teeth as he stirred his steaming pots; but that
was all in the past, and my heart was all in the future.

We approached Leith harbour at daybreak. As we entered the
Firth of Forth a pink glow spread across the sky behind us, and cast
an illumination on the water. Inland were the familiar outlines of
the Castle and of Arthur's Seat, with the Pentlands rolling darkly
beyond. I had sent a letter to Rowley, instructing him to await me at
the dock, and I scanned the quayside as we approached. I could just
make out a small figure half hidden beside some herring barrels,
and was sure that this was Rowley, though such reticence did not
become him. I raised a hand; he looked pointedly in another direction. 'Damnation,' thought I, 'what tricks has he been learning in
my absence?' I signalled more urgently; he retreated into the shadows. It seemed I would have to carry my own baggage, which was
not at all what I considered appropriate. I vowed the re-education
of Rowley as soon as I laid hands on him.

I was no sooner on dry land than I became aware of the stares of
two men whom, in my irritation with Rowley, I had not noticed
before. The taller had thin and bandy legs; the other had a swarthy
face with eyes deep in the shadow of his brow. Recognition came
instantly, not of their faces but of danger, for there was something

in the very tilt of their chins that spoke of hostile intent. At that moment a familiar voice hissed in my ear.

'This way, Mr. Anne, sir, quick. They ain't gentlemen, them two. Not at all, they ain't.'

Rowley pulled me behind the herring barrels, but the two men were between us and the road to Edinburgh, and were already coming in our direction. Rowley picked up my bags and began to run, bent low, dodging between barrels and around coils of rope, leaping over rusted anchors and fish baskets. I could only follow. Seconds later I heard a shout; the two men must have reached the point where they had last seen me, only to discover that I had vanished. I had dreamed of the moment when I would set foot on shore, when, with Rowley in attendance, I would proceed in a hired carriage to Swanston, where Flora would be waiting, and Ronald would warmly greet a brother-at-arms and future brother-in-law, and even Miss Gilchrist would melt to the extent of a smile of welcome. The dream was shattered: I was on the run again.

Rowley paused for breath behind some fishing nets hanging up to dry. 'I've had my eye on them two. I didn't like the look of them one little bit,' he panted.

A glance behind showed the two gentlemen searching the harbour debris. 'They're furrin,' said Rowley. 'Speak a peculiar lingo. I got close enough to hear.' He grinned, and looked expectant of praise.

'French, doubtless,' I said drily.

Rowley failed to catch my tone, but nodded vigorously, and added, 'French, that'll be it. You can't trust 'em, Mr. Anne, sir. They're slippery, they are. The old gal, I mean Mrs. MacRankine— she's been like a mother to me, Mr. Anne, sir, really she has—the old gal don't hold much with Frenchmen. It's the Pope, you see. The old gal, I mean Mrs. MacRankine, don't care for the Pope.'

'Rowley, this is hardly the time to discuss the predilections of the good Mrs. MacRankine. I mean to put some distance between myself and these two gentlemen. I suggest you follow at your leisure.'

The shore was busy now with carts and seamen, and further along I could see what appeared to be the bustle of a fish market. I put my hands in my pockets and affecting an insouciance I did not feel strolled into the stream of traffic. Behind me lumbered a cart pulled by a pair of heavy horses; beside me a fishwife made her way with a basket of herring on her back. I blessed the presence of the two barefoot children in front of me, and of the man who had not yet slept off the previous evening's entertainment. The latter was disposed to be rather more sociable than in normal circumstances I would have welcomed; now his hand on my arm and his bleared and unshaven visage uncomfortably close to my own were a boon. 'Shfine morning,' he said, giving my arm an intimate squeeze. 'Been at shea for nine months,' he confided. 'Whalesh. Big as chur-chesh. Ishebergsh. Big as cathedralsh.'

I nodded in polite agreement. He stumbled against me, and lurched back onto both his feet again. 'Nuff baleen for ten thoush-and shtaysh, ten timesh ten thoushand.'

We continued in silence for a few yards, he leaning on my arm, and breathing the stale fumes of celebration into my face.

'Near froshe to death, near froshe—' And he stopped in his tracks, looked at me with a smile of beatific innocence, and sank slowly to the ground. His head came to rest against a bollard; he closed his eyes. As I continued on my way I heard him muttering, 'Big as churchesh, big as cathedralsh.'

I did not venture a look back, but walked on at a moderate pace until the noise and smells of the fish market enveloped me. Where Rowley was I could not guess: I supposed he knew his business. Amongst the stalls and carts of the market I was importuned on all sides. Herrings and haddocks lay in glistening heaps. Baskets of oysters were thrust under my nose; live crabs and lobsters stared vengefully as I pushed my way past.

I paused; where was Rowley? And where now could I go? Any part of Edinburgh that had known me was now barred. If Alain had knowledge enough of my movements to have men posted at the port he would be watching elsewhere. Under pretence of examin-ing a handsome turbot I glanced about me, and there were my two compatriots, searching doorways and vennels as they came. I turned abruptly, and found myself face to face with a large, broad-faced man with the fingers of each hand thrust into the gills of a salmon. Inspiration came unbidden: gold was the most reliable passport to safety.

'A guinea,' said I, 'for your salmon and your coat.'

'Done,' said he, clearly a man of the market, if not of the world.

Moments later there emerged out of the crowd a man who might have been marked by his deportment as a gentleman, but whose threadbare coat and pair of salmon indicated a tenant farmer bringing home supper to his family. I could only hope the transfor-mation did not deceive the elusive Rowley. I followed the curve of the shore, the salmon depositing their scales on the skirts of my coat, thus embellishing the masquerade. When I reached a narrow wynd between tall houses I risked another look around me. There they were, quartering the fish market now; but there was no sign of my rascal servant.

I had disguised my fine apparel with the garb of a worker on the land; my bags had experienced a sea-change indeed, and had become finned creatures; my boy had effected a disappearance that might be thought magical. I was reflecting thus when my French friends grew tired of the smell of fish and withdrew some distance for a conference. After some deliberation Bandylegs retraced his steps to the quayside; the other came on. I could not stop to wait for Rowley.

The sea in front of me and the clustered masts of the ships brought to mind the delights of Cramond, and I bethought me that, as I must go somewhere, anywhere that was not the Edinburgh I knew or Swanston, I would set forth for that pleasant place. I slipped up the wynd, a salmon still hanging from either hand, and by way of back streets followed the line of the shore, until the houses thinned and I found myself in the green countryside. Here I considered I had no further use for my salmon, and laid them tenderly on the grass, where I hoped they might prove a prize for some hungry wanderer. At Newhaven fishing boats were drawn up on the shore, and there was a dank smell of fish and seaweed in the air. There was one boat drawn up further than the rest, and turned with its keel in the air. A figure was perched on the hull, one leg crossed over the other, for all the world like an overgrown and earthbound Puck. His hat was drawn down over his face, but nothing could mask the grin that brightened under it.

'How the devil did you get here?' I enquired, noting at the same time that my baggage was stowed beside him.

Rowley raised his hat and the grin widened.

'Hurl in a cart, Mr. Anne, sir. Easiest way, sir. Them Frenchies were too busy looking for you to take notice of me in the back of a cart full of straw.' He carefully removed a fragment of this material from his sleeve. 'I thought, where's he going to make for this time?' I thought, he ain't going to the old gal's, thats for sure, and he ain't going to Mr. Robbie's, and ain't going to Swanston. And he ain't going knocking on the Castle door. Where else, I asked meself, where else does Mr. Anne know? Why, I thought, he knows Cramond. So Cramond it is, sir, and here I am.'

He jumped to his feet, picked up the bags, and began to whistle as he strode forward.

'Rowley,' I said, 'I am pleased to see you, and I'm pleased that life with Mrs. McRankine has not slowed your wits.'

'Not a bit of it, sir. Me wits are pretty sharp, sir. Them Frenchies was 'anging about in St. James Square, that's how I knew 'em. And the other one, the other viscount, he's in town. I saw him in Leith Street, skulkin', I'd say, sir, with his curls covered up by a 'at. He's not here for his 'ealth, sir.'

We were walking briskly now, on the road to Granton; for the moment there was no sign of pursuit.

'Well, Rowley, I am grateful to you. Assuredly, my cousin is not in Edinburgh for his health, and not for my health either. He cannot set the law against me now; I fear he has something more dangerous in mind.'

'Not—not *murder*, Mr. Anne, sir?'

'Indeed, Rowley, I do not believe my cousin would hesitate over so small a thing as the mere deprivation of life. What is a man's life when gold is at stake, and an estate and a fine house? Confound him, how dare he come between me and my inheritance, between me and my bride?'

Anger boiled inside me as I thought of how all my plans had been frustrated. Even now, Flora would be wondering at my absence, and imagining storms at sea, or worse. I saw her at the window, watching for a carriage; I felt her agitation as I failed to appear, and Ronald no doubt taking pleasure in my perfidy. I saw Miss Gilchrist pursing her lips over her needlework. I shuddered at the general replacement of my image with that of Major Chevenix.

As if reading my thoughts Rowley interjected, 'I could take a message to Swanston, Mr. Anne, sir.'

I thought for a moment; the temptation was great, but the risk was great also. Rowley was involved enough in my quarrel; I would not send him on an errand that might lead to his apprehension by a desperate man. 'No, Rowley,' said I. 'Let us wait. Before very much longer my cousin Alain and I must come face to face; I feel it in my bones. The fates have decreed that this island cannot accommodate us both, and it will not be I who leaves, either dead or alive.'

'Bravo, Mr. Anne, sir. I'm with you all the way, you can count on me. They're slippery, them Frenchies, sir, and I don't care for 'em.'

We walked through a countryside lit by summer sunshine. In the fields crops of barley and oats were beginning to ripen. On our right we looked across the firth to the hills of Fife, bathed in a blue-green haze.

'I like it almost as much as England, sir,' was Rowley's comment. I was in mind of Rowley's prejudice against the French, which would have to wait until such time as I could improve his education, and forebore to remark on the superior qualities of France. Yet I now know that, on the rare occasions when Scotland is released from her vile weather, the country can be almost civilised, and I can almost understand how it has come to produce giants such as Sir Walter.

We reached the inn at the Cramond Brig in apparent safety. I went in to secure supper and lodging, leaving Rowley outside. Sitting hunched by the fire, in spite of the warmth of the sun, was a man in black, who looked up as I entered, to reveal a brown face and coal black eyes. As I spoke to the landlord he slowly rose, and at the same time Rowley was suddenly at the door. I read his message in his face, bowed to the landlord, murmured something about a change of plan, and retreated. Outside the inn were my two compatriots astride sweating horses; behind us was the man in black.

'Rowley,' I whispered, 'leave the bags and run,' and suiting my own actions to my words I took to my heels. There was a shout and a rattle of hooves. Rowley led the way, down the path by the river that led to the shore. The horses were slowed by trees and the narrowness of the way. When we burst out onto the shore we saw the tide was out, and the causeway to Cramond island seemed to beckon.

'No, Rowley,' I panted. 'We'd be trapped like lobsters in a pot.'

Then the horsemen were on us, and I saw the gleam of a weapon. I turned to face the first horse and grabbed its bridle with both hands, forcing it back and dodging as Bandylegs slashed with his sword. Rowley, with commendable presence of mind, tore off his hat and waved it in the face of the second horse, which plunged aside and nearly unseated its rider. Then he seized the leg of my assailant and struggled to dislodge him. In the melée I let go of the bridle, the horse reared up, its rider lunged at Rowley, whose ferocious yell indicated a hit. It sent the horse rearing again, and to my amazement Rowley jumped back, apparently unharmed, and flapped his arms like a monstrous bird while still screaming like a banshee. Then he turned and was off like a cannon ball. As the startled horses slipped on sand and seaweed I too turned tail.

Rowley was brought up short by the river bank. 'I can't swim, Mr. Anne, sir!'

'I'll swim for both of us,' said I. 'You can't stay here.'

I propelled him into the water and the two of us floundered into the centre of the channel; but it was not so deep that we were forced to swim. As we reached the further bank I looked back and saw the horses being urged into the river. Behind, at some distance, stood the man in black, motionless, but he had been joined by another, a figure I knew instantly. Unlike his companion he could not keep still, and shook a frilled fist. Even with the river between us I was sure I caught the whiff of scent: it was my cousin.

We scrambled up the bank, and his words followed us. 'You cannot escape me, cousin. You are a fraud and a counterfeit. You are a coward. Why don't you face me? Only a guilty conscience runs away.'

I stood looking at him, almost overcome with loathing, yet almost sorry for him, too. He walked up to the river bank, and I could see his face clearly.

'You are a coward, my dear cousin,' he repeated more calmly. 'You surprise me. You cheated me; you took advantage of an old

man; and now you are running away. You are an insult to the blood
of Saint-Yves.'

'Cousin,' I replied, 'it is deceit and duplicity that is an insult. It is
no fault of mine that my uncle could not stomach a spy in the
family. I have no cause to be concerned about my honour.'

'I am astonished you show no desire to defend it.'

'Don't, Mr. Anne, sir. He'll cheat, like he did before. He's not
worth a fight, sir.'

'My dear Rowley,' I said in a low voice, 'I am not disposed to argue
with you, but I think we have a fight on our hands whether or not he
is worth it.' I raised my voice. 'Call off your dogs, cousin. If you care
to join me on this side of the river we can seek a less public spot to
play out the final act.'

Some of the villagers of Cramond had been attracted by the
sounds of struggle and had now gathered near the river bank to witness the drama. Although their presence offered some protection I
had no wish to postpone the inevitable. Alain looked around him.
The two horsemen had pulled up in the river, just a few yards from
us. The man in black stood a pace or two from my cousin, still
silent, still motionless. Alain spoke to him, and he replied briefly,
looking all the while at me; I half expected a signal that would
unleash the hounds, although I trusted that, in the full light of day
and in the presence of bystanders, they would have held back from
actual bloodshed. But then I recalled the flash of a sword; and I had
a suspicion of pistols.

Alain turned and walked along the bank to a small jetty where the
ferry boat that plied between the river banks was tied up, the ferryman having stopped to enjoy what had promised to be a fine spectacle. The man in black followed a few paces behind. There were a
few peremptory words to the ferryman, money changed hands, and
they stepped in to the little craft. When they stepped out on the
other side the horsemen had not moved. As my cousin and his
black shadow climbed the path towards us I said again, 'Cousin,
call off your dogs. There are two of us; we have need of only two of
you.'

It was the man in black who gave the order. 'Wait for us on the far
bank,' he said, lifting his hand in what seemed to be a gesture of dis-
missal.

'I don't like the look of *him*, sir,' Rowley muttered beside me.

The horses splashed back to the Cramond bank and took up their
position there, their riders still smouldering with anger.

'Well, cousin,' said Alain, 'will you lead the way? There must be
some spot in this barbaric country where we can pursue our business in private.'

I knew the path led towards the Queen's Ferry, some three or four miles distant; there would doubtless be some deserted stretch of shore where we could accomplish whatever was necessary. We walked in single file, I in front followed by Rowley, then my cousin, with the man in black bringing up the rear. No words were exchanged. I had time to reflect that I had no weapon and that Alain did not appear to be armed. I surmised, from the outline of his coat, that the man in black had a pistol in his belt. Were we to fight a duel with our bare hands, or was some treachery afoot? I thought of the Castle, and of Goguelat; but here I had no means to improvise a weapon.

We skirted a stark, unadorned castle looking out to the firth and came at last to a stretch of sandy beach. Apart from the cries of gulls and oyster catchers there was no sound, and no footprint had sullied the expanse of sand. This was the place. I walked out onto the sand and turned to face my cousin. He lifted his lip in a sneer, and one hand played with the ruffles on his shirt.

'You are a coward, cousin,' said he, 'a disgrace to the upstart general you admire so much.'

'And you are a dishonourable cheat, an insult to your family.'

'We will see who is the more worthy of the name Saint-Yves.'

'I have no weapon,' I said.

He raised his hands. 'And I, too, am unarmed. We are well matched.'

The man in black watched us with the ghost of a smile on his face, the only expression he had betrayed, while Rowley, pale and anxious, completed the square with his back to the sea. Alain and I removed our coats; I thought he would be impeded by his frills, but he paid them no heed. For a few seconds we held each other's gaze; then, suddenly, he launched himself at me and we were grappling on the sand. Greed and jealousy lent strength to my cousin's limbs, and twice I was nearly thrown to the ground. I heard his breath rasp in his throat. He lunged again, but this time I was too quick for him, and stepped aside so that for a second he was off balance. Instantly I took advantage, and had him down on one knee in the sand and was poised for the final throw.

'A knife! Mr. Anne, sir, he's got a knife!'

I hurled myself at Alain; Rowley's urgent cry only fuelled my anger. I felt a hot pain as Alain's knife raked my side, and at the same time a pistol shot rang out, and I heard the thud of hooves. Pain incensed me further, and I flung Alain to the ground with such force that the knife dropped from his hand. In an instant I had it in mine. He lay winded in the sand, and I stood over him with the blade of the knife inches from his throat.

'A step nearer and he's dead,' I cried. I was aware of Rowley close beside me. Slowly I raised my eyes: there was the man in black calmly recharging his pistol. The horsemen had reined in their mounts, but both had drawn their swords. I knelt beside by cousin, with the blade now touching his skin.

'For the last time, my dear cousin, I ask you to call off your dogs. Bid them go home, or they will never see their master alive again.' I sliced off a ruffle from his shirt and tossed it into the air. The man in black stood with his pistol pointed towards the ground. I felt the warm spread of blood on my side.

'Stay close by me, Rowley. I wager that first bullet was meant for you.'

'That it was, sir, and strike me sky-blue scarlet if I go down to a Frenchie's pistol.'

'Come, come, cousin, you are slow. Where is your tongue? You were all too ready to use it a moment ago. Bid your dogs go back to France. If they hurry they'll catch the evening tide.' I cut off another ruffle and sent it after the first.

'Damn you, Anne,' my cousin croaked, 'may you roast in hell for this.'

'All in due time, Alain. If damnation is to be my destiny I wager I'll be in good company. Now, to the purpose; do not keep me waiting.'

Alain raised his hand in a feeble gesture. 'Go, go,' he said weakly.

'Louder, *mon brave*, they cannot hear you.'

'Go. Return to Leith; wait for me there.'

I looked up, but did not take the knife from his throat. 'You heard your master,' I said. '*Filez. Allez-vous-en.* My hand is none too steady.'

The cavalry moved off, first Bandylegs, then the other, turning their horses' heads back towards Cramond. The man in black looked thoughtful, and, I judged, a trifle disappointed; then, with the hint of a shrug, he pushed his pistol into his belt and followed. I watched until they were all three out of sight, and all sounds of their going had ceased. Whatever my cousin was paying them, it was not enough to buy their loyalty. I looked down at Alain, white faced, with beads of sweat on his temples.

'Now, my dear Alain, there are no witnesses. Would you blame me if I chose to finish the matter here and now? I am sure you would be tempted to do the same.'

'O Mr. Anne, sir!' I had, for a moment, forgotten Rowley. 'O Mr. Anne, sir, you can't *kill* him. You can't kill him *now*, sir.'

'No,' I sighed, 'you are right, Rowley. I can't kill him, though I have no doubt I will have cause to curse my kind heart. Well, cousin, what is your promise worth, I wonder? Do I let you go? Will you give me your word that you will leave the country at once, and never return?'

I got to my feet, determined not to show the pain this caused.

Alain still lay sprawled in the sand; I balanced the knife carelessly.
'You have my word,' he said, with something like a groan.

'Well, Rowley,' said I. 'Promise or no promise, I think we will now
make our way to Queensferry, and enjoy my cousin's company for a
little longer. I will feel more comfortable when I am sure his friends
are not planning a reunion in this vicinity.'

And so we took the path to Queensferry, my cousin reluctantly in
the van, spurred by the knife in my hand, and Rowley completing
the procession. Behind us on the sand was the imprint of our
encounter, here and there coloured red. The sun was low in the
west, and sent a warm glow across the firth. Sails skimmed the
water in the evening breeze, and as we approached the town we
saw the ferry midway between the two shores. At last we came out
of the trees and saw the Hawes Inn before us. There I bade farewell
to Alain, in the profound hope that I would never set eyes on him
again, and watched him make his way wearily up the long brae on
the road back to Edinburgh.

I, too, was weary, with the pain I had disguised and with loss of
blood. We found in the pleasant burgh of Queensferry a doctor,
who examined my wound and dressed it, and assured me I had been
spared serious injury. Gold silenced any questions the doctor
might have been disposed to ask.

We came out into the High Street in the quiet darkness of a summer night, and repaired to the Hawes Inn. Rowley had shared the
dangers of the day, and shared my supper. When his head began to
nod over his ale I sent him to his bed, and finished my bottle of
excellent claret alone. Tomorrow at first light I would set forth for
Swanston, and I prayed that my beloved Flora would forgive my
tardiness.